Pa YA
Ward, Dayton.
 Open secrets
30049002510213

AUG   2009

P9-BTN-162

"Gangway! Make a hole!"

Atish Khatami shouted the commands over the wail of the
red alert sirens as she sprinted down the curving corridor
of Deck 5 on her way to the nearest turbolift. Ahead of her,
crew members already moving to their assigned battle
stations cleared the center of the hallway, some even
flattening themselves against bulkheads in order to provide
the captain free passage. Rounding a turn, she nearly
bowled over a hapless lieutenant who was trying to vacate
the turbolift. The younger officer managed to dodge her
and thereby avoided being body-slammed into the wall as
Khatami plunged into the lift.

"Bridge!" she called out as she gripped one of the car's
quartet of control handles and the doors closed behind her.
An instant later she felt the slight push from below as the
lift began its ascent. Reaching for the comm panel positioned just inside the door, Khatami activated the unit.
"Khatami to bridge. Report."

"*Stano here,*" replied the *Endeavour*'s first officer.
"*Sensors have picked up three Klingon warships at extreme range, but they've altered course to intercept us,
and they're coming fast. I've raised shields and readied
weapons crews.*"

PIQUA PUBLIC LIBRARY
CHILDREN'S DEPT.

DISCARD

DISCARD

PIQUA PUBLIC LIBRARY
CHILDREN

STAR TREK®
VANGUARD

OPEN SECRETS

DAYTON WARD

Story by
Dayton Ward & Kevin Dimore

Based upon Star Trek
created by Gene Roddenberry

PIQUA PUBLIC LIBRARY
CHILDREN'S DEPT.

Pa YA
Ward, Dayton.
Open secrets
30049002510213

POCKET BOOKS
New York   London   Toronto   Sydney

The sale of this book without its cover is unauthorized. If you purchased this book without a cover, you should be aware that it was reported to the publisher as "unsold and destroyed." Neither the author nor the publisher has received payment for the sale of this "stripped book."

Pocket Books
A Division of Simon & Schuster, Inc.
1230 Avenue of the Americas
New York, NY 10020

This book is a work of fiction. Names, characters, places, and incidents either are products of the author's imagination or are used fictitiously. Any resemblance to actual events or locales or persons, living or dead, is entirely coincidental.

™, ® and © 2009 by CBS Studios Inc. All Rights Reserved.
STAR TREK and related marks are trademarks of CBS Studios Inc.

This book is published by Pocket Books, a division of Simon & Schuster, Inc., under exclusive license from CBS Studios Inc.

All rights reserved, including the right to reproduce this book or portions thereof in any form whatsoever. For information address Pocket Books Subsidiary Rights Department,
1230 Avenue of the Americas, New York, NY 10020.

First Pocket Books paperback edition May 2009

POCKET and colophon are registered trademarks of Simon & Schuster, Inc.

For information about special discounts for bulk purchases, please contact Simon & Schuster Special Sales at 1-866-506-1949 or business@simonandschuster.com.

The Simon & Schuster Speakers Bureau can bring authors to your live event. For more information or to book an event, contact the Simon & Schuster Speakers Bureau at 1-866-248-3049 or visit our website at www.simonspeakers.com.

Cover art by Doug Drexler

Manufactured in the United States of America

10 9 8 7 6 5 4 3 2 1

ISBN-13: 978-1-4165-4792-1
ISBN-10:   1-4165-4792-4

IN TRIBUTE
Joan Winston
(June 19, 1931–September 11, 2008)
You knew it all along, Joanie,
but Star Trek *does indeed live.*

AUG 2009

2003

AUG

HISTORIAN'S NOTE

The main events take place in 2266 (ACE). This is just after the *Starship Enterprise*'s encounter with the First Federation ship the *Fesarius* ("Corbormite Maneuver") and approximately three weeks after the disappearance of the Jinoteur system and the publication of a story that reveals many of the carefully guarded secrets of the Taurus Reach (*Star Trek: Vanguard—Reap the Whirlwind*).

Operation Vanguard:
Current Status

THE TAURUS REACH: A largely unexplored region of space, situated between the borders of Federation, Klingon, and Tholian territory. It is here that Starfleet has discovered the remnants of an ancient, incredibly powerful civilization, the Shedai, with links to one of the Federation's most mysterious adversaries, the Tholians. Also discovered is the Taurus Meta-Genome, a complex strand of deliberately engineered DNA that seems to hold the key to genetic manipulation and perhaps even artificial world-building on a scale never before imagined. The scientific and martial potential of unlocking this knowledge quickly becomes obvious, and Starfleet launches a mammoth exploration and research effort into the region. As the investigation continues, Starfleet scientists uncover an enigmatic energy waveform in the Jinoteur system, which is believed to be the homeworld of the long-dead race. This waveform, working in concert with the meta-genome, might well be the key to unlocking all of the Taurus Reach's many secrets.

STARBASE 47: A massive, self-sufficient Federation deep-space station constructed in the Taurus Reach. The station is the focal point of activity in the region, a command base for Starfleet vessels assigned to the sector as well as a way station for Federation colonists

xii   Operation Vanguard: Current Status

heading into the region. Operating beneath this cover,
the station's larger, classified mission is to spearhead
the investigation of the Taurus Reach. As tension grips
the Federation's political relations with the Klingon
Empire and the Tholian Assembly, Starbase 47 stands
poised knowing it could become a flashpoint in an
interstellar conflict.

COMMODORE DIEGO REYES: Commanding officer of Starbase
47, as well as the person overseeing the mission to
discover the secrets of the Taurus Reach. A man of
strong conviction and principles as well as an
unwavering loyalty to Starfleet and the Federation,
Reyes has found himself gripped in a crisis of
conscience. The secret nature of his mission and the
potential it carries to destabilize the relations between
the Federation and its neighbors has forced him to take
questionable and even illegal actions. Forced by
circumstance and political expediency to cover up the
truth behind the destruction of the *U.S.S. Bombay,* a
starship assigned to Starbase 47, Reyes is later forced
to lay waste to the entire surface of Gamma Tauri IV in
an effort to contain a Shedai threat. The action, which
results in the deaths of thousands of Federation and
Klingon colonists, eventually leads Reyes to allow the
publication of an exposé by journalist Tim Pennington
that reveals much of the truth behind the Shedai and
the menace they represent. As a consequence of this
decision, Reyes is arrested and charged with violation
of Starfleet regulations, and now awaits court-martial.

LIEUTENANT COMMANDER T'PRYNN: Starbase 47's
intelligence officer. T'Prynn is charged with ensuring
the secrecy of Operation Vanguard, a task she undertakes

with unwavering and even ruthless efficiency. Unknown to anyone, T'Prynn has suffered severe mental trauma for decades, the result of a violent mind meld she endured during an abortive marriage ceremony on her home planet of Vulcan. Since that time, she has carried within her mind the consciousness of Sten, her fiancé whom she killed during ritual combat. The pressures of this continuous mental struggle, coupled with the trauma of losing her lover, Anna Sandesjo, finally become too much for T'Prynn, and she falls into a deep coma. As station doctors attempt to ascertain her condition and search for a cure, the war she has waged within her own mind continues unabated.

LIEUTENANT MING XIONG: The young, idealistic scientist assigned to Starbase 47 and given the enviable task of learning the truth behind the Taurus Meta-Genome and the Shedai civilization that created it. His passion for learning and exploration are at first challenged and eventually dampened as he comes to understand the true power of the Shedai and the potential it represents not only to the Federation but also its enemies. Still, he retains hope that unearthing and even sharing the mysteries of the Taurus Reach might help to forge new ties between the interstellar powers.

TIM PENNINGTON: An investigative journalist working for the Federation News Service and assigned to cover the Federation's activities in the Taurus Reach. Pennington's investigations have already brought him afoul of Lieutenant Commander T'Prynn, who sacrifices the reporter's professional reputation as a means of covering up what really happened to the *U.S.S. Bombay*. Ostracized by his employers as well as the majority of the station's crew, Pennington soon finds himself befriended by the unlikeliest of allies, the shady trader/merchant Cervantes Quinn. Pennington and Quinn find themselves partaking of several unusual adventures before fate brings the reporter face-to-face with the truth of the Taurus Reach and the supreme race of beings that once called it home. Armed with these startling revelations, the journalist unleashes an exposé that shatters the veils of secrecy surrounding Operation Vanguard and the very real threat the Federation now faces.

AMBASSADOR JETANIEN: A Rigelian Chel and the Federation's diplomatic attaché assigned to Starbase 47. A wise and learned statesman with a firm belief in the Federation's bedrock principles and ideals, Jetanien also is driven by an intense need to forge some form of enduring legacy to mark his life and career. Necessity requires the ambassador to foster several bold diplomatic overtures with the Klingons and the Tholians, but it's ambition and ego that compel him to do everything possible to salvage such proceedings even as the political climate between the Federation and the Klingon Empire continues to deteriorate.

THE SHEDAI: The enigmatic architects of an ancient hegemony that once spanned the Taurus Reach. At first believed to be extinct, the Shedai in fact were once all but destroyed as a result of civil war. Some survivors of the once-mighty civilization have lain dormant in stasis for thousands of years, waiting for an opportunity to rule again. A few of those survivors have awakened in response to the arrival in their space of Federation and other curiosity seekers, viewing the interlopers as a threat to be annihilated. A lone agent, the Wanderer, has begun systematically pursuing and destroying outposts on worlds once ruled by the Shedai. However, another agent, the Apostate, has split from his peers, disagreeing on this course of violent action. Though the Apostate succeeds in crippling the remaining Shedai, it remains to be seen if they can rally their forces for one more attempt to return to power. Meanwhile, the Wanderer, the one Shedai capable of interstellar travel without assistance from the astonishing technology her people once commanded, continues her mission to rid the Taurus Reach of all who would seek to exploit the power of the Shedai.

The Taurus Reach
2267

PROLOGUE

"Red alert. The station is now on red alert. All hands to battle stations. This is not a drill. Repeat. This is not a drill."

The lifeless feminine voice of the computer droned over the sound of alarm Klaxons blaring through Starbase 47's command center. Jon Cooper emerged from his office, a quick glance all he needed to size up the scene around him. Each of the duty stations was manned, and a check of the center's primary situational displays told him that all defensive systems had been activated and currently were functioning at full capacity. It was only the second time since the station had been declared operational that its deflector shields and weapons had been brought online for anything other than a readiness exercise.

As Cooper crossed the deck, the alarm sirens faded, though the harsh crimson alert indicators continued to flash. After ascending the steps two at a time to the supervisor's deck, he noted that the station's commanding officer had yet to arrive. "Status report."

"Sensors are picking up six Klingon *D-7* battle cruisers approaching the station, Commander," replied Lieutenant Haniff Jackson from where he sat at "the hub," the platform's conference table into which had been integrated eight workstations, each tied into the station's primary systems and from which almost any aspect of Starbase 47's operation could be monitored and controlled. The computer interface seemed tiny and frail beneath the security chief's massive dark-skinned hands. He was hunched over his console, his red uniform tunic stretched across his broad torso to the point that Cooper was sure it simply would rip to shreds if Jackson flexed his muscles. "They're coming in weapons hot and deflector screens powered up. Our ships have formed a perimeter around the station and are holding position."

Looking to where Lieutenant Judy Dunbar sat at another of the hub's stations, Cooper asked, "I don't suppose they're responding to hails?"

The communications officer shook her head, looking up at Cooper and brushing a lock of light brown hair from her eyes. "No, Commander."

It had only been a matter of time, Cooper knew. In recent months, the political situation with the Klingons had been steadily deteriorating, with many Federation diplomats and Starfleet military experts concluding that the mounting tensions with their longtime adversaries—as well as the isolated yet increasingly frequent confrontations—would escalate to open hostilities. Cooper was not surprised when the Code One alert from Starfleet Command reached the station, notifying all ships and installations that the Federation, for all intents and purposes, now was at war with the Klingon Empire.

Even now, in the few days that had elapsed since the alert was dispatched, skirmishes between Starfleet and Klingon vessels were on the rise all along the border. In one of the more distressing reports Cooper had read, two Klingon cruisers had attacked and destroyed a Starfleet hospital ship in the Kalinora Sector, claiming that it actually had been engaged in espionage. Assaults on other ships, as well as forward observation outposts, unmanned subspace communications relay stations, and even one starbase, had been reported. Starbase 47, given its location away from well-traveled Starfleet patrol routes and its proximity to Klingon space, also offered a tempting target for enemy attack, and that did not even take into account the empire's increased interest in the Taurus Reach.

"Let's see them," Cooper said, looking up from the hub to the array of large rectangular viewing screens dominating the upper portions of each wall of the command center. In response to his order, Jackson keyed a string of commands to his workstation, and the images on several of the screens shifted to show varying views of the different approaching enemy vessels.

"They're breaking formation and moving to equidistant positions around the station," Jackson reported. "Current distance is seven thousand kilometers." To emphasize his point, the security chief pointed to one of the overhead viewers, which currently displayed a tactical schematic of the station and the surrounding region. The image depicted a large blue circle representing the station at its center and four smaller circles corresponding to the Starfleet vessels that would form the first line of defense should the situation escalate to that point. Six fiery red arrows maneuvered around it in formation—the Klingon vessels.

Feeling a knot tightening in his gut as he watched the deployment continue to unfold, Cooper saw his mounting anxiety mirrored in the faces of the command-center staff. The pulsing indicators on the screen might put forth the notion that the odds were almost even despite the greater number of Klingon ships, but Vanguard's executive officer knew better. The *U.S.S. Endeavour* was the largest and most powerful of the four Starfleet vessels at the station's disposal, but from there, things began to slide very much toward the Klingons' favor. The *Endeavour*, along with the *Locknar*-class frigate *Akhiel* and the *Saladin*-class destroyers *Hannibal* and *Theseus*, was all the ship-based firepower that could be mustered to the station's aid when it became clear that an enemy attack was imminent. The *Miranda*-class *Buenos Aires* was away from the station on assignment, and the only other available Starfleet ship, the *Sagittarius*, had been ordered to remain within the relatively safe confines of its hangar bay. The tiny scout-class vessel would be no match for a Klingon battle cruiser and did not possess armaments necessary to play even a supporting role in what might well end up being a brutal battle.

"Receiving a hail from the *Endeavour*," reported Dunbar, her eyes narrowing as she listened to the communication being filtered through the Feinberg wireless receiver in her left ear. "Captain Khatami's requesting instructions."

Cooper drew a deep breath in an effort to quell his growing unease. It had been a long time since he had seen combat, and he never had experienced a situation that required him to protect a stationary target. Though Starbase 47's own defenses and those of its accompanying starships should be enough to hold off the worst of any imminent Klingon attack, there were no reinforcements if things went sour.

Always the optimist, aren't you?

"Try to raise the Klingons one last time," Cooper said, nodding to Dunbar as he gave the order. Then the sound of turbolift doors opening behind him caught his attention, and he turned to see the station's commander, Rear Admiral Heihachiro Nogura, stepping into the command center.

Thin and lean, the Asian man paused on the center's main floor, standing calm and composed amid the furious activity taking place around him. Cooper knew that the admiral had seen and managed his share of crises, and that experience appeared to be guiding him now as his eyes took in all of the information presented on the various viewscreens around the room. Watching Nogura now, Cooper even felt his own tension ease just a bit.

The respite was short-lived.

"We're being targeted," Jackson called out, his voice rising in volume. "All six cruisers are locking weapons on the station. Our ships are maneuvering to intercept."

This was it. War had come to Vanguard.

"Notify Khatami and the others that they're clear to engage the moment any of the enemy ships opens fire," ordered Nogura as he climbed the steps to the supervisor's deck and moved to stand opposite Cooper on the other side of the hub. Cooper knew that the admiral—who seemed to possess almost Vulcan-like hearing—likely had picked up every word spoken by anyone in the command center since exiting the turbolift. "Jackson, have engineering transfer power from all nonessential systems to the shields." Nogura spoke the words with a quiet yet palpable authority, with no excitement or even a hint of worry or uncertainty.

Settling into one of the hub's empty seats, Cooper used its workstation to call up the latest status from each of the station's primary systems. He felt his heart rate increasing, sensed his breaths coming quick and shallow in anticipation of what the next minutes might bring. Feeling a rush of warmth, Cooper reached up to tug at the neck of his uniform tunic. To him, it seemed as though the temperature in the command center was increasing by the second.

Then intense heat washed over his fingers, and he jerked his hands away from his workstation, flinching at the sudden, unexpected pain. At the same time, he realized that his chair also was growing hotter, and he pulled himself to his feet. All around the command center, personnel were rising or stepping back from their stations, wearing mirrored expressions of shock as they looked to the upper deck—and Admiral Nogura—for guidance.

"What's happening?" Nogura asked. He, too, had stepped away from the hub, and Cooper now saw the air shimmering over the table as heat radiated upward.

Jackson shook his head. "I don't know, Admiral." He leaned closer to his workstation, studying the status monitors. "All weapons systems on the station are offline. The same with our ships." Frowning, he added, "And the Klingons, sir." Looking up, his brow was knit in confusion. "What the hell's going on?"

Any response that Nogura or anyone else might have made was cut off by a faint, high-pitched whine beginning to reverberate through the command center. Cooper looked around for the sound's possible source but saw nothing out of the ordinary. The whine became a howl, its intensity increasing with each passing second, so much that everyone in the room pressed his or her hands to ears in futile efforts to stifle its piercing assault.

"Where's it coming from?" Dunbar shouted over the din, her eyes squeezed shut.

At the point where Cooper was sure his eardrums would burst, the sound faded. In its place, an orb of light appeared above the center of the conference table, growing in size and brightness. Cooper watched as it stretched and elongated until it took on the outline of a humanoid life-form. Within seconds, it coalesced and solidified, with facial features, hair, and clothing emerging from the light. When the glare faded, all that remained was what appeared to be a human male, perhaps seventy Earth years of age, with deep creases in his forehead and around his eyes and mouth. His dark hair and beard were streaked with gray, and he wore a simple short-sleeved brown tunic with ornamental white stitching around its neck and down to the center of his chest. As he gazed out at the command-center staff, the man's eyes seemed heavy with sadness.

More like resignation, Cooper thought.

"It looks like a projection," Jackson said.

Stepping forward to better study the apparition, Nogura asked, "But where's it being transmitted from?"

It was the apparition that replied.

"My name is Ayelborne, of the planet Organia," the figure said, clasping his hands before him. *"At this moment, the military forces of your Federation and the Klingon Empire have converged in orbit above my planet, as well as elsewhere in space, ready, if not eager, to wage war. Were you to confine your hostilities to yourselves, we would be content to allow you to destroy each other. However, your conflict threatens millions of innocent lives, and that is something we cannot allow. At present, all of your instruments of violence now radiate a temperature of three hundred fifty degrees. They are inoperative. These same conditions exist within both of your star fleets. There will be no battle."*

"Are you kidding me?" Jackson asked, exchanging with Cooper an expression of disbelief.

Ayelborne continued, *"As I stand before you now, I also stand upon the home planet of your Federation and the home planet of the Klingon Empire. Unless both sides agree to an immediate cessation of hostilities, all of your armed forces, wherever they may be, will be immediately immobilized."*

Cooper felt his jaw slacken as he began to comprehend the enormity of what he was hearing. Who was this Ayelborne? What planet was Organia, and what kind of race that called it home could impose its will with such force and confidence? Were these mysterious beings friend, foe, or self-appointed overseer?

"You must understand," Ayelborne said, *"that we consider interference in the affairs of others to be most distasteful, but you have left us no choice. To that end, you will soon be contacted again, at which time the nature of our mandate will be made clear, and you will be offered paths to assist you in finding peace with each other."* For the first time since the projection had appeared, Ayelborne's features hardened from an almost paternal expression of disapproval to one of cold determination. *"The choice of which path to follow is entirely yours to make, and the consequences for your decision will rest solely with you."*

He said nothing more, and a moment later, his human appearance dissolved into the orb of blinding light, and those in the command center covered their ears again as the high-pitched whine returned. The light pulsed as it brightened, and Cooper shielded his eyes from the glare until it and the ear-piercing sound faded as though they never had existed. No one on the supervisor's deck spoke, apparently content to stand silent and absorb the astonishing revelation they had just witnessed.

Finally, Nogura broke the quiet. "Well," the admiral said, turning to Cooper as he clasped his hands behind his back, exuding the reserved demeanor that seemed to drape over him like a comforting blanket, "that's certainly going to make things a bit more interesting."

One Year Earlier

1

All was silence in the Void.

Despite tireless searching, the Shedai Wanderer heard nothing, just as she had since arriving on the lifeless moon she now called home. How long had she been here, listening for the songs that logic told her might never come?

The Conduit that was part of this moon remained dormant. It, along with all of the others throughout the realm once ruled by the Shedai, was dead, as they had been from the moment the First World departed this dimensional plane, taking with it the *Serrataal*. Without energy and guidance channeled outward from the First World, the Conduit could offer her nothing. The vast technology and resources it commanded and which were embedded within the moon's very core were inaccessible, protected by fail-safes that had activated the moment contact with the First Conduit was breached.

She was fortunate in that she had managed to traverse the immense distance separating this moon from the heart of the Shedai realm before all power was lost. Had that happened while she was still in transit, she likely would have been destroyed, crushed by the forces of space-time rushing in to fill the narrow gap forced open for only fleeting moments by the First Conduit. Despite escaping annihilation—at the hands of the Shedai Apostate and the collapsing Conduits—it had taken every bit of energy the Wanderer possessed simply to make her desperate, headlong journey to this desolate place. Now she was trapped here, powerless to do anything except search for any sign of her people while waiting for her strength to return.

And where was here?

Looking toward the stars, she saw the equally dead planet around which this moon orbited. It had taken her some time to sift through her memories and recall that this star system was among those most distant from the First World, near the outer periphery of what had been the vast realm once ruled by the Shedai. The Wanderer remembered with little interest that the barren world had once been home to a thriving civilization. For reasons she could not remember, the inhabitants had seen fit to exterminate themselves by means of a protracted conflict. Generations of unremitting warfare had destroyed both the people and the planet from which they had sprung. Whatever value the world might once have possessed had been lost long ago, first to violence and finally to time.

Wait . . .

Something touched the Wanderer's consciousness, startling her from her ruminations, and it was an additional moment before she realized that the Conduit had called to her. No, she decided, that was not accurate. Turning her attention to the ancient construct, she confirmed that it remained inert. None of its power systems was active, though a closer inspection revealed that the Conduit had indeed received some kind of faint, erratic energy pulse. Had the *Serrataal* returned already? She found that unlikely.

When another chime made its presence felt, this one just as faint as its predecessor, the Wanderer focused her mind on it, reaching out with her thoughts to grasp it. Fading into nothingness, it evaded her. Whatever she was sensing, it was far too weak and disjointed to have come from any *Serrataal.* This was something different.

Feeling new purpose resonating through her, she redirected her concentration, once again attempting to reach outward, toward the distant stars, seeking the source of this fleeting, mysterious contact. Even as her consciousness protested this new demand on her still-depleted strength and she registered yet another momentary hint of song emanating from the Conduit, instinct told her who was responsible for these startling new sensations.

Telinaruul.

Without the Conduit to guide her, the Wanderer was unable to determine from where the feeble signal had originated. Still, she was certain it came from one of the worlds that now seemed to be infested with *Telinaruul* who bore little resemblance to those beings who once had been subordinate to the Shedai. While she and her people had spent that unmeasured period locked in slumber, their realm had been invaded by these inferior beings. At first, the Wanderer was convinced that the *Telinaruul* could easily be punished for their impudence, either defeated in battle and run off or obliterated altogether.

That underestimation had nearly been her undoing during one encounter with them. On the barren, ice-covered world they had defiled with their very presence and upon which they had seen fit to plunder the Conduit erected there, the *Telinaruul* had very nearly destroyed her. They possessed knowledge and technology far superior to what she remembered from before the long sleep that for so long had claimed the Shedai. While their abilities alone were insufficient to overcome the power she wielded, the Wanderer had come to realize that their intellect was not to be misjudged. She would not do so again. When next she encountered them, she would do so with all of the force she could bring to bear, leaving nothing to chance. She vowed that the *Telinaruul* would be crushed.

For that to happen, she would have to escape this lifeless rock, which had become her prison.

Taking stock of her condition, the Wanderer knew that her strength was far from restored. Her escape from the First World had weakened her to a degree she had never before experienced. Even the encounters with the *Telinaruul* on other Shedai worlds that had left her depleted for reasons she still did not understand had not approached this level. In the time that had passed since her arrival here, she had recovered only a fraction of the energy necessary to escape this moon. Without the Conduits to aid and guide her, simply channeling her mind to listen for the songs was difficult. Any attempt to journey from the moon, even to the closest destination, would be an undertaking of such magnitude that the physical toll on her would be second only to the immense mental strain she would endure. Indeed, she knew the risks were so great that the passage might drive her to insanity, if she even survived at all.

None of this mattered, of course. Her loyalty to the *Serrataal* demanded that she take whatever action was available to her. The *Telinaruul* must be purged from all that once was Shedai. Once that was complete, the Enumerated Ones could return to their former glory.

The very thoughts, burning as they did in her mind, fueled the Wanderer's emergent powers. Soon, she knew, she would be ready.

2

Briana Pham leaned back in her seat, feeling the vibrations of the *Bacchus Plateau*'s massive engines as the ship made the transition from warp speed to impulse power. The reverberations played across every surface of the compact bridge, rattling loose deck plates and even causing her coffee mug to tremble in the makeshift holder she had fashioned for it on her chair's right armrest. Pham likened the shift to the vessel releasing a heavy sigh at the end of a protracted exertion. As always, she was unable to resist reaching out to give her helm console a reassuring pat.

"There, there, you big baby," she said, her tone mocking. On the viewscreen before her, she watched streaks of multihued light recede to distant points against the impenetrable black curtain of space.

To her left, her copilot and second-in-command, Joshua McTravis, smiled and shook his head. "One of these days, you're going to do that, and she's going to buck you right out of that seat."

"Maybe," Pham replied as she reached up to brush a lock of her long black hair back from where it had draped across her eyes, "but not today." She had no worries about the ability of the vessel to get her crew and her cargo wherever they needed to be, on time and in one piece. The ship had more than proven its mettle as part of her family's deep-space transport business for four generations, benefiting from the loving care lavished upon it by engineers such as the two she currently employed as part of her crew. Compared with some of the longer hauls the *Plateau* had endured during its many years of service, the three-month

PIQUA PUBLIC LIBRARY
CHILDREN'S DEPT.

journey at warp five from Rigel X had been a walk in the proverbial park.

"Warp drive is shut down," McTravis reported, sitting up in
his chair and running his fingers across his own console. "We're
at point seven, passing through the fourth planet's orbital plane."
He pointed to the trio of display screens dominating the section
of console that sat between them. "Sensors show no other ship
activity in the system, save for what look to be two transports in
orbit above the colony."

Pham nodded, satisfied. "That's good to hear. Make our
course for standard orbit." Reclining in her seat, she allowed herself to relax, if only a bit. After the uneventful voyage from Rigel,
Pham wanted nothing more than for the *Plateau* to complete its
latest contract assignment with an equal lack of excitement. From
what she knew of their current destination, the colony on Lerais
II was less than a month old, but it already was expanding at a
pace far greater than similar settlements spread throughout the
Taurus Reach. Still in its infancy, the colony also had managed to
escape the turmoil that had engulfed other planets in this region
of space.

Thanks to subspace news feeds received while the *Plateau*
was in transit, Pham and her crew had read of Gamma Tauri IV's
utter destruction at the hands of a joint bombardment carried out
by Starfleet and Klingon vessels. According to the incredible
story published by the Federation News Service, the order to annihilate the planet had come from the commander of the massive
starbase constructed in the Taurus Reach in a bid to contain what
had been described as a threat from an unknown species. By all
accounts and according to the latest FNS reports, the potential
threat to Federation security was on a scale unlike anything encountered in the history of human space exploration, dwarfing
even the Earth-Romulan conflict of more than a century ago.

And yet here we are, Pham mused, *flying head-on right into
the thick of it.*

The unsettling revelations that had come in the wake of the
tragedy that befell the colony on Gamma Tauri IV, along with the

other news of increased traffic by Klingon vessels throughout the region, had done little to assuage her unease about traveling through what might well be evolving into the epicenter for interstellar conflict. While the situation had been anything but tranquil from the outset—something Pham and her people knew firsthand from previous contracts with other Taurus Reach colonies—these latest developments were something else altogether. News disseminated via the FNS and messages received from other transport vessels traversing the region were saying the same thing: the Klingons were on the move, spreading out and tightening their grip.

With this in mind, she had discussed with the *Plateau*'s crew the possibility of abandoning their contract and reversing course. It was a notion with which she naturally disagreed, of course. Though born on Earth, she had spent less than a third of her life in her home country of Vietnam before following her father to space and eventually succeeding him as the *Plateau*'s master. Hard-won experience had taught her that uncertainty and even danger were occasional realities of the job, which was not to be abandoned in the face of adversity. Despite her own unwillingness to abandon the obligations to which she had committed herself and her ship, she knew she could not simply continue the voyage without giving her people opportunity to voice their concerns.

To a person, every member of the vessel's company had rejected the notion of turning back. Like Pham herself, several of her shipmates had spent their entire lives in this business, following in the footsteps of several generations who had aided in the Federation's expansion into even the minuscule portion of the galaxy that had been explored. For them, it was a simple issue: a contract was a contract.

Doesn't mean we have to be stupid about it, Pham reminded herself. *Let's get this over with and get the hell out of here.*

As if the *Plateau* itself might be agreeing with her, a green indicator light at the center of the navigation station began flashing in time to a steady, repeating beep. Reaching across his own

PIQUA PUBLIC LIBRARY
CHILDREN'S DEPT.

console, McTravis touched a control, and the tone halted. He took a moment to study the array of gauges and readouts before clearing his throat.

"Entering standard orbit." He tapped another series of buttons. In response, the image on the viewscreen shifted to that of a lush, green world. "There it is: Lerais II. Not a bad-looking planet, at least compared with some of the other dirtballs we've seen out here."

Pham shrugged. "According to what I've read, this is one of the more promising candidates for large-scale farming." Looking to the screen, she noted the layers of clouds obscuring portions of the planet's four major landmasses and snowcaps highlighting both poles. "If the experts are right, in a couple of years, this planet might well find itself at the center of a whole new agricultural boom."

"You sound almost envious," McTravis countered, his tone teasing. "Thinking about staking a claim?"

Rolling her eyes, Pham could not resist a smile. This conversation, or some variant, echoed around the *Plateau*'s bridge whenever she voiced knowledge of or—heavens forbid—even interest in any of the numerous planets they visited, to the point where either she or McTravis could recite both sides of the discussion with the passion and verve of seasoned performers.

"I just might surprise you one of these days," she said, in keeping with how the verbal volley usually ended. After all, both she and McTravis knew that making a home on some far-flung planet was an unlikely possibility for either of them, or most of the *Plateau*'s crew, for that matter. While Pham took every opportunity to enjoy the fresh air and unrestricted freedom offered by any port of call after a long voyage, like her longtime friend and partner, she was most at home in space.

Not that a decent nonreconstituted meal or a long, hot bath along with a bottle of wine won't go unnoticed or unappreciated, she reminded herself. Those things and more awaited the crew on the planet below, but only after they handled the more pressing business. *Get back to work.* Leaning forward in her seat, Pham

PIQUA PUBLIC LIBRARY
CHILDRENS DEPT

keyed the ship's communications system and opened a standard hailing frequency.

"New Anchorage Control, this is the transport vessel *Bacchus Plateau*. We are entering standard orbit and are ready to receive landing instructions at your convenience." With her initial greeting complete, Pham touched a control on the panel above her head to transmit the *Plateau*'s identification codes and shipping manifest to the colony's orbital traffic administrator.

After a brief pause, a deep masculine voice blared from the bridge's intercom, "Bacchus Plateau, *this is New Anchorage. Welcome to Lerais II. According to our logs, you're almost a week early. Hope your trip was uneventful.*"

"That's one word for it," McTravis replied, unworried that his comment might be picked up by the comm system. Pointing to one readout situated on the console between them, he added, "We're receiving landing information now."

"Bacchus Plateau," continued the voice from New Anchorage, "*Orbital Tracking has cleared you for landing maneuvers. You are authorized to commence powered descent to the designated coordinates.*"

"Acknowledged, New Anchorage," Pham replied. "Preparing to initiate landing sequence." Closing the comm circuit, she initiated a cross-check of the provided coordinates against a quick sensor scan and landing information she had been given upon accepting the job. New Anchorage was situated just less than one hundred kilometers inland from the northern coastline of the continent straddling the equator in Lerais II's eastern hemisphere. Within seconds, Pham was able to confirm the *Plateau*'s intended target. The coordinates coincided with the area of land designated for what would evolve into the colony's main industrial district—specifically, a vast open tract adjacent to what eventually would become a commercial transportation hub. At present, the facilities were rudimentary, consisting largely of whatever equipment the settlers had brought with them and the small, functional buildings they had erected since arriving. Still, Pham knew that in just a few short years, the planet would be capable of offering full landing support as well as maintenance and repair services to incoming vessels both on the surface and in orbit.

Until then, ships like the *Bacchus Plateau* were on their own, trusted by the residents of Lerais II not to plow into their colony while attempting to land.

"Okay, Josh," Pham said, reaching for her console and keying the instructions to transfer the coordinates to the helm and activate the automated landing protocols. "Here we go."

A crimson alert indicator flashed on her station, accompanied by a shrill alarm whine that echoed across the confines of the bridge.

McTravis pointed to one of the sensor displays. "Proximity alert. There's another ship, coming in fast." Hunching over the console, he scowled. "It just dropped out of warp, and damned close. Whoever they are, they must be idiots or suicidal."

What the hell? Her stomach churned in reaction to the abrupt turn of events. There were many reasons for ships not to travel at warp close to planets, including the possibility of flying into said planets or even another vessel in orbit. "Sensors," she ordered.

"Already on it," McTravis replied.

Keying the hailing frequency once more, Pham called out, "New Anchorage, this is the *Bacchus Plateau*. We've got other traffic up here. What's the story?" Without her conscious control, Pham's right hand tapped the controls to cancel the landing sequence. Her fingers already were beginning to enter the commands to give her full helm control.

"*Plateau, this is—*"

Static belched from the speakers, drowning out the voice of the New Anchorage orbital control tech. Wincing at the assault on her ears, Pham slammed her hand down on the switch to close the frequency, once more plunging the cramped bridge into merciful near-silence.

"We're being jammed," McTravis said, grunting through gritted teeth. "Whoever it is, they don't want us talking to—"

Pham heard his sharp intake of breath and snapped her head in his direction in time to see the look of disbelief on her friend's face. Prying his eyes from his console, McTravis turned to her, and Pham watched the color drain from his face, the expression of astonishment twisting into one of horror.

"It's a Klingon ship," he said, his voice barely a whisper.

Sitting at his workstation within the tiny, dimly lit room that—for now, at least—served as New Anchorage's orbital tracking control center, Colin Rella blinked in horrified disbelief as the animated symbol representing the *Bacchus Plateau* on his sensor display screen disappeared.

"Oh, my God."

A second indicator, depicting the other, still-unidentified vessel that had appeared without warning, continued on its flight path, and Rella watched as the ship maneuvered into a standard orbital track. He had already requested a sensor scan from the communications center, and now he cursed the slower turnaround that was part and parcel of civilian sensor equipment. If he had been aboard the Starfleet science vessel he had called home for five years before resigning his commission to join the colonization effort on Lerais II, he already would have received confirmation of what his gut already was telling him.

"Colin," said Gwen Casale, calling through the doorway separating the comm shack from the tracking center, "it's a Klingon ship. *D-7*-class, according to the database."

Of course it is! Just such a possibility had been on everyone's mind from the moment the Federation News Service had reported increased Klingon ship movements throughout the Taurus Reach. The incident at Gamma Tauri IV was still fresh in everyone's mind, and many of the Lerais II settlers were on edge. A good number of those had opted to return to Federation space, and all available passenger berths aboard the transport freighters were reportedly booked. Cot space in the cargo holds now was going fast, and even Rella was considering taking one of those slots for himself, though now it appeared that it might not make any sort of difference. Even a single Klingon vessel would be more than capable of destroying the unarmed merchant ships hovering like sitting ducks in orbit.

As for what might be in store for those still on the planet's surface, Rella held no illusions. He had seen reports of what happened to the populations of worlds the Klingons chose to conquer. But would the empire be so bold as to take aggressive action against any world with a Federation presence?

We're not Federation, Rella reminded himself. *Well, not really.* Though the colony's leader had not taken the extraordinary step of renouncing Federation citizenship, they still had deferred most of the aid offered both by colonization assistance agencies and by Starfleet. Still, a vessel dispatched from Starbase 47 and carrying a contingent from the Corps of Engineers had come to support the settlement's initial setup and construction efforts. The ship's captain had graciously acquiesced when asked by administrators to leave the bulk of the work to the colonists themselves, but not before transporting to the surface a cargo bay's worth of tools and other equipment, along with an open-ended offer to return and render further help if and when asked.

I wish that ship was here now, Rella mused, *along with a few dozen of its bigger brothers and sisters.*

"Alert the administrator's office," he said, hearing the slight tremble in his own voice as the realization of what had just happened continued to sink in. "And get me the other transport ships." Tapping a string of controls on his console, he adjusted the image on his sensor displays so that he could now see the other vessels' orbital tracks. So far, the Klingon ship did not seem interested in pursuing them.

Someone behind him opened a door, flooding the darkened room with harsh sunlight that washed across his console and obscured his view. Squinting at the sudden change in illumination, Rella spun in his seat, holding up his hand to shield his eyes. "What in the name of . . . ?"

Silhouetted in the doorway was the squat, portly figure of Pehlingul, one of the engineers who was currently working to upgrade the sensor transceiver arrays on the roof of the building. The Tellarite was engaged in a bout of frantic gesturing, apparently to anyone who might take notice.

"Something's happened up in orbit!" he said. He pointed a pudgy thumb over his shoulder. "You need to come see this."

Rella was the first to leave his station, following the agitated engineer through the door and out into the courtyard that served as New Anchorage's town center. Flanked on all four sides by uneven rows of interim prefabricated single-story structures, the square would soon be supplanted by the permanent buildings being erected nearly a kilometer to the east. Outside, dozens of other colonists had emerged from the various buildings and were gazing upward. No sooner had Pehlingul emerged from the cover of the canopy mounted above the door than he was pointing toward the heavens.

"Up there. Look!"

Barely visible behind the thin haze of clouds obscuring what otherwise was a beautiful, springlike afternoon, Rella could make out at least a dozen faint streaks of light arching across the brilliant blue sky, all originating from a single point. At the heads of most of the contrails were dazzling balls of fire, remnants of the *Bacchus Plateau* breaking up as they plummeted from orbit.

Around him, Rella heard reactions of horror and disbelief from some of the colonists, most of whom, of course, did not yet know the reality of the situation currently unfolding far overhead.

"What happened?" someone asked from behind him.

Another colonist answered, "One of the transport ships. It has to be. Maybe they suffered a warp-core breach?"

Rella said nothing, the truth churning his gut, as did anticipation over what might happen next.

He jerked at the touch of a hand on his shoulder and turned to see Gwen Casale staring at him, her face a mask of worry and mounting terror.

"Colin."

Whatever else she might have said seemed to die in her throat, and Rella saw her expression change an instant before he caught sight of the column of harsh crimson energy that had appeared in the courtyard. Within seconds it coalesced into the form of a humanoid figure. As the new arrival's body solidified and the effects of the transporter faded, a chorus of surprised and startled gasps and several cries of alarm echoed around the square.

"Dear Lord," Rella heard Casale say in a croaked whisper.

The Klingon had to stand nearly two meters tall by Rella's estimation. There was no mistaking the martial nature of his attire, which consisted of a dark tunic beneath a silver vest cut from what Rella knew was a lightweight, flexible variant of chain mail. Dark, patterned trousers were tucked into polished black leather boots, the tops of which reached to the Klingon's thighs. He was broad-shouldered and muscled, with long black hair falling past his shoulders and a prominent array of brow ridges dominating the top of his head. A massive sidearm, a disruptor pistol, was strapped to his right hip, and the palm of his left hand rested atop the pommel of a long sheathed blade.

Without thinking, Rella reached out and pulled Casale to him. She did not resist, wrapping her arms around his waist.

"Earthers and your assorted lapdogs," the Klingon said, his deep baritone voice bouncing off the temporary buildings' thermoconcrete walls, "my name is Komoraq, commander of the Imperial vessel *M'ahtagh*. This planet has been claimed by the Klingon Empire. We established our presence here some time ago. You are therefore trespassing." Holding out his hands, he seemed to shrug. "It is unfortunate that your ship did not announce your presence in the system prior to making planetfall. As it happens, my vessel's sensors malfunctioned and registered your freighter as an enemy ship arming its weapons against us. An unfortunate oversight, to be sure. However, in the interest of preserving whatever fragile peace our respective governments and their political puppets treasure, I will offer you a single opportunity: leave, or be destroyed."

Cries of incredulity and denial erupted from the growing crowd. Rella found it unlikely that Komoraq was intimidated or even impressed by the protests, and there certainly was no outward appearance of the Klingon's even registering the display.

Still, it was obvious that he had anticipated such resistance, if not something more aggressive.

"You growl like mongrel dogs, Earthers, and I can smell the fear you hope to hide," he continued. "Perhaps some of you are considering brandishing a weapon and striking me down from the shadows. Should that come to pass, know that my crew will not rest until every living thing is dead, and every trace of your colony is wiped from the face of this planet."

"The Federation won't stand for this!" someone yelled from the crowd.

"This is an act of war!"

Komoraq seemed to consider those along with other comments and epithets. He even nodded in apparent acknowledgment, allowing the tirades to continue for a moment before raising his right hand. Incredibly, the assembled colonists fell silent at the unspoken request.

"It would be wise for you to channel your anger and fear into the energy required to pack your belongings and depart this world." He paused, unleashing a smile that revealed uneven rows of jagged yellow teeth before waving his hand with dramatic flair. "Once I return to my ship, you will have one standard day to be gone. Anyone still on the surface one heartbeat after that deadline will die. The choice is yours. Make it a wise one."

From his belt, the Klingon retrieved a palm-sized device that Rella took to be a communicator. An audible chirp filled the air before Komoraq uttered something all but unintelligible into the unit.

"M'ahtagh. HIjol!"

An instant later, the stark, fiery-red transporter beam enveloped the Klingon, and he disappeared, the only trace of his having been among the colonists the distinct prints his boots left in the soft earth of the courtyard. In the wake of Komoraq's departure, a subdued buzz of halting, uncertain murmuring filled the compound as colonists looked askance at one another, anxiety and dread weighing on them all like a stifling blanket.

Behind him, Rella heard Pehlingul say, "He can't be serious."

"Tell that to the crew of the transport he just shot down," Casale snapped.

Rella was astounded at the Klingon captain's unchecked audacity. Starfleet would learn of the *Bacchus Plateau*'s destruction, to say nothing of whatever might happen here during the days to come. Would they stand idly by and allow the empire to wrest control of the planet for their own ends? Of course, to Rella, the real question was whether the Federation considered Lerais II important enough to risk declaring interstellar war.

I wouldn't bet on it.

"So, that's it?" the Tellarite engineer pressed. "We just give up and run away like scared children?"

Lifting his head to stare transfixed once more at the dissipating cloud of debris that was all that remained of the ill-fated merchant vessel, Rella shook his head in resignation. "Better scared than dead."

3

Commander Jon Cooper sat behind the desk that until three weeks ago had belonged to Commodore Diego Reyes, poring through the twenty-sixth of forty or so personnel requests from different members of the station's crew—transfer applications, recommendations for promotion or personal commendations, requests for extended leave, and other administrative drivel. These had followed status reports, one submitted by each of the station's fifteen department heads, which, in turn, had followed five intelligence briefing memos.

All of that, and he had been in his office less than an hour. It was not shaping up to be a good day.

Paperwork never had been Cooper's strong suit, and the administrative duties that came with the role of Starbase 47's executive officer gave him more in this arena than could be accomplished by two people working full-time. In the weeks that had passed since he had assumed temporary command of the station, the correspondence demanding his attention seemed to be multiplying at an exponential rate. Though he knew that he would be replaced just as soon as Starfleet could assign a flag officer to the station and transport that person out here, Cooper wondered if he would survive that long. It was as though the mass of documents, reports, memos, and position papers he faced each morning was a living thing, threatening to expand until it consumed him, the office, and possibly even the station itself.

How the hell did the commodore do this every day and not blow himself out an airlock?

It had been difficult to take on the duties of which Reyes had been relieved, especially given the circumstances under which that action had occurred. Despite the amount of time that had passed, Cooper knew that the station's crew still functioned beneath a cloud of shock and uncertainty. The vast majority of people assigned to Starbase 47 had been blissfully unaware of the true purpose for its presence in the Taurus Reach. Naturally, many of them now wondered if they had been placed on the forward edge of a new battleground, soon to fight a war for which they were woefully unprepared, against an enemy they did not understand and who by all accounts outclassed them on every level.

As for Diego Reyes, the commodore remained in confinement since his arrest. Though visitors were permitted, Reyes had made it clear that he wished no contact from any member of the station's crew, particularly the senior staff. At first, Cooper had thought this was simply a matter of ego or embarrassment, but it was Ambassador Jetanien who told him that the commodore was actually looking out for his crew. Anything they might discuss would be subject to deposition when the court-martial began, and Reyes had taken great pains to ensure that only those persons with absolute need-to-know about Starbase 47's true mission were so informed.

Including T'Prynn, of course.

Many of the actions taken by the station's intelligence officer remained cloaked in mystery. Investigators from Starfleet and even Starbase 47's lead officer from the Judge Advocate General Corps, Captain Rana Desai, had already conducted thorough searches of the Vulcan's quarters and office, to no avail. Her computer files were sterile, offering no clue to the activities she had been conducting in secret, allegedly in defense of Starfleet and Federation security interests. Such information had to be stored somewhere, or perhaps Lieutenant Commander T'Prynn simply carried it around in her mind, which at this moment was being held captive by the coma into which she had fallen three weeks ago. Frequent updates from the station's chief medical officer, Dr. Ezekiel Fisher, and the physician assigned to oversee T'Prynn's care, Dr. Jabilo M'Benga, had offered no change in the commander's condition.

The second she wakes up, she'll be held in irons, Cooper mused. *Maybe they should just move her bed to the brig and be done with it.*

The intercom positioned at the corner of the desk chirped for attention, and he heard the voice of his assistant, Ensign Toby Greenfield. *"Commander, Ambassador Jetanien is here to see you, sir."*

Setting aside the data slate containing the latest mind-numbing report, Cooper sat up in his chair and stretched the muscles in his back. The fact that he was already performing such a therapeutic action at this early hour was yet another indicator of how he expected the rest of his day to unfold.

As if you don't already have enough clues.

"Send him in, Ensign," Cooper said, rising from his chair as the door slid aside to admit the towering figure of Ambassador Jetanien, dressed as always in the flowing, ornately designed robes of his office.

"I'd say good morning, Ambassador," Cooper said by way of greeting, "but I think we can agree it's not good for a lot of people."

"Commander," Jetanien replied, "your gift for understatement rivals that of Commodore Reyes. I take it you've read the security briefing with respect to the incident on Lerais II?"

Cooper nodded. "First thing this morning." The report had provided only the sterile, matter-of-fact accounting of the Klingon attack on the colony, with an additional report appended by the station's colonial liaison, Aole Miller, detailing the impacts of the incident from the perspective of the settlers, who even now were in the process of abandoning the colony they had worked so hard to establish. "I'm still waiting for updated information from Starfleet Intelligence. Do you have any idea what happened? Are the Klingons' claims legitimate? Did they plant their flag on that planet first?"

"We received no such notification," the ambassador replied, "though the Klingon Diplomatic Corps is saying it sent official notice to its counterparts on our side months ago." Jetanien then emitted something that sounded to Cooper's ear like a dog sneezing. "Surely the colonists would have said something if they'd detected any signs of Klingon occupation. And why would the Klingons wait until the colony was almost up and running before revealing their presence?"

"Maybe they didn't want anyone to know they were there," Cooper said. "You think the Klingons have found Shedai technology there?"

"It's certainly a possibility," Jetanien said. "The planet was not found to contain traces of the Taurus Meta-Genome; that doesn't rule out Shedai influence. Also, it offers little in the way of strategic value, as far as Federation or Klingon security interests are concerned. Its natural resources are plentiful, though nothing remarkable such as dilithium. Still, it harbors great agricultural potential, and the colony wanting to settle there was a good fit."

At first, the practice of allowing legitimate colonization efforts to act as unwitting camouflage for Starfleet's clandestine research into the origins of the Taurus Meta-Genome had seemed innocuous. However, when it became obvious that the Tholians were greatly opposed to Federation expansion into the region, which was followed by Klingon spies obtaining information revealing Starfleet's intentions in the Taurus Reach, Cooper had begun to wonder when or if such a strategy might backfire. That doubt had been confirmed with horrific force at Gamma Tauri IV. When the truth of the cover-up for Starfleet operations was revealed by Pennington, he and Aole Miller had been besieged by communiqués from colony administrators across the Taurus Reach, demanding to know if their planet was one that might be of interest for Klingon, Tholian, or even Shedai attention. Several colonies founded on worlds known to possess Shedai artifacts were already in the process of relocating or being abandoned altogether as the settlers returned to the relative safety of Federation space.

Lerais II, officially, had not been listed as one such planet.

"I'm betting we were wrong about the Shedai not having a

presence there," Cooper said, sighing as he shook his head. "If we'd known, the colony might have opted to leave before something like this happened."

"Colonial Liaison Miller has already had extended discussions with his counterparts on Earth," Jetanien said. "They're backpedaling with respect to the Klingons' asserted rights to the planet. According to them, it's still in dispute, but early indications are that there was to be no contesting the claim."

"The Klingons didn't have to blow an unarmed freighter out of the sky to make their stand," Cooper said, reaching up to rub the bridge of his nose. "What a waste." Coffee, he decided, was the prescription best suited to helping him at the moment. He rose from his chair and moved toward the food slot built into the office's rear bulkhead.

"It's worth pointing out that this colony had all but renounced Federation citizenship," Jetanien said after a moment. "Though they did so with far more aplomb and civility than the settlement on Gamma Tauri IV, the result was the same: they unfortunately removed themselves from the umbrella of Starfleet protection."

Waiting for the food slot to dispense his coffee, Cooper snorted. "You think that's what Starfleet should tell the families of the people on that freighter?" The slot's door slid up, revealing a steaming mug, and he reached for it. "Somehow, I'm thinking that won't go over so well." After taking a sip of the coffee and deciding it would do, he asked, "So, UFP Colony Administration's washing their hands of this one?"

"It would make sense," Jetanien said. "Given the current political climate between the Federation and the Klingons, particularly over the situation here in the Taurus Reach, Starfleet's thinking may be that contesting this move by the Klingons now is buying us more trouble than we can handle at the moment."

"I have to say, Ambassador," Cooper countered, "that I'm getting pretty tired of hearing that argument. Appeasing and not wanting to make waves—for the Klingons or the Tholians or whomever else we might piss off in the coming days—is not really the job I signed up for." He returned to his chair, dropped into it, and took a long drink of his coffee, enjoying the taste of the thick, hot liquid as it coursed down his throat. He held the mug under his nose, allowing the brew's enticing aroma to play at his nostrils. For just this moment, he could almost forget the mounting pressures of the day. Almost.

"It is, however, the job I've been given, Commander," Jetanien said. "Federation and Klingon diplomatic attachés have been meeting for several weeks, with one of the key issues being territorial expansion. The Taurus Reach has factored prominently in those discussions, and there's been little progress made. Suffice it to say that if—or when—relations with the Klingons deteriorate to the point of war, the Taurus Reach likely will be one of the main fronts in such a conflict."

Cooper nodded. He already knew much of this, of course, given the daily intelligence briefings he received. There were other issues in play with regard to the tenuous tug-of-war that could laughingly be called the state of political relations between the Federation and the Klingon Empire, but the Taurus Reach was fuel thrown on a smoldering fire.

"If this keeps up," he said, "I'll have to recommend to all of the colony administrators that they evacuate. Some are considering it, and others have already given orders to start packing. There are several holdouts, though. Some have renounced Federation citizenship. Others are just being stubborn." He shook his head. "And we both know that being stubborn will get you dead." Cooper contemplated the effects of a mass exodus of Federation colonists from the Taurus Reach. The Klingons likely would consider that open season on the planets left behind, particularly those chosen for their strategic value or the resources they offered.

"There is one other thing," Jetanien said, shifting his position and stepping closer to the desk, the string of high-pitched twittering he verbalized indicating to Cooper the Chel's discomfort with what he was about to say. "I have spoken with my Klingon counterpart, Lugok, via back channels. The High Council will soon be demanding the extradition of Commodore Reyes. They want him tried in their courts for what happened at Gamma Tauri IV and Jinoteur and a few other comparatively minor offenses."

Cooper felt a knot tighten in his gut. The Klingon legal system, to say nothing of their notions of justice, was not something he wanted to experience firsthand. That the Klingons were making this kind of noise about Reyes spoke volumes about how angered they were at the commodore and the actions he had taken.

"I suppose it's too much to hope for them to accept that he's standing court-martial and is likely to spend a significant portion of the rest of his life in prison?"

After spewing another string of derisive clicks and snorts, Jetanien replied, "I suggest you refamiliarize yourself with the concept of Klingon honor, Mr. Cooper. In my experience, it is a fluid, ever-evolving notion, though some things remain absolute. The Klingons feel they have been wronged in battle, and in their view, there are precious few avenues available for recompense."

"That's a fancy way of saying they want their pound of flesh," Cooper added, "and they'll be particular in how they go about getting it."

Jetanien nodded. "Well put, Commander."

Listening to the ambassador's counsel and trying to order it within the teeming mass of information clogging his mind with respect to the current problems he faced, Cooper took a moment from all of that and reminded himself of the location of the nearest airlock.

4

"I have to say, I really love what you've done with the place," said Ezekiel Fisher, making a show of looking about the station's brig in dramatic fashion. The walls, deck, and ceiling all were painted in the same drab, utilitarian, gray color scheme dominating the bulkheads in nearly all of Starbase 47's duty areas. Fisher had always hated gray. Fifty years spent serving aboard various Starfleet vessels and space stations had done little to alleviate that opinion.

Sitting atop the cot that was his cell's dominant piece of furniture and with his back against the far wall, Commodore Diego Reyes regarded Fisher with the now-familiar sour scowl that seemed to have become his default expression. "That one was old when Napoleon was in prison," he said, making no move to rise from the cot. "If you're going to keep coming down here to visit me, is it too much to ask that you bring fresh jokes?" Filtered through the speaker grille set into the wall to Fisher's right, the commodore's voice was imbued with a hollow, artificial quality enhanced by the omnipresent hum of the force field separating the two men.

"Napoleon?" Fisher asked, allowing a small grin to tug at the corners of his mouth. "You know, that comparison almost works." He shrugged. "Well, other than you being much too tall." Eyeing the dull orange jumpsuit Reyes had been given to wear during his confinement, he added, "And he was a snappier dresser."

Reyes gestured toward the hatch leading from the holding area. "Do me a favor. Knock on that door, tell Lieutenant Beyer to come in here, and have her shoot me with her phaser set to maximum."

"She's getting some lunch," Fisher replied. "Said to hold off on that sort of thing until she gets back."

Shifting his weight on the cot as though seeking a more comfortable position, Reyes grunted. "Well, I suppose you can stay, then."

"I'm honored." Fisher moved to the single chair that was the only piece of furniture on his side of the force field and lowered his lanky frame into it.

"Did you come all the way down here to insult my wardrobe?" Reyes asked.

Fisher shook his head as he made himself comfortable. "Well, that's one reason. Another is that I thought you might like to know that the Klingons have demanded your extradition." That news had spread with unbridled haste, adding to the tense atmosphere already permeating the station.

"Well," Reyes said, "it's certainly nice to be loved." He released a tired sigh. "Still, Starfleet might be doing themselves a favor by handing me over to the Klingons. You can bet they'll execute me when their trial's over, and they won't waste a lot of time worrying about classified information or any of that crap. Everybody wins."

"That would make a twisted sort of sense, I suppose," Fisher replied. "Can't have that. It's not every day they get to keel-haul a commodore. You have to be paraded around in front of God and everybody before they get around to making an example of you, which, at the rate they're going, should be sometime next century."

Reyes expelled a forced, humorless chuckle. After a moment, he asked, "How's T'Prynn?"

"Same as before," Fisher replied. "M'Benga's been at it night and day for the past three weeks, trying to get some answers. He thinks somebody on Vulcan must have some idea about her condition or whatever might have brought it about, but so far, nobody's talking."

"Another life I might have saved," Reyes said, "if I'd just opened my mouth."

Fisher considered several responses but chose instead to say nothing. While it was true that Reyes holding up the release of T'Prynn's classified medical records had hampered M'Benga and Fisher's efforts to diagnose the Vulcan officer's condition, Fisher himself was not entirely convinced that having such information would have mattered. Whatever illness gripped T'Prynn, the doctor suspected it had a great deal less to do with physical maladies than with the largely unexplored regions of the Vulcan mind.

Now you're starting to sound like M'Benga.

When Reyes said nothing else after several seconds, Fisher decided to try changing the subject. "So, have many visitors?"

"No," Reyes replied, his gaze shifting so that he stared at the floor between them. In the weeks that had passed since his arrest and confinement to the station's brig, the commodore had allowed exactly one person other than his lawyer to visit him: Fisher. Members of the senior staff had made several attempts, all of which were rebuffed. Commander Cooper, Reyes's executive officer and the unfortunate soul currently tasked with running the station until a formal replacement was assigned, had been ordered by Starfleet Command not to communicate with the commodore. In spite of that directive, he had relayed messages through the brig's security staff, limiting his missives to queries about procedures and protocols. Reyes had allowed that much but had otherwise rejected almost all outside contact.

The silence hanging in the air between the two men was beginning to feel awkward, Fisher decided. "Has Rana been to see you? Even in an official capacity?"

Reyes shook his head. "Neither one of us thought it would be a good idea. She's the ranking JAG officer aboard the station, and even if she doesn't play a role in my court-martial, she'll at least be called to testify. It'll be hard enough on her without any perceptions that she's going easy on me."

Nodding in silent agreement, Fisher folded his arms across his chest as he leaned back in his chair. Captain Rana Desai, Starbase 47's senior representative from Starfleet's JAG Corps, had faced the unenviable task of arresting Reyes and filing the charges Starfleet had leveled against him. Disobedience of lawful orders, releasing classified information to unauthorized personnel, and conspiracy were the most serious offenses, any one of which would be sufficient to end Reyes's career. The most serious allegations surrounding his allowing journalist Tim Pennington to publish a scathing exposé about what had happened to the Jinoteur system as well as on Gamma Tauri IV—thereby presenting restricted information to the public—likely would send the commodore to prison, possibly for the rest of his life.

That Desai and Reyes also had been lovers for months before these unfortunate events—a fact that remained unknown for now to all but a precious few souls aboard the station—only served to complicate matters. While their relationship might be a secret now, Fisher held no illusions of that continuing once whatever legal proceedings that awaited Diego Reyes began in earnest.

So, Fisher mused, *I suppose I should cut the man some slack if he feels a bit grumpy.*

"How's your lawyer treating you?" he asked. "He seems like a decent enough fellow."

"Spires?" Reyes nodded. "He's a good man, very committed to the cause and so on and so forth. It's a shame he's got no chance of winning. Once we get past all of the legal smoke and mirrors, the charges are pretty clear-cut."

Reaching up to stroke his short, trimmed beard, Fisher said after a moment, "Well, maybe not to some people. Even Jetanien, as by-the-book as he can be, isn't ready to give up. I can't believe he hasn't punched his way through the wall to see you by now, Starfleet order or no."

"He wouldn't do that," Reyes replied. Shrugging, he added, "Well, yeah, he would, if it were anyone else but Rana who'd told him not to. They both know what's coming, and Jetanien's no good to anyone sitting in here next to me."

Fisher knew that the Chelon ambassador was one of the few individuals who had known from the very beginning the nature of Vanguard's true purpose: understanding the ancient civilization and technology of the Shedai. Even as Starfleet's brightest young scientific and engineering minds worked toward that goal, Jetanien and his legal cadre from the Starfleet Diplomatic Corps labored to preserve the fragile political ties that currently existed between the Federation and the Tholian Assembly, as well as the Klingon Empire. The Taurus Reach was of interest to all three parties. While the Tholians harbored great apprehension about the region and its former rulers, the Klingons were simply intrigued by whatever had attracted the Federation's attention.

Now that pretty much anyone in the galaxy capable of reading Federation Standard was aware of at least some aspects of what was going on out here, Fisher knew that the problems facing Vanguard's crew would only get more complicated.

"You'd think they could at least let you out of that box," he said, indicating Reyes's cell with a wave of his hand.

Reyes shrugged. "Be it ever so humble."

"You're still a flag officer," Fisher countered, his irritation beginning to mount, "and we're on a damned space station, for crying out loud. Confining you to quarters should be good enough. Where the hell else are you going to go?"

Pushing away from the wall, Reyes moved to the edge of the cot so that his boots rested on the floor. "Rana said she put in that request about five seconds after I was locked up, but she never got a response from Starfleet. I'm guessing no one back there wants anything to do with me these days, so here I sit."

Fisher frowned as he surveyed the commodore's living arrangements. Other than the cot on which Reyes sat, there was also a straight-backed chair, bolted to the deck before a narrow shelf that might charitably be called a desk. A small viewing screen was mounted to the bulkhead above the desk, equipped with a rudimentary interface that Fisher knew would allow the cell occupant to access a very limited section of the station's library computer banks and permit communications—all overseen by security personnel. The cell's only other noteworthy feature was the toilet, separated from the rest of the compartment by a waist-high privacy partition.

"So, you just sit in here until they decide what to do with you." Fisher shook his head, snorting in disgust.

"Until after the trial, anyway," Reyes replied, reaching up to scratch the side of his face. "After that, well, most Federation penal colonies have pretty decent accommodations these days." Pausing, he said nothing for a moment before offering a tired shrug. "Of course, they might hold the court-martial in San Francisco, and the brig there is first-rate."

"And that's the other news I brought you," Fisher said, leaning forward in his chair. "The court-martial is going to be held here."

Reyes seemed to take this revelation in stride. "Makes sense. The lawyers will have to interview damn near everyone on the station. Easier to do that here than shipping everyone back to Earth or another starbase. After all, we've still got our oh-so-secret mission to keep up with." He rose from his cot and began to pace the width of the cell—all six paces of it. "Then there's convening the trial board. They'll all have to be flag rank, commodores or better. Getting four of them who can be pulled away from their regular duties will take time. Hell, just getting them out here could take months."

He halted his pacing and turned to look at Fisher.

"So, what it boils down to is that my fate will be decided by four desk jockeys with nothing better to do for the next six months." Nodding toward the door, he added, "I'd rather Beyer just finish her lunch and come put me out of my misery."

It would be easy to interpret Reyes's remarks as simple fatalism, but Fisher knew better. The commodore had made no effort to deny or diminish his responsibility in the face of the charges against him. He fully expected to face harsh penalties for his actions and seemed ready to welcome whatever fate might be in store for him. Though he looked tired, Fisher could see that in spite of everything his friend had brought down upon himself, Reyes appeared more at ease than he had been in years.

It was his curious calm that worried the doctor.

5

T'Prynn stood alone in the wasteland, listening to the howling wind as it whipped sand across her face and through her hair and the folds of her desert soft suit. Despite the lack of stars or a moon in the night sky, a strange violet luminosity surrounded her, and what she saw was desolation. Barren low-rise hills and rolling dunes stretched to the horizon in all directions, the faint illumination casting long shadows.

As always, this place did not seem familiar, though it reminded T'Prynn of the foothills leading into one of the mountain ranges that formed the perimeters of Vulcan's Forge on her home planet. She had visited that region only once, in childhood as a student participating in a field excursion for a geology class, and she still recalled the fear that had gripped her during the group's encounter with a wayward *sehlat*.

T'Prynn now felt a similar stab of anxiety as she stood, alone in this place, waiting. Again.

Feeling the weight in her hands, she looked down at the *lirpa* she wielded. A staff of dark polished wood, it featured an oversized curved blade at one end, offset by a blunt metal weight on the other. The weapon's heft offered a measure of comfort, which T'Prynn knew was illogical but chose to embrace regardless. In another time and place, she would have rebuked herself for the flurry of emotional reactions she was allowing to detract from her focus. Now was not the time for such distraction.

Movement in the dunes caught her eye, and she looked up to see a lone figure approaching her. Clad in dark robes from head to foot, the new arrival also carried a *lirpa* in his right hand, its blade gleaming even in the weak indigo light that surrounded it and him. He covered the distance between them with long, assertive strides, and as he drew closer, T'Prynn recognized the crest and other traditional symbols woven into the front of his robe. The embroidery highlighted the wearer's lineage and ancestral history, and once again, T'Prynn considered the price she might well have paid had she agreed to join that family, as well as the penalty she had long endured for refusing to do so.

The figure stopped when less than ten meters separated them, reaching up with his left hand to push back his hood, revealing the face that had haunted her every moment since she had held his head in her hands and broken his neck.

Sten.

"We meet at the appointed place, T'Prynn," he said, his expression inscrutable but his tone mocking the ritualistic words that were part of the many ancient, time-honored marriage ceremonies still performed by many Vulcans. Lifting his *lirpa* so that he could grip its staff in both hands, Sten regarded her with his fierce gaze. "Do you finally agree to submit?"

T'Prynn shook her head. Her answer was the same as it had always been, from which she had never wavered over the decades and which she would speak until her dying breath. "Never."

"So be it," Sten said, and for a fleeting instant, T'Prynn—as she always did at this point—thought she detected the barest hint of resignation in her bondmate's voice. Then the time for reflection was over, as Sten charged, his *lirpa* raised and its razor-sharp edge aimed at her.

Expecting the feint, T'Prynn was ready when Sten abruptly stepped to his left, lowering his weapon and attempting to swing it beneath her guard. T'Prynn twisted her own *lirpa* downward, blocking the attack and forcing his blade away from her body. The move left Sten's torso exposed, and she jabbed forward, trying to take advantage of the opening, but her former lover was too quick and too well trained in this particular fighting art.

Sten recovered his stance, twirling his *lirpa* in his hands until its blade was near his left hand. Lunging forward, he swung the weapon up and over his head, bringing it down straight at her head. T'Prynn was only just able to lift her *lirpa* in defense, every bone in her body trembling from the force of the onslaught. Their blades locked, she kicked at him, her boot stomping into his midsection with all of the strength she could muster. It was enough to push Sten back and gain her some maneuvering room, but the respite lasted only seconds, as he recovered, adjusting his grip on his *lirpa* and renewing his attack.

He thrust the weapon forward, and T'Prynn reacted, dropping her arms in an attempt to block, failing to see that his maneuvering was a ploy. At the last instant, Sten pulled back the *lirpa,* dropping its blade and pushing forward yet again, this time getting inside her reach. T'Prynn felt the sting as the finely honed metal sliced across her abdomen. Gritting her teeth and releasing an audible groan at the sudden pain, she brought up her *lirpa* once more, swinging around its blunt end and catching Sten just above his right elbow. She heard the sound of bone cracking beneath the force of the blow. Sten staggered to his left. He loosed his grip on his weapon and let its blade fall to the sand as he lost his balance and dropped to one knee.

T'Prynn lurched forward, sensing her opportunity and ignoring the pain in her belly as she readied for another swing. Sten jerked himself upright, his right hand extending toward her, and at the last instant, she realized what he had done. Sand showered her face, stinging her eyes and catching in her nose and mouth. Gagging and spitting to clear her throat, T'Prynn reached up with one hand to wipe her eyes, backpedaling away from Sten and trying to keep him in her line of sight. When she looked up again, Sten was nowhere to be seen. Rubbing sand from her face, T'Prynn searched but could find no sign of him. Even the sand where they had fought appeared undisturbed, with no footprints or tracks to tell the story of their brief skirmish.

"Submit," she heard his voice call out, carrying over the wind.

Gripping the *lirpa* in her hands ever tighter, she screamed her reply. "Never!"

Dr. Jabilo M'Benga sat alone in Isolation Ward 4 of Starbase 47's sickbay, which was darkened save for the feeble illumination offered by the work light over his desk. So engrossed was he in the stack of reports that he had allowed to accumulate in his office—paperwork for which there never seemed to be sufficient time except for late at night, well after his normal duty shift had ended—that several seconds passed before he became aware of the telltale string of beeps echoing across the room. Their volume was subdued, barely carrying over the music M'Benga had set to play over the room's internal communications system.

Turning in his seat, M'Benga's gaze shifted to the ward's only patient and the biofunction monitor positioned above her bed. Bathed in the soft crimson light cast down from a small lamp he had found in her quarters, T'Prynn seemed almost regal as she lay unmoving on the bed, covered with a thermal blanket designed to offer a semblance of the desert warmth she might experience on her home planet. The Vulcan's expression remained as vacant as it had been when M'Benga and Dr. Fisher found her, collapsed near Vanguard's main hangar deck.

From where he sat, M'Benga could make out the one indicator on the bio monitor that deviated from the others. Unlike those designated for a patient's pulse, blood pressure, respiration, and other autonomic actions—all of which hovered just above the minimal levels needed to sustain life—the gauge denoting the detection of brain-wave function had spiked, bouncing up and down along its column of status markers as the monitoring equipment detected heightened activity.

"Hello," M'Benga said, rising from his chair and crossing to the biobed. He watched as the indicator rose to its highest level, remaining there for several seconds, as though fighting to free itself from the constraints of the monitor's display. Based on the readings, T'Prynn's mind, or at least a portion of it, was working overtime.

As part of his routine examination of the equipment overseeing his patient, M'Benga also checked the small, shallow clay bowl he had set on the nightstand next to her bed. A thin wisp of smoke drifted up from a coil of incense resting in the bowl, releasing a pleasing, earthy fragrance that reminded M'Benga of Vulcan's arid climate. It also did a wonderful job of masking the smell of cleansing agents used to disinfect and sanitize the sickbay patient areas. Knowing that incense was often used by Vulcans as a means of facilitating meditation, he had placed the bowl near T'Prynn in the hopes that she might sense its presence even while locked in her deep coma. So far, he had detected no reaction from her to this or any other external stimuli, but M'Benga figured there could be no harm in continuing the holistic regimen.

He activated a computer interface terminal at the side of T'Prynn's bed. "Computer, this is Dr. M'Benga. Begin recording."

"Recording," replied the feminine voice of the station's main computer system.

M'Benga cleared his throat before reciting, "Personal log, stardate 1573.9, time index 2137 hours. Notes on patient T'Prynn. Medical scans indicate increased mental activity, similar to that recorded on three earlier occasions. Computer, append links to appropriate entries from my log, using keywords 'T'Prynn' and 'coma' as search arguments."

There was a momentary pause before the computer replied, *"Acknowledged."*

"As before, I'm unable to determine the cause of this latest spike in activity," M'Benga continued, watching as the gauge began dropping until it came to rest at one of its lowest levels, an indication that T'Prynn's mind was returning to its state of near-catatonia. "Duration of latest active period was just less than two minutes. REM sleep has been ruled out, because of patient's current condition. Dream state is possible, perhaps even probable, as a consequence of the trauma the patient seems to have suffered. I have not yet ruled out the possibility of this being the effect of a healing trance, as would be normal for Vulcans who have sustained significant physical or psychological damage."

He had paused, considering his next comments, when he heard from behind him the door to the ward sliding open. He was not surprised to see Ezekiel Fisher entering the room. The station's chief medical officer seemed preoccupied, which M'Benga could not fault, given that Fisher likely was returning from one of his frequent visits to see Commodore Reyes.

"Good evening, Doctor," M'Benga offered as Fisher strode toward him.

Fisher nodded. "Evening, Jabilo," he said, his attention on the bio monitor above T'Prynn's bed. "No change, I take it?"

"You just missed another spike in mental activity," M'Benga countered, nodding toward the monitor. "It only lasted a couple of minutes, but it was just as intense as the other occasions." Sighing, he reached up to wipe grit from his eyes. The first mild protests of fatigue were calling, but he ignored them. "I've racked my brain trying to figure this out. I've run through every kiloquad of data in the computer's medical banks, both here and at Starfleet Medical, and come up dry. The doctors I've been able to reach on Vulcan haven't been of much help, either." He shook his head. "According to her file, she was suffering from those episodes for *decades*. Someone on Vulcan had to examine her at some point, if not offer some course of treatment."

"We both know how tight-lipped Vulcans can be," Fisher said, crossing his arms and reaching up to stroke his beard.

M'Benga released a mild chuckle. "You don't know the half of it." During his medical internship on Vulcan, he had come to learn a great deal about not only Vulcan physiology but also the shroud of secrecy that seemed to permeate so much of their culture. Only after working in such close proximity to Vulcan physicians had he begun to penetrate the opaque veneer that protected Vulcan society from the peering eyes of "outworlders."

Regarding him for a moment, Fisher said, "You look like hell. When's the last time you had a decent night's sleep?"

M'Benga shrugged. "I do all right." As had become his habit, he would seek a few hours' sleep in one of the ward's unused patient beds, wanting to be close at hand in the unlikely event that T'Prynn's condition changed to any measurable degree. Stepping away from the bed, he crossed the room toward his desk and indicated the computer terminal with a wave of his hand. "I do have one lead that hasn't hit a dead end just yet."

He reached the workstation and keyed a command string to bring up a log of communiqués he had received in recent weeks. "A friend of mine, a Denobulan physician who also interned at a Vulcan hospital, suggested that this could be the result of a mind meld that was forcibly interrupted. If, for instance, she was subjected to a meld against her will and that meld was broken, her own mind may have rallied in some sort of self-defense. If the other party's melding abilities were far superior to her own, she may not have been able to extract herself from the union without inflicting severe psychological damage to herself."

"That's an interesting leap you just made there, Doctor," Fisher said, pulling another chair closer to the desk and taking a seat. "What makes you think she was forced into a meld?"

Pointing to the computer screen, M'Benga replied, "Something my friend said. Remember what I told you about T'Prynn and the marriage challenge she underwent, where she ended up killing her fiancé in ritual combat?"

Fisher added. "Just don't ask me to say its name."

M'Benga ignored the joke. "Part of the original betrothal process involves a mind meld when the parties are children. Another meld takes place during the actual marriage ceremony. So, I started wondering, what if, during the *Koon-ut-kal-if-fee*, T'Prynn's fiancé tried to force her to meld. Maybe she killed him in a desperate attempt to break that meld. That would almost certainly have some debilitating effects." He shrugged. "Of course, without being able to talk to anyone on Vulcan about this, it's just a theory." To that end, he had sent all manner of messages to the Vulcan Science Academy, including a complete dissertation of his hypothesis. He had yet to receive a response to any of his queries.

"So," Fisher said, "what's the next step?"

Stifling a yawn, M'Benga shook his head. "For now? Continue to monitor her treatment and hope that she actually is in some form of healing trance. That, or fly to Vulcan, kidnap one of their doctors, and shanghai him back here."

"You could take her to Vulcan," Fisher said.

It was a thought M'Benga had considered himself, more than once. "It's almost nine weeks' travel from here." Nodding toward T'Prynn, he added, "Before I subject her to that, I'd like to verify that someone will be willing to help her when we finally get there."

Fisher said, "If she never comes out of that coma, someone on Vulcan likely will want her taken there, anyway. You might be speeding up the inevitable."

"Maybe," M'Benga replied, hearing his uncertainty lacing the single word. Still, the bio monitors overseeing T'Prynn's condition told him enough to keep going. He was certain that somewhere deep in the recesses of her tortured mind, T'Prynn was fighting to escape whatever gripped her. Even if he could not offer assistance, he still wanted to be here when—if—she managed to claw her way to consciousness.

"Something inside her simply refuses to give up," he said, studying T'Prynn's still form once more, "and I don't plan to give up on her, either."

6

Though it often had a calming effect on his stomach and even went so far as to alleviate the collected stresses of a given day, the bowl of chilled Coferian oyster broth offered nothing for Jetanien on this night.

It probably has more to do with my choice of drinking companions. That, the Rigelian Chel ambassador decided, to say nothing of the subject of the conversation in which he currently was engaged. Jetanien pushed his bowl to the far corner of the desk and returned his attention to the tabletop viewer before him. On the screen, a burly Klingon regarded him with a look of disdain to which the ambassador had become all too accustomed.

"Lugok," Jetanien said, reining in his growing exasperation and attempting to retain his composure, "how in the name of all that is civilized and sane do you think the Federation is going to react to this?"

The Klingon ambassador shrugged. *"I imagine it will do what it always does: flail about, decrying the action as hostile, and make stern noises about swift and unforgiving retribution, all while quietly hoping something more serious comes along with which to occupy their attention. Earthers have no stomach for conflict, Jetanien. We both know that."*

An aggravated rattle exploded from Jetanien's oversized proboscis. "You've been reading too much of your own propaganda, Lugok. If anything, humans have proven themselves to be among the most brutal of known sentient species. When provoked, they can and will fight, particularly in defense of those things they hold dear. Your ship attacked an unarmed *farming* colony, Ambassador. They obliterated a defenseless freighter for no reason."

Not responding immediately, Lugok instead reached for something out of range of the viewer's video pickup, and Jetanien watched as the Klingon brought a stout, wide-based mug to his mouth. When he pulled it away, a red film was visible on his mustache, which he wiped away with the back of his hand. *"Rest assured, Ambassador, that if the empire truly had viewed this willful encroachment on our territory as of any real concern, the colony itself would simply have been removed, rather than allowed to leave unmolested. As for the freighter, it was a regrettable error, I admit. Our vessel's sensors were overdue for refit with more modern systems. However, it's worth noting that the Earther colony was trespassing on a world already claimed by the empire."*

Feeling his ire rising, Jetanien cleared his throat. "Lugok, setting aside the apparent fact that no sign of Klingon presence on the planet was detected prior to the colony's establishment, tell me this wasn't retribution for what happened to your people on Gamma Tauri IV."

"This was not retribution for what happened to our people on Gamma Tauri IV," Lugok said, his expression so neutral, so impassive, that Jetanien wanted very much to reach through the display viewer and throttle the Klingon. *"Believe that, or don't. Either way, it is no concern of mine."*

While he did not say so aloud, the Chel suspected the real reason for the empire's interest in the planet, to say nothing of its willingness to use any means to defend that interest. Could it be that Lerais II was home to Shedai technology? There would, of course, be no way to determine that without a comprehensive sensor scan, something a colony transport would have been unable to accomplish. As had been demonstrated on several occasions, the Shedai artifacts found on other worlds throughout the Taurus Reach were curiously immune to detection unless one knew precisely what was being sought.

And if I'm right, the Klingons will never allow a Starfleet ves-

sel with the proper equipment anywhere near that planet. Indeed, Jetanien decided, such an act might well spark another, larger confrontation.

For the first time since their dialogue had begun, Lugok abandoned his relaxed posture and leaned forward until his grizzled features all but filled Jetanien's screen. *"Unless I'm mistaken, there is no treaty between our governments requiring the empire to notify the Federation of its activities, particularly in open territories. It is unfortunate that your colonists suffered from a simple technical malfunction, but there is little to be done about that now. Perhaps if a greater level of trust existed between our two governments, this tragedy might have been avoided."*

Though the words almost sounded sincere, there was no mistaking Lugok's expression. The Klingon either was lying about the destruction of the freighter or was simply regurgitating whatever story had been fed to him by a superior. Either way, the ambassador appeared not to care.

"Trust, you say?" Jetanien countered. "Is this the same trust that involves placing an undercover agent aboard this station? Within my *own* staff?"

Again, Lugok shrugged, appearing to be considering a nap. *"Opportunity presented itself, Ambassador. Are you suggesting that such action is beneath your vaunted Federation?"*

The revelation that the late Anna Sandesjo, one of his trusted aides, had actually been a Klingon intelligence operative surgically altered to appear human had come as a shock to Jetanien. Other members of his staff had discovered Sandesjo's true identity even before it had come to T'Prynn's attention. He had been considering just what to do with the covert agent, whether to expose her and have her arrested or find some way to monitor, if not direct, her activities for his own uses. T'Prynn had beaten him to that decision, further surprising him by converting Sandesjo into a double agent working for her.

For all the good that ended up doing for us. Given the length of time Sandesjo had served on his staff, how much damage had she caused to Federation security interests before Jetanien had discovered her and T'Prynn had converted her? Despite the precautions T'Prynn was sure to have taken, could they be sure that the Klingon agent had not continued providing real, actionable intelligence to her superiors? Jetanien was certain that all of the ramifications of this security breach had yet to be felt.

"Jetanien," Lugok said, *"we appear to be dancing around the important issue dangling before us. At first, we believed that your unrestrained expansion into the Gonmog Sector was carried out for the Federation's usual arrogant, selfish reasons, but of course, we both now know the real purpose of your presence here."* He pointed one large finger at Jetanien, and the Chelon imagined it coming through the screen to poke him in his chest. *"Your fumbling and indecisiveness have angered an enemy that threatens both our peoples. You can hardly fault the empire for pursuing its own interests in the region, especially now that we may well be searching for some weapon with which to defend ourselves from this adversary you've provoked."*

As irritating as Lugok could be, Jetanien knew he was right. Starfleet's mission to uncover the truth behind the Shedai had come with tremendous, unforeseen costs. The demonstrations of their power on planets throughout the Taurus Reach, including most recently the staggering disappearance of the entire Jinoteur system, was sending shock waves throughout the Federation and beyond. Now, with the Klingon Empire aware of the secrets buried within the Taurus Reach, Starfleet's original mission to determine the origin of the meta-genome had changed. The quest for unparalleled scientific discovery was now a mad dash to secure technology and weapons with the potential to shift the balance of power throughout the galaxy, possibly for centuries to come.

"Well, as you say, the Shedai are a threat to both the Federation and the empire," Jetanien said, his beak punctuating his words with rapid staccato clicks. "To that end, it would seem logical that our peoples come together in joint defense against this menace."

Throwing back his head, Lugok released a hearty, thunderous

laugh, which seemed determined to overload the viewer's audio ports. Once he settled down, he leaned back in his chair. *"Yes, that's quite a fine idea you have there, Jetanien. We will join hands and stand up to our mutual enemy. Assuming we prevail, what are we to do in the aftermath of our glorious victory?"*

"Surely," Jetanien replied, "this unprecedented alliance to protect our common interests might be viewed by any rational person as the foundation for a stronger, longer-lasting relationship between our two peoples? There is much good we can accomplish, Lugok, if we could only pledge to work together rather than against each other."

Once more, Lugok smiled. *"You're at your most entertaining when you propose such fantasies, Jetanien. We Klingons are not fools; we understand that you only now come to us after your failed attempts to hoard the alien technology for yourself. It is but the latest in a string of deceptions foisted upon the rest of the galaxy by your Federation. They are a gang of weak cowards who lack the fortitude to face their enemies in battle. Instead, they would rather attempt to defeat their foes by boring them to death with their words, hiding behind lies and treachery."* Once more, he leaned forward, his eyes boring out from the viewer as they locked with Jetanien's. *"It has not worked for you on any other front, Ambassador, nor will it work for you here."*

Forcing himself not to react to Lugok's baiting, Jetanien still could not discount the words of his counterpart. The divide between the Federation and the Klingon Empire had been widening for some time, long before the latest developments here in the Taurus Reach. Even now, as he conversed with Lugok, teams from the Federation's Diplomatic Corps were locked in protracted negotiations with similar representatives from the empire. Key among the many issues being debated were agreements with respect to territorial expansion by both parties. For years, Klingon officials had maintained that the Federation's outward growth threatened to constrict the empire's ability to do the same. Instead, they were being forced in directions where the possibilities of finding planets rich in the various natural resources required to maintain their society's standard of living dwindled. In the Klingons' eyes, this was tantamount to an attack on their very civilization, and while the Federation struggled to reach some form of mutual accord that might avert interstellar war, the Klingons, of course, seemed all but eager for what many on both sides saw would soon devolve into inevitable, open conflict.

Jetanien knew this was to be expected, given the empire's long heritage of enhancing its power and influence through conquest and enslavement and the great honor Klingons placed on the warriors who served as the instruments of that expansion. If Federation diplomats held any hope of bridging this massive ideological gap, it lay in finding some form of common ground, some means of earning the Klingons' respect. Jetanien also was certain that as negotiations ran on longer, the likelihood of winning that appreciation through words rather than demonstrative action grew very slim indeed.

"This discussion is getting us nowhere," he said after a moment. "Lugok, you and I may not be friends, but at least we have cultivated a respectful professional rapport. The fact that you and I continue to correspond when our governments would have us turn our backs on each other is proof enough of that. Surely, there must be something we can accomplish, some example we can offer our peoples to show that war does not have to be our destiny."

As he raised his massive hands, Lugok's face for the first time took on an expression of regret. *"There are limits to my influence, Jetanien. Circumstances have changed, both here and elsewhere. It seems that fate would prefer the course we now travel."* He looked off to his right, as though someone or something else had caught his attention. *"There are other matters to which I must now attend, Ambassador, but with luck, we may soon revisit this discussion."* Without waiting for any acknowledgment, Lugok severed the connection, his image on Jetanien's viewer now replaced with the seal of the United Federation of Planets and the words "Communication Ended."

Jetanien sighed. *Klingon stubbornness. How many times has Diego warned me about it?*

For a moment, his thoughts turned to his friend, still held prisoner in the station's brig. Commodore Reyes had refused most visitors' attempts to see him, and intellectually, Jetanien knew it was an appropriate stance to take. With a court-martial looming, the less anyone spoke to Reyes directly, the better off those people would be if and when they were summoned to testify.

None of that made Jetanien feel any better. Though there was precious little he could do for Reyes at this point, it had not saved him from the many sleepless nights he had spent in contemplation, examining the situation from every angle and hoping he might stumble across something previously overlooked.

He could not dwell on that now, he reminded himself. For the moment, he had far more pressing matters to address.

7

The disc sailed through the air, arcing over the heads of the children running to catch it. As it fell back toward the ground, it was caught by a girl with long brown hair pulled back into a ponytail, who snagged the disc with one hand while sprinting across the grass. She pulled up, arresting her forward motion as she looked for a teammate. The other kids had closed the distance now, the other six members of her team vying for position on the field against the seven children acting as their opponents. Members of the girl's team, wearing white shirts, bobbed and weaved around the kids wearing black shirts and trying to block or defend against any of them catching the disc. The field of play had shrunk now that the white team was nearing the goal line. One more throw would be enough to secure a score.

"Here! Over here! I'm open!"

From where she sat on the grass to one side of the area marked off for the playing field, Carol Marcus watched as her son, David, broke free of the boy trying to cover him and sprinted for the end zone, waving his hands above his head. Tall for his age, he stood nearly a head above his playmates. His blond curls were matted with sweat, and his face was flushed with exertion, but the boy—like his companions on the field—seemed not to care. All that mattered at the moment was the game.

Youth, Carol mused, watching with pride as David feinted right before darting to his left, avoiding his defender and leaving himself wide open as the brown-haired girl hurled the disc in his direction. It was low, but David compensated, diving toward the

ground and catching the disc in both hands before sliding across
the grass, well inside the end zone.

"Bravo!" Carol called out. Rising to her feet and allowing the
book resting in her lap to fall to the grass, she applauded as David
and his team celebrated their score. Their shouts of joy and excitement carried across the open expanse of park lawn making up
this section of Fontana Meadow. For a brief moment, Carol could
almost forget that they were not in a real park on Earth but instead
taking advantage of Starbase 47's terrestrial enclosure.

She smiled, watching as the defending team walked the length
of the field toward the opposite end zone, the teams preparing to
put the disc back into play. Some of the kids had been throwing
the disc around to one another when she and David arrived at the
park, and David had accepted their invitation to join in. Once
enough children had shown up, they divided into teams and commenced playing, one team trying to advance up the field by passing the disc, with the other team defending by trying to intercept
or knock down the disc. Though Carol had been watching the
game for ten minutes, she had no idea what it was the kids actually were playing.

"They seem to be having a good time out there."

Recognizing the voice, she turned to see Ezekiel Fisher standing behind her, dressed in beige trousers and an oversized maroon shirt. His hands were in his pockets, and his attention was
focused on the playing field as David's team threw the disc down
the field to their opponents. Once again, the game was on.

"Dr. Fisher," she said, turning toward him.

"Zeke," replied the station's CMO. "That's what my friends
call me, anyway."

Marcus nodded. "Zeke, how is it that kids can run at full speed
all afternoon and never seem to get tired?" she asked as Fisher
stepped forward. "I can't remember the last time I had that kind
of energy."

"The power of youth," Fisher said, chuckling as the disc flew
across the field with kids chasing after it. "If you don't mind my
asking, Doctor, how old is your son?"

"Please, call me Carol," Marcus replied as she bent to retrieve her fallen book. "He'll be six in a few weeks."

Fisher nodded. "Tall for his age."

"He's growing like a weed, and he's got a bottomless pit for a stomach," Marcus said. "Do you have kids?"

"Oh, my, yes," the physician replied. "Two sons and a daughter. They all have children of their own, all of them older than young David over there." He paused, his gaze shifting to look somewhere across the meadow. "Saying that out loud just made me realize how old I really am."

Marcus laughed, enjoying the conversation and how at ease she felt around the doctor. After a moment, she asked, "Was it hard for them, following you around as you moved from one duty assignment to another?"

"A lot of the time," Fisher replied, "they and my wife stayed at home on Mars while I was doing the Starfleet shuffle. I think a stable home life worked better for the kids, rather than being uprooted every couple of years. Doesn't mean I don't regret not being around more when they were growing up." He nodded toward the field. "How's David adjusting to life here?"

Shrugging, Marcus said, "He seems to be doing okay. Leaving friends and a school he liked back on Earth was hard, and he sulked a bit the first couple of weeks we were here, but he's been making friends." She looked about the park. "It doesn't hurt to have all of this to take advantage of. It's not Earth, but at least it's roomy. I think the last space station I was on would fit in a closet here." She could sense where Fisher's questions might be leading. "It's probably harder on him, following me all over the place, without his father around. Unfortunately, that's not an option."

Fisher seemed satisfied not to pursue the discussion in that direction. Instead, he said, "Well, he looks as if he's adjusting well enough. If he's got half your strength, he'll do just fine." Turning to her, he asked, "So, what about you? How are *you* adjusting?"

"I feel like a first-year intern all over again," Marcus said, releasing another laugh. Glancing around to be sure that her words would not carry to unwelcome listeners, she said, "I thought I had at least a decent idea of what I was getting into when I signed up for this, but boy, was I wrong." Her original assignment had been to review all of the data and materials pertaining to the Shedai and their technology as collected by Lieutenant Ming Xiong and his team of research scientists, debrief Xiong and his people, and then take copies of all of that information and establish a second, secure facility. The result would be two independent groups, continuing the work begun here in parallel, as an added measure of security over all of Operation Vanguard.

Her ramp-up period was taking longer than she had expected, owing mostly to the incredible progress made by Xiong and his team. Despite the obstacles they faced as they worked to decipher the secrets of the Shedai, the information they had gathered was as staggering as the potential it represented. The Shedai's apparent ability to control matter and energy in flawless harmony—manipulating and shaping it into any desired form or configuration—carried with it the possibility of advancing current knowledge across every field of science and technology. Whoever unlocked the mysteries surrounding that power and those who once wielded it might single-handedly affect the destiny of the galaxy for centuries to come.

The key to solving that mystery was the Taurus Meta-Genome and the mysterious energy waveform found in the Jinoteur system that seemed to share some of the incredibly complex DNA string's characteristics. Xiong and his people had made some progress, and even Dr. Fisher himself had contributed several insights, but Marcus knew there still was a long way to go. Pieces of the puzzle remained to be found.

"I've spent nearly every waking moment up to my eyeballs in the data collected by Xiong's team," she said. "Even though a lot of what we're talking about is within my field of expertise, I still feel as if I'm in over my head." Pausing, she looked around again, satisfied that there were no eavesdroppers within earshot. Still, she kept her voice low. "If we're ever going to get a handle on this meta-genome, we'll have to expand our understanding not only of genetics but also of artificial intelligence and astrophysics, and that's just the tip of the iceberg. Compared with the Shedai, we're like *Homo erectus* emerging from a cave into modern-day San Francisco."

Turning her attention back to the field where David and his friends continued to play, Marcus laughed once more, and it dawned on her that she had laughed more in the past few minutes than she had in weeks. Given the schedule she had been keeping and the magnitude of the work in which she was ensconced, she had not had much cause for laughter.

I should enjoy it while I can, she mused. *Who knows when any of us might get another chance?*

8

"Space. The big empty."

Standing next to Lieutenants Ming Xiong and Stephen Klisiewicz at the science station on the bridge of the *U.S.S. Endeavour,* Captain Atish Khatami turned at the voice of Anthony Leone as the ship's chief medical officer emerged from the turbolift. Making his way toward her, he carried a data slate in his left hand. The physician was dressed in standard-duty trousers but with the more casual blue short-sleeved tunic often worn by members of the ship's medical staff. Though the *Endeavour*'s previous captain, Zhao Sheng, had preferred a certain level of formality here, Leone was the one person who always was able to flout that rule with impunity. His long friendship with the late captain likely was the primary reason, and Khatami also knew that Leone simply did not give a damn about most Starfleet rules or regulations, at least those that did not directly pertain to the practice of medicine.

Good enough for me, Khatami mused.

"Morning, Captain," Leone said as he drew closer. Holding up the data slate, he offered the device to her, his features scrunched into his trademark expression of cynicism. "My status report, detailing the latest developments in my ongoing investigation into whether the current state of the Jinoteur system—or the lack of a system with said name—might have any harmful medical effects on the crew."

Already knowing what she would see, Khatami suppressed a chuckle as she took the data slate from Leone and held it up to read its display. Confronting her was an empty screen.

"Same as yesterday, I see," Khatami said, playing the game.

Leone grunted. "And the day before, and the day before that. You've broken through my encryption scheme and discovered the subtle pattern. Excellent. I've never been known for my powers of precognition, but I'm willing to bet tomorrow's report will look a lot like today's."

Behind her, Khatami heard both Xiong and Klisiewicz struggling to contain their laughter. They had been spectators of this banter between her and the doctor for the past several days, and Klisiewicz had even admitted that it was one of the high points of his mornings.

"I appreciate your diligence, Doctor," Khatami said, offering a wide grin to Leone as she handed him back the data slate. "Mr. Xiong and Mr. Klisiewicz were just making their own cases to me that we've spent more than enough time here."

Leone nodded, his face pinched as he regarded the two lieutenants. "Well, lay it on me, and don't go easy on the fourteen-syllable words. It's not as if I'm in a hurry or anything."

"It's pretty simple, Doctor," replied Klisiewicz after getting a go-ahead nod from Khatami. Turning from his station, the science officer adopted a formal resting stance, his hands clasped behind his back, his expression neutral as he regarded Leone. "We've been here nine days, and in that time, we've detected no debris, gravimetric anomalies, or variances in background radiation of any kind. We've detected no hint of the energy-wave patterns Xiong and the *Sagittarius* recorded during their time here or any indications of active Shedai technology."

Next to him, Xiong added, "As far as every sensor and scanner on this ship is concerned, to say nothing of four hundred thirty pairs of eyes staring through portholes, it's as though the Jinoteur system never existed." The young Asian man shook his head. "We have no explanations."

No matter how many times Khatami heard some variation of this report, it never ceased to amaze her. An entire solar system vanished without a trace? She had read the reports submitted by both the captain of the *Sagittarius* and Xiong, who had become

Starfleet's leading expert on the Shedai in the time since the discovery of the Taurus Meta-Genome. Both reports detailed how representatives of the Shedai, an enigmatic race that apparently had ruled over a significant portion of the Taurus Reach thousands of years ago, had attacked members of the *Sagittarius* crew while the ship was marooned on the system's fourth planet. Mere days later, one of these representatives, some über-powerful being known as the Apostate, had made the Jinoteur system disappear. Whether that meant the star, planets, moons, and other astral bodies had been sent to some other plane of existence, had simply been destroyed, or had been subjected to something else entirely was unknown. What kind of power would be required to bring about any of those events? How far would a species have to evolve—physically, mentally, and technologically—to wield such power? Even Xiong's detailed accounting of the incident, which he had witnessed firsthand, had done little to assist Khatami in understanding just what it was that the Federation, the Klingons, the Tholians, and anyone else in the Taurus Reach were facing.

We are way, way out of our league here.

"So, why are we still here?" Leone asked.

Klisiewicz shrugged. "At this point, we're hoping we might find some indications of where some of the Shedai went. According to Ensign Theriault on the *Sagittarius,* the Apostate told her that thousands of Shedai could be scattered across the Taurus Reach, likely spread to planets containing caches of their technology such as what we've found on Erilon, Ravanar, and other worlds."

"Even acting alone and without benefit of the influence apparently provided by the Jinoteur system," Xiong said, "these individual Shedai still pose a major threat." Khatami watched as the lieutenant's face fell, as though recalling an unpleasant memory. "Captain, you'll recall what we faced on Erilon?"

"Only too well," Khatami said, her voice low as she recalled the tragic events of *Endeavour*'s first mission to that ice-bound world and the deaths that had come at the hands of a lone Shedai warrior. Among the casualties was Captain Zhao, whose death had opened the door for Khatami's promotion and ascension to *Endeavour*'s center seat.

A horrible way to get promoted. The thought evoked images of the good friend and trusted mentor she had lost that day, along with other members of the *Endeavour*'s crew and people from the science team assigned to investigate the Shedai artifacts on Erilon.

"I take it we haven't had luck finding anything on that front, either," Leone said. He asked Khatami, "How long are we supposed to stay out here, anyway?"

Khatami frowned. "We've been given no end date, but I'm about ready to throw in the towel and set course for home."

"Now we're talking," Leone replied. "You've seen my other reports, Captain. The crew's been operating at warp nine for weeks without a break. Efficiency is starting to slip, though the department heads are doing a pretty good job of holding things together. Still, my staff has treated more than a few cuts and bruises resulting from fights belowdecks." He shook his head, clearly disgusted that the physical and mental well-being of the people in his care was anything less than ideal. Khatami knew from long experience that Leone was not keen on standing around, unable to do anything to rectify such a problem. "They need some downtime, Captain, and soon."

Khatami nodded. "I appreciate your report, Doctor, as well as your continued efforts to keep things on track." Looking to Xiong and Klisiewicz, she said, "Gentlemen, unless you can give me some compelling reason for us to remain here, I'm advising Vanguard of our current status and requesting authorization to return to base."

She watched as the two young science officers exchanged looks. Neither man wanted to admit that they were all wasting their time, but it was not as though they had been given any say in the matter. The Shedai were the ones to blame for all the tail chasing that had ensued in the aftermath of their abrupt disappearance.

"Considering our notable lack of progress," Klisiewicz said, "I think our time would be better utilized elsewhere, Captain."

Xiong added, "I've been thinking that with the Shedai apparently having gone dormant, this might be a good time to return to the sites on Erilon or Ravanar. There's still much to be learned about their technology."

Frowning, Leone said, "Didn't you just say there might be renegade Shedai on some of those planets?" He looked at the other officers. "If I'm the only one here who thinks going back to those places is a really bad idea, I'm scheduling a bunch of psych tests after lunch."

"Of course, there's a risk," Xiong countered, eyeing the doctor with what Khatami recognized as a well-hidden air of irritation, "but if we're to have any chance of understanding the Shedai and their capabilities, we need to continue our hands-on research. I can't see that we have any other choice."

Khatami knew that while scientific curiosity fueled the young lieutenant, recent events in the Taurus Reach had altered his perspective on why he was out here. Originally, his attitude had been that the knowledge they would uncover as they researched the Taurus Meta-Genome should be shared by all, perhaps to the benefit of thousands of species spread across the galaxy. That noble desire had been tainted by the stark realization of what might happen to the galaxy—and those thousands of species—if an enemy such as the Klingons discovered a way to wield the power once commanded by the Shedai.

"Points well taken, Mr. Xiong. I suggest you begin coordinating with Dr. Marcus back on the station and have her begin whatever preparations you'll need from her to support a return visit to one of those locations. I'll inform Commander Cooper with my next report. Thank you, gentlemen."

The informal meeting was over, and as Xiong and Klisiewicz returned to their work, Khatami turned and stepped down into the bridge's command well. To her left, she saw Leone hovering near the curved red railing separating the bridge's upper and lower sections. "Something else on your mind, Doctor?" she prompted as she settled into the command chair.

"Just what I said before, Captain," Leone replied, the fingers of his left hand fidgeting with the data slate he still carried. "Shore leave. The sooner, the better."

"All in good time, Tony," Khatami replied. "Besides," she said as she leaned back in her chair, looking over her shoulder at Leone, "something tells me we'll be spending plenty of time on the station once we get back."

Stepping closer so that his voice would not carry across the bridge, the doctor said, "You mean the business with Commodore Reyes?"

"Yes," Khatami replied. "I expect the senior staff will be deposed, but they'll have to do it quickly, given our operational tempo. I wouldn't get your hopes up of spending all of your shore leave enjoying yourself."

Leone's face screwed up into one of his trademark sarcastic scowls. "Getting verbally abused by a lawyer? I haven't had that much fun since my second divorce. As long as they let me drink during the deposition, I'll be fine." Without waiting for a rebuttal, the doctor signaled a farewell gesture to Khatami before turning and disappearing into the turbolift at the back of the *Endeavour*'s bridge.

Suppressing the smile that always seemed to come whenever Anthony Leone opened his mouth, Khatami glanced over her shoulder toward the communications station. "Lieutenant Estrada," she said, "let's prep a message to send to Vanguard."

9

*"Greetings, Dr. M'Benga. I am Sobon. It has come to my atten-
tion that you seek the assistance of someone skilled in the treatment of certain psychological ailments known to affect Vulcans
on rare occasions. I believe I may be able to offer such assistance."*

M'Benga touched a control on the wall-mounted keypad next
to the main viewscreen in Commander Cooper's office and
paused the visual playback. The image on the screen froze, depicting an aged, withered Vulcan. His white hair was long, pulled
back away from his tanned, lined face. He was dressed in a simple beige garment, a form of robe that M'Benga recognized as
that typically worn by older healers as well as *Kolinahr* high
masters.

"I did some checking on him," M'Benga said, turning to
where Cooper sat behind his desk. Occupying one of the chairs
before the desk, Fisher regarded him with his hands clasped in
front of him. "Sobon at one time was one of the most respected
physicians at the Vulcan Science Academy. In the early twenty-
second century, he was a member of the science contingent working on Earth. He was somewhat of a maverick back then, one of
the few Vulcans who advocated a closer cooperative relationship
with Earth. He championed sharing more information in a number of areas, particularly medicine. Because of him, human medical science made several leaps in a very short period of time,
developing cures or treatments for a number of debilitating dis-
eases. The gradual increase of human life spans over the past
century can be traced directly to Sobon's efforts."

Fisher said, "You said he was respected at one time. Does that mean he's not carrying that kind of clout anymore?"

"He resigned from the science academy more than forty years ago to pursue other interests," M'Benga replied. "Continuing his mental studies, he attained the level of adept, a master of the mental healing arts. Soon after that, he rejected that title and position, and since then, he's been living and working as a healer at a commune tucked away in the L-langon Mountains. From what I've been able to learn, the village is pretty isolationist. There are several communities like it scattered around the planet, shunning most contact with the rest of Vulcan society. The closest parallel I can think of is the Amish religion on Earth."

Leaning forward in his chair, Cooper said, "Parallel in that they eschew modern technology and conveniences and fly under most people's radar?"

"For the most part, yes," M'Benga replied.

Fisher asked, "If that's the case, then what is it they think they can do to help with T'Prynn's problem? I'm going to guess that whatever passes for a hospital in that mountain retreat isn't equipped for this sort of thing."

"That's where this starts to get interesting," M'Benga replied. Turned back to the viewer, he tapped the control to resume playing the recorded message he had already viewed half a dozen times before bringing it to the attention of Fisher and Cooper.

On the screen, the image of Sobon said, *"I am familiar with T'Prynn's condition from my tenure at the Vulcan Science Academy. The Adepts of Gol attempted on many occasions to assist her, to no avail. However, their conservative natures have always prohibited them from considering certain unconventional methods of treatment for severe psychological ailments such as this. While T'Prynn's condition is unique in my experience, I believe I still can offer assistance."*

The message ended with Sobon offering a perfunctory salutation, after which M'Benga turned and moved across the room toward the chair situated next to Fisher's. "I've received a follow-up message. He's invited me to bring T'Prynn to his commune on

Vulcan so that he can attempt treating her with some kind of ancient ritual involving a very powerful form of mind meld."

"You know, I've been meaning to ask, is there anything on or about Vulcan that's not ancient?" Fisher asked.

"I think they have a restaurant or two in the capital city that have only been open for about a year or so," M'Benga said, taking a seat in the remaining chair.

Cooper asked, "Do we really need to transport T'Prynn to Vulcan? Is it even safe to do that? Why can't this Sobon come to us?" Before M'Benga could answer, the acting station commander held up a hand. "Wait, let me guess. Since he's some kind of monk, he's sworn off space travel."

"That's about the size of it," M'Benga replied. He had already tendered such an offer to Sobon, and the Vulcan healer had promptly refused.

"What about this mind meld or whatever it is?" Fisher asked. "Do we know anything about it?"

M'Benga shook his head. "I searched every database I could think of—including one or two on Vulcan no outworlders are even supposed to know about—and found nothing. Of course, Sobon didn't tell me much about it, not even what it's called. He also says he hasn't heard of it being performed in centuries. He only knows about it because he's had forty years to spend irritating the rest of the Vulcan science and medical community. He seems to derive a great deal of satisfaction from researching and putting forth theories and papers regarding the benefits of arcane holistic treatment methods, most of which were abandoned about ten minutes after Surak started making a name for himself. Most of the science academy views him as something of an irritant."

"The more I hear about this guy," Fisher said, "the more I like him."

Cooper said, "So, you want transport to Vulcan?" He looked to Fisher. "That okay with you?"

"Seems like an avenue worth exploring," replied the station's CMO. Eyeing M'Benga with a wry grin, he added, "It's not as though I'm getting a true replacement so that I can retire anytime soon, right?"

Returning the smile, M'Benga replied, "Not if I can help it." He had applied for a transfer to ship duty some months earlier, but Starfleet had yet to approve or deny his request. At last check, the personnel offices on Earth were processing his application, but medical officer berths aboard starships were hard to come by, particularly aboard those vessels tasked with long-duration exploration missions. Though Vanguard's hospital was one of the leading facilities of its type, it *had* been jammed into the middle of a space station. M'Benga wanted to go out into the galaxy, not wait for it to come to him. It was the reason he had joined Starfleet in the first place.

Cooper emitted a mock sigh as he regarded Fisher. "Finding you a replacement. It's just one more thing on my list of things to do before I die of old age, which, by my calendar, should be sometime next Thursday."

"How much longer until *your* replacement arrives?" Fisher asked.

Shrugging, Cooper said, "Supposedly on the way and should be here in a couple of weeks. I don't even know who it is at this point. All I know is that he or she is a flag officer, and Starfleet's not in the habit of publicizing the travel habits of its commodores and admirals, especially these days." He reached up to rub the bridge of his nose, and M'Benga noted the dark circles beneath the commander's eyes. Cooper had shouldered immense responsibility during these past weeks, despite his reputation as a competent executive officer. He had, in effect, been engaged in prolonged on-the-job training to take over for Reyes if necessary, but the abruptness of the commodore's removal from command had hit everyone hard, Cooper harder than most. Still, the commander had risen to the occasion with all of the adroitness and professionalism Reyes obviously had seen in the younger man when selecting him to be the station's second-in-command.

"Make whatever preparations you need," he said to M'Benga.

Fisher said, "To be honest, I'm really not sure whether to wish you luck or not. If you're successful, and T'Prynn's able to recover from . . . whatever it is that's wrong with her, Starfleet's going to court-martial her at the earliest opportunity."

M'Benga shook his head. "Not my concern. My only priority is providing my patient with the best possible care. If that means I cart her off to Vulcan, then so be it."

"I can't argue with that," Cooper replied, nodding, "and that means I do wish you luck, Doctor."

"Thank you, sir," M'Benga replied, his mind already turning to thoughts of the tasks that lay ahead of him. He was moving into areas of medicine he did not feel qualified to address and was uncomfortable with the notion of placing the welfare of his patient in the hands of someone he did not know and for whom no one of any standing in the Vulcan medical and scientific communities would vouch. Though he considered himself proficient with regard to Vulcan physiology and treating physical ailments unique to the species, the shroud of mystery surrounding Vulcans' formidable mental disciplines and telepathic abilities was one area M'Benga had never before tried to penetrate.

You keep saying you want to explore, he chided himself. *Now's your chance.*

10

Tom Walker's place was all but deserted save for a few die-hard leftovers from the midday lunch rush, which suited Tim Pennington just fine. This was actually his favorite time of day to visit the small, unassuming bar located in Stars Landing, the residential and commercial center of Starbase 47's massive terrestrial enclosure. It allowed him to hole up in one of the establishment's semi-private booths without any distractions but the occasional refill of the drinks he nursed while working. Though the bar was his preferred place to unwind with a drink, he had only paid sporadic visits during the past few weeks. He was overdue, he decided.

"Afternoon, Allie," he offered to the attractive female bartender leaning against a counter behind the bar as he crossed the floor toward her. She was dressed in a black leather vest, under which she wore no shirt, and matching pants. "How's things?"

Allie shrugged. "The usual. Quiet time, at least until the evening shift change. You?"

Pennington walked up to the bar, leaned forward, and rested his elbows on its smooth, worn surface. "You know me. I'm a feather on the wind; where fate takes me, I know not."

"Uh-huh," Allie replied, pushing away from the counter and moving toward the cooling units beneath the bar. "I figured you were keeping a low profile or something." She retrieved a bottle of beer—his favorite brand—and turned back to the wall behind her to get a glass, giving Pennington an opportunity to admire her shapely posterior for perhaps the thousandth time since arriving on the station.

"I usually kill people for less than that," Allie said, and

Pennington looked up to see her eyeing him with a wicked smile via the reflection in the mirror behind the bar. She stepped back to the bar, tilted the glass, and began pouring into it the contents of the bottle. "I only give you a pass because you've never tried to grab it, but don't push your luck." She filled the glass to the three-quarters point and handed it to him.

Holding the glass up in salute, Pennington smiled. "I would never dream of doing so, my dear."

Allie moved to another section of the bar, took a cleaning cloth from a shelf, and began to wipe down the polished wood. "So, where've you been? I haven't seen you around much lately. Seeing someone behind my back?"

"That explains a bit of it, yes," Pennington replied, sipping his beer. It was only partially a lie. The relationship he had struck up with Vanessa Theriault, the adorable redheaded ensign from the *U.S.S. Sagittarius,* had been enjoyable for its first few days, cooling a bit once Pennington's stories about the truth behind the Taurus Reach and the arrest of Commodore Reyes began to take hold.

"I guess if I were in your shoes," Allie said as she continued the time-honored tradition of wiping down the bar, "I might keep a low profile, too. I can't imagine it's fun with everyone blaming you for everything that's going on around here."

No one had actually come to him to express displeasure at what he had written, but Pennington knew the sentiment existed. On a rational level, he did not begrudge the reactions his stories had generated among the station's crew members, many of whom held Commodore Reyes in high regard. Likewise, he could not in good conscience blame Theriault for keeping her distance. She was Starfleet, and in the eyes of many of her fellow officers, Pennington had attacked them and perhaps everything for which they stood. He did not see it that way, of course, just as he did not see Diego Reyes as a villain and had avoided portraying him as such. If anyone saw the commodore in that light, it was Starfleet—or a handful of people at its highest levels of power, at any rate.

"Can't say as I blame them," Pennington said, thinking of the reactions that had come about in the hours and days immediately following the Federation News Service's publication of the story he had written after the Jinoteur incident. The threat he had revealed about the mysterious aliens and the ramifications it held for this part of the galaxy, if not the entire Federation, were staggering. Was it hyperbole to say that the very nature of humanity's place—along with those of the inhabitants of many planets who had become allies in the century or more since Earth had fled its cradle and raced faster than light to the stars— was in question? Was all of that simply to be wiped away should this powerful new face emerge from whatever hole they had hidden themselves in, enraged and bent on vengeance?

As for Theriault, she had not said anything to make Pennington believe that their relationship was over and, in fact, had seemed to accept his explanation that Reyes himself had authorized the writing of the FNS stories and even helped in getting them transmitted to the news service, rather than acting in his expected role of censor as a means of facilitating internal security. As far as Pennington was concerned, Diego Reyes was a man of courage and principles, who had sincerely believed he was doing the right things for the right reasons, until it became clear—in the commodore's eyes, at least—that such was not the case. The actions taken by the seasoned officer after that realization could only be described as heroic. In his heart, Pennington wanted to believe that even those in Starfleet who soon would decide his fate felt the same way, even if the letter of the law forced them to view Reyes as a criminal.

"Oh, by the way," Allie said, snapping her fingers, "I almost forgot. I've got something for you." Looking between the bar and the counter and back again, she frowned as she searched for something Pennington could not see. "It's around here somewhere." After a moment, she grunted in satisfaction, reaching beneath the bar. When her hand reappeared, it held what Pennington recognized as a standard blue computer data card. "Your buddy Quinn left this for you."

Pennington frowned, puzzled. "Quinn? Is he all right?"

"Seemed okay when I saw him last night," Allie said. Then her brow furrowed. "Come to think of it, though, he has been a little off the past couple of weeks. I hate to admit it, but I think I liked him better when he was drunk all the time. At least then he was predictable."

Pennington chuckled at that. His unlikely friend and traveling companion, Cervantes Quinn, had indeed undergone some kind of change in the time since their joint and very memorable venture to the Jinoteur system. They had done good work there, as makeshift rescuers of the besieged crew of the *Sagittarius,* which had sustained massive damage while reconnoitering the system's fourth planet. In payment for their good deeds, Lieutenant Commander T'Prynn had dissolved the debts Quinn owed, not only to her but also to the ruthless Orion merchant prince Ganz. While Pennington hesitated to think of Quinn as a "new man" thanks to these developments, he liked to believe that the wayward scoundrel might well have taken the first few steps along the path to some form of a better, more fulfilling life.

It occurred to Pennington that he had not seen Quinn since early the previous day. He had been in the midst of inspecting the *Rocinante,* the dilapidated hunk of scrap metal and baling wire he proudly called his ship. When Pennington had asked if Quinn was preparing the tramp freighter for some new job he might have taken, the freelance cargo hauler had replied that it was always prudent to be ready, particularly in his line of work.

Reaching across the bar, Pennington took the data card from Allie. "Thanks. Mind if I use one of the comm stations?"

Allie shook her head, gesturing toward the back of the bar with her free hand. "Knock yourself out. But hey, if he died and left you everything in his will, you're cutting me in for a slice, understand? I figure it's the least he owes me after all the pawing he's done since he showed up here."

"I'll see what I can do," Pennington replied, pouring the last of his beer from the bottle to his glass. Holding up the now-empty bottle, he asked, "Put this on my tab?"

"Count on it," Allie replied, without looking up from where she had busied herself with something beneath the bar.

At the back of Tom Walker's place was a quartet of personal communications vestibules, each ensconced within its own shell of opaque, soundproof glass. None of them was occupied, and Pennington chose the one farthest from the bar's main room. He closed the compartment's door behind him and settled onto the backless stool in front of the compact audiovisual communications unit. The unit itself was a simple design, featuring a compact viewing screen, a keyboard, and a data card slot. Pennington took the card Allie had given him and inserted it into the slot, then reached for the pad next to the viewer and touched a control to read the card's contents.

An instant later, the grizzled image of Cervantes Quinn filled the screen. His black and gray hair had been cut, washed, and groomed into something resembling a presentable style. The beard stubble that habitually darkened his cheeks and jawline was gone, and there was an alertness to the man's eyes that Pennington had only seen on rare occasions since the pair's improbable friendship had formed.

"You look almost human, mate," Pennington said to no one, his voice echoing in the cramped vestibule as, on the screen, Quinn began to speak.

"How're they hangin', newsboy?" he said, breaking into one of his trademark leering grins. *"I know this probably comes off lookin' a bit like a Dear John letter, but rest assured, I haven't dumped you for a younger reporter."*

"As if I had reason to worry," Pennington quipped.

On the viewer, Quinn's smile faded a bit. *"Listen, you're smart, so you probably guessed this, but I've been doing a lot of thinking lately. I guess some of those touchy-feely types would call it soul-searching, but my pappy used to just call it takin' a good long look in the mirror. We both know I've had my share of screwups, and for whatever reason, someone or something has seen fit to give me what amounts to a second chance. I may be stupid, but I'm not crazy, so I think it's high time I did the smart thing whenever somebody gives me a gift like that."*

He smiled again, gesturing toward himself with his right hand. *"I clean up pretty good, don't I? Too bad you're not here to smell the fancy cologne I bought. It's curling the paint right off the walls of the ship. But taking a bath more than once every other time I get kicked out of a bar is just the start. I've got some places I need to go, some people I need to see, and some things I need to work out. I guess it's what you call a midlife crisis of conscience or something."*

Realization was beginning to dawn in Pennington's mind. "Oh, don't tell me you've . . ."

"By the time you get this message, I'll be gone," Quinn said, confirming the journalist's budding suspicions. *"The stuff I need to do I have to do alone. Besides, you probably don't need me hangin' around, crampin' your style, now that you're back in the news business. I saw the look on your face when you got your street cred back with the FNS, and you've been milkin' that for all it's worth for weeks now. As much fun as you're havin', I know it pisses you off that you weren't able to report about that First Federation business."* He leaned forward, his expression taking on a conspiratorial air. *"Between you and me, newsboy, those guys are amateurs compared with what we found running around in the Taurus Reach. You're still number one in my book, even if your stories are getting bumped to back pages for the moment. Wait until something crazy happens out here again. Your bosses'll be on you like—well—like me on a bottle of scotch.*

"Anyway, I'm not one to wax philosophic or get all choked up about this kind of thing, but I want you to know, Tim, that you've been a good friend . . . a better friend than I deserved, to be honest, and one of these days, I promise I'll tell you exactly what that means. Once I get some of this other baggage behind me, I'll be back, so tell Tom and Allie not to let you drink all the good stuff while I'm gone." He paused before reaching up and tapping his fingertips to his head in mock salute. *"Stay out of*

trouble, and keep doin' what you're doin'. It makes for enter-taining readin' on these long trips."

The image went dark a second or two later, leaving Penning-ton alone in the vestibule to contemplate what he had just heard. At first, he was somewhat disappointed and even angered at Quinn's unilateral decision to leave without even saying good-bye, but that reaction was short-lived. His friend had obviously reached some type of crossroads in his life, and the path he had seen necessary to follow would be different from the road on which Pennington found himself. Would those two courses inter-sect again in the future, as they had when circumstances had cast them together in the first place?

Their friendship had been an interesting one from the start, coming as it had while Pennington dwelled in the lowest, darkest pit of personal and professional despair. He hesitated to describe as interesting the experiences they had shared in the weeks that followed—traveling to Yerad III to fetch Ganz's irritating Zakdorn accountant, Sarkud Armnoj, fetching the Klingon sensor drone, and then being hijacked by rivals of Quinn's, to say nothing of the insanity that was their visit to the Jinoteur system—but they had helped to forge the odd bond the men now shared.

Despite his initial regret at not being able to offer farewells to Quinn in person, Pennington had to admit that he admired his friend's seeming new resolve. The man had made the difficult decision to exorcise his internal demons through direct action, which was to be admired.

You've got a demon or two of your own, mate, Pennington reminded himself. *T'Prynn.*

The very thought of her name caused his gut to tighten. Though he had not forgiven her for the sabotage she had wrought on his career—damage he was really just beginning to recover from, even with his recent successes at FNS—he could not bring himself to hold on to the hate that had festered within him when he learned what she had done. Watching her collapse on the hangar deck and having learned of her condition, Pennington could muster only pity for the stricken Vulcan. Of course, he now knew that her actions against him likely had prevented a war with the Tholians, a good thing on any occasion but more so given the Federation's current political climate with the Klingons.

So, maybe—just maybe—you should cut her some slack?

Perhaps, Pennington decided, it was long past time he purged his own demons.

11

Diego Reyes sat at the table in the center of the drab gray meeting room, saying nothing. He was content to stare into his coffee cup, watching the dark brown liquid swirl as he stirred it with a swizzle stick. As far as he was concerned, it was likely to be the most productive task he accomplished all day.

It was as depressing a room as any he had ever seen. Even his cell was warm and welcoming by comparison. One of three such rooms in the station's security section, it was designed for interviews or interrogations of criminal suspects and private conversations between detainees and their legal counsel. Unlike the food slot in his cell, however, the unit installed in these rooms provided food and drink at any time of day, not just at mealtimes.

The coffee tasted the same.

"Commodore?" a voice asked for the third time, preceded by a soft, polite clearing of the speaker's throat.

Resigning himself to the fact that he would not be allowed to sit and enjoy his coffee in silence, Reyes looked up from the cup and into the wide, questioning eyes of the room's only other occupant, Commander Nathan Spires.

"What?"

Taken aback by the gruff response, the young officer shifted position in his chair and made a show of reviewing whatever it was he had displayed on his data slate. Clearing his throat again, he leaned forward until his elbows rested on the metal table's polished surface. "I thought we might begin to work on your defense, sir."

"Seems to me we did that already," Reyes replied, returning his attention to his coffee, which—he was finally forced to admit—looked only slightly more appealing than it tasted.

Spires nodded. "As you may recall, sir, we made no progress during my first visit. Perhaps it slipped your mind, but—"

"That's twice in two sentences that you've questioned my mental faculties, Mr. Spires," Reyes said, locking eyes with the lawyer. "I hope that's not a precursor to you suggesting that my defense should be based on my being insane or simply a moron."

He watched as Spires's jaw clenched in reaction to the verbal jab, but to his credit, the lawyer did not rise to the bait. Still, Reyes could see this was a man who was used to controlling the situation around him.

Saying nothing for a moment, Spires instead reached for his own coffee and took a sip. "I take it you don't consider that a viable option, Commodore?" he asked as he returned his cup to the table.

"Hell, no, I don't," Reyes snapped, allowing the first hints of genuine irritation to creep into his voice. "Listen to me very carefully on this point, Commander, for the one thing that well and truly pisses me off is having to repeat myself: I am not insane, and I was fully aware of my actions when I undertook them, as well as any potential consequences. Am I making myself clear?"

"Perfectly, sir," Spires replied, his tone clipped and formal. He placed the stylus for his data slate on the table, clasped his hands before him, and leveled an unflinching stare at Reyes. "Permission to speak freely, sir?"

Reyes shrugged. "Knock yourself out."

"Why am I here, sir?"

Finally, Reyes thought. *There's a pulse in there, after all.* Keeping his expression neutral, he asked, "Do you have something better to do?"

"As a matter of fact, I do." Before Reyes could respond to that, Spires plunged ahead. "Don't get me wrong, Commodore. I want this case. I specifically *asked* for this case. I want to help you, if I can, but at the end of the day, it doesn't really matter. Whatever happens to you, my résumé will look a lot better for having accepted the challenge of representing you in the face of overwhelming odds."

His expression revealed nothing, but Reyes felt a slight rush of satisfaction as he listened to the commander unload a small portion of the frustration he undoubtedly had buried beneath his veneer of outward calm. The commodore had no problem with ambition in a younger officer; it was a trait to be nurtured and harnessed for constructive purposes. Spires's blunt honesty was also a quality Reyes could appreciate. Too few junior officers, in his opinion, suppressed the instinct to speak their minds when a situation warranted it, even when pressed to do so by a superior.

None of this meant that Reyes actually liked the man, of course. Not yet, anyway.

"You have to know that your fate has largely been decided already," Spires continued. "The charges against you are rather straightforward. We might be able to argue our way out of the disobedience charge, and we might even be able to get the conspiracy charge dismissed. But releasing classified information? There's no way around that, sir. The last time we spoke, you seemed to have accepted the inevitability of the situation, and from what I've been able to gauge so far, that hasn't changed." He picked up his stylus and began to twirl it between the fingers of his right hand. "For me, this begs the question of why you simply haven't entered a guilty plea and dispensed with the need for a court-martial in the first place."

Having drained the rest of his coffee before offering a reply, Reyes finally said, "Because I really *don't* have anything better to do." Sensing that Spires might try to stab him with the stylus, he held up his hand. "Not because I want to screw with you, Commander, though I admit I've decided it's a nice bonus. You said it yourself. Pleading guilty does away with the need for a court-martial, which means they can throw me in a hole, and they get to do it without anyone else having to break a sweat. I'm not about to let that happen, at least not without a fight. I want a chance to speak my piece."

He rose from his chair and moved across the room to the food slot. After punching the sequence for a new cup of coffee, Reyes turned from the unit to face his attorney again. "Now, I've told you everything I can relating to the charges against me, and you've had two weeks to read every scrap of data you can get your hands on. What I haven't heard yet is what you plan to do with all of that information. I'm not interested in throwing myself on the mercy of the court, Commander. I want people to know how big this thing is, why we're here, what we hope to accomplish, and the real price we've paid in pursuit of that goal." He tapped his chest with the fingers of his left hand. "I don't expect to win, but I aim to make some noise, and I expect you to be right there beside me, doing your best to piss off anyone and everyone they line up against me."

The time he had spent in isolation had given Diego Reyes plenty of time for long and thoughtful reflection. Did he regret the actions he had undertaken? No. His remorse came from knowing that he could have, *should* have, acted sooner, *before* the situation could escalate to the point of costing so many innocent lives. He mourned the loss of the *U.S.S. Bombay* and its crew, destroyed in battle against Tholian vessels. He grieved for those members of the *Sagittarius* who had died on Jinoteur IV, crushed beneath what was now known to be only a minuscule demonstration of the awesome power wielded by the Shedai. As he lay awake on the cot in his cell, images of Jeanne Vinueza, his former wife and administrator of the colony on Gamma Tauri IV, haunted him every night before finally allowing him to drift off to fitful sleep.

After several moments spent in silence, Spires finally took up his stylus again and began writing on his data slate. "Well, then, where to begin? As for why you allowed that reporter to write about a classified Starfleet operation, as I said, that will be our toughest battle. I need to do some further research, of course, but from where I sit right now, it seems our best chance is to push for the idea that at least some of the orders you were following weren't legal." He paused, his stylus hovering above the data slate as he seemed to review what he had just said aloud. "For that to work, though, we'd have to demonstrate that you had no reason to believe the orders you were following were illegal. I take it you're still against that strategy?"

"Absolutely," Reyes replied. While others could be blamed for establishing the parameters by which the Federation had established such a marked presence in the Taurus Reach, the choices he had made at Gamma Tauri IV rested solely on his shoulders. The cost of that decision was his to pay.

He had made some small measure of recompense by allowing Tim Pennington to publish a recounting with as much detail as he could muster of the events the journalist had experienced while on Jinoteur IV. Pennington had acquitted himself with distinction on that occasion as he and his friend, a civilian merchant named Cervantes Quinn, had accomplished nothing less than save the *Sagittarius* and its remaining crew members from a Klingon vessel and the awesome power and weaponry the Shedai had wielded on that world.

Thanks to Pennington, much of the truth behind that incident was no longer a secret, and countless billions now were aware—at least to a degree—of the immense threat lurking within the Taurus Reach. Steps had to be taken to prevent further loss of innocent life. That meant either finding a way to combat the Shedai or retreating from this area of space altogether and leaving it to its original masters while hoping they would not seek vengeance for any wrongs they perceived as having been inflicted on them.

Before any of that could happen, the truth, all of it, must be revealed.

Weighing Reyes's answer, Spires nodded after a moment. "You realize that the court-martial is likely to be closed proceedings, sir. Even with what's already been leaked to the public, Starfleet will still want to restrict as much information as possible about Starbase 47 and Operation Vanguard."

Reyes knew that Spires was currently working from a disadvantage stemming from that very desire, in that he had not yet been granted access to all of the information he would require in order to mount his defense for the coming court-martial. The commodore wondered what the young lawyer's reaction would be once he received that opportunity and reviewed all of the files pertaining to Starbase 47 and its mission in the Taurus Reach.

If he's smart, he'll hop the first transport home.

"People will still find out, Commander," he replied. "They might not need to know absolutely everything about what we're doing, but they need to know when we screw up, particularly when it costs innocent lives. I'm tired of creating lies and stories to cover our asses out here. That's not the mission I signed up for, and that's not what Starfleet's supposed to be about. I don't think that *is* what it's about, but I was dumb enough to get caught up in the machine. There are others caught the same way, because they were blinded either by duty or by conscious choice. Either way, the public has a right to know about them, just as they're going to find out about me."

Neither man said anything for several moments, the only sound in the room being the low, ubiquitous warble of Vanguard's massive power generators, far below them in the belly of the station's secondary hull. When Spires spoke again, he did so while tapping the end of his stylus along the tabletop.

"So," he said, releasing a small sigh, "you basically just want to be a pain in the ass."

The commander's deadpan delivery caught Reyes off guard, but then he laughed, the first time he could remember doing so in weeks. It was a wonderful feeling.

"I've always been a pain in the ass, Commander," he replied, wiping the corner of his right eye. "Now I just want more people to know about it."

Nodding with what Reyes took to be a new sense of determination, Spires said, "I think we can do something with that, sir. I'm still not saying we have any chance of winning, mind you." He shrugged. "But at least it'll be entertaining."

Okay, Reyes decided, *now I'm starting to like you. A little.*

Spires glanced down at his data slate. "I've got about an hour or so before I'm supposed to meet Captain Desai and discuss—among other things—my clearance for reading classified data. Until then, might I suggest that we refocus our efforts here, Commodore?"

As he turned his attention back to the task at hand, Reyes could not help thinking about Rana Desai. He thought of her often, of course, but he tried only to recall their private times together, rather than the unpleasant reality of what they both now faced.

I wonder how she's dealing with all of this?

12

"Commodore Reyes, through conscious thought and deed, will-fully allowed a member of the press to become aware of classified information. In doing so, and by further allowing that journalist to publish a story containing this information, he violated Starfleet regulations. Worse, his actions carry with them the possibility of placing innumerable innocent lives at risk, to say nothing of the unrest and even panic he may well have inflicted upon countless citizens throughout the Federation and beyond."

Her words echoing within the chamber that served as the courtroom facility assigned to Starbase 47's contingent from Starfleet's Judge Advocate General Corps, Captain Rana Desai paced a circular path around the witness stand at the center of the room. It consisted of a lone empty chair sitting on a compact square dais, with a high backrest and a biometric computer inter-face. The chair was positioned so that it faced the judge's bench, a raised, curved desk designed to seat four board members, stan-dard procedure for Starfleet court-martial proceedings.

Pausing in her rehearsed remarks, Desai stared at the bench and tried to imagine the faces of the officers who would make up the board. With each of them ranked commodore or higher and with line experience as starship captains, as well as commanding offi-cers of their own starbases or Starfleet ground installations, Desai knew that she would not be able to rely on cold, hard facts to make her case. These would be men and women who had lived the same life as Diego Reyes and had experienced many of the same chal-lenges and dangers that filled the commodore's personnel file. They would be fair and just, but not to the point of favoritism or vindictiveness. Whatever fate they might decide for Reyes, it would be in keeping with both the letter and the spirit of Starfleet regulations. Her job would be to present her case in such a fashion that the board members would feel no recourse but to decide in her favor.

Piece of cake, right?

"Captain Desai?"

Hearing her own name snapped her out of her reverie, and she turned to see the room's only other occupant, Lieutenant Holly Moyer. One of the junior officers assigned to her JAG office, the auburn-haired young lawyer was seated in a chair positioned against the room's left wall. She regarded Desai with an expression of concern.

"Is everything all right, ma'am?"

Desai blinked away the last vestiges of distraction that had claimed her for a moment. "Yes. Sorry, Lieutenant. I was . . . thinking about something else for a minute there." Clearing her throat, she resumed her circuit around the witness stand. "Now, then, where were we?"

"Inflicting panic upon the citizens of the Federation and beyond," Moyer replied, looking down at the data slate resting in her lap and her copy of Desai's opening statement. "Before we move on to the next part, I think we should revisit this piece. If you'll permit me, ma'am, it seems too general and maybe even a bit melodramatic."

Desai offered an appreciative nod after a moment. "You're right. We need to be more explicit here. A nondescript threat sounds like fear mongering or just plain pandering. Make a note to append highlights from some of the information we're starting to get from various colonies. How some of them are reconsidering their decisions to proceed without Federation or Starfleet aid, the couple that have already pulled up stakes and evacuated, that sort of thing. Nothing too sensational—that they're taking these actions is enough without having to embellish things."

Moyer nodded as she made the notations. "What about that incident with the Klingon ship and the colony on Lerais II? Should we bring that up?"

"Not during opening statements," Desai countered. "It has nothing to do with our case. If it comes up at trial, we'll deal with it then. Otherwise, let's keep it focused." There was enough to consider and address as she continued the effort to shape her trial strategy. Clouding the central issue with unrelated details and irrelevant tangents would only bog her down rather than give her the momentum she would need to see this through.

Moyer said without looking up from her notes, "The section where you describe the specific charges is good, but I wonder if you might change the order? Move the disobedience and conspiracy, and build up to his release of the classified data."

"Ramp up for a big finish?" Desai asked, unable to mask the wry grin pulling at the corners of her mouth. Shrugging, she added, "It's not a bad idea, actually, especially since I expect those two charges to be either dismissed or at least lessened." The conspiracy charge would be hard to press, given that her investigation had failed to reveal a single other soul aboard the station who might have known about Reyes's decision to give journalist Tim Pennington such free rein. The disobedience charge would come down to a discussion about whether Reyes believed the orders he had flouted were legal, ethical, or moral. This, of course, would solicit questions about the identities of other, superior officers who may well have issued unlawful directives with respect to Operation Vanguard. Desai suspected that the board members would want to avoid wading into that particular quagmire, not because they were interested in supporting any kind of cover-up but rather because it would detract from the purpose for which they had been assembled. Desai knew it was possible that further legal proceedings would be launched against other officers, but only after the final disposition of Commodore Diego Reyes was determined.

Therefore, she decided, the charge of releasing classified information to the public, and making it stick, was where this case would be won or lost.

"Okay," Desai said, "we'll rework that section, too, but I want to be careful during that part. No overwrought theatrics and just enough fire and brimstone to hammer home the point without overdoing it."

From behind her, another voice called out, "But it's the fire and brimstone that makes these things interesting."

There was no mistaking the speaker, and Desai turned in that direction to see Ezekiel Fisher watching her from the rear of the courtroom. Occupying one of the chairs against the back wall, Vanguard's chief medical officer slouched in his seat, his long legs stretched out before him and crossed at the ankles. His arms were folded across his chest, and he was—as he always seemed to be—stroking his thin, gray-peppered beard. Glancing at Moyer, Desai was certain that the lieutenant's expression of surprise mirrored her own. Neither woman had heard him enter the room. How long had he been sitting there?

How the hell does he always do that?

"Fish," Desai said, employing the nickname she knew he hated and tolerated only from her, "you really shouldn't be in here." Making her way around the witness stand toward him, she realized how sharp her words may have sounded. With a smirk, she added, "How did you get in here, anyway? Were you some kind of ninja in a past life or something?"

Shrugging, the doctor replied, "I was a ninja in a past life. Don't worry, I've only been here a minute or so. I managed to miss the rest of your fiendish plot to overthrow the universe, or whatever the hell it is you two are doing in here."

Desai released a humorless chuckle. "Okay, so you're not spying for the other side. Why *are* you here? Isn't there a baseball game or a chess match or a couple of kids playing hide-and-seek you could be cheering on somewhere?" She indicated the courtroom with a wave of her hand. "I didn't think this was your kind of thing."

His features taking on an expression of feigned shock, Fisher replied, "Are you kidding? Two opposing sides taking the field of battle, each armed with skills and healthy doses of guile and grit, facing off in the ultimate showdown of good versus evil, with the fate of a man's very life at stake?" He waved away Desai's suggestion. "All we need is for that boatload of Orion pirates to lay odds and take bets, and we're set."

When Desai laughed this time, it was from deep within her, and she felt the stresses of the day lift from her shoulders, if only for a moment. "Thanks. I needed that. Now, why did you really come down here?"

"Just wanted to see how you were doing," Fisher replied.

Something in his voice and the look in his eyes told Desai he would prefer to have the rest of this conversation in private. She looked over her shoulder, a nod to Moyer enough to tell the lieutenant that Desai needed a minute alone with the doctor. Fisher waited until the younger officer departed the room before saying anything else.

"How are you holding up, Rana?"

"Fine," Desai replied, hoping her response sounded more truthful to her friend than it did to her own ears.

Fisher's eyes narrowed in suspicion as he regarded her. "Uh-huh." He lifted his right leg until it was parallel to the floor. "And if you pull this leg, it plays one of those fancy piano numbers I always hear coming out of Manón's." Rising from the chair, he stepped forward and placed his hands on Desai's arms. "This is me talking, kid. It's okay to let the shields down."

Reaching up to pat his right hand, Desai replied, "I'm dealing with it as best I can, Fish. I don't really have a lot of choice in the matter." The truth was that she had been expecting something like this to happen, had even been planning for it, to face head-on the prospect of Diego Reyes, her lover, standing trial. That said, it still was taking every scrap of willpower and determination not to succumb to the overwhelming need either to run to Reyes and hold on to him for support or simply to crawl under her bed and wait for all of this to pass.

Well, you can't do the former, she chided herself for what felt like the hundredth time, *and there's no way in hell you're doing the latter. Stop whining, and do your job.*

"I know that look," Fisher said, squeezing her arms in his gentle yet reassuring hands. "You just kicked yourself in the ass, didn't you?"

Desai laughed again, pulling away from her friend before reaching up to wipe the lone tear she felt in the corner of her eye. "Yeah, I sure did. I was probably overdue for that, anyway." Releasing a tired sigh, she looked up once more at Fisher's weathered visage. "How is he, Fish?"

"About the same, I suppose," Fisher replied, offering another shrug. He indicated the courtroom with a nod of his head. "Ready to get on with it. He's resigned himself to whatever happens. I don't think he gives a damn about himself, but he's sure as hell worried about you."

She nodded. "I'm worried about him, too." She and Reyes had agreed not to see each other until after the trial. Now more than ever, their personal relationship could not be allowed to interfere even to the slightest degree with her carrying out her duty. Anything less would invite scrutiny and accusations of misconduct, which would do nothing except make the case against Reyes that much stronger. She knew the only way to see him was to get this unpleasant business over with, as soon as possible.

So, get on with it.

To his credit, Fisher said nothing as she once more waged this battle within herself, waiting in respectful silence until she once more found her bearing. Drawing what she hoped was a cleansing breath, Desai reached out and patted Fisher's chest.

"I should probably get back to work."

A small smile broke through Fisher's veneer of calm and poise. "Me, too." He began crossing the room, then stopped and turned back to her. "By the way, I lied before. I heard most of your opening remarks. If you're worried about not being taken seriously at the trial, don't be. Just do what you're supposed to do, and you'll be fine."

Desai regarded him with a fresh look of uncertainty. "Even if it means nailing his ass to the wall?"

Moving toward the exit once more, Fisher did not pause as the doors opened for him. "If that's your job, then yes," he said as he left the room. "Diego would expect nothing less."

"Damn you," Desai called out as the doors closed behind the doctor. "I knew you were going to say that."

13

Sunrise on Cestus III.

Standing in the expansive courtyard that was the center of the newly established Federation outpost on this world, Captain Daniel Okagawa drank in the crisp morning air, which contained none of the humidity that would saturate it later in the day. The temperature was cool but not uncomfortably so, and there was a serenity in his surroundings that reminded him of camping trips he had taken with his father. An early riser since childhood, Okagawa had always enjoyed mornings and the brief periods of tranquility they offered before the day's business took over. He looked to the sun, which was just beginning to peek above the mountain range bordering the colony's eastern flank, casting long shadows across the courtyard and the dozen or so free-standing buildings scattered within it. A mix of Starfleet personnel, civilian colonists, and contracted engineering and colony support staff moved between the various structures and the ring of buildings positioned just inside the tall, reinforced thermoconcrete wall forming the settlement's perimeter.

"I've been meaning to mention, Commodore, that I find the wall to be an interesting design aesthetic," Okagawa said to his companion, Commodore Howard Travers, as the pair emerged from the colony's administration building. "You don't typically see that sort of thing anymore."

"Call me outdated," Travers said, smiling as he placed his hands on his hips. "It reminds me of a castle or forts the army built to protect settlers pushing across the American frontier in the 1800s. That appeals to the kid in me, I suppose." When he smiled, Okagawa could see a hint of mischief in the commodore's eyes. Travers was a tall, thin man, who seemed almost to be swimming in his gold Starfleet uniform tunic. His blond hair moved a bit thanks to the gentle breeze coursing over the compound, and his smile reminded Okagawa of the Cheshire cat.

"Truth be told," Travers said as they walked farther out into the courtyard, "I didn't have much input into the colony's design. When I was first told I'd be leading it, I met with the designers to go over the construction blueprints, and they'd already been working with the general layout. Constructing the buildings and living quarters into the base of the wall itself offered a better degree of protection from the weather, particularly the sand storms we're liable to get."

Okagawa nodded in agreement, having already experienced one of the milder storms that had pushed through the area several days ago. "I'd be lying if I said I wanted to hang around long enough to see one of the nastier storms pop up."

"And I'd be lying if I said I was happy to see you go," Travers replied, pausing to offer morning greetings to a woman walking past them, whom Okagawa recognized as one of the civilian contractors assigned to help with establishing the colony. "We couldn't have accomplished as much as we did in such a short time without your people, Daniel."

Smiling with unreserved pride, as he often did whenever his crew's efforts were praised, Okagawa offered a congenial nod. "That's very kind of you to say, sir. They're not the most by-the-book bunch you'll ever meet, but they're second to none if you want something built, rebuilt, torn apart, or augmented to within an inch of its life."

It was true that the complement of technical specialists from Starfleet's Corps of Engineers currently assigned to his ship, the *U.S.S. Lovell,* was as eclectic an assemblage of unorthodox officers Okagawa had ever encountered. Indeed, upon first being notified that he would be placed in command of the all-but-ancient *Daedalus*-class vessel and its crew of engineers, his first reaction had been to verify that he was not being punished for some as-yet-unexplained transgression. Okagawa had believed the entire *Daedalus* class was retired from service decades earlier, after a long and proud operational record as the workhorse vessels of a still-burgeoning Starfleet in the mid- to late twenty-second century. He was surprised to find not one but three such ships on active duty, all of them assigned to the Corps of Engineers.

Travers laughed at Okagawa's remark. "You're not kidding. That talented band of tinkerers is something else. I know coming here is more than a bit off the beaten path with respect to your other assignments, but I hope you won't mind if I ask for you and your crew by name the next time we need this kind of help."

"It'll be our pleasure, Commodore," Okagawa replied. The *Lovell* and its crew had arrived at Cestus III sixteen days earlier, under orders from Starbase 47's interim commanding officer, Jon Cooper, and in response to a request submitted by Travers for such assistance. The Cestus star system actually resided just beyond the boundaries of the Taurus Reach and, as such, would normally fall outside the area of responsibility overseen by Vanguard and the ships assigned to the space station. Still, the need for the type of specialized assistance the *Lovell*'s engineering contingent could provide had been legitimate.

Travers said, "Even colonies at the far end of nowhere need running water and functioning toilets. Sure, we could've gotten the kinks worked out and taken care of all of the 'settling in' adjustments on our own, but it would've taken months to iron everything out."

Okagawa smiled at that. The *Lovell*'s crew had certainly done its share of diagnosing and correcting problems in much of the outpost's essential infrastructure, including irrigation for the agricultural center and supplying water for the more than five hundred people living within the compound itself. They also had found several deficiencies in the colony's central computer and communications systems, including more than a few issues with the systems that would oversee defense. "Well," he added, "we both know that location is precisely why Starfleet made sure we were the ship sent out here."

Cestus III's location, with its proximity to Klingon space, made the planet an important asset with regard to Starfleet monitoring of Klingon ship movements. With the Klingons paying heightened attention to the Taurus Reach, it was all but certain that vessel traffic would come from this general direction. Positioning an observation outpost here strengthened the ability to provide early warnings in the event of increased activity that might prove dangerous to Federation interests in the region. The planet's location and apparent value in the larger intelligence and defense hierarchy would make it a tempting target, and Starfleet had already factored that into the travel routes for starships assigned to patrol the sector. That was reassuring, Okagawa thought, particularly if the unthinkable occurred and the Klingons—or some other, yet-unknown enemy—decided to come calling.

Hearing approaching footsteps, Okagawa turned to see a member of his crew, Ensign Jeffrey Anderson, walking toward him. The captain knew from experience that the younger man was not a morning person, even without the ensign's red-rimmed eyes accentuating that fact.

"Good morning, Commodore," Anderson said to Travers before turning his attention to Okagawa. "Captain, Commander al-Khaled asked me to let you know that all of our equipment has been beamed back to the *Lovell,* and most of our landing parties have returned as well. He and Lieutenant T'Laen are still in the computer center, working out a few stubborn bugs, but otherwise, he says we should be able to depart on schedule."

Okagawa nodded at the report. "Thank you, Ensign." To Travers, he said, "If anyone can figure out what's got your computer in a bad mood, it's T'Laen." The young Vulcan lieutenant was an accomplished computer-systems expert, holding high proficiency and classification ratings on nearly every type of Federation computer hardware and system currently in use. As for Mahmud al-Khaled, the *Lovell's* second-in-command and leader of the ship's Corps of Engineer contingent, he was an accomplished specialist in his own right, a master of many technical disciplines that had proven invaluable on more than one occasion.

"By the way, Anderson," Okagawa said, frowning a bit, "why didn't you just beep my communicator?"

He watched as the ensign's face reddened in apparent embarrassment. "Well, sir, thereby hangs a tale." He reached to the small of his back with his left hand, retrieved his communicator, and held it—or, rather, what remained of it—up for Okagawa to see. "I had a bit of a problem earlier this morning."

"What the hell happened?" Travers asked, his eyes wide with confusion as he beheld the bent and twisted outer casing of what once had been a standard-issue Starfleet field communicator. Its gold flip-top antenna grid was creased down the middle, and the sides of the unit itself also were curved inward, as though the device had been held in a vise.

"I happened, Commodore," Anderson replied, holding up his empty right hand. "I'm still getting the hang of reflexive responses with this thing. It's great if you want me to punch a hole in a wall for a new power conduit, but don't ask me to hold eggs or shake your hand. At least, not yet."

Okagawa said, "Ensign Anderson sustained some rather serious injuries during our time on Gamma Tauri IV. His arm is a bionic prosthesis." To the casual observer, the synthetic replacement limb passed for the real thing. It was only upon close inspection that the arm's artificial nature was revealed.

"Wow," Travers said, nodding in appreciation. "Gamma Tauri IV. I'd almost forgotten your ship was involved in that."

"I'd like to forget about it myself," Okagawa replied. The incident was still fresh in his mind, of course, where he suspected it would remain for the foreseeable future. Drawing a deep breath, he tried to shrug off the troubling reminder of that tragic mission.

"Is there anything else I can do for you, sir?" Anderson asked. "I'd like to see about replacing my communicator, along with . . . a few other things I oversqueezed last night."

Unable to resist teasing the younger man a bit and anxious for some levity to lighten his momentarily darkened mood, Okagawa said, "Late night, Ensign?"

Anderson shook his head. "Long day that continued well into the night, sir. In fact, do I get to count today as part of yesterday, or do clocks just explode when you try to cram that many hours into them?"

"Feel free to avail yourself of your bunk as soon as Mr. al-Khaled says you're done," Okagawa replied. "It's a long trip back to Vanguard, and I imagine everyone will be trying to catch up on missed sleep." The crew had been working almost around the clock for two weeks, and he knew the strain was beginning to show. He had already fielded al-Khaled's request for shore leave on behalf of the entire ship's complement once the *Lovell* returned to Starbase 47.

"Understood with utter exhaustion, Captain," Anderson said, emphasizing his retort with a mock salute before turning to leave.

Turning back to Travers, Okagawa extended his hand. "Commodore, thank you for the hospitality. It's too bad all of our hosts don't have your manners."

Travers laughed as he took the proffered hand and shook it. "If you like, I can come up with a few more things for your people to fix. I might even be able to keep you here for Saturday's big cookout."

Patting his midsection, Okagawa replied, "A few more meals like what you've been feeding us these past couple of weeks, and I'll have to put my entire crew on a diet."

Pennington entered the reception area of Starbase 47's hospital, only to find it empty. Even Jennifer Braun, the attractive young woman who acted as a receptionist and with whom he sometimes flirted, was nowhere to be seen. No one sat at the reception desk, and no one waited in the patient area to be seen by one of the station's medical staff. The place seemed abandoned.

Can't say I blame them, he thought, wrinkling his nose as he caught a whiff of antiseptic cleanser that seemed imbued in the DNA of any medical facility. "Hello?" he called out in a voice only an octave or so higher than a normal conversational tone, his words carrying down the short passageway, which he knew from his previous visits led to offices, patient wards, and labs.

A door opened at the far end of the corridor, and Pennington watched as Braun emerged, her soft footsteps echoing in the hallway. Seeing him, she smiled as she moved toward her desk.

"Good morning, Mr. Pennington," she said, "It's nice to see you again."

The journalist nodded. "A pleasure to see you again as well, my dear." He offered his most charming smile. "I hope they're not working you too hard today."

"I was helping Dr. M'Benga," Braun replied, lowering herself into the chair behind the desk. "He's with T'Prynn, of course."

"Of course." The doctor seemed to have spent every waking moment—and perhaps more than a few not-so-waking moments—overseeing his Vulcan patient from the first moments after she had suffered whatever event had affected her. Nodding in the direction of the patient-care wards, Pennington asked, "Is everything all right? Has there been some change in her condition?" He had come to visit T'Prynn on several occasions during the past weeks, only to find her in almost exactly the same position of repose as when he had last seen her.

He noted how Braun paused before replying. "There's been no change, but Dr. M'Benga is preparing for a new course of treatment. I should probably leave it to him to say anything else about that."

"I understand completely," Pennington offered. He was not family or even a close friend. Neither Braun nor M'Benga was obligated to tell him anything, though the doctor had at least been considerate enough to update him on T'Prynn's condition every few days, the details of which had not changed since her initial collapse. "Thank you, Jennifer," he said, turning to head toward the patient ward where he knew T'Prynn was receiving care.

"You can thank me by taking me to dinner sometime," Braun said from behind him, and when he paused to look over his shoulder, he saw the inviting smile on the young woman's face. She bobbed her eyebrows, and Pennington could not resist returning the smile.

"I'll do that," he said, nodding to her before turning and resuming his walk down the hallway.

He entered Isolation Ward 4 expecting to confront the same scene that had greeted him on his previous visits: T'Prynn lying unmoving in her bed, the medical equipment arrayed around her tirelessly monitoring her condition, and some piece of music from M'Benga's private collection piped through the room's intercom system. Instead, he found the doctor supervising what looked like preparations for moving T'Prynn and the plethora of monitoring devices that had become her entire world these past weeks. Around the stricken Vulcan's bed, three nurses—two men and one woman—were loading some of the equipment onto antigrav transport carriers. To one side sat a stretcher, apparently waiting for T'Prynn to be transferred to it.

Looking up at Pennington's approach, M'Benga nodded in formal greeting. "Mr. Pennington, I apologize for not notifying

you personally, but I'm afraid I can't allow any visitation today."
He looked tired, standing a bit stoop-shouldered and with dark
circles under his eyes. It was easy to discern that the prolonged
strain of overseeing T'Prynn's care—regardless of any progress or lack thereof—was beginning to take its toll on the young
doctor.

Frowning as he watched the team of nurses working over
T'Prynn and the bedside equipment, Pennington asked, "Is
something wrong?"

M'Benga shook his head, his attention divided between Pennington and the data slate in his hand. "No. In fact, there's been
no change at all in her condition, which is why I've opted to try a
different approach to her treatment." He paused, using the stylus
in his right hand to jot a note. "I'm preparing to transport her to
Vulcan."

His eyes widening at this news, Pennington asked, "Really?"

"Yes," M'Benga replied. "I've done all I can for her, so I've
gotten permission to take her there, where I hope one of their doctors can help me." He shook his head, casting his eyes toward the
floor as though ashamed to have to say what came next. "Whatever's happened to her, it's beyond anything I've ever dealt with,
even during my internship on Vulcan."

"Don't beat yourself up too badly, mate," Pennington offered.
"It takes a good man to know when he needs to ask for help. Lord
knows I might have fared better if I'd done that myself once or
twice." Nodding toward T'Prynn, he asked, "When do you
leave?"

"Fourteen hundred hours," the doctor replied. "Commander
Cooper's authorized my using one of the station's long-range personnel transports, which I'm having outfitted to support this
equipment. Between that and various other supplies, there should
be just enough room left over for me and a few books to read."

From the pocket of his jacket, Pennington took out the object
he had been carrying around with him since purchasing it two
days earlier. It was sheathed in a piece of beige material similar
to canvas, which he unwrapped to reveal a palm-sized disc of

polished bronze, upon which was engraved an elaborate geometric design. Its edge was engraved with a string of what Pennington had learned were Vulcan glyphs. Offering it to M'Benga, he asked, "Do you think there might be room for this?"

The doctor looked down at the object in Pennington's hand, his eyebrows arching with interest. "A mandala."

Pennington nodded. "I bought it from a Vulcan vendor in Stars Landing. According to him, it's supposed to help with meditation or something."

"More or less," M'Benga said. "You focus on it to help quiet your mind and your emotions, removing barriers or distractions that might prevent you from concentrating on the reception and application of logic."

"It seemed kind of hokey to me," Pennington replied. "I mean, considering how well disciplined most Vulcans are, it's odd that they'd need some kind of trinket to help them."

Shrugging, M'Benga said, "You'd be surprised. Vulcans are known to employ a wide range of meditational aids, from mandalas to art, music, and even games."

"I'll take your word for it." Handing the bronze medallion to M'Benga, Pennington said, "Anyway, I thought it would be a nice gift for her, when she . . . you know . . . wakes up."

M'Benga nodded in understanding as he accepted the mandala. "*Like* isn't the right word, but I'm sure she'd appreciate it, just as I appreciate the time you've spent with her. You've told me you two weren't especially close, but that doesn't seem to have stopped you."

Once more, the heart-wrenching scene of T'Prynn collapsing beneath the weight of whatever trauma now plagued her came surging to the forefront of Pennington's mind. Juxtaposed against that was the sting of betrayal he still felt when contemplating the actions the Vulcan had taken against him in the name of preserving the truth behind the *U.S.S. Bombay*'s destruction. He also remembered the evening—months ago now—when he had seen T'Prynn come to his apartment in Stars Landing. Though she had left before even knocking on his door and they ended up not meeting on that occasion, her actions and body language suggested that she might have been guided by guilt, something Pennington still found hard to believe. Had she come to apologize? The reason for her visit remained a mystery, a question for which he sought answers. Also an enigma was the nature of the odd bond he seemed to feel with her. What kept bringing him back to visit her? What did he expect to get from his time here? Try as he might, Pennington failed to find explanations for that.

"I guess you could say we've unfinished business, Doctor," he finally said, his eyes lingering on T'Prynn's unmoving form. Would someone on Vulcan really be able to help her, and if so, to what extent? Was it possible for her to emerge from her coma free of any debilitating effects? If so, what would happen to her after that? Surely, Starfleet would have some say in that matter.

"Doctor, I'd like to travel with you to Vulcan."

The words came out without Pennington's conscious bidding, and he blinked in astonishment even as they left his mouth. He was almost certain the expression of surprise on M'Benga's face mirrored his own.

"I don't know if that's appropriate," the doctor said, frowning.

Nodding, Pennington replied, "I know, I'm not family, and we're not even good friends, but the truth is that . . . for reasons I'm not really sure I understand myself, I care about what happens to her."

M'Benga's eyes narrowed in suspicion. "Setting aside for the moment the fact that we're going to *Vulcan,* a planet not known for welcoming outsiders—particularly when it comes to anyone observing some of the more private aspects of the culture, such as medical care—how do I know I'm not going to read all about this on the Federation News Service?"

Pennington held up his hands. "Word of honor, Doc. I'm not going as a reporter. This isn't about exploiting her condition in order to grab a headline. I *want* to go, as . . . as someone who just gives a damn." After watching M'Benga's features tighten as he contemplated the pros and cons of this notion, he added, "Besides, it's a long trip. You might enjoy the company."

Another moment passed as M'Benga considered Pennington's request and turned his attention to his nurses and their continued preparations to move T'Prynn. Then he asked, "What about this business with Commodore Reyes's court-martial? Won't they want you to stick around for that?"

"Reyes's lawyer has already deposed me," Pennington said, "and Captain Desai won't want me anywhere near the trial. I'm a hostile witness. Reyes didn't offer me any classified information or make available any member of Starfleet to corroborate my article. Everything in that piece is as I saw it happen with my own eyes. I haven't been subpoenaed to testify, and I'm a member of the press, so they can't confine me to the station. I'm free to go wherever I want." Naturally, it occurred to him that a subpoena might well be coming and that Reyes's lawyer just had not yet gotten to it, but Pennington saw no reason to make it any easier for Starfleet to hang the commodore.

To hell with the lot of 'em.

After a moment, his expression remaining almost Vulcan-like, M'Benga asked, "I don't suppose you play chess, do you?"

Pennington could not help the smile beginning to warm his own features. "Just tell me where and when to show up with my board, mate."

"As I said," M'Benga replied, "fourteen hundred hours. Docking Bay four. Pack lightly."

"You got it," Pennington said, clapping his hands together and turning toward the exit. Already, his mind was racing with the list of tasks he needed to accomplish in the handful of hours remaining before the transport's scheduled departure. Pausing, he turned to look over his shoulder. "Thanks, Doc. I appreciate this."

"Don't mention it," M'Benga said, his attention already returned to his data slate and the preparations he was overseeing. Glancing up one final time, he added, "But if you snore, I'm kicking you out the airlock."

15

"Gangway! Make a hole!"

Atish Khatami shouted the commands over the wail of the red-alert sirens as she sprinted down the curving corridor of Deck 5 on her way to the nearest turbolift. Ahead of her, crew members already moving to their assigned battle stations cleared the center of the hallway, some even flattening themselves against bulkheads in order to give the captain free passage. Rounding a turn, she nearly bowled over a hapless lieutenant who was trying to vacate the turbolift. The younger officer managed to dodge her and avoided being body-slammed into the wall as Khatami plunged into the lift.

"Bridge!" she called out as she gripped one of the car's quartet of control handles and the doors closed behind her. An instant later, she felt the slight push from below as the lift began its ascent. Reaching for the comm panel just inside the door, Khatami activated the unit. "Khatami to bridge. Report."

"Stano here," replied the *Endeavour*'s first officer. *"Sensors have picked up three Klingon warships at extreme range, but they've altered course to intercept us, and they're coming fast. I've raised shields and readied weapons crews."*

The report was completed just as the turbolift slowed and the doors opened, revealing the *Endeavour*'s bridge. Khatami exited the lift just as Lieutenant Commander Katherine Stano glanced over her shoulder and rose from the captain's chair.

"Sensors indicate they're *D-7* cruisers," Stano said. "They'll be on us in less than two minutes, Captain." Her expression was neutral, but Khatami heard the concern in her exec's voice.

"Maintain course and speed," Khatami said as she stepped down into the command well, her eyes looking to the viewscreen and taking in its image of stars streaking past as the *Endeavour* cruised at warp six. She asked, "Have they attempted to hail us?"

Stano shook her head, and a lock of the dirty-blond hair she wore in a short bob fell across her eyes. "No, Captain, nor have they responded to our hails. They're still approaching on an intercept course, maintaining a loose formation. Their weapons are hot."

"Well, of course they are," Khatami replied, offering a humorless grin to her first officer as she settled into the center seat. Behind her, Stano left the command well and moved to the engineering station near the turbolift, taking up the duties she normally performed when she and Khatami were both on the bridge.

At the communications station, Lieutenant Estrada turned in his seat. "Captain, we're still receiving no responses to our hails."

"Keep after it, Lieutenant," Khatami ordered. She knew it likely was a fruitless gesture, but she wanted it on record that every peaceful overture was attempted when and if the situation deteriorated during the next few minutes.

And what are the odds of that?

"One of the ships is breaking formation," reported Lieutenant Klisiewicz from the science station. He looked up from the console's hooded sensor viewer. "It's accelerating to warp seven and coming right at us. Intercept in forty-three seconds."

Khatami did not have to look around her to know that the anxiety her bridge officers were feeling was heightening with each passing second. The *Endeavour* was still a long way from home, and three ships against one were not good odds, even if the one vessel was a *Constitution*-class starship. Forcing her own unease from her mind, she straightened in her chair.

"Are they targeting us?"

Turning back to his sensor readouts, Klisiewicz shook his head. "No."

At the helm console, Lieutenant Neelakanta asked, "Captain, should we target?"

"Negative," Khatami replied. Something was off here. It was a gut reaction, one she could not explain. "Maintain course." Glancing toward Klisiewicz, she asked, "What about his two friends?"

When the young science officer looked at her this time, a frown clouded his features. "They've adopted a parallel course, Captain, holding distance one million kilometers port side, aft."

"You think they're screwing with us?" asked Stano.

"We know they've been doing it with civilian traffic," Khatami replied. She had read several reports during the past several weeks, detailing accounts of merchant or colony vessels being harassed by Klingon warships, not just in the Taurus Reach but all along the border separating Federation and Klingon territory. No shots were fired, and no communications were exchanged, so the reasons for the odd behavior remained unknown. "There've been no reports of them going after Starfleet ships. Not yet, anyway." Starfleet had no way to know if the Klingons were itching to provoke a fight, a move that essentially would void the ongoing, if largely stalled, diplomatic talks between the Federation and the empire. Khatami figured it was something far simpler, and Klingon ship captains were getting restless and looking for some means to alleviate boredom as they patrolled unfamiliar space far from home.

As opposed to just curling up with a good book.

The next moments passed in silence, save for the omnipresent chatter of the various bridge systems and the occasional voice from the intercom offering some form of status report, before Klisiewicz again spoke. "Here they come. They're matching our course and speed, Captain."

"Onscreen," Khatami ordered, an instant before the aspect on the main viewscreen shifted to show the Klingon *D-7* battle cruiser as it angled toward the *Endeavour* on what appeared to be a collision course. It was an incredibly dangerous maneuver at warp speeds, one that lasted mere seconds before the Klingon ship veered to its right, offering a sidelong view of the menacing vessel. From this distance, every seam of every hull plate was clearly visible as it sailed past, arcing out of view.

From over her left shoulder, Khatami heard Stano say, "Somebody tell me I'm not the only one who needs a diaper change."

"They're playing chicken," Khatami said, rising from her chair. Even as she spoke the words, the alert indicator at the center of the helm and navigation console began blinking a deep crimson. "Hell of a thing to do at warp seven."

"One of the other ships is coming in for a fly-by," reported Klisiewicz. "Same trajectory as the first one."

Khatami nodded. "They're trying to provoke a reaction, hoping we might blink or, better yet, open fire." The thought of spending the last three days of their return journey to Vanguard being hounded by Klingons did not sit well with her. In fact, the idea of spending the next three minutes so engaged irritated her, and her annoyance mounted as she watched the image of the Klingon ship growing larger on the main viewer.

"Mr. Neelakanta, target their warp nacelles. Don't use the computer; you'll have to do it manually. Do *not* engage weapons. Mr. Estrada, the instant we have target lock, I want you to broadcast a tight-beam signal on all frequencies, directly at the Klingon ship. Channel it through the navigational deflector. I want it to bounce off their walls and rattle their teeth. If you blow out a window or two, I'll promote you right here and now."

"Aye, Captain," replied the communications officer. "What do you want the message to say?"

Crossing her arms as she studied the image of the oncoming ship, Khatami said, "Back off." As the Klingon ship drew closer, she heard a telltale beeping from Neelakanta's console.

"Nacelles targeted, Captain," reported the helmsman, and Khatami nodded in approval. Achieving a target lock without assistance from the ship's fire-control systems was no easy feat.

"Sending the tight-beam message," said Estrada.

The reaction on the viewer was immediate, with the Klingon

vessel abruptly changing its course and even accelerating as it hurled past the *Endeavour*.

"That's got their attention, Captain," Klisiewicz called out. Khatami looked to her science officer, who was leaning over his sensor viewer. The unit's cool blue light played across his face. "All three ships are veering off."

"I'm picking up comm traffic between the ships," said Estrada. The lieutenant sat with his eyes closed, the fingers of his left hand held against the Feinberg receiver in his ear. "I think you rattled their cage, Captain."

A chorus of satisfied chuckles and other indications of approval sounded around the bridge, but Khatami ignored them. "Klisiewicz, any indications that they might be coming about?"

"Negative," replied the science officer. "They're making a beeline out of here at warp seven." He turned from his console, his expression one of satisfaction. "Looks as if you spooked them, Captain."

Khatami shrugged, "Even three on one isn't a guarantee against a ship of the line." From a weapons and defense perspective, the *Endeavour* and her sister starships were theoretically capable of standing up against three *D-7* cruisers, but it was a hypothesis tested only on rare occasions. In those instances, it had come down to the experience and shrewdness of the vessel's commander as much as the capabilities of the ship itself.

"The big question now," said Stano as she moved from her station to stand at the curved red railing, "is how long the Klingons are going to keep up this nonsense."

As she returned to her seat in the captain's chair, Khatami felt the first hints of fatigue as the adrenaline of the past moments began to fade. "They'll keep it up until they get the reaction they're looking for."

When that happened, all bets would be off.

16

After much careful deliberation, most of which had been carried out while consuming a sizable portion of his personal, private supply of bloodwine, Captain Komoraq decided that he truly was beginning to hate this planet.

Standing on a plateau, the highest point on the small island that was the focal point of Klingon presence on this world since the *M'ahtagh*'s arrival, he surveyed the lush landscape around him. At first glance, the island seemed nothing more than a tranquil haven, one among a vast archipelago far from the shores of the nearest continent and surrounded by brilliant azure water. Yes, Lerais II, as the Earthers called it, had much to offer, if one were interested in such pursuits as farming or fishing. The world teemed with vast untapped natural resources, a temperate climate, and numerous plant and animal species never before encountered. Were he a colonist, Komoraq could see the allure of making a home on a world such as this. As a scientist, he would appreciate the unparalleled opportunities the planet presented.

However, he was not a farmer or a fisherman or a scientist. Indeed, he despised farmers and fishermen, and the only reason he tolerated scientists at all was that he happened to call one his wife. Still, there were days, such as today, when she and those like her made Komoraq give more than a passing thought to destroying the entire planet and them along with it.

Releasing a grunt of frustrated resignation, he turned and proceeded down the narrow trail that members of his crew had cut through the lush tropical undergrowth. Following the path as it descended from the plateau along the side of the hill, Komoraq made his way to the ravine, which was all but concealed from the air by the canopy of towering trees covering the island's northern quadrant. It took several bends and turns in the trail before the Klingon captain found himself standing at the entrance to the structure that had no business here, in what poets—including his wife—would call unblemished paradise.

Seemingly carved from a single piece of what appeared to be obsidian glass but which Komoraq knew was a still-unidentified substance, the edifice was thousands of years old, if the sensor readings recorded by his wife and her cadre of science specialists were accurate. Rising only a handful of meters from the soil, the visible portion was but a fraction of what lay embedded in the ground beneath Komoraq's feet. The entrance, as impressive as it was in its elegant simplicity, belied the wondrous contents to be found within. Scans had determined this to be the center of the planet's collection of mysterious alien technology, much like what had been discovered on other worlds throughout the Gonmog Sector. According to the collected sensor data, nothing hidden beneath the surface at this location had been disturbed for millennia. It all lay untouched, waiting for its creators or anyone else fortunate to find it.

Now, all I need is for my wife and her gaggle of sniveling bookworms to figure out how to make any of it work.

After crossing the threshold and entering the structure's foyer, Komoraq proceeded down a narrow corridor, which also appeared to have been cut with uncanny precision from whatever material had been used to build the place. Just as with the external façade, the passage showed no visible seams or any means of fastening together sections or components. Others might even view the corridor itself as a work of art, but Komoraq was not one to waste time on such useless observations.

"Someone, anyone, please tell me that you've discovered something of worth," he called out, his voice echoing off the smooth, opaque walls as the passage opened into a larger chamber.

Present in the room were six Klingons, five males and one

female. Komoraq knew the males only in passing, recognizing their faces from the crew's personnel database. They were scientists rather than warriors, so he had never considered it necessary to bother learning their names. They were occupied with various tasks, huddled around a collection of portable computer workstations on field desks and equipment containers transported down from the *M'ahtagh*. Ignoring them and whatever they might be doing, he directed his attention to the lone female in the room. "Alleviate my doubts, my mate, and convince me that you've found the source for powerful new weapons that will make us rulers of the empire."

From where she stood hunched over what he recognized as the control panel of a portable dynamic energy-mode conversion unit—the type normally used by engineering and repair crews when a situation required directing power on a level generated only by a vessel's warp engines—his wife, Lorka, turned from her work toward him. As she straightened and rose to her full height, Komoraq noted that her dark hair, which she wore in a short, utilitarian style, and her face and uniform were lightened by a thin coat of fine dust. The scowl darkening her features told him that she was in no mood for any of the playful banter he was unable to resist employing whenever she was immersed in her work.

He smiled, baring his teeth. Her reactions never failed to excite him.

Shaking her head, Lorka directed an expression of disgust toward the dust covering her as though noticing it for the first time. Rivulets of sweat had drawn lines in the filmy grime, and Komoraq tensed as his nostrils caught her scent. He had always thought her at her most beautiful whenever she was ensconced in her element, her thoughts not at all on him and instead focused on the tasks before her.

"Maintain your bearing, my captain," she said, obviously recognizing his expression. "We've no time for such distractions." She pointed to what Komoraq recognized as a darkened control console, one of the room's few notable features. "As for progress, there's been precious little of that. This cursed machinery defies our every effort to understand it, much less activate it."

It was the same report he had been hearing, with little variation, since they'd come to the planet more than two months ago, well before the arrival of the meddlesome Earther colonists. Since they had discovered the ancient chamber and its promise of unheralded secrets and potential, some type of energy generation source had been in operation, supplying minimal power to the equipment stored within the underground cache. Lorka and her teams had only just begun to study the amazing find when, without warning, all power routing ceased to function. All attempts to restore operations, or even to understand what had caused them to cease, had failed.

There were theories that this was related to the incredible disappearance of an entire star system deep within the Gonmog Sector, which might well be the center of power for the ancient race that supposedly had once ruled this region of space. It was a hypothesis supported by intelligence reports from spies within Starfleet, as well as the Federation's own public media outlets, if one series of astonishing news reports was to be believed. Members of the mysterious civilization had already been encountered on other worlds, usually with alarming results and putting to rest any notions that they had ceased to exist long ago. Was their influence so far-reaching that they could command the destruction of entire planets and solar systems on a whim and channel energy to planets scattered across light-years of space? If they possessed even a fraction of that power, Komoraq knew that made them an enemy far more formidable than anything yet encountered by the Klingon Empire.

He frowned as he studied the panel, which had only a minimal array of features. No display screens or controls adorned the console, which instead was dominated by a collection of crystals of varying sizes, shapes, and colors. None of the crystals was illuminated or pulsed with anything indicating a power source, and no patterns or methods to the crystals' arrangement presented themselves. "It's a mechanism, is it not?" he asked, waving one hand toward the device. "We know that much from previous encounters with this technology."

"Of course," Lorka replied, making no effort to hide her disdain at having to discuss these concepts with someone who did not possess any appreciable degree of scientific or engineering knowledge. "But on those occasions, the crews who studied the finds also had at their disposal whatever energy source generated power to the equipment. Since the power source behind this technology stopped functioning, we no longer have that luxury."

Grunting in irritation, Komoraq shook his head. "Surely, there must be a means of accessing its innards and providing our own power."

"How fortunate that we have you here to provide such unrivaled insight," Lorka replied, sneering so that he saw her rows of uneven, sharp teeth, "for certainly we would not have thought to consider that notion ourselves." Before Komoraq could respond to the verbal jab, she cut him off, gesturing to indicate the chamber around them. "We've been unable to find anything resembling a power junction or an access conduit or even a door, as though this entire structure were one monstrous mountain of crystal or glass or whatever this substance is."

The room was comparable in size to the *M'ahtagh*'s largest cargo hold, with a high, arched ceiling that, like the walls and even the floor, was made of the same damnable, forbidding substance. One of the landing parties under Lorka's direction had positioned a series of six portable lighting columns around the chamber's perimeter. While illumination allowed him to see the room's contents, Komoraq could not help noticing yet again that the light caused absolutely no reflection in the walls, floor, or ceiling, as though whatever material used to construct them were absorbing the energy and leaving no trace.

Lorka paused a moment, drawing a deep breath as though to compose herself, before returning her attention to her husband and the inert console. "According to the scans I've made of everything we've found down here, this panel is the key. My readings suggest that it harbors a type of biometric or possibly even bio-neural interface, embedded within a crystal lattice, which I assume forms a power-distribution network, though it's not one I've encountered before."

"Let us pretend I understood nothing you just said," Komoraq said, his grin laced with an underlying menace. "What does all of that mean?"

Her hand moving as though of its own free will to the sheathed *d'k tagh* knife she wore on her left hip, Lorka regarded him with smoldering annoyance. "If you were not my husband, I would have killed you long ago." Despite her words and expression, Komoraq noted the way her eyes regarded him. Though she would never admit it while life still coursed through her body, she enjoyed their verbal jousts as much as he did, as they often served as a momentary respite from the demands of her duties.

None of that meant that Lorka would not later seek reprisal for his role in this discussion, of course, and Komoraq found himself rather looking forward to making good on that debt.

"It means that a form of direct energy transfer is required, through this console," she said, moving to stand once again before the panel. "Without whatever piece of technology is missing to complete the connection as originally intended, we've been forced to experiment with alternative methods. None of our portable generators seems to possess the required output levels, so I've decided to attempt powering it via direct energy transfer from the ship."

Komoraq was familiar with the notion, having seen a similar tactic employed to transmit power from an orbiting vessel to ground-based weapons emplacements such as crewed disruptor cannons and related armaments. Frowning, he asked, "Wouldn't there be a risk of damaging or destroying the mechanism?"

Lorka nodded. "Possibly, but I find it unlikely. Based on everything I've learned from my sensor scans, the technology used to construct this equipment is quite robust. All indications are that it is more than capable of channeling even the maximum power we might direct at it. What is in question is compatibility. There may be frequency or other calibration issues to resolve, even if this console recognizes our power signature."

Without waiting for permission to proceed, she reached to her belt for the communications device on a clip next to her *d'k tagh*. Pressing the control to activate the unit, she growled, *"M'ahtagh,* this is Science Officer Lorka. Is that pathetic excuse for a chief engineer ready to transfer ship's power?"

"Yes," a deep voice replied through the communicator's speaker grille, offering nothing else. After a moment, the voice added, *"He has completed his adjustments to our deflector relay and is standing by for your order to proceed."*

"Very well," Lorka said, stepping toward the portable energy converter. Komoraq watched as she reached for a control to activate the unit, at the same time verifying that she had properly aligned its transceiver assembly to direct the energy it would be converting toward the alien control panel. "Proceed."

The room was abruptly filled with a high-pitched whine as the energy converter began receiving the power transmission from the *M'ahtagh.* The reaction by the alien technology was immediate, with the console's array of crystals flaring to life, accompanied by a synchronized string of melodic tones echoing within the chamber. Then he noted a telltale vibration in the floor beneath his boots, along with a hum beginning to resonate throughout the chamber. Around him, recessed lighting panels began to brighten, very dim at first but growing in intensity with each passing moment.

Studying the readouts on her portable scanner, Lorka said, "I'm picking up power signatures from somewhere beneath us. It looks as if other systems are activating."

"You've done it," Komoraq said, watching the display with no small amount of excitement.

Wielding a portable scanner, Lorka shook her head. "I don't think so. There are too many fluctuations in the power transfer to the console. The energy we're providing isn't truly compatible with this technology." She looked over her shoulder, barking orders to one of her team members to adjust the settings on the energy converter's control panel.

Komoraq watched as the illuminated console began to sputter

and flicker. Several of the crystals went dark, followed almost as quickly by others, until all of them once again lay dormant. Along with the panel itself, the oddly enticing litany of almost musical tones faded. The overhead lighting was extinguished, and the reverberations in the floor beneath him quieted as well.

Lorka, uttering one of her preferred strings of colorful oaths, turned to the converter, pushing aside her subordinate and taking over the task of calibrating the unit. Her efforts yielded only fleeting results as the panel reactivated for a moment, a shorter version of the light show playing out across the console's surface before it again went dark. When she made further adjustments to the converter, the alien equipment revived once more but only for a few seconds.

Holding out her scanner, Lorka stepped closer to the panel, shaking her head in disgust as she reviewed the readings. "It's as though it shut down deliberately," she said after a moment. "I don't understand. Some kind of defense mechanism to prevent intrusion by unauthorized users?" With a final grunt of rage, she threw the scanner against one obsidian wall, and the unit exploded into dozens of pieces that scattered across the floor. She punctuated her angry display with another chorus of profanity.

"What?" Komoraq asked.

Shaking her head, Lorka replied, "I picked up no residual readings whatsoever. For whatever reason, the console decided the power I was sending to it wasn't compatible with its systems and shut everything down." She released another enraged growl. "Just as on the other planets where this technology has been discovered, without this key component being active, we won't be able to access any of the structure's lower levels."

She did not have to complete her thought. Komoraq knew precisely what she had not put into words. The lower levels housed the truly remarkable examples of the ancient race's wondrous technology. If this planet possessed a global defense system comparable to ones seen on other worlds in the Gonmog Sector, then it harbored a weapon capable of ensuring the Klingon Empire's supremacy throughout the galaxy.

Assuming that those who created the weapon don't decide to use it on us and the planet itself, he mused. There already had been examples of such power being unleashed even in the brief time that had passed since both Federation and Klingon ships had ventured into this region of space. Since learning of this technology and the potential it offered, Komoraq had spent many evenings imagining what he might accomplish with such weaponry under his direct control. There would be no limit to what he might achieve, but now he was sensing the enormous opportunity beginning to slip from his grasp.

"We need to find some way inside," Komoraq said through gritted teeth as he bit back his mounting frustration. "If we're unable to wrest control of this technology from the belly of this cursed planet, I'll have destroyed a Federation freighter and forcibly evicted one of their colonies for nothing except my own amusement."

He had been informed by his superiors that the High Council was not pleased with the methods he had employed to secure Lerais II in the aim of the empire. Though he had made the uncharacteristic gesture of sparing the Earther colonists and allowed them to evacuate the planet without incident, annihilating the freighter still had served to exacerbate the tense political situation with the Federation. Between his own actions and other incidents involving imperial and Starfleet ships in recent weeks, subspace communications were being choked with rumors of war with the empire's longtime adversaries. While the Council seemed to welcome that possibility, they were proceeding with any planning toward that goal with a slowness that enraged Komoraq's warrior blood. Still, there would be calls for increased vigilance to protect Klingon interests in the Gonmog Sector as more Federation ships came to the region. There would soon be other, more pressing duties to which he and his crew must attend. With that came the likelihood that another, less deserving commander of some other, less distinguished battle cruiser might seize for his own uses what Komoraq himself had failed to secure.

For the first time since he had entered the chamber, Komoraq felt his wife's hand on his arm. "We will find a way, my husband," Lorka said, "but you know that I cannot make any reliable estimates. These types of mysteries are not typically solved on any discernible timetable."

Pausing, she added, "The artifacts we found on Mirdonyae V are in better condition. The planet is also more isolated than this one. We should continue our research there."

Komoraq emitted a dissatisfied grunt. "Unfortunately, my wife, even your best efforts may not be good enough." No, he decided, they needed something more, something that had been unavailable to them. Offering his beloved wife a leering grin, he felt a small rush of anticipation as he considered how best to proceed. "What we need just now is a fresh perspective."

17
INTERLUDE

Pain and exhaustion gripped the Shedai Wanderer, threatening to crush the withering vestiges of life to which she clung as she all but fell to the dead world that was her destination.

Without the Conduit to guide and support her, it had taken nearly all of the energy she had been able to gather during her exile on the distant moon even to reach this far. By the standards of travel to which she long ago had become accustomed, journeying to this planet should have been simple. She knew it to be on par with the sort of exercise a mentor might give to a child just learning to control the great powers commanded by the Shedai. Instead, the voyage had drained most of her strength, nearly leaving her stranded without corporeal existence and dispersed to the void between stars.

She took in her surroundings, searching her memories for information on the world she would now call home, at least until she regained enough strength to make another attempt at travel. Like the moon she had left behind, this planet also was lifeless, though for much different reasons. All around her, the Wanderer saw remnants of the civilization that once had thrived here. The ruins of a great city stretched to the horizon in all directions, the artificial structures and other technological constructs lying abandoned and crumbling for aeons, if her memory served her. Far above, the sky was black and brilliant, though it and the stars that filled her vision carried a crimson tinge, owing to the large red sun dominating the spectacular scene. The planet's atmosphere had been burned away, a casualty of the nearby star having gone nova, an event that likely had snuffed out this world's population in an instant.

It took a moment, but in short order, the stories came forth from her memory. A great empire—Tkon, the Wanderer now recalled—had once owned this planet. Now all but extinct, its influence had covered a vast segment of space, nearly rivaling that of the Shedai. The Tkon, according to the legends, were but one of the very few peoples to resist any effort at conquest, including submitting to the will of the Shedai. Tales and folklore regarded them as a more than worthy adversary. Had they survived the disaster that had befallen their homeworld, they might well have unseated the Shedai as the dominant power in this area of the galaxy. While legends suggested that some paltry shadows of the once-mighty Tkon people might still remain scattered through space, their empire would never rise again.

Unlike the Tkon, the Wanderer knew, the Shedai would return. When that might happen remained uncertain, of course, as did the nature of their resurgence, but that they would emerge once again to stake claim to their place as rightful rulers was not in doubt.

Whether the Shedai would be worthy of that authority was also a question demanding resolution. After all, the galaxy had changed, evolved, while the Shedai had lain dormant. Would the civilizations that had emerged and advanced during that time willingly subjugate themselves to such rule? Based on what she had seen just since her own awakening, the Wanderer found this unlikely. Despite her unwavering loyalty to the Enumerated Ones, she also had learned to doubt the inherent assumption that all others existed simply to serve the Shedai. Such thinking was dangerous, she knew, and would not endear her to the *Serrataal* when they finally returned. That did nothing to keep the thoughts from taking hold in her mind, commanding her focus and requiring answers.

Dishonorable notions and other ephemera were pushed aside without warning as the Wanderer realized that something else was drawing her attention. Another presence, distant and faint but still detectable, called out across the Void.

The Apostate. As I roam free, so, too, does my enemy.

Directing a few precious strands of the depleted energy she had strived so untiringly to gather, the Wanderer reached out, pushing past faraway stars in search of her adversary. Her mind tingled with the fleeting contact, and in that instant, she knew that the Apostate had done as she had feared and as the Maker had warned them all. Deception and treachery were the ways of the Apostate, and he had exercised them with utmost effectiveness. He had removed the Enumerated Ones and the key to their power from this spatial plane under the pretense of forcing the Shedai to an evolving galaxy. Now he was free to pursue his true agenda, whatever that might be.

The Wanderer had known fear only on rare occasions throughout her long life, but nothing she ever had experienced could compare to the terror she felt at the thought of facing the Apostate again. She knew that their next meeting, wherever and whenever it took place, would likely be her end. Her only hope was the return of the Enumerated Ones from whatever distant realm they now inhabited.

Where are you?

18

Jon Cooper exited his office at a full run, mere heartbeats after the first red-alert siren echoed through Vanguard's command center. The din lasted only a moment, as he saw Lieutenant Haniff Jackson signal toward Lieutenant Judy Dunbar, the center's communications officer and his companion on the supervisor's deck.

"Shut that off!" Jackson shouted over the alarms. "Call battle stations."

Cooper crossed the room toward the stairs leading to the supervisor's deck. He took the steps two at a time until he reached the hub. "What've we got?"

"Unidentified vessels just dropped out of warp, Commander," Jackson replied. "Distance three hundred sixty million kilometers. They're not on a direct intercept course, but they're definitely heading in our direction."

Glancing at the sensor display monitors dominating Haniff's station at the hub, Cooper saw that the lieutenant had already ordered the station's deflector shields raised and weapons energized and placed on standby. "Any idea who they are?"

"Three ships," replied Ensign Kail Tescar from where he stood at another station, leaning over a hooded viewer. "Sensors identify them as Tholian in design, sir."

Tholian? "What are they doing here now?" Cooper asked as he and Jackson exchanged confused frowns. As far as Cooper knew, there had been no Tholian vessels near the station for weeks, since just after the incident in the Jinoteur system. The reclusive race had seemed content to draw even further in on itself, which did little for the advancement of diplomatic talks between the Tholian Assembly and the Federation. Despite that, they at least had not seen fit to cause trouble, for either Federation or Klingon vessels traversing the Taurus Reach. At the time, that had been enough to keep Cooper happy.

Glancing down once more at the hub's active sensor displays, he felt that mild contentment beginning to melt away.

It was fun while it lasted.

"We're picking up weapons fire, Commander," Tescar said. Still hunched over his viewer, the young, lanky ensign paused as he studied the information being fed to the viewer via the station's vast sensor network. "Two of the ships appear to be firing on the other. That ship's warp engines look to be disabled, and it's flying what I think is an evasive course toward the station." He looked up from his station, and Cooper saw that the man seemed more than a little nervous. Cooper found it hard to blame the ensign, especially considering that Tescar was less than a year out of Starfleet Academy and still adjusting to his first deep-space assignment.

Hell of a way to earn your stripes, kid.

"Just the three ships?" Cooper asked.

Tescar nodded. "Yes, sir. Sensors show no other traffic that we haven't already accounted for."

Across the table from Cooper, Jackson frowned. "Why the hell would they be firing on one of their own ships? That doesn't even make any sense."

"Tell me anything about a Tholian that does make sense," Cooper countered. "Tescar, what's the condition of the pursued ship?"

The ensign took a moment to recheck his sensor readouts before responding. "Besides their warp engines, I'm picking up fluctuations in what I think is their life-support system. Their weapons appear to be offline as well."

Just behind him, seated at another station at the hub's opposite end, Lieutenant Dunbar looked up from her console. Her right hand moved to the Feinberg receiver she wore in her ear. "Commander, we're being hailed by the Tholian ship."

After exchanging another surprised glance with Jackson, Cooper nodded to the communications officer. "Open a channel."

"Federation starbase." A shrill, high-pitched voice blared from speakers recessed into support columns around the supervisor deck's perimeter. *"I am under attack and request your assistance."*

"This is going to be fun," Jackson muttered as he took a seat at his own station.

Scowling, Cooper moved around the hub until he stood behind Dunbar. "Tholian vessel, this is Commander Jon Cooper aboard Federation Starbase 47. Please identify yourself, and state the nature of your emergency."

"My name is Nezrene," the Tholian responded, *"and I bring knowledge you may find helpful. I—"*

The rest of the transmission exploded into a burst of static, loud enough that Dunbar grunted in protest as she yanked the receiver from her ear. "Damn, I hate it when that happens."

"What?" Cooper asked.

Dunbar shook her head. "The frequency's being jammed, sir. Probably from one of the pursuing ships."

"Distance from the station less than two hundred fifty million kilometers, sir," Tescar reported. "The ship is still evading the worst of the attacks, but it won't last long on its own."

"Commander, did I hear that Tholian say her name was Nezrene?"

It took Cooper an extra moment to realize that the question came not from one of his officers on the supervisor's deck but rather from somewhere down on the command center's main floor. Looking over the railing, Cooper saw the imposing visage of Ambassador Jetanien glaring up at him, the mandibles that formed the Chel's beaklike bill moving up and down in a frantic motion suggesting that the diplomat was more than a bit anxious. Where in the hell had he come from, and how had he gotten out of the turbolift and across the room without drawing anyone's attention? And why had he chosen to come up here now?

"Ambassador?" Cooper held up a hand in warning. "This really isn't the best—"

"I'm aware of the situation, Commander," Jetanien snapped, clicking his manus in evident irritation. "I wouldn't be so stupid as to bother you at a time like this if I didn't think it was important. Now, did that Tholian say her name was Nezrene?"

Nodding as he tried to keep his attention focused on the situation at hand, Cooper said, "Yes, she did." He paused before offering a frown. "At least, I think it was a she."

"You need to grant that ship safe harbor, Commander," Jetanien said, having moved to stand at the bottom of the stairs leading up to the hub, as his large form would not allow him to climb the steps to reach the upper deck.

I bet he'd get up here if I pissed him off enough.

His eyes narrowing in confusion, Cooper asked, "Other than the obvious reason that it's a ship in apparent distress, Ambassador, what aren't you telling me?"

Several agitated clicks erupted from the Chelon's mouth before he replied. "Because that Tholian may provide us unequaled insight into the Taurus Reach."

So much for shore leave.

Leaning forward in her chair at the center of the *Endeavour*'s bridge, Atish Khatami forced the inappropriate thought from her mind and returned her attention to the situation at hand. All around her, the members of alpha shift's bridge crew were focused on their stations, and the tension they exuded hung in the air like a stifling blanket.

"We've cleared the docking port, Captain" called out Lieutenant Neelakanta without looking up from his helm console. "We're free to navigate."

Khatami nodded, pleased at the report. Unable to resist a final jab before getting down to business, she said, "Well, it's not as though we even had a chance to tie up or anything."

Her observation was not far from the truth. The *Endeavour* had just returned to Vanguard the previous day, only to receive orders from Commander Cooper not to utilize one of the docking bays in the station's massive primary hull section. Instead, the starship was directed to one of the external ports ringing the docking wheel at the center of the secondary hull. Khatami had at first been confused by the instructions, but Cooper's reasoning had been straightforward and—as evidenced by events currently unfolding—remarkably prescient.

"Bring us about," she ordered. "Lay in that intercept course, and engage at full impulse. Shields up, and place weapons on ready status."

Neelakanta replied, "Time to intercept is less than two minutes, Captain."

Within moments of Cooper's order to take any and all necessary action to protect the apparently rogue Tholian vessel, the *Endeavour* was away from the station and ready for battle. This, too, was an unexpected dividend from the starbase commander's orders, given his concern about the increase in activity throughout the Taurus Reach in recent weeks. According to the daily security briefings Khatami had received from Cooper's staff, long-range scans had even revealed Klingon vessels at extreme range—presumably to conduct their own sensor sweeps of the station and other ships traversing the region. To this end, the *Endeavour* had standing orders to dock at one of the external ports and, while moored, to maintain a crew complement sufficient to undertake combat operations in the event that an emergency arose in proximity to the station.

I like the way you think, Cooper, Khatami mused. *Just remind me never to play poker with you.*

"Mr. Klisiewicz," she said, glancing toward the science station, "what's the condition of the ship they're chasing?"

At his console, Klisiewicz leaned over so that he could peer into the hooded viewer. "If it had deflector shields, they're down. Sensors are picking up damage all along the hull, but so far, it's still intact."

Khatami asked, "What about life signs? Just the one?"

"Yes," the science officer replied. "It's a smaller ship, probably some kind of scout vessel. The other two ships are of the cruiser design we're more familiar with."

More familiar with.

The phrase rolled around in Khatami's mind. So far, Starfleet's dealings with Tholian vessels had been limited. Individually, Tholian ships presented only limited tactical challenges to most Federation starships. It was when they worked in concert, operating in groups of three or more, that they began to present a more imposing threat, even to larger and more powerful adversaries such as *Constitution*-class starships.

From behind her at the communications station, Lieutenant Hector Estrada said, "Captain, I'm picking up a new signal. It's coming from one of the other Tholian ships."

Khatami frowned. "This ought to be good. Let's hear it."

A harsh, clipped voice burst from the bridge speakers. *"Federation outpost, this is the* Battle Cruiser Vin'q Tholis, *representing the Tholian Assembly. The vessel we are pursuing is stolen property, and its pilot is a known fugitive. Attempting to assist this criminal or in any way obstruct us from retrieving this vessel and its pilot will be considered an act of aggression against our government."*

The voice was a pitch or two deeper to Khatami's ear than that of the first Tholian to contact the station, Nezrene, but the similarities in pronunciation and inflection were acute. Was it her imagination, or did she detect a slight hint of fear behind the aggressive demands?

Over the same communications channel, Khatami and the rest of the bridge crew listened as Commander Cooper responded, *"Tholian vessels, this is the commander of Starbase 47. Be advised that you have entered Federation space without authorization. The vessel you are pursuing has requested asylum on this station, and I now apprise you of our intentions to grant that sanctuary. You are therefore ordered to cease fire and alter your course heading immediately. Any attacks on this station or any ship under its protection will be considered hostile acts, and we will take all necessary measures to defend ourselves. Acknowledge."*

"Any response to that from the Tholians?" asked Khatami.

From behind her, Estrada replied, "No, Captain."

"How delightfully unexpected," retorted Lieutenant Commander Bersh glov Mog, the *Endeavour*'s chief engineer, from where he sat at his station.

Despite the tension she could feel mounting around the bridge as she looked over her shoulder at the burly Tellarite, Khatami could not help the wry grin she felt warming her features. "Don't tell me *you* think *they're* being rude, Mog?"

The engineer shook his head. "Rude? That would require them actually answering our hails. No, I think they're just being insufferable asses."

"Thanks for clearing that up," Khatami said as she returned her attention to the main viewscreen. "Okay, look sharp, people. Things are going to get very interesting in the next couple of minutes. Klisiewicz, what are they doing?"

The science officer turned to face her. "Still giving chase, Captain. They'll cross the station's outer defensive perimeter in less than a minute."

"That's why we're here, Lieutenant," Khatami said. Cooper's orders had been quite clear on this point: protect the fleeing Tholian vessel at all costs. The station's defenses would likely be far more than a match for the other ships, but it would be the *Endeavour*'s responsibility to ensure that they never got that close. Glancing over her shoulder at Estrada, she said, "Lieutenant, hail the Tholian ships, and let them know that the path to Vanguard goes through us."

All around her, Khatami sensed her blunt, no-nonsense message having the desired effect as a new burst of determination seemed to course through everyone on the bridge. From the overhead speakers, she heard the litany of status reports coming from stations throughout the ship, notifying the bridge that they stood ready to face whatever tasks or challenges the next minutes might bring.

The responses of her crew as they readied themselves filled Khatami herself with a familiar confidence, the sort that could be cultivated only from leading into the unknown those who had placed in her their faith that she would do right by them. Since taking command of the *Endeavour* after the tragic death of its former captain, Zhao Sheng, Khatami had struggled to see herself as deserving of that sacred trust. In those few short months, circumstances already had given her ample opportunity to demonstrate her worthiness. Despite their success on those occasions, Khatami knew that as a leader, her ongoing responsibility was to continue reinforcing the bond to this crew, which once had been Zhao's but now was charged to her.

"Captain," said Estrada, "I've sent the message on a repeating loop, but we're not getting any responses to it."

Khatami had only a moment to cast a knowing look at Mog before Klisiewicz suddenly exclaimed, "We're being targeted!"

No sooner were the words out of the science officer's mouth than the entire ship shuddered around Khatami. Her hands flailed for her chair's armrests, barely preventing her from being tossed to the deck. Overhead, the bridge's main lighting flickered for a moment before returning to full illumination, and the distraught howl of the red-alert Klaxon wailed across the bridge.

"Evasive maneuvers!" Khatami shouted over the din. "Damage report!"

Using the sensor viewer to hold himself steady, Klisiewicz replied, "Direct hit on forward shields. No damage."

Yeah, but those Tholian weapons still pack a mean punch. As though striving to emphasize her thought, the ship bucked again as the *Endeavour*'s shields absorbed another strike. All around the bridge, display screens and lighting blinked in chaotic fashion. Khatami waved toward the viewscreen. "Target those ships, and fire at will, but aim to disable only. And give me a tactical view."

Neelakanta nodded without looking up from his station. "Aye, Captain." The lieutenant's fingers were almost a blur, moving across the console's rows of controls as though possessed of their own will.

"In case you were wondering, Mr. Estrada," Mog said from where he still sat at the engineering station, "that was the Tholians responding to our hail."

Ignoring the comment, Khatami focused her attention on the computer-generated schematic now on the main viewer. The *Endeavour* was displayed as a bright blue circle at the image's center, and the trio of Tholian vessels appeared as red arrowheads in the screen's upper right quadrant. The tactical plot updated with each passing second as the other ships' positions and distances changed in relation to the *Endeavour*.

"Stubborn, aren't they?" she asked as she watched the pair of cruisers maintaining their aggressive pursuit of the smaller and weaker scout ship.

At the helm, Neelakanta nodded. "And slippery, too. Even with computer targeting, I'm having trouble locking on."

"Captain," Klisiewicz called out, "the smaller ship just took another direct hit! I'm reading a total loss of power onboard as well as a hull breach. It's venting atmosphere."

Damn!

"Get us in there, helm," Khatami ordered without hesitation, still hunched forward in her chair and for the first time noticing the dull ache that had formed between her shoulder blades. "Put us between that ship and its pursuers."

On the viewer, Khatami watched as the *Endeavour* changed course, maneuvering toward the stricken craft. In front of her, Neelakanta stabbed the control on his console to fire phasers, and Khatami felt the minor thrum in the deck plating as the starship's massive weapons came to bear.

"Substantial damage to both ships' shields," reported Klisiewicz. "They're breaking off their pursuit and taking evasive action."

Excellent, Khatami thought. Maybe now they had breathing room, if only a little bit. Considering her options and knowing that most of them would take more time to implement than the damaged Tholian ship might have left to it, she looked to her chief engineer. "Mog, can we extend our shields to protect that ship?"

Turning from his station, the Tellarite replied, "It will weaken our overall shield strength somewhat, but I should be able to compensate by rerouting power from nonessential systems." He nodded toward the viewscreen. "That's liable to irritate our friends out there."

"Do it. We only need it long enough to tractor the ship into our shuttle bay." She had considered using the transporter but ruled that out, owing to Tholian atmospheric requirements and the unlikely event that the damaged ship's lone occupant would be wearing any sort of environment suit.

"We're within range of the damaged ship, Captain," reported Neelakanta.

Khatami nodded. "Mog, extend our shields." To Neelakanta, she said, "Lay down a full phaser spread. No need to hit them. Just keep them off our backs."

"Extending now," the engineer replied. A moment later, he added, "They're inside our shield envelope. Activating tractor beam." Looking over his shoulder, he released an irritated grunt. "I don't recommend sitting still while I do this."

"Neither do I," Khatami replied. "Neelakanta, get us back to the station." Part of her rebelled at the thought of tucking tail and leaving the other ships to chase after them, but securing the renegade Tholian's safety took precedence.

Not getting ourselves blown up is pretty important, too.

Klisiewicz said, "They're coming back around." He paused, not looking up from his viewer before adding, "It looks as if they're splitting up, trying to flank us."

"They're hoping to catch us in a cross fire," Khatami replied. "Mog, get that ship into the shuttle bay. Helm, continue evasive, and keep up the cover fire."

Thanks to the *Endeavour*'s inertial dampening system, only the shifting tactical plot on the main viewer offered any clue to Khatami that the starship was responding to the helm officer's commands. On the screen, the red arrows representing the two

Tholian vessels appeared to be buzzing like flies around the larger ship.

And just as annoying, too.

"Captain," Klisiewicz called out, "I'm picking up weapons fire from Vanguard! They're laying down cover fire for us." After a moment, he added, "The Tholian ships are breaking off. Looks like the cavalry's here."

"They were always there, Lieutenant," Mog said, grunting in amusement. "They were just waiting for us to get our act together and start home."

On the screen, Khatami watched the pair of pursuing vessels veer away from the *Endeavour*. She allowed herself a small sigh of relief as the tactical view updated to reflect the ships' departure from the immediate area and—presumably—well out of the region.

"Captain," Estrada said from behind her, "I'm picking up a new hail from one of the Tholian ships." Without waiting for direction from Khatami, the communications officer keyed a control that allowed the incoming message to be heard through the bridge intercom.

"Federation outpost, the fugitive you now harbor is a threat not only to us but to you as well. By interceding in our affairs, you invite whatever consequence should befall you. Rest assured that this matter will not serve to improve the current diplomatic relationship between our two peoples."

There was a distinct crackle as the connection was severed, and on the main viewscreen, the images of the Tholian vessels continued to move away from the *Endeavour* until they vanished altogether from the tactical display.

"I guess this means they won't be coming by for dinner?" Klisiewicz asked.

Heavy footfalls rattled the deck plating behind Khatami, and she looked up to see Mog stepping into the command well to stand beside her. "Something tells me we just gave Ambassador Jetanien a whole new set of headaches," he said, punctuating his observation with a grunt of concern.

Khatami leaned back in her chair, contemplating this latest development in what over the past months had proven to be anything but a smooth, peaceful relationship between the Federation and the Tholian Assembly. Already strained—possibly to the breaking point—the tenuous understanding between the two powers would be tested further by what had happened here today.

19

As she stood in the drab, utilitarian chamber onboard the massive Federation space station and regarded her hosts, Nezrene finally felt the first easing of the anxiety that had gripped her for so long.

My instincts were correct, she decided, sensing the warm blue auras of confidence emanating from her visitors and beginning to wash over her. *These people can assist me.*

"Nezrene," said the large, Rigelian Chel as he towered over her, "my name is Jetanien, and I am a Federation ambassador. It is a pleasure to meet with you today." He indicated with his massive manus the human female dressed in a Starfleet uniform who had accompanied him into the room. "This is Ensign Vanessa Theriault, who you may recall had a most memorable encounter with the Shedai on Jinoteur IV."

It took an additional moment for the communications system's translation protocols to convert the Chel's words from Federation Standard to native Tholian, after which Nezrene turned her attention to the human, Theriault. "You are the one from the First World, who pleaded for the release of the *Kollotaan* from Shedai servitude?"

The human made a motion with her head, which Nezrene understood to be a gesture of affirmation. "That's right."

Though neither the Chel nor this human possessed even the most rudimentary telepathic capabilities, Nezrene still sensed, as she had on the First World, the female's genuine concern for the welfare not only of Nezrene herself but also of her shipmates from the *Lanz't Tholis,* who had been abducted by the Shedai and forced to serve them. It was a fascinating dichotomy, Nezrene decided, particularly given the lengths to which Tholia had gone to preserve from the Federation the secrets of the Shedai and its roots in her people's history.

Humans are strange creatures, Nezrene reminded herself.

"On behalf of my people, I thank you," she finally said, hoping the translation would carry with it her inflections of gratitude.

"Nezrene," Jetanien said, "it is my duty to ask why you've come to us. Surely, you understand that your very presence here threatens the already fragile peace currently enjoyed by our people and yours."

"Both of our peoples have allowed themselves to be guided by fear," Nezrene said. "Tholians fear the return of the Shedai, and that dismay has translated into extreme xenophobia with respect to other sentient species. Your Federation senses an opportunity to avail itself of ancient technology it does not understand, while at the same time struggling to prevent your enemies from benefiting in similar fashion. None of that is of importance any longer. We must set aside our differences if we are to have any hope of preventing the Shedai from conquering us all."

Surprisingly agile for his size and mass, the Chel began to walk around the room's perimeter, his manus clapping together as an odd yet lyrical string of clicks emanated from his prominent proboscis. "And you are here because you wish to foster some kind of cooperation between our peoples with the goal of fighting the Shedai?"

How little these beings truly understand, Nezrene mused.

"You cannot comprehend the power of the Shedai," she said. "Their sphere of influence once spanned star systems throughout this part of the galaxy, which they moved between as easily as you or I might traverse the rooms and passageways of this space station. The attempts you have made toward understanding the technology they once commanded are nothing, the merest fraction of the true power they wielded. And yet what you have seen—if employed in direct action against you—would be more than enough to crush your Federation and anyone else who dared to oppose them."

Jetanien made a noise that Nezrene took to be one of irritation. "Then why *are* you here?"

Continue as you have, she reminded herself, *and there will be no going back. Are you prepared for what might result?*

Yes, Nezrene decided, forcing away the harsh crimson flare of anxiety. The time for change had long passed.

"I offer to help you find the understanding you lack," she said. "The secrets of the Shedai are too important to remain buried beneath the veneer of mystery and fear. My people have dreaded the Shedai's reawakening for aeons and have no desire to return to the existence of slavery and servitude from which we sprang. We cannot act alone against our former oppressors, and at the same time, we must prevent the exploitation of the power they once held by those who also would threaten us. There are others like me who believe your Federation possesses not only the capacity to understand what we offer you but also the purity of spirit needed to utilize such knowledge with the required benevolence."

The magnitude of what she proposed did not appear lost on either the Chel or the human. Nezrene sensed the disbelief radiating from both of them, even as they struggled to cope with the notion of equalizing the opportunities presented here with the impacts they surely would have on their own people. Nezrene knew she was navigating a treacherous slope. She also found it ironic that it would be the Federation—a body whose core principles included not imparting advanced technology to lesser-developed civilizations so as to avoid disrupting their natural development—that would benefit from what she proposed. Surely, gaining the knowledge of the Shedai would have some massive, long-term effects on whatever course of evolution and advancement the Federation currently traveled.

And the alternative? Subjugation, or destruction, not only for the Federation but for Tholia as well.

"What you suggest cannot help but be the foundation for a

long-term pact of peace and cooperation between our civilizations," Jetanien said after a moment. "However, conscience dictates that we also admit the possible risks. We are talking about a fundamental shift in our understanding of a great many subjects, many of which we are only just beginning to explore. We must work together, Nezrene, if we are to find the delicate balance needed to help both of our peoples deal with the immediate threat, as well as determining how this alliance will affect us all in the future."

Though she did not share Jetanien's optimism, Nezrene drew comfort from the Chel's words. That he not only was able to consider the potential for danger represented by embracing the knowledge of the Shedai but also possessed the integrity to voice those concerns aloud caused a glow of intense satisfaction to warm her. *Perhaps we have chosen wisely, after all.*

Despite that confidence, Nezrene knew that this was only the first of many steps along a far-reaching path. Together, they could learn the secrets of the race that imprisoned her people so long ago.

"Then, my new friends," she said, "let us begin that process today."

20

T'Prynn rolled to one knee, her eyes and the numerous cuts on her face and hands stinging from the sand. Her mouth was dry from prolonged exertion, made worse by the unrelenting heat beating down on her from the harsh Vulcan sun. The side of her head pounded from the attack she had only partially managed to parry, and something wet trickled down her face. She wiped her temple with her free hand, her fingers coming away tinged with dark green blood.

The whistle of the *ahn-woon* slicing through the air warned her of the next attack, and T'Prynn rolled to her right just as she felt the heavy leather sling wrapping around her neck. The weighted ball on the end of the weapon struck just her chin, and she managed a single cough before the strap was pulled tight. She felt the leather contracting around her throat an instant before she was yanked backward, off her feet, and down onto the sand. Her body angled downward along the hill, disrupted sand shifting beneath her.

Clawing at the leather with her free hand, T'Prynn tried to bring her own *ahn-woon* to bear in a useless gesture of counterattack. Her adversary's weapon dug into the skin of her neck, choking off her air. Then a shadow fell across her, blocking out the sun, and she looked up into the face of her enemy.

"You will submit, T'Prynn," said Sten, hissing the proclamation through clenched teeth. He dropped to one knee beside her, keeping the *ahn-woon* taut in his hand as he pulled it ever tighter around her neck. "It is inevitable." As she lay locked in his grip, the wind began to intensify, whipping sand through her clothes and across her exposed skin.

"I . . . refuse." She bit the words, forcing them past her constricted throat and parched lips, all but shouting to be heard above the increasing wind.

Her right arm snapped upward, bringing with it her own *ahn-woon* and the heavy orbs attached to each end. Sten's reflexes were superior, and he reached up to block the attack, but his movements and his position along the slope of the hill forced him off balance. Momentum brought him closer to T'Prynn, causing the strap in his hand to loosen. She grabbed it with her other hand, pulling it with all of her flagging strength. It was enough to carry Sten's body forward, though now T'Prynn grabbed him and lurched from the ground, rolling after him as he fell face-first into the sand. An animalistic cry of rage escaped her as she landed atop his body, her weight not nearly enough to pin him. With her free hand, she lashed out at his head, landing blow after blow in rapid succession. Stunned by the sudden, ferocious attack, Sten could only attempt a clumsy defense. T'Prynn ripped his *ahn-woon* from around her neck and bolted to her feet, the wind ripping at her body as she pressed her right boot to the back of Sten's skull and forced his face into the sand. Sten's body jerked, his hands and feet spasming as he fought to free himself. She felt him struggling to raise himself and brought up her foot only to stomp down on his head once again.

"Die!"

As she moved to repeat the attack, Sten snapped upright, regaining his feet in a single, fluid motion. Green blood streamed from the wounds in his head, and sand stuck to his face, and T'Prynn saw the fires of hatred burning in the eyes of her betrothed.

"I will die," he said, his words echoing above the howling wind, "but not before I take what is mine."

"No!" another voice called out above the mounting storm. "You will die defeated, broken, and alone, with my hands on your throat and my blade in your heart."

Surprised, T'Prynn turned to see Anna Sandesjo, her long red hair billowing about her face, her pale, soft features contrasting against the dark leather of her formfitting Klingon warrior's uniform. In her hands, she held what T'Prynn recognized as a *bat'leth*, a ceremonial Klingon weapon. The curved sword, with its trio of grips along the blade's outer edge, seemed almost too large for Anna's hands, though she wielded it with the strength and confidence of a practiced master.

Anna.

Love, anguish, remorse. T'Prynn was awash in a sea of raw emotion as she beheld her former lover. How could she be here, now, in this place? Like everything else here, Anna's presence made no sense.

Before T'Prynn could react, Anna twirled the *bat'leth* in her hands, the blade slicing through the thickening clouds of sand blowing about her, before lunging forward and charging up the hill toward Sten. She loosed a fierce battle cry, spittle flying from her lips as she raised her weapon above her head.

Drawing a knife from a scabbard along his left hip, Sten held the blade before him and beckoned Anna with his free hand. "Yes!" he shouted, welcoming the new challenge.

"Wait!" T'Prynn called after Anna, but there was no response as both she and Sten faded into the blinding sandstorm.

The sound of one of the medical monitors beeping jolted Pennington from his fitful slumber. He had fallen asleep sitting in one of the chairs in the room designated for T'Prynn's quarters, and now he had a crick in his neck.

"Damn," Pennington whispered as he rose from the chair, his right hand pressing against the side of his neck as he crossed the room to T'Prynn's bed. Studying the bio monitor behind her head, he recalled what Dr. M'Benga had taught him about the different indicators. One small arrowhead traveling along a column of numbers—the one labeled as monitoring a patient's brain-wave function—had ascended to the top of its scale, indicating a sudden increase in activity. According to the readings, T'Prynn's mind was churning at something approaching warp speed.

"Good Lord." His eyes widened as they alternated between the monitor and T'Prynn. As far as he could determine, there were no outward signs of change in the Vulcan woman's body. He saw no muscle spasms or even a telltale movement of eyes beneath their lids, which might indicate dreaming. She remained completely inert, with only the machines and her slow, shallow breathing to indicate that she was anything other than dead.

M'Benga had mentioned similar events having occurred since T'Prynn's collapse, but this was the first time it had happened in the five weeks following the *U.S.S. Yukon*'s departure from *Starbase 47*. The doctor had told Pennington to be on the watch for such changes in monitored activity, stressing that such instances were irregular, infrequent, and impossible to predict.

"What's going on in your head, lady?" Pennington asked, wondering, as he had during his other visits, if she might be able to hear him when he spoke to her. As always and as he had come to expect, there was no response. After a moment, the gauge began to settle, dropping three-quarters of the way down the scale before coming to rest at what Pennington had learned was T'Prynn's "default level," the monitors recording her elevated mental activity even while in the grips of her coma. The tone that had awakened him also fell silent.

Pennington heard the door slide open behind him and turned to see M'Benga enter the room. The doctor was frowning as he inspected the readouts on the assorted displays around the bed. Beyond the doorway, Pennington saw one of the *Yukon*'s security personnel standing guard. One of the conditions of T'Prynn's release to M'Berga's custody was that she remain under watch at all times.

Looking to Pennington, M'Berga asked, "A spike?"

"Yes," replied the journalist, rubbing his stiff neck. "Craziest thing I've ever seen. How can her mind jump into overdrive like that and she not twitch the slightest bit?"

Crossing his arms, M'Benga said, "Her mind is in a state of chaos. According to what Sobon told me, it's been divided into two parts, thanks to the mind meld she shared with her fiancé all those years ago. It was forcibly interrupted for reasons unknown, and she's been suffering the effects since then."

"After so long," Pennington said, "do you think this Vulcan

healer can really help her? Wouldn't the damage be too great, after all these years?"

M'Benga shrugged. "I really don't know. Sobon seems to think that he can help her, but to be honest, I never bought into everything some of their doctors tried to teach us about Vulcan mental-healing techniques. That said, at this point, I'm willing to try anything."

There could be no faulting the doctor's commitment, Pennington decided. Only someone so dedicated would undertake a nearly nine-week voyage through space with his patient in order to attempt a controversial course of treatment, which, according to M'Benga, was not even recognized by the sizable faculty of the Vulcan Science Academy.

Dedicated or crazy, Pennington reminded himself. *And look at the pot calling the kettle black.*

"I feel so bloody helpless," he said, shaking his head. "I just wish there was something I could do." It was an odd sensation, especially considering the lingering anger and distrust he still felt toward the stricken Vulcan. He wondered what she might say to him if and when she ever awakened and was able to confront him about their joint sordid past and the conflicted feelings raging within him.

She'd tell me I was being illogical, he guessed.

As he stuck his hands into his pants pockets, the fingers on his right hand brushed across smooth metal, and he extracted the mandala. Its burnished surface reflected the dim lighting and the multihued indicators from different bio monitors, casting an odd kaleidoscopic pattern of colors across T'Prynn's face. After a moment, he reached out and laid the medallion on her chest, just above where her hands rested.

"Here," he said, his voice low. "I bought it for you, anyhow." Looking up at M'Benga, he shrugged, offering a sheepish, humorless grin. "Stupid, I know."

"Every little bit might help, I suppose," the doctor replied.

Pennington nodded. "I suppose." He looked down at the comatose T'Prynn, whose outward peace belied her relentless inner struggle.

21

"Admiral on deck."

Cooper issued the command with snap and precision as he stood next to Jetanien, and he and the officers from the senior staff—Lieutenant Haniff Jackson and Dr. Fisher—came to positions of attention just as the doors leading to the docking port's access gangway parted. Standing alone in the foyer just beyond the doors was a slender Asian man of shorter-than-average height, dressed in the standard-duty uniform of a Starfleet flag officer. His once-black hair was liberally streaked with gray and styled in a brush cut, and his face was tanned and lined. Despite his obvious advanced age, his deep blue eyes seemed to miss nothing as they took in everything around him, and when he stepped through the doors and onto the station, it was with the confident stride of a man comfortable with his own abilities.

Rear Admiral Heihachiro Nogura.

"You must be Commander Cooper," he said, moving to stand before the younger man. "Permission to come aboard, sir?"

"Permission granted, Admiral. Welcome to Starbase 47." Until the moment the personnel transport had entered the station's docking bay and its captain had contacted Cooper, the commander and the rest of the crew had not even known the identity of the officer sent to replace Commodore Reyes. The whereabouts and schedules of several high-ranking Starfleet officers were considered classified information, especially for a select few individuals. Nogura numbered among that small group, owing in large part to the fact that very little in the way of Starfleet tactical planning took place without his input. He was one of a handful of specialists entrusted with the responsibility of developing, coordinating, and putting into motion any policies and strategies that involved the use of military force. Considering the current political climate in which the Federation found itself as it faced potential threats from several quarters, people like Nogura were invaluable assets. His presence here spoke volumes as to the importance of Operation Vanguard.

Taking the admiral's proffered hand and shaking it, Cooper said, "I'd like to introduce key members of my senior staff." He made quick introductions before indicating Jetanien with his free hand. "And this is Ambassador Jetanien, our diplomatic envoy."

"A pleasure to meet you all," Nogura said. "I look forward to getting to know you better as we move forward." In his left hand, the admiral carried a computer data card, which he handed to Cooper. "Commander, these are Starfleet's orders assigning me as commanding officer of this facility and returning you to your position as executive officer. Your reassignment is by no means a statement of Starfleet's lack of faith in your abilities. On the contrary, I'm counting on you to help push me through the inevitable settling-in adjustments I'll have to make."

Cooper nodded. "Understood, sir."

"I've been keeping updated with the reports you've been filing," Nogura said, "but for now, give me the highlights. For example, what's the latest with the Tholian we're protecting?"

Not wasting any time, is he? After glancing around to ensure that no one without the proper security clearance was within earshot before responding, Cooper nodded to Jetanien.

In a subdued voice, the ambassador said, "She's under the supervision of Dr. Marcus and Lieutenant Xiong, who currently head up our primary research team." Indeed, the Tholian, Nezrene, had spent almost all of her time with Marcus and Xiong in the Vault, the top-secret research facility hidden deep in the bowels of the station, working to understand the various artifacts and information recovered from planets now known to have existed once under the rule of the Shedai.

"That research facility," Nogura repeated, also mindful to

prevent his voice from carrying. "Its security hasn't been compromised?"

"No, Admiral," replied Lieutenant Jackson at Cooper's prompting. "It and its contents remain classified."

Nogura nodded in approval. "Excellent. We've got more pressing concerns out here. Now, my understanding is that both the *Endeavour* and the *Sagittarius* are away from the station, with neither ship due back for some time?"

Cooper said, "That's correct sir. The *Endeavour* is on security patrol and won't return for at least three weeks. *Sagittarius* was sent to perform a low-profile recon probe based on some new intelligence we received about Klingon ship activity, and she'll be back in six days." After a moment, he added, "Both ships, as well as the *Lovell,* have been getting run pretty ragged, Admiral."

"I know," Nogura replied, "and I'm already taking steps to fix that. Until then, they'll just have to do the best they can, but we'll see about not overextending them any more than absolutely necessary for mission-critical assignments." He paused, reaching up to cover his mouth as he stifled a yawn. "Pardon me, Commander, but I'm afraid my aging body doesn't cope as well as it once did with long-duration space travel. It probably doesn't help that the bunk they gave me is smaller than the bed my grandson sleeps in. I'd like to grab a shower, a decent meal, and a real bed for a few hours before we dive into everything."

"Absolutely, sir," Cooper said.

Jackson added, "Quarters have already been prepared, Admiral, and I'll see to it that your belongings are delivered there. All of the latest reports, including detailed information on the topics we've just discussed, are available to you at the personal workstations in your quarters and your office."

Cooper asked, "Admiral, is there anything else you need from me at this time?"

"Actually, there is. I never cared for all the pomp and circumstance of a formal change-of-command ceremony, and I'm sure the crew has better things to do. So, if it's all the same to you, I'm opting to forgo the formal song-and-dance routine and get down to business."

Hearing such an unpretentious request, particularly when it came from an officer of Nogura's rank and standing within the upper echelons of the Starfleet Command hierarchy, filled Cooper with relief, but it was Fisher who could not pass up the opening Nogura provided.

"The crew will be devastated to hear that, sir, but we'll do our best to deliver the news gently and soften the blow."

When Nogura laughed, it was from his belly, and the results echoed off the curved corridor walls. His whole face seemed to expand to accommodate the full smile that took over his features. "Nicely played, Doctor." Nodding once more to the group, he said, "Thank you, all. I won't keep you from your duties any longer."

"Aye, sir," Cooper said, before indicating to Jackson that he should accompany the admiral to his quarters. Nogura and Jackson departed, leaving Cooper alone with Jetanien and Fisher.

"Not what I expected," Fisher said.

Jetanien loosed a litany of chirps and clicks. "Don't let appearances fool you, Doctor. Admiral Nogura's reputation is well earned. His list of diplomatic and military achievements is as lengthy as that of the advances he's guided in the realms of science and exploration. Given the situations we face out here, he is an ideal selection for commander of this station."

Not liking the way that sounded, Cooper nevertheless could not disagree. Nogura was known for his by-the-rules approach, but he had incited no small amount of controversy with his propensity to serve not the cold, lifeless words used to construct the rules but rather the spirit imbued in them.

Cooper's attention was drawn to the sound of footsteps descending the gangway from the docking area, and he looked up to see a woman, also dressed in the duty uniform of a Starfleet flag officer. "Admiral on deck," he called out, drawing himself back to a formal stance as the woman crossed the threshold separating docking port from the station itself. She wore black trousers and a red tunic, rather than the skirt version that had become the standard-duty uniform for female personnel, and she carried a polished black briefcase in her left hand. Her brown hair was cut in a short, feminine style that did not descend past her collar, and Cooper noted the gray highlights around the temples and scattered across the top of her head. Crow's feet were visible at the corners of her eyes, and a few wrinkles bordered her mouth. Cooper knew that she was in her mid-fifties, but only because he had done some preliminary research upon learning that she was en route to the station.

Here we go. The thought elicited a knot of anxiety in his gut.

"Permission to come aboard, Commander?" she asked as she moved toward Cooper.

"Granted, Admiral," Cooper said. "Welcome to Starbase 47. I'm Commander Jon Cooper, executive officer." He quickly introduced Fisher and Jetanien.

The admiral nodded. "Gillian Moratino, Starfleet Judge Advocate General Corps. I'm here to preside over the court-martial of Commodore Reyes." With the hint of a smile on her lips, she asked, "I'm guessing you've been expecting me?"

"Something of an understatement, Admiral," Jetanien said.

"I get that a lot."

Cooper knew of Moratino only thanks to information he had retrieved from the main computer. By all accounts, she was a competent jurist, having presided over numerous courts-martial of varying size and scope, always comporting herself with restraint as she dispensed her rulings with a firm yet fair observation for the rule of law. She was well known for having little tolerance for courtroom theatrics, preferring instead that the focus of the case remain on facts and pointed testimony. Given the furor surrounding the charges against Reyes and the attention his court-martial already had generated within the media, as well as Starfleet and the civilian populace, Cooper viewed Moratino as an ideal candidate to keep the trial proceedings from devolving into a circus.

"Is there anything I can do for you, Admiral?" he asked.

A sly grin graced Moratino's features. "I hear you've got one or two decent places to get a drink around here. One of those'll do nicely, especially if they can offer a meal that doesn't come out of a food slot."

"Manón's Cabaret, Admiral," Cooper replied. "It's a civilian establishment, but it's become the de facto officers' club." His inner cynic was already telling him that within twenty-four hours, word would circulate through the crew that the woman who might well decide Commodore Reyes's fate had arrived. If that were true, then Moratino would want one last, quiet meal before everyone on the station realized who she was.

Looking to Jetanien, Cooper asked, "Ambassador, would you be so kind as to escort the admiral?"

The Chel bowed his head. "It would be my honor. I'm told the Tarellian snail stew is especially tasty this evening."

"That sound you heard," Fisher said, "was my appetite venting into space."

22

Lieutenant Holly Moyer, hunched over her desk as she had been for the past five hours, finally forced herself upright and released a groan of fatigue. She pushed away from the forbidding stacks of reports, legal briefs, data slates, computer data cards, and other clutter concealing the surface of her desk and raised her arms over her head, the muscles in her back and shoulders thanking her as she interlocked her fingers and reached for the ceiling. That accomplished, she brought her hands to her head and massaged her temples, certain that at any moment, her head might simply explode in protest.

You make that sound like such a bad thing.

Her day had been spent much like however many—Moyer had stopped counting—had passed since Captain Desai had assigned her to assist in the prosecution of Commodore Reyes. The days began early, *very* early, and continued well into the evenings, to the point where on several occasions, Moyer had forsaken returning to her quarters in favor of collapsing on the sofa in her office for a few fitful hours of sleep. True rest evaded her, though, as her mind continued to process the voluminous amounts of information relating to the commodore's case. Meals, when she ate them, were taken at her desk, though she did manage to escape her office each day for a precious respite at the gymnasium, which also allowed for a shower and a fresh uniform following her workouts.

There's really nothing like a life of leisure.

Rising from her desk, Moyer reached across the administrative quagmire and retrieved her coffee mug. It was the same dark maroon vessel, emblazoned with the symbol of Starfleet's Judge

Advocate General Corps, that she had acquired while still attending law school. With its wide, thick base, molded handle, and insulated exterior, the ceramic mug had withstood three years of studies plus a tour at Starbase 11, associated moves, and numerous attempts to supplant it by other, lesser contenders. It had survived long enough to find itself at the hind end of explored space, flanked on all sides by just a few of the Federation's more formidable enemies, and now was facing perhaps the most daunting task of its owner's young career.

Okay, Moyer decided, shaking her head in response to the wayward stream of thoughts. *You* definitely *need more coffee.*

The doors to her office slid aside, and she exited into the "bullpen," the large open area located at the center of the JAG offices and harboring the lawyers' cadre of legal and administrative assistants. Moyer stopped short as she glanced around the room, noting that most of the bullpen's dozen desks were unoccupied, their individual lamps extinguished. Even the overhead lighting had been dimmed, and it took her an extra moment before she glanced at the chronometer over the main exit and remembered that it was well past normal duty hours.

Only two of the desks held any signs of habitation. The one closest to her belonged to her own assistant, Ensign Christopher Pimental, who was elsewhere at the moment. The other desk, at the far end of the room and closest to Captain Desai's office, belonged to her assistant, Lieutenant Deborah Simpson. Its personal lamp shone down upon the lieutenant's own collection of files and reports, and the desktop computer monitor also was active, displaying a jumble of text Moyer could not decipher from this distance. As for Simpson herself, Moyer presumed she was in Desai's office, bearing the brunt of the captain's latest round of prosecutorial preparations.

Moyer actually smiled at that, knowing that Desai was pushing herself far harder than anyone else in the office as arrangements and strategizing continued for what everyone on the station believed would be one of the most followed and scrutinized Starfleet courts-martial in the history of the Federation.

Being a bit melodramatic, aren't we?

Sighing, Moyer headed toward the galley at the rear of JAG's suite of offices and conference rooms, nearly bowling over Ensign Pimental as the other officer rounded a turn in the corridor. Pimental, nimble and quick to react, sidestepped to avoid the collision while protecting the mug of coffee he carried.

"I'm sorry, Lieutenant," Pimental said with a sheepish smile. "I didn't see you there." He was a tall human, with close-cropped black hair that was receding back across the top of his head. His gold uniform tunic stretched across his muscled chest and shoulders, and not for the first time did Moyer consider what he might look like without it.

At ease, Lieutenant.

Shaking off the errant observation, Moyer waved away his apology. "No, it's my fault. I wasn't watching where I was going." Holding up her own coffee mug for emphasis, she added, "I'm afraid I'm cruising on automatic pilot."

"I know what you mean, ma'am." His expression changed, and Moyer realized that he was making a grand effort to stifle a yawn. After blinking several times, he returned his attention to her. "Sorry about that. Today's been a long year."

Moyer laughed, enjoying the brief diversion. "I know it's been a tough haul these past few weeks, but all we can do is just keep pushing ahead."

She knew that the trial preparations were hard on everyone in the office. From a strictly legal standpoint, there was little to be said in defense of Commodore Reyes and the actions he had committed, but that did not detract from the simple fact that she knew of no one who did not respect the man as an officer, a leader, or a human being. In private, there had been much admiration voiced for the bold and likely career-ending steps Diego Reyes had taken to allow the truth about the alien threat to be made public. Of course, such praise was all but stifled in the face of the numerous apprehensive conversations held with regard to what this truth meant to every single person currently living aboard Starbase 47.

Were we better off not knowing? Moyer dismissed the question. As any Vulcan might tell her, it would be illogical to waste time dwelling on what might have been. Better to direct that energy elsewhere. *Yes, but not without coffee.*

"Time to get back to it," she said, turning once more in the direction of the galley as Pimental made his way back to his desk. She had taken only a few steps before she heard the JAG office's main doors opening. Moyer was surprised to see a stocky, barrel-chested Tellarite, dressed in a gold Starfleet tunic and carrying a standard-issue briefcase, enter the room. His tunic sported captain's stripes as well as the chest insignia of Starfleet Headquarters, and while he appeared shorter than Moyer herself, there was no mistaking the air of authority surrounding him.

Tell me this isn't who I think it is.

"Good evening, Captain," she said, depositing her coffee mug on the desk closest to her as she crossed the bullpen to greet the new arrival. "Welcome to Starbase 47's JAG offices. I'm Lieutenant Holly Moyer, one of the junior legal officers assigned here. How may I help you?" As she drew closer and got a better look at the Tellarite's face in the room's subdued lighting, Moyer realized that she had indeed recognized and correctly identified him.

Uh-oh.

"Good evening, Lieutenant," the Tellarite replied, his words clipped and formal. "I am Captain Mosh zelev Sereb. I have been dispatched to this godforsaken boil on the posterior of space by order of Starfleet Command, and I am here to see Captain Desai. I was told she would be here." Making a show of subjecting the entire room to a scathing visual inspection, Sereb returned his gaze to Moyer and grunted in derision. "Well, where is she?"

Swallowing the lump trying to fight its way into her throat, Moyer replied, "She's in her office, sir." Indicating Desai's office door with a nod of her head, she added, "I'll get her right away." She activated the intercom on the nearest switch and connected to Desai's office, alerting the captain of her visitor. All the while, her imagination swam with the possibilities of why Sereb had been dispatched to Vanguard from Earth.

This cannot be good.

After a moment—which seemed to take an hour to pass—the doors to Desai's office parted, and the captain emerged, Lieutenant Simpson following her. There was a determined set to her jaw as Desai crossed the room to stand before Sereb, folding her arms across her chest.

"I'm Captain Desai," she said, her tone so low and reserved that her normally clipped London accent was all but absent. "How may I help you?"

Instead of responding immediately, the Tellarite reached into his briefcase and extracted a red computer data card, which he offered to Desai. "These are the Starfleet Judge Advocate General's orders removing you from the prosecution of Commodore Reyes and assigning me in your stead."

Accepting the data card, Desai nodded. "Well, that was expected." She paused, examining the card as though attempting to divine its contents. "It would've been nice if JAG had made this decision before my staff and I spent the past month working twenty-hour days to prepare our case."

Sereb's stout nose wrinkled up and down, and he released a short grunt. "What is that human expression? The wheels of justice grind slowly, do they not?" Then, in a way that Moyer considered most out of character for a Tellarite, he actually seemed to take on a sympathetic air. "You should not consider this an impugning of your integrity or professionalism, Captain. No one is questioning your character or ability to prosecute this case. Starfleet simply believes it imperative to avoid any appearance of impropriety while adjudicating a trial of this magnitude."

Sure took them long enough, Moyer mused. For JAG to send Sereb all the way from Earth, it meant that Starfleet itself and perhaps even the Federation Council were serious about seeing this to the end. There would be no cover-up, no attempt to mitigate or sidestep the issue. Diego Reyes would be facing one of the most formidable prosecutors in the Starfleet legal community. Mosh zelev Sereb's reputation was well known; he had never lost a case, even on those rare occasions when he acted as defense counsel. His ethics were beyond reproach, and he coupled a brusque manner born of Tellarite stubbornness with an unrelenting approach to trial work. Reyes's attorney, Commander Nathan Spires, would have his work cut out for him.

Desai's features remained fixed and impassive, but Moyer could see in her eyes that the captain appeared to be having some difficulty accepting something she had to have seen as inevitable. Even with the long days spent in virtual seclusion as they worked to prepare their case, Moyer had been certain of this as well. Desai had revealed to Starfleet JAG her personal relationship with Commodore Reyes almost from the moment it had become clear that she would have to place him under arrest. To her credit, she had offered to recuse herself from the case, stating the obvious conflict of interest and the perception of bias from the public if she were to remain as prosecutor. Rather than accepting her offer, JAG had waffled, citing concerns about the station's remote location coupled with the strain of making available sufficient officers of flag rank needed to sit on a court-martial board. Meanwhile, Desai and her people had turned to their work.

Her gaze once more locked with Sereb's, Desai nodded. "My assistant will see to it that you're provided with everything my staff and I have put together. Have you brought a staff or an assistant with you?"

"No," Sereb replied, indicating the data card in Desai's hand. "Also included in the orders are instructions allowing me to select from your office whomever or whatever I require to assist me." Glancing over his shoulder, he added, "Lieutenant Moyer comes with high recommendations, and it would be imprudent to waste the effort she's exerted in preparing for this case. Therefore, Captain, if you have no objections, I request that she assist me."

It took a moment for that to sink in, and when it did, Moyer could not help the expression of shock that she knew appeared on her face. "Excuse me?" she asked. Then, realizing her slip, she immediately cleared her throat and reclaimed her bearing. "I'm sorry, Captain." The idea of assisting Sereb was exciting and terrifying at the same time. Serving as the distinguished attorney's aide would, of course, be quite an entry in her service record—but on this case? All of the discomfort she had been squelching, the unease as the reality of putting Commodore Reyes before a court-martial, came rushing back at her. Until this moment, she had been able to treat it as something abstract, possibly not coming to pass. Sereb's presence reinforced that it was real, it would happen, and she would be one of the instruments that would decide the fate of a man she greatly respected.

I think I'm going to throw up.

"Very well," Desai said, offering a curt nod. Turning her attention to Moyer, Simpson, and Pimental, she added, "See to it that Captain Sereb receives any assistance he requires." Taking her leave of the Tellarite, she returned to her office, the doors closing behind her.

To Moyer, Sereb said, "We'll begin at oh-seven-hundred hours tomorrow morning. Please see to it that I have an office at my disposal, and bring all of the case work prepared to date. I don't know if it will be useful, but it will be a start. Good evening."

As he turned to leave, his briefcase brushed against the nearby desk, catching Moyer's coffee mug and sending it tumbling to the deck, where it clattered against the duranium plates, shattering into dozens of pieces of disjointed ceramic shrapnel.

Eyeing the mug's remnants, Sereb released another snort. "Not the best place to put something like that, I suppose. Please offer my apologies to its owner." He nodded once more to Moyer before turning and exiting the JAG offices, leaving Moyer to stare at her destroyed coffee mug.

If that's not an omen, I don't know what is.

23

It took every last ounce of his formidable will to keep Ganz from hurling the data slate across the room. Instead, he settled for simply crushing it in his hands.

The sound of plastinium cracking echoed in his office, followed by pieces of the data slate raining down on Ganz's desk. Wiping his hands together to rid them of any remaining bits of shrapnel, the Orion looked down at himself, then brushed from his robe the few shards that had fallen on him.

"Feel better?" asked Zett Nilric from where he stood on the other side of the desk. One of Ganz's most trusted assistants aboard his ship, the *Omari-Ekon*—with trust being a relative concept, of course—he held his hands clasped behind his back, smiling so that his black teeth reflected from the light of Ganz's desk lamp. As always, the Nalori assassin was impeccably dressed in a dark blue, well-tailored suit that, to Ganz's trained eye, appeared to have been designed from Andorian silk. The shoes he wore were polished to a high gloss, as black as the opaque, glistening orbs that were Zett's eyes.

"I'll feel better when the captain of that freighter is standing in front of my desk," Ganz replied, moving from around his desk to the well-appointed bar dominating one wall of his office.

"That's not likely to happen," Zett said. "He and the crew were arrested, the vessel and its cargo impounded."

Ganz did not bother to offer Zett a drink as he poured one for himself; the Nalori never imbibed any alcohol, at least not while anyone was watching. It was yet another of Zett's rigid, unwavering habits, and it was that self-control that made him such a valuable asset in Ganz's organization. In this line of work, one could not afford to be surrounded by undisciplined subordinates. At best, they could lose you money. At worst, they might get you killed.

"There was a lot of money tied up in that ship's cargo holds," Ganz said, turning from the bar with his drink in his massive left hand. The shipment had consisted of various prohibited items—weapons, illegal alcoholic beverages, pharmaceuticals, computer equipment, and so on—which ordinarily required special permits to transport. Any of the components on their own would attract scrutiny from an attentive border-patrol ship, but all of that seized at one time aboard a single vessel? Such a find would raise questions that might lead back to Ganz's organization, if not to Ganz himself.

He took a long pull from the glass, enjoying the burn and sting of the Aldebaran whiskey as it flowed down his throat. Soothing warmth cascaded to his belly, and for a moment, at least, his anger was subdued. Finally, he asked, "How did this happen, at Arcturus, of all places?"

"They didn't actually make it to Arcturus," Zett said, his voice low and even, as always. "The *Valinor* was two days out when it was intercepted by a Starfleet vessel on patrol in that sector."

Ganz released a grunt of irritation. "That's the point. What was a Starfleet ship doing in that sector at all? Since when does the Federation care about anything within ten light-years of Arcturus?" The planet's location, on the fringe of Federation territory and close to the borders of both Romulan and Klingon space, made it an ideal center of free commerce, as none of the three interstellar neighbors seemed at all interested in dealing with the system and the type of travelers it attracted. It also was a key stop along travel routes utilized by smugglers and pirates of every stripe, drawing all manner of business transactions, both legitimate and illicit.

Making a show of examining the dark nails on his right hand, Zett said, "Relations between the Klingons and the Federation are tense at the moment. It therefore makes sense that Starfleet would increase its presence and attention all along the border. I understand there may even have been an incident with a Romulan ship."

Very little surprised Ganz, but that new bit of information did. "Really?" he asked, taking another sip of his drink. "After all this time? Not a single Romulan ship has ever visited Arcturus, and that's right next door to their border, or any of the other free-trade planets, but now they're crossing into Federation space?" He had no idea what might prompt such a drastic change in behavior from the notoriously reclusive Romulan Star Empire, which had been—as far as was generally known, anyway—ensconced in a sort of self-imposed isolationism for more than a century. It had been that way since the signing of the peace treaty between them and the coalition of planets formed by the humans and a few staunch allies, the act that had signaled an official end to the Earth-Romulan War of the mid-twenty-second century.

He waved away his own question. "I don't care. If the Romulans want to come picking a fight with the Federation, I'm happy to stay as far from that as I can, but only if we figure out that there's no money to be made. What I care about is the *Valinor*. This could be a bad sign." If the freelance merchant freighter his organization had contracted—after passing through several intermediaries, shadow companies, and legitimate business fronts designed to disguise the flow of information and currency to and from Ganz himself, of course—had made it all the way to Arcturus as planned, he would have been free and clear. Arcturus pledged allegiance to no government and, in fact, possessed no ruling body of its own. It was simply a hodgepodge of unregulated commerce, where rules were few and the inhabitants policed their own problems in whatever manner they saw fit. For someone in Ganz's chosen line of work, where transactions relied on avoiding the scrutinizing eye of watchful governments, possessing contacts on Arcturus was vital to any sort of prolonged success.

The *Valinor*'s captain had committed a grievous error in allowing his ship to be intercepted and boarded in Federation space. If the man had not already been under arrest, Ganz likely would have put a bounty on his head.

"I'll need a complete manifest," Ganz said as he crossed the room back toward his desk, "and we need to get a message to the buyers. Let them know we'll have to work out an alternative arrangement."

"They're not going to like that," Zett said. "You know how they are."

Nodding, Ganz dropped into his chair and took another sip of his drink. "They're jumpy, but they'll have to learn to live with this one. If the Federation is breathing down our necks, we're all going to have to play things a bit smarter for a while." He did not like failing to honor the deals he brokered, not because of any sense of fair play but because it was simply bad business.

"Some of our competitors may not see the need for such patience," Zett offered, flicking at a piece of lint that had found a temporary home on his left lapel.

"Then we'll have to teach them patience, one way or another," Ganz replied before upending the glass and finishing the drink.

The sound of his door chime caught his attention, and he looked up as the door slid aside to admit Neera, his most trusted companion and his lover. The sensuous Orion woman was dressed in a beige gown with a plunging neckline and slits on both sides that exposed her legs all the way to her hips. The rest of the gown hugged her figure like a second skin. She glanced toward Zett, and Ganz recognized her attempt, almost yet not quite successful, to hide her disdain for the Nalori. Without a word of greeting to the assassin, she leveled a stern glare at Ganz.

"You have a visitor. The admiral Starfleet sent to replace Reyes is here and wishes to speak with you."

Zett said, "Well, that's certainly interesting."

"Indeed," Neera replied. "Should I tell him to schedule an appointment?"

Leaning back in his chair, Ganz nodded. According to his sources, the ship transporting the human admiral from another Starfleet outpost had arrived the previous evening. Surely, the person now assigned to command Starbase 47 had more pressing matters demanding his attention than coming here?

"No," Ganz said. "I'll see him now. Show him in." A glance down at his desk reminded him of the remnants of the crushed data slate still lying there, but he shrugged at the sight of them. There was nothing illegal or untoward about destroying his own private property, after all. Otherwise, nothing damning was to be seen in his private office.

Confident with that assessment, he was in the midst of fixing himself another drink when the door again slid open, this time to allow entry to the Starfleet admiral. To Ganz's surprise, the human appeared to have come alone. Was it a gesture of trust, an attempt to demonstrate that this was not to be a confrontation, or was the man simply a reckless idiot?

Reckless idiots don't get to be Starfleet admirals.

Standing a few paces inside the door, the human turned to regard him. In Ganz's estimation, this admiral was a diminutive specimen even by Terran standards. The lines in his face bore mute testimony to a long career, as did the easy, self-assured manner in which he seemed to carry himself.

"Mr. Ganz, is it?" the admiral said by way of greeting, though Ganz noted that he did not move to shake hands as so many humans always did. Instead, he kept his hands at his sides. "I'm Admiral Nogura, now in command of this station. Thank you for seeing me on such short notice."

"My pleasure, Admiral," Ganz replied, turning from the bar. "May I offer you something to drink?"

Nogura shook his head. "No, thank you. I don't wish to take up too much of your time. My reason for being here won't take long."

"An attitude I can certainly appreciate," Ganz said as he moved toward his desk, glancing toward Zett as he did so. The Nalori's expression, as was often the case, was unreadable.

Indicating the detritus on the desk with a wave of one hand, Nogura said, "Technical problems?"

"The warranty expired," Ganz replied, once more taking his seat. There was no other chair in the office and therefore no reason to invite Nogura to sit. "What brings you to my ship this morning, Admiral?"

Nogura's expression wavered not one iota. "I'm here to tell you that life as you know it is over."

The blunt statement caught Ganz almost by surprise. At the last instant, he was able to school his features and his body language to reveal no reaction to the admiral's words. He even forced himself not to blink as he processed what he had just heard. "I beg your pardon?"

"Your days of running about unchecked and using Starfleet's good graces as cover to manage your various enterprises are over," Nogura replied, maintaining his own steadfast bearing. "A new sheriff in town means new rules. My rules."

Ganz's first thought was that he could crush the puny human's windpipe with one hand with little effort. His second thought was that Zett could cut the man's throat and be back standing beside the deck before the first spray of arterial blood. Finally, he decided that either of those scenarios would require disposing of a body that likely would be reported missing in short order.

Nogura seemed to entertain similar thoughts. "I've been around the galaxy a time or two in my day, Mr. Ganz, and I'm aware of the sorts of 'accidents' that can happen to people aboard Orion pleasure ships like this one. So, don't think I walked in here on my own. I have a security detail ready to storm this vessel if I've not returned to the station ten minutes after I first boarded. By my count, we have slightly over six minutes."

"This ship is sovereign Orion territory," Ganz said, despite himself. "My government would not appreciate you seizing it under force of arms." He generally was not one to tolerate such arrogant behavior from anyone, let alone anyone standing within his inner sanctum. Only the braid on the admiral's sleeve and the promise of what it represented kept the Orion seated and maintaining a civil demeanor.

For the first time, Nogura adjusted his posture and crossed his arms, and his eyes never left Ganz's. "We both know that the Orion government prides itself on maintaining its neutrality. If the Federation files a protest alleging illegal activities carried out by an Orion citizen while in Federation space, your government will drop you like a hot rock. Either way, you'd be stuck dealing with Starfleet." He moved forward, just a couple of steps but enough that Ganz sensed Zett tensing in anticipation.

"However, it might be your lucky day. I have a proposition for you."

Of course, Ganz thought, now allowing a small smile. "I thought you might."

Nogura said, "We both know that civilian ships have easier access to areas that ordinarily don't react well to the presence of Starfleet vessels. *Arcturus,* for example." The added emphasis on the planet's name spoke volumes of its own, though once again, Ganz forced himself not to react.

"Besides," the admiral continued, "with the political landscape shifting the way it is these days, it helps to have contacts on these worlds where we might not otherwise be welcomed. There's something to be said for people willing to do certain types of favors or enter into mutually agreeable business arrangements that, although unseemly or unrefined, are still occasionally necessary."

Ganz set his drink down on his desk before clasping his hands and interlacing his fingers. "The sort of arrangement you're describing often ends up costing people in my line of work a lot of money. It sometimes gets them killed."

"All true," Nogura countered, nodding. "On the other hand, if such a relationship were in place, one could find oneself enjoying an increased profit margin, to say nothing of the hassles you'd avoid, such as having your freighters filled with contraband cargo seized by border-patrol ships. That actually happened to some poor bastard just the other day." He made a show of shaking his head in mock grief. "Terrible. Simply terrible."

All right, Ganz decided. *He's definitely not an idiot.* In fact, Nogura seemed to be one shrewd bastard, with an air of arrogance that belied his tiny frame. There were only two good reasons to display such bravado: either you were bluffing, or you knew you held the winning hand. If Nogura was as clever as he seemed to think he was, then this was no bluff.

"Even if I were to consider something of this nature," Ganz said, now working to maintain his composed façade and present the appearance that nothing Nogura had said to this point was a shock, "I'd need certain assurances."

"You have my assurance," Nogura replied, "that if you don't accept this arrangement, your ship, your crew, and your own fat ass will be off my station before lunch."

Ganz forced down his rising ire. He paused to ensure that his response would be measured before replying. "I'd need time to think about it."

Nogura shrugged. "Take your time. You've got ten seconds."

Now, Ganz stood. "Admiral, I've been most cordial with you this morning, but I'm not used to being talked to in this manner aboard my own ship. I advise caution at this juncture." Glancing to Zett, behind whose eyes he knew lurked a desire to put this insufferable human in his place, he added, "For *everyone.*"

If Nogura was worried about the Nalori, he revealed no hint of his fear. "Time's up. What's your answer?"

"If I were even suspected of assisting Starfleet with anything," Ganz replied, "every one of my rivals would paint a target on my back. I'd be signing my own death warrant. Even being docked at your station wouldn't save me from that." The truth was that he could see the advantages on several levels that would come from such an arrangement, but he could not allow himself to be browbeaten into accepting the offer as extended by this human. Such action would send the wrong message, which definitely would be bad for business.

This also was a matter of pride, Ganz admitted. It could not happen in this manner. Not here, aboard his own ship, in the presence of a subordinate—Zett, of all people. Ganz simply could not allow it.

"That's a no, I take it?" Nogura asked.

There was no choice. "Correct."

The admiral nodded. "So be it. You have two hours to be off my station and on your way out of its sensor range, or I'm seizing it and everything and everyone aboard." With that, he turned and headed for the door, exiting the office without another word and leaving Ganz in the grips of anger threatening to explode from within him.

"What do you want to do?" Zett asked after a moment.

Ganz's immediate answer was to ball his right hand into a fist and slam it down on the desk. He felt its metal surface give just a bit beneath the force of the blow, the echo from the strike reverberating off the walls of the office. Staring at the door through which Nogura had left, he contemplated all of the ways he could have the admiral killed before he left the *Omari-Ekon* and returned to the space station. Instead, he turned his gaze to Zett and beheld the Nalori's unreadable expression and his own reflection in the assassin's eyes.

"Start packing."

24

"So, you're telling me . . . what, exactly?"

Leaning back in his chair, with his arms folded and his feet resting on the drab metal table, Reyes regarded Commander Nathan Spires as the attorney, visibly disturbed by the news he had just received and imparted, paced the length of the interview room. His normally well-groomed hair was disheveled, a consequence of running his hands through it.

"Captain Sereb is a force of *nature,* Commodore," Spires said, continuing to pace. "That he's here is a clear sign that Starfleet is leaving nothing to chance and pulling no punches with respect to your court-martial." Pausing, he held up a hand. "They're not throwing you to the lions or anything like that, but they want to be sure that every last detail of this trial is aboveboard." He shrugged. "That won't be especially hard in this case, given Sereb's credentials. Call him gruff, call him rude, call him insufferably arrogant in the finest Tellarite tradition, but unethical he most certainly is *not.*" Shaking his head, he moved to the table, took a glass of water from where it sat next to his briefcase, and drained its contents.

Reyes, of course, had been expecting Starfleet to replace Desai as the prosecuting attorney. Even though very few people in her chain of command would be so foolish as to question her integrity and commitment to carrying out her duty, no matter how unpleasant, Reyes was confident that someone at Starfleet Headquarters would demonstrate sufficient humanity—and common sense—to relieve Desai of the responsibility of doing her best to send him to prison for the rest of his life.

Small favors, I suppose.

Reyes brought his feet off the table and leaned forward in his chair. "What're you trying to tell me, Commander? I should just give up now? Throw myself on the mercy of the court and so on?"

"Of course not, sir," Spires countered, waving away the suggestion. "I'm just trying to make it clear that our battle has gotten that much harder. After all, unlike Captain Desai, Sereb has no personal connection to you, no reason to offer anything in the way of—"

"Belay that, Commander," Reyes snapped, cutting off Spires with such volume and force that the commodore could almost see the blood drain from the other man's face. Rising from his seat, he pointed a finger at Spires's chest, and when he spoke again, the words came out dripping with undisguised menace. "That's the first and last time I ever want to hear you so much as think that Captain Desai isn't and hasn't been conducting herself in accordance with Starfleet regulations, particularly with respect to this court-martial. Do I make myself absolutely clear?"

Swallowing the obvious lump in his throat, Spires nodded once. "You do, sir. My comments were out of line, and I apologize."

Reyes frowned as he watched the commander resume his pacing. Was this other lawyer, Sereb, really so formidable? Even if that were the case, Spires, from Reyes's admittedly layperson's viewpoint, seemed a rather effective attorney in his own right. During the past weeks, whether spent together in conference or with Spires working alone to interview relevant witnesses and review computer files, the commander had demonstrated a seemingly unwavering focus, determined to do his level best to mount an effective defense for Reyes.

"You sound scared, Commander," he said, returning to his seat. "You said this Sereb was a stickler for the rules. That means I'll still get my chance to answer questions, to say my piece, right?"

Spires cleared his throat. "You'll get your chance, sir, and then he'll hang you with your very words." As though anticipating Reyes's reaction, he held up both hands in a gesture of supplication. "Commodore, with no disrespect intended toward Captain Desai, this needs to be said. Captain Sereb is one of the most effective prosecutors in JAG. He doesn't lose. He's *never lost,* and the only thing he seems to like more than winning is how thoroughly he can dismantle an opponent *while* he's winning. That includes the defendant *and* the defense attorney."

Releasing a tired grunt, Reyes shook his head. "Sounds like someone Jetanien might like." For a moment, he was amused by the image of the bombastic Rigelian Chel facing off against a Tellarite in a no-holds-barred verbal joust.

Maybe we could sell tickets.

After a moment, Reyes shrugged. "Okay, then, so we have to work that much harder to get ready for this guy. I need to check my calendar, but I'm pretty sure I can work in any extra time you think we'll need." The way he saw it, he had nothing to lose, no matter whom Starfleet put up to prosecute him. If Spires was right about his new opponent, Sereb would not only welcome any attempt to present a forthright defense based on facts, but he would also relish any victory he attained in the face of such opposition. Regardless, Reyes at least would get his day in court, his opportunity to put a face to the secrets and mystery surrounding Starfleet's presence in the Taurus Reach.

"There's something else to consider," Spires said, abandoning his fruitless pacing and returning to the table. He retook his seat, his eyes boring into Reyes. "It goes without saying that Sereb will be performing due diligence as he prepares for the trial. That means he'll have access to every record and order issued by anyone briefed into Operation Vanguard. At this point, we have no way to know whether his attack will concentrate solely on you or if he might widen his focus to include any superior officers responsible for the orders you carried out—or disobeyed, as the case may be."

Reyes scowled as realization dawned. He had no desire to call out superior officers as a means of strengthening his own defense and had resolved not to volunteer such information. Would Sereb employ a scorched-earth policy during the court-martial in his quest to convict the commodore, disregarding anyone and anything possessing even a tangential connection to the Vanguard project?

Both men's attention was drawn by the sound of the interview room's doors sliding open to admit Captain Rana Desai. Starbase 47's senior JAG officer strode into the room, her arms locked at her sides and her expression one of utter determination.

"Rana," Reyes said, rising from his chair. It had been more than a month since he had last seen her, in the days immediately following his arrest, and she looked more radiant to him than ever. Her gaze shifted to him only for a moment, but in that instant, he saw every bit of the love and anguish he knew she felt for him, coupled with prolonged fatigue buried beneath layers of duty and protocol. Then her attention returned to Spires, who also had gotten to his feet, his features a mask of indignation.

"Excuse me, Captain," Spires said, rising from his seat. "I'm in the middle of a private meeting with my client."

Instead of answering him, Desai turned back to Reyes. "I've come to offer my services as your defense counsel, Commodore."

The blunt statement caught Reyes off guard. "Are you serious?"

"I beg your pardon?" Spires asked, and Reyes watched as the commander's mouth literally fell open. "Am I being relieved?"

Shaking her head, Desai answered, "Not at all. However, the accused *does* have the right to decide who'll be handling his defense at trial." Looking once more to Reyes, she asked, "Commodore?"

Still unsure what to think or believe in the face of his lover marching into the room and apparently taking charge of the situation, Reyes did not offer an immediate reply. Instead, he closed his eyes and shook his head, as though doing so would erase what had to be a hallucination. When he opened his eyes and saw Desai still standing before him, he frowned in lingering disbelief.

"I don't understand," he said. "Rana, the scuttlebutt even works its way down here sooner or later. You've been spending the past month setting up your case against me. I know you're only doing your duty, but are you telling me you're ready to shift gears just like that?"

Desai actually rolled her eyes. "You know I love you, Diego, but you can be such a moron sometimes. I wasn't preparing a case against you. I've spent all of this time figuring out everything they might throw at you so that I can *defend* you."

Scowling, Reyes said, "That doesn't even make sense."

"Under normal circumstances," Desai replied, "as the senior JAG officer on the station, I'd be tapped to act as prosecuting attorney during a court-martial, but there was no way Starfleet was going to let me go to trial against you. It was only a matter of time before I was replaced, but it's not my fault they took their time relieving me." She shrugged. "So, I used my staff to help fortify a prosecutor's case against you, then spent my nights countering everything we thought up during the day."

"And just what in the name of hell do you think *I've* been doing these past weeks?" Spires asked, making no attempt to hide his umbrage. There was no mistaking the commander's wounded pride, and Reyes decided he could not blame the man. No one liked to be thought of as dispensable or replaceable. In Spires's case, though he and Reyes had gotten off to a rocky start, the young lawyer had expended great time and effort crafting a defense for the commodore, so it was only natural that he would feel resentful and defensive at the idea of being cast aside.

Returning her gaze to Spires, Desai replied, "No disrespect toward you, Commander, but I honestly believe that I'm the person best qualified to represent Commodore Reyes at trial. I possess a greater knowledge of the classified aspects of Operation Vanguard than you do, to say nothing of my familiarity with those members of the station's crew who know of the project."

His expression clouded with bitterness, Spires said, "I suppose your personal relationship with the commodore would be of some help as well."

Desai countered, "Yes, Commander, that will also be useful." To Reyes, she said, "But there's something else. He doesn't think you can win. Maybe you can't, but *I'm* not ready to admit that yet." She indicated Spires with her thumb. "He already has."

"I beg your pardon," Spires said, his face reddening, and Reyes saw that it was taking every scrap of the man's self-control to maintain his bearing. "Captain, with all due respect, how dare you—"

"You *have* admitted that you can't win," Desai said, cutting him off. "If not aloud, then at least to yourself. Somewhere, in the back of your mind, you've decided that his conviction is a foregone conclusion. You've been thinking about pulling your punches in that courtroom in order to avoid angering anyone who might have a say in your future." She leaned closer, her gaze boring into him. "Tell me I'm wrong."

With Spires rendered speechless, at least for the moment, Desai turned to Reyes, her eyes burning with determination. "What do you say, Commodore?"

Despite her passion and verve, as far as Reyes was concerned, there still was one very important point to consider. "Rana, there's no telling what could happen to you or your career. Let's face it, I'm damaged goods. I'm poison. You're probably better off staying as far away from me as possible."

"Don't think I haven't thought of that," Desai replied, and Reyes saw the ghost of a smile playing at the corners of her mouth. "Make no mistake. They're going to crucify you. They're going to draw and quarter you, serve you up on a platter, and leave your guts for the buzzards, but whatever happens, I want to be the one standing next to you."

That was good enough for Reyes. Turning to Spires, he saw that the commander already knew what he was going to say.

"Nothing personal, Mr. Spires, but you're fired."

25

Jetanien had always prided himself on his ability to control a situation, be it the most informal gatherings or the most intense diplomatic negotiations. Successfully harnessing and channeling the energies and desires of others with whom one was engaged was a powerful asset to any politician, and the Chel had spent a significant portion of his professional life honing this and other vital skills. He was well aware that it was ego more than anything else that drove him in this manner, and with a few notable and still-painful exceptions, such talents had served him well throughout his career.

None of that, however, seemed enough to compel Admiral Heihachiro Nogura to set down his cup of green tea and get on with whatever reason he had called Jetanien and Commander Cooper to his office.

"Admiral," he prompted for the second time.

As he had done after Jetanien's first attempt, Nogura held up his free hand, not looking up from the data slate he studied while taking another sip of his tea.

With nothing else to do, Jetanien glanced at Cooper, offering a mild sigh before directing his attention to the data slate that gripped the admiral's attention. The ambassador attempted to read the text visible on the face of the device, but Nogura had reduced the display's brightness so that the data appeared as little more than a jumble. The data slate was one of several arrayed on Nogura's desk—the desk that had once belonged to Diego Reyes. While he waited, the ambassador noted that Nogura had wasted little time removing those few personal items with which the commodore had decorated the office, apparently having opted not to replace them with any of his own. Was there some hidden meaning to the lack of individualization? Perhaps the admiral knew or at least believed his assignment to Starbase 47 to be temporary.

It would not be out of the question, Jetanien knew, given Nogura's standing within the upper echelons of Starfleet Command. With the ever-tenuous relationship between the Federation and the Klingon Empire, Starfleet's preparations for possible conflict continued at a rapid pace. Nogura was one of a handful of flag officers who almost certainly would be involved in planning any protracted offensive or defensive campaigns should war become a reality. Starfleet even had gone so far as to ensure that, for reasons of security, the admiral was separated from other such officers at all times. Jetanien was all but certain that Nogura's presence here was part of that overall strategy, as much as someone of his experience and skill was needed to oversee Operation Vanguard.

The ambassador had no desire to remain standing in this office until that unfortunate event came to pass.

"Should I have my breakfast delivered here," he asked after a moment, "or simply dispense with that and place an order for lunch?"

Cooper's face went pale in response to the question, but Nogura seemed unperturbed by the verbal jab. His only reaction was to return his teacup to its saucer and clear his throat before leaning back in his chair. He said nothing at first, taking a moment to regard Cooper and Jetanien with bright, sharp eyes. Finally, a slim grin creased his weathered face.

"I have to say, Ambassador, you are as your reputation describes you. I'm sure that forthright demeanor of yours works for you most of the time." He reached once more for his tea, taking a long sip before setting the cup down. "It might even have worked with Commodore Reyes, but it won't do anything except annoy the hell out of me. Consider that free advice to apply toward our working relationship going forward. I trust I'm being clear on this point?"

Bristling at the rebuke, which he knew he had brought on himself, Jetanien nodded. "You are, Admiral. I apologize for my conduct. It will not be repeated."

"Excellent," Nogura said, picking up the data slate from which he had been reading. "Now, since this is the first time the three of us have been able to meet since my arrival, allow me to congratulate both of you. You've faced remarkable challenges these past weeks, particularly you, Commander Cooper, stepping into Commodore Reyes's shoes and making it look easy." Looking to Jetanien, he added, "Ambassador, your efforts not only with the Klingon and Tholian delegations but also with our resident Tholian guest also haven't gone unnoticed. While it might go without saying that the success of this station and its mission is a direct result of your being here, I'm saying it anyway. Thank you both, and I can only hope such extraordinary work will continue."

"Thank you, sir," Cooper replied, offering a curt, formal nod.

Jetanien added, "My staff and I will pursue every diplomatic option available to us, and once those are exhausted, we will not stop until we find new avenues to explore."

Nogura nodded in apparent satisfaction. "That's good, because I'm afraid things are only going to be getting busier. As you already know, the Klingons are on the move throughout the Taurus Reach."

"Indeed," Jetanien said. "Despite the limited number of ships they're able to spare, the empire seems determined to engage in wholesale land grabbing."

Cooper added, "From a tactical perspective, it's easy to see the lines being drawn. Klingon ship captains also seem hell-bent on testing us as they keep pushing through the region."

"They want to see if we're willing to challenge their claims on whichever planet they plant their flag," Nogura replied. "With limited exceptions, they seem satisfied to stick to resource-rich worlds that are uninhabited."

Jetanien chirped before saying, "That won't always be the case. Sooner or later, they'll begin subjugating populated planets and enslaving the indigenous inhabitants. The unfortunate reality of life under Klingon rule."

"Both the *Endeavour* and the *Sagittarius* have been conducting patrol missions to planets claimed by the empire," Cooper said. "According to Captain Nassir on the *Sagittarius,* they've already established a strip-mining operation on one planet in the Conana system." He shrugged. "The whole planet isn't much more than a giant dilithium crystal."

"They're not just causing problems here," Nogura said, "but all along the border as well, and I'm afraid there's more bad news." He reached for another data slate on his desk. "It seems someone else has taken an active interest in the goings-on out here." He held up the unit for Cooper and Jetanien to see. "This is a report I received just this morning from Starfleet Intelligence. It details an analysis of a collection of what looked to be spaceship wreckage recovered several weeks ago by the *Lovell* and her Corps of Engineers team. As you may recall, they were sent to the Palgrenax system to investigate the remains of the planet that we believe was destroyed by one of these Shedai global superweapons I've been reading so much about."

"Yes, sir," Cooper responded. "We'd received briefings that the Klingons had claimed the system and subjugated the preindustrial civilization indigenous to the system's only Class-M planet. The *Lovell* retrieved what it thought were remnants of a Klingon ship, but an on-site analysis followed by a more detailed inspection here on the station revealed that the hull plating we recovered didn't match any known Klingon vessel configuration. In fact, it didn't match anything in any of Starfleet's recognition databases."

"It does now," Nogura countered, holding up the data slate in his hand for emphasis. "Last week, the *U.S.S. Enterprise* made contact with and engaged a previously unknown type of vessel. That ship was also destroyed, and the *Enterprise* collected pieces of the wreckage. Their science officer forwarded his own analysis of those samples to Starfleet Command, who found themselves with a mystery of their own, since the material from the ship they encountered matches that from the one apparently destroyed near Palgrenax. Both ships were Romulan."

"Romulan?" Cooper said, his complexion growing pale. "Seriously? After all this time?"

Nogura nodded. "Looks that way. The report from the *Enterprise* is alarming, to say the least."

"To the best of my knowledge," Jetanien said, "no contact with a Romulan ship has been recorded for more than a century, since the armistice after the war."

Following that protracted conflict, and the signing of the tenuous peace treaty still enjoyed by both sides, Romulans had all but gone into total seclusion. Numerous theories abounded about the reason for the self-imposed isolation, most notable being shame at having been equaled or even bested by what the Romulans had perceived to be a vastly inferior foe. After his studies of the reclusive interstellar power, which admittedly were based largely on century-old intelligence briefings, battle reports and transcripts from the few diplomatic meetings that took place before the peace treaty's enactment, Jetanien had come to another conclusion. He did not believe that embarrassment or wounded pride had anything to do with the Romulans' choosing to absent themselves from the interstellar political stage. Rather, he was all but certain that they simply had been biding their time, refining the weapons and technology that had failed to serve them during the war and waiting for such time as their onetime adversary offered a weakness or other opening that might be exploited.

Had the Federation, after all these years, finally offered such an opportunity?

As though reading his mind, Nogura said, "The ship destroyed by the *Enterprise* had been attacking observation outposts positioned on our side of the Neutral Zone. Three of those outposts were destroyed by this single vessel, which, according to the *Enterprise*'s captain, was carrying some form of high-energy plasma weapon."

Leaning forward in his chair, the admiral tossed the data slate so that it landed on top of several of the others on his desk.

"And it gets better. It seems our old friends have improved on their cloaking technology, at least to some degree."

"They've advanced to the point where their ships are undetectable?" Jetanien asked. From what he had read about the cloaking, or "stealth," technology employed by the Romulans more than a century ago, the power requirements necessary to envelop an entire vessel in a dampening field that rendered them invisible not only to the eye but also to sensors were huge. It was an obstacle the Romulans had only partially overcome in the twenty-second century, and that incomplete success was but one of the reasons Earth and its allies had stood a fighting chance during the war.

Nogura shook his head. "They've made improvements, yes, but according to Commander Spock, there are still some weaknesses to be exploited. He was able to track the Romulan vessel even while it was cloaked, but only after he knew what to look for. What we don't know is whether the Romulan ship figured this out and communicated it back to its home base. If it did, then you can bet that Romulan scientists are already working to figure out where they went wrong so they can fix the problem and improve the cloaking technology even further."

"I take it neither the cloaking nor the weapons technology was salvageable after the *Enterprise*'s encounter?" Jetanien asked.

"No," Nogura replied. "The Romulan commander set his ship to self-destruct after it was disabled. Preliminary analysis of the hull remnants found near Palgrenax indicates a similar fate for that vessel."

Cooper shook his head. "If the Romulans are in the Taurus Reach, then they're interested in a lot more than just testing our borders."

"Agreed," Nogura replied. "Naturally, no formal means of communicating with their government are in place, so we've no way of contacting them and hearing their official denial of any activity in Federation space."

"Well," Cooper said, "they got wind that we're up to something out here somehow, sir."

Jetanien released a series of sharp clicks to indicate his agreement. "The commander is right, Admiral. They must obviously have suspicions about our own presence here. The challenge we now face is determining how much they know and how they are getting their information."

"Oh, yes," Nogura said, as though remembering that his wastebasket required emptying, "there's one *more* thing. It seems that Romulans bear a striking resemblance to Vulcans. In fact, and again according to the *Enterprise* science officer, it's entirely possible that the two races are related."

"Good God," Cooper said, his mouth falling open in unrestrained shock. "We have evidence of this?"

The admiral shrugged. "It's supposition at this point, but Vulcan High Command is verifying Commander Spock's report. Begrudgingly, I might add. It would appear that this is a sore subject with those Vulcans who are even aware of the connection."

Shaking his head, Jetanien tried to imagine the impact such a revelation might currently be having on the Vulcan people, to say nothing of how this might be viewed by their interstellar neighbors. As a long-valued ally of Earth and a founding member of the Federation, would Vulcan and its storied civilization now be looked upon with suspicion and fear by those once called friends? The ambassador suspected that such paranoia would be short-lived, owing in large part to the very loyalty and trust that had been forged over nearly a century before the Earth-Romulan War and only strengthened as that conflict was waged.

"If they were reluctant to talk about it before," Cooper said, "I can only imagine what they'll be like once Starfleet Intelligence gets on this."

"Indeed," Jetanien added. "They doubtless are already considering the possibility of Romulan spies in our midst, possibly posing as Vulcans. That they may have had such operatives among us for more than a century will only add to their anxiety." It would, Jetanien believed, be little different from what Starfleet currently faced with respect to the rampant rumors of surgically altered Klingon agents operating in Federation space.

Nogura rose from his chair, clasped his hands behind his back, and strolled from behind his desk. "If you're saying our lives just became a good deal more complicated, Ambassador, then I'm afraid I'll have to add understatement to the long and distinguished list of skills you seem to possess."

Jetanien grunted, ignoring the admiral's gentle wit. As if his own mission here was not difficult enough, the ramifications of yet another interstellar power vying for the secrets of the Shedai were almost too much to contemplate.

And yet, at the same time, the Chel could not resist considering the challenges and even rewards for whoever might forge some new foundation of understanding and—dare he think it—cooperative spirit between the Federation and another longtime adversary.

Intriguing, he thought, *to say the least.*

26

"Well, if there's any added bonus to getting you out of the brig," said Desai as she studied Reyes, a smile playing at her lips and a mischievous glint in her eyes, "it's that they let you change clothes. Orange most definitely was *not* your color."

The commodore said nothing as he retrieved two cups of coffee from the food slot in his quarters. "I'm just happy to be getting decent coffee again. It took weeks for Farber and his crew of engineers to get that damned thing working right." Setting one of the cups near Desai's right arm, he took his own coffee and moved to a chair on the opposite side of the small, oval-shaped dining table in one corner of his quarters. With a sigh, he lowered himself into the chair, leaned back, and sipped the steaming beverage. It was his own personal recipe, derived after weeks of fine-tuning the food slot's programming with the help of the talented wizard Isaiah Farber. After placing his cup on the table, he moved his hand to smooth the lines of his gold uniform tunic. He had to admit that the familiar material felt good against his skin. Seeing himself in the mirror after he had finished dressing that morning, he almost had begun to feel like his old self.

Almost but not quite.

Looking around, Reyes was struck by the seeming immensity of his quarters. During the months he had spent here—before his extended stay in the station's brig—the rooms assigned to him as his home away from home had always felt even more like a prison than the one from which he had recently been released. Now the suite felt cavernous. It was a natural reaction, given the length of his incarceration, which had been terminated and replaced with house arrest at the order of Admiral Moratino. It was far better than the brig, but of course, he was anything but free. The presence of the security guards outside his door, along with the requirement that he remain confined to his quarters except for agreed-upon sojourns to the station's fitness center—which could occur only during a set time when no other personnel were utilizing the facility—shattered any such illusion.

"I'm guessing that even though the admiral showed me this little bit of mercy," Reyes said as he held his coffee mug between his hands, "I can't count on her having a soft spot for me, can I?"

Looking up from one of the data states on the table before her, Desai regarded Reyes with a frown of mock irritation as she reached for her coffee. "Hardly, Diego. Admiral Moratino will follow the regulations to the letter, but she's also fair. She has no problem exercising any option or leeway available to her under the Uniform Code."

Reyes nodded, thankful for his judge's apparent compassion, especially given that she had also granted Captain Sereb a thirty-day continuance in order to meet his stated requirement to interview and depose numerous Vanguard personnel. The outspoken Tellarite attorney naturally had protested Desai's resulting request to have Reyes moved to house arrest, using as justification the severity of the charges against the commodore. Admiral Moratino had sided with Desai, given that Reyes—at the present time—only stood accused of the crimes listed against him. Until and unless he actually was convicted of the charges, the judge had seen no need to treat him with anything less than the respect due a Starfleet flag officer. However, even before Reyes could release a sigh of relief at that decision, Moratino had made it clear that neither he nor Desai should view it as any sort of bias in favor of the commodore.

I'll take what I can get.

"I'm planning follow-up interviews with the senior staff later today," Desai said. She pointed to one of the data slates before her.

"Then, tomorrow, I plan to talk with the *Sagittarius* crew. Given the events they witnessed on Jinoteur, there are some conflicts in individual statements. Understandable, considering what they went through, but I don't want to leave anything to chance. If there's even the slightest crack in our strategy, Sereb will force it wide open, and we'll end up fighting with our backs to the wall."

"Isn't that when you're at your best?" Reyes said, allowing a hint of innuendo to creep into his voice. Despite the court-martial hanging over his head and the very real repercussions he likely was to endure, it felt almost too easy to slip back into old routines. Sitting here in his quarters, wearing the uniform for which he always had felt unmitigated pride—until recently, of course—drinking coffee with the woman who had brought him a happiness he had not known for far too long, it took almost no effort to resume such enjoyable pastimes as teasing his lover.

Desai, for her part, was not amused. He saw her jaw tighten as she began to tap her data slate's stylus along the tabletop. "You need to be serious, Diego. When it comes to Sereb, we can't afford the slightest chink in our armor. Once he finds that hole, we'll spend all of our time just parrying whatever attacks he sets up to keep us from the most important matter at hand, and we'll look weak and guilty doing it. It'll just make his case appear that much stronger."

"So, he likes to play mind games," Reyes said, pursing his lips. "Feints and dodges and whatever else he can dream up to keep you off balance." He shook his head, grunting in irritation. "Have I mentioned how much I hate lawyers?"

As if on cue, the door leading from his quarters opened, and he and Desai turned to see Captain Sereb himself marching into the room, silver briefcase in hand. Behind the Tellarite, one of the two security guards stationed outside his door, Lieutenant Beyer, regarded him with a look of shock and apology on her face. Reyes remained seated, but Desai bolted from her own chair, her expression one of surprise and newly blossomed anger.

Sereb released a derisive snort. "You may go now, Lieutenant."

Beyer ignored him, her attention still focused on Reyes. "Commodore, I'm sorry, he—"

"No problem, Lieutenant," Reyes replied, raising a hand to silence her. "It's fine. We'll take it from here." Waiting until Beyer offered a sheepish nod before backing out of the room and allowing the door to close after her, he turned his attention to Sereb.

"Please, *do* come in, Captain."

Before the attorney could respond to the obvious sarcasm, Desai cut him off. "What's this about? How dare you just barge into someone's private quarters without invitation? Particularly when they belong to my client?"

Sereb grunted. "The commodore is still in the custody of station security, is he not? Regulations grant me access to accused prisoners at my discretion."

"If you want unfettered access to me any time you damned well please," Reyes said, keeping his voice low and tight and refusing to rise from his chair, "then make your case to the judge, and get me thrown back in the brig. Until then, you request permission to enter *my* home just like anyone else. Otherwise, they'll be adding an assault charge to my sheet after I dropkick your ass through the nearest bulkhead. Do I make myself clear, *Captain*?"

After a momentary pause, during which Reyes figured the lawyer was contemplating the pros and cons of pushing this issue, Sereb finally nodded in agreement. "Understood, Commodore. I apologize for my rudeness. It will not happen again." He glanced around the room before adding, "I was told you both would be here, and in the interest of expediency, I thought it would be more convenient if I just came to you rather than setting up a meeting at a later time."

Casting a glance in Desai's direction, Reyes replied, "Well, golly, why didn't you say so in the first place?" He indicated one of the table's two remaining chairs. "Coffee?"

"Given the circumstances, I don't believe that would be appropriate," Sereb said, clearly caught off guard.

Reyes shrugged as he leaned back in his chair. "That's me. Mr. Inappropriate."

"Diego," said Desai, her tone and the narrowing of her eyes telling Reyes that she wanted to move this along. Turning to Sereb, she asked, "What can we do for you, Captain?"

"It's what *I* may be able to do for *you,*" Sereb replied as he moved around the table to the chair. He set his briefcase on the table and did not sit down. "Obviously, Starfleet is interested in dispensing with this matter as quickly and cleanly as possible. With that in mind, I've been given significant latitude in order to bring about such a resolution." As the Tellarite spoke, Reyes noted that he seemed to have recovered some of his earlier bluster but was still reining himself in, to a degree.

"I take it you're proposing some kind of plea bargain?" Desai asked, and Reyes heard the hint of skepticism lacing her words.

Sereb nodded. "Exactly. The offer, were I to tender it, would be simple: I move for all but the charges of releasing classified information to be dismissed. Plead guilty to the remaining charge, and I request that no incarceration be levied against you. Your Starfleet career would, of course, be over, and you would lose any and all benefits and standing afforded a retired officer of your rank."

He forced his features to remain fixed and impassive, but Reyes still felt the kick to his gut as he absorbed Sereb's offer. Of course, he had expected to be offered a choice like this, but being stripped of everything for which he had served and sacrificed for his entire adult life was almost too much for him to contemplate.

Fortunately, Desai knew this, too. "You seem to be forgetting some very important facts, Captain. If we can demonstrate that the orders under which Commodore Reyes was operating were illegal, then you don't have a case. Perhaps that's what you're worried about and why you're so eager to offer up such a *generous* plea deal?"

Sereb appeared unruffled by her remarks. "I forget none of those things, Captain, just as I do not forget that you are an accomplished and respected attorney. Because of that, I'm confident that we both know just how fragile your stance with respect to legal or illegal orders will be. If this is the strategy you elect to follow, then you do so at great peril to your client."

Before Desai could answer, Reyes held up his hand. "What about my staff? What happens to them?"

Looking across the table at him, Sereb asked, "Except for Lieutenant Commander T'Prynn, there appears to be no willful impropriety or wrongdoing on the part of any other member of your staff." Snorting, he reached up with one massive paw to wipe his stout, porcine nose. "Charges *have* been filed against T'Prynn, but until or unless the commander emerges from her coma, there is nothing else we can do."

Reyes was, of course, troubled by the thought of any proceedings that might be launched against his intelligence officer—assuming she ever regained consciousness and only if she somehow managed to avoid any serious or prolonged damage induced by her affliction. Despite that, Reyes wondered if Sereb's offer was something he could accept. In truth, he had been trying to prepare himself for just such a decision for weeks, attempting to come to terms with what it might mean for his life going forward and especially any future he hoped to share with Rana.

Screw it, he decided. *You're old enough to retire, anyway, right?* He knew it was going against everything he had been telling himself for weeks, to say nothing of what he had communicated first to Commander Spires and then to Rana, but what he had been trying to ignore during that time—the single thought that had been gnawing at him during those uncounted hours alone in his cell—was that he simply was tired and wanted all of this to be over. With it done, perhaps he and Rana, assuming that her own career aspirations did not preclude a continuing relationship with him, might settle somewhere, build a life and a home together, and maybe even start a family. He knew Rana was hesitant at the notion, but perhaps this sort of life-altering event was just the thing to renew the infrequent, fragmented conversations they had shared on this topic.

Long past time to seize the day, I suppose.

With a slow, resigned sigh, Reyes finally looked to Desai and nodded.

"Diego," she said, her face a mask of concern, "are you sure about this?"

"Yeah. Maybe it's best for everyone involved. You and I both know they've got me. It's just a matter of how much they want to beat on me before they finally throw me in a cell somewhere." He sighed. "Why go through all of that when I can just put it all behind me? Everybody would probably be better off." The words were sour in his mouth. He despised the idea of compromising, particularly with anyone he considered an enemy. For purposes of the court-martial, Sereb was that opponent, and realizing that the best course of action for all concerned was to agree to the attorney's proposal made Reyes feel both anger and defeat.

After a moment, Sereb offered a perfunctory nod, his blunt nose moving up and down in rapid fashion as he folded his beefy arms across his broad chest. "Excellent. I thought as much."

Frowning in confusion, Reyes glanced at Desai, whose eyes narrowed in suspicion. "I beg your pardon?" she asked.

"Well," Sereb replied, "as you say, we've got you, and it's just a matter of degrees at this point. I simply wanted some firsthand insight into the defendant I will be prosecuting." To Reyes, he added, "You are fully culpable for every charge against you, Commodore, and it's my duty to prosecute you to the fullest extent of Starfleet regulations, which is precisely what I intend to do."

He was sizing me up. The bitter thought pounded in Reyes's mind in response to the realization of what he soon would be facing in the courtroom. *Cunning bastard.* He saw that Desai had drawn herself up to her full height. Her hands had balled into fists, which she kept locked at her sides.

"How dare you come in here and ambush my client under false pretenses," she said, her already crisp accent taking on a brutal, clipped quality underscoring the anger she clearly was trying to keep at bay. "This meeting is over. We'll see you in court, Counselor."

Sereb reached for his briefcase, and Reyes was certain that he caught a hint of smugness crossing the Tellarite's pudgy features. "Indeed you will. Good day." With a formal nod, he turned and exited the room. Reyes and Desai watched him until the doors closed behind him.

27

"So," Nogura said as he took in the expansive area of the Vault and nodded in appreciation, "this is where the fun happens."

All around him, nearly a dozen Starfleet officers and civilian scientists busied themselves at computer workstations or in several of the laboratories and offices he could see from where he stood inside the office currently occupied by Dr. Marcus. In this part of the station, which on technical schematics appeared as an area devoted to environmental-control and waste-extraction systems, was housed the sum total of knowledge that Starfleet had collected with regard to the Shedai and the Taurus Meta-Genome.

"I suppose that's one way to put it," replied Marcus from where she stood behind her desk, looking over one of the numerous reports littering her office. The room itself was not that large, and its limited space was cluttered with boxes, reports, data cards, and other managerial flotsam.

Numerous ongoing efforts ensured the facility's secrecy. As far as the vast majority of Starbase 47's Starfleet and civilian contingents were concerned, the Vault did not exist. The people working here appeared on personnel rosters as assigned to other sections throughout the station, though most fell within a rather nondescript group known as Logistical Studies, with Marcus listed as the civilian section head. Plans currently were under way to create a mirror site at another, undisclosed location, but for now, Starfleet's efforts to understand the mysteries of the Taurus Reach were spearheaded by the people hidden away within this core of the station.

Marcus stepped around her desk and moved for the door. "If you'll follow me, sir, I think we've got something you'll find very interesting."

"I'd imagine that term fits pretty much everything in this room," Nogura said as he fell in step beside her, and the pair proceeded down the Vault's central corridor. "At least, it seems that way according to what I've been reading."

Marcus nodded. "You don't know the half of it." She gestured to the labs they passed. "When I think about what's out there for us to find, compared with what we actually know at this point, it boggles the mind. You've read the reports, Admiral, so you know we're not exaggerating when we say we may be on the cusp of expanding our knowledge a hundredfold in so many different areas of science and technology. It's all out there, waiting for us."

"We have but to understand how the key fits the lock containing all of this information," Nogura said, repeating a phrase he had come across on several occasions, in reports submitted by Dr. Marcus as well as Lieutenant Ming Xiong.

"Exactly," Marcus said. "The problem is that the meta-genome is so complex, and when we couple that with the manner in which the Shedai apparently interact with their technology, we're talking about quantum leaps of scientific advancement." She paused, sighing and smiling in what Nogura took to be something approaching embarrassment. "I'm sorry, Admiral. I tend to get excited about my work."

"I hadn't noticed," Nogura replied wryly. In fact, he was quite aware that there seemed to be an energy permeating the room, something palpable enveloping the effort being expended here. The people around him were driven to understand the mysteries they had been tasked with solving. One of the things that had interested him upon reading the regular Vanguard updates was how young everyone seemed. Carol Marcus was in her early thirties, according to her personnel file, and Lieutenant Xiong was even younger. Nogura had no issues with age as far as the people under his command were concerned; indeed, he welcomed the diversity of experience and attitudes, as well as the vigor and unbridled passion that youth often contributed to undertakings of this type. What interested him was how such people might come to cope with the knowledge that even at their young age, they were involved in one of the greatest scientific endeavors in the history of civilization. With so much of their lives still ahead of them, would they be driven to find something of even grander scale in which to invest their efforts, perhaps as a means of proving—whether to themselves or to anyone else—that their potential had not already peaked and that they still had so much to offer?

In other words, what do you do for an encore?

Near the end of the corridor was a door flanked by a pair of security guards, who came to attention upon seeing Nogura. The admiral acknowledged the men, but Marcus ignored the Starfleet protocol and reached for the security keypad on the bulkhead next to the door. She placed her thumb on a biometric sensor. A red indicator at the top of the keypad turned green, and the door slid aside to reveal another laboratory, one that did not feature any walls of transparent aluminum.

"After you, Admiral," Marcus offered, standing to one side and allowing Nogura to enter the room. He was greeted by the sight of a young Asian man sitting at a computer workstation, wearing a blue uniform tunic with the rank stripe of lieutenant on the sleeves. His dark, tousled hair was a bit longer than regulation, and his entire appearance made it seem that the lieutenant had not slept the previous night. Also in the room was a Tholian, dressed in what Nogura recognized as one of the environment suits they wore when outside their native atmospheric conditions. The Tholian seemed engrossed in a piece of unfamiliar equipment, but when the lieutenant looked up and saw Nogura, he immediately rose to his feet.

"Admiral," he said, nodding.

Nogura crossed the room, extending his right hand in greeting. "Lieutenant Xiong, isn't it?"

"Yes, sir," Xiong replied, and Nogura noted the dark circles under the other man's eyes.

"You look tired, son," the admiral said. "When's the last time you slept?"

Xiong smiled. "What day is it, sir?"

"We're all a little behind in that department, Admiral," Marcus said, "but I think it's been worth it." She indicated the Tholian with a gesture. "With Nezrene's help, Mr. Xiong has made what we believe is a major breakthrough with our efforts to understand Shedai technology."

At the mention of her name, Nezrene turned to face the group. A string of indecipherable clicks and chirps echoed in the small room before her native language was converted to Federation Standard. "Greetings, Admiral. I have not yet had the opportunity to extend my thanks to you for continuing to allow me sanctuary here."

Nogura nodded. "Ambassador Jetanien spoke most highly of you. I appreciate everything you're doing to assist us." Looking first to Xiong and then to Marcus before smiling, he added, "Though I must confess I'm not at all sure that I understand just what it is you're doing."

"That's what you have us for," Marcus said. "Mr. Xiong, why don't you show the admiral what you've come up with?"

"Of course," Xiong replied. "Admiral, as you know, we've run into several obstacles while trying to understand the Shedai artifacts we've found. One of the theories I've put forth is that the unique crystalline nature of their physiology is a key component to interfacing with their technology. I believe this lends itself to a form of biometric interface, though of a sort far beyond anything we've developed. I think the Shedai are able to access their versions of electronic pathways directly, with the physical-equipment components acting as little more than interface conduits. For all intents and purposes, the Shedai are able to channel themselves directly through their computers and communications."

Marcus said, "Mr. Xiong's theory was given some weight after Dr. Fisher's examination of a Shedai body brought back from Erilon. It was the doctor who also discovered the ancestral link between Tholians and the Shedai. It's this similarity that allowed the Shedai Apostate—that's what Nezrene calls it—to utilize several captive Tholians while on Jinoteur, including Nezrene, and force them to interact with Shedai technology on that world."

Nogura asked Nezrene, "You understand this technology?"

"To a very limited degree, Admiral," replied the Tholian. "While under the control of the Apostate, we were forced to operate within very stringent parameters. We were portals for the Apostate, our minds acting as surrogates for his thoughts, rather than exercising any independent control."

"I don't think I like the sound of that," Nogura said, his mind conjuring various unpleasant depictions of what such an experience might entail.

Nezrene pointed to the equipment she had been working upon when Nogura arrived. "We have been experimenting with this console, which we found in one of the underground chambers on Erilon." The component was approximately one meter in length and about half that in width. It was only a few centimeters thick, leading Nogura to believe that it was merely one piece of a larger piece of equipment, perhaps too large to be transported.

"Based on what we've already learned from previous expeditions to Erilon and Ravanar IV," Xiong said as he crossed the room toward Nezrene, "we've been able to make very limited inroads into understanding their technology. However, if my theory about a biometric interface is correct, then we're going to be limited by our very physiology in making real use of such equipment. We may be able to fashion an artificial substitute, but I believe that will only get us in the door. After that, we're still lost."

Marcus pointed to Nezrene. "However, Nezrene's Tholian physiology is much closer to that of the Shedai. Nezrene's been able to interface directly with this piece of equipment, which we've linked to our testing stations here in the lab in such a way that we can record various responses as power is fed to it."

I like where this is going, Nogura thought.

"And you're able to comprehend what it is you're experiencing?" he asked Nezrene.

The Tholian replied, "Somewhat." She indicated the console with one appendage, which Nogura noted had been free from the confines of Nezrene's environment suit. "This interface contains several points of access embedded in its surface. They mean nothing to beings with physiologies like humans, but for my species, they are easy to ascertain, and they provide a natural port of entry as far as accessing the equipment is concerned." Demonstrating her point, she reached out and touched the console, which immediately flared to life. Nogura was able to make out several graphical displays, none that made any sense to him.

"Remarkable," he said.

Nezrene continued, "As I have explained to Lieutenant Xiong, the experience is much like what I endured while under the Apostate's control, but without him forcing me to certain paths and actions, I am uncertain how to proceed once I am integrated with the console."

"Integrated?" Nogura repeated.

"I become one with the machine," Nezrene said.

Xiong said, "Based on her descriptions, it sounds like an out-of-body experience." He pointed to the alien console. "On some level, she's actually *inside* that thing."

Nogura frowned, trying to wrap his head around this idea. "So, your theory of them somehow projecting themselves into whatever it is they call their version of a computer network is correct?"

"Possibly," Xiong said. "Or it could simply be a case of using telepathy and psychokinesis to operate such equipment, rather than actual physical contact or even voice commands. Whatever it is, it's centuries beyond even our most advanced experimental computer systems. Imagine the possibilities of instantaneous, seamless integration between computer and user."

"I don't have to," Nogura countered. "I've read the reports of the Shedai attacks on Erilon, Gamma Tauri IV, and Jinoteur." What could the Federation do with technology on this scale?

More important, what would their enemies do with it? Looking to Marcus, he said, "I bet I can guess where this is going."

"We have to go back to one of the Shedai planets," Marcus replied.

Xiong added, "We can only do so much from here, Admiral. To make any real progress, we'll need to conduct hands-on research with equipment like what we found on Erilon and Ravanar. Those computer systems are integrated into the entire planet, and if we're to believe just some of what the Shedai can do, they're capable of establishing networks between those planets and all of the others they once controlled."

"They may still be out there," Nogura replied, crossing his arms. "We've seen what they're capable of. I'm not sure I want my people exposed to dangers like that again."

"Sir," Xiong said, "we're talking *real-time* connections, Admiral, across dozens, perhaps hundreds of light-years. The uses for that kind of technology are countless, and if the Shedai are able to project themselves into their computer conduits, then we're talking about an ability to move between worlds the way you and I cross a room. We have to understand it, if only as a means of countering it. What if the Klingons, or someone else, learn to manipulate it?"

An interesting observation, Nogura decided, coming from someone who by all accounts was driven first and foremost by the quest for knowledge for knowledge's sake. Of course, Nogura thought the young man's experiences on Erilon and Jinoteur likely had changed his outlook about what understanding the Shedai meant from a scientific standpoint. Reality had a way of doing that.

He has a point. We can't stand by and do nothing, not while the Klingons are sniffing around. There simply was too much at stake.

Finally, Nogura nodded. "I agree, it's worth the risk." Looking to Xiong, he said, "Gear up, Lieutenant, and dress warm. You're heading back to Erilon."

28
INTERLUDE

Anger, an emotion she had not felt in some time, filled the Wanderer, her mounting rage made all the more acute because she remained powerless to act on it.

The arrogance of the Telinaruul *continues unfettered.*

After several tentative probes into the Void, she had returned weakened and even discouraged by her seeming inability to break the limitations imposed on her by the absence of the First Conduit and those who controlled it. Once again finding temporary solace on the dead world that had belonged to the Tkon, the Wanderer had regained enough of her depleted energies that she was able to sense disturbances within what should have been the lifeless, dormant system of Conduits. At first, she had allowed hope to wash over her, thinking for a fleeting moment that the Enumerated Ones had returned, but such anticipation was quickly dashed as the Wanderer realized that what she had detected was not the bold, unequaled power of those to whom she pledged eternal loyalty. That strength and those who wielded it were still lost to her, absent from this spatial plane and perhaps never to return.

Instead, what the Wanderer felt were the most fleeting permutations, hesitant and clumsy efforts that carried with them a familiar tinge, one she detested. The *Telinaruul* once again were attempting to gain access to technology they could not possibly hope to understand. Focusing her mind toward the source of the activity, she realized that the *Telinaruul* had returned to one of the planets on which they had discovered a Conduit, the ice-bound world where she had first encountered them. She vowed not to underestimate them again. The intruders would pay for their insolence.

While she once had believed without exception in the supremacy of the Shedai, the Wanderer now was forced to admit that the *Telinaruul* were not to be so easily dismissed. In their unchecked lust to obtain the secrets of the Shedai, the infiltrators had overcome the confines of their vastly inferior intellect and made tangible progress in the brief span of time since their arrival in this region of the galaxy. The very nature of their primitive life-forms and their simple incompatibility with Shedai or even Tholian physiology would continue to present the most formidable obstacles, but based on her previous skirmishes with them, the Wanderer believed them capable, in time, of finding some means of bridging that gap.

Of course, without the First Conduit to provide guidance and oversight, the individual portals located on different worlds throughout the realm of the Shedai were all but useless. Therefore, any inroads made by the *Telinaruul* to understand and exploit Shedai knowledge and technology would remain limited.

Would they not?

That uncertainty now fueled the Wanderer, driving her to regain her former strength and free herself from her self-induced isolation. Only then could she carry on with her singular purpose of defending that which belonged to the Shedai, acting in their stead until they chose to return.

They will not return.

From some distant point in the void, another presence called to her, intruding upon the Wanderer's thoughts. The voice of the Apostate reached across space and time, taunting her.

You are alone, as you always will be. Those to whom you pledge loyalty are gone. They will not save you. Their time has passed, as has yours.

The Wanderer felt anger grip her once more, just as the Apostate knew would happen. Despite herself, she could not hold back her own response.

You, too, are alone.

She sensed the Apostate laughing at her bravado. *You possess much courage and spirit for one so young. Then again, I also remember how you fled like a frightened child when I gave you the opportunity. When we meet again, do not hope for similar leniency.*

Before the Wanderer could summon another reply, she felt an abrupt disturbance in her thoughts as the link with the Apostate was severed. Wherever he was, he had tired of the exchange. Though weakened, he remained confident in his abilities and his purpose, dismissing her as though she did not exist.

The Wanderer seethed at his arrogance, her frustrations made all the worse by the knowledge that she was powerless to refute him.

Pushing away her irritation and striving not to dwell on the Apostate, the Wanderer instead marshaled the still-pitiful energies under her control, beginning the arduous task of preparing for yet another journey.

29

There was hot, Pennington decided, and then there was *Vulcan*.

The initial merciless blast of midday desert heat had caught the journalist in the face the instant the *Yukon*'s passenger-access hatch cycled open, and things had only worsened after that. Even now, hours later and with the sun low on the horizon and just beginning to slip behind the distant range of mountain peaks, the temperature remained uncomfortable. It was at least somewhat tolerable here when compared with the stifling heat that seemed to envelop Vulcan's capital city, Shi'Kahr, earlier in the day. Pennington also knew that the heat would abate as sunset turned to night, but that seemed small solace at the moment.

"We've been here eight hours," he said as he paced the width of the small, sparsely furnished reception room in which they had been directed to wait. "I think I've already lost ten bloody kilos in water weight."

Sitting in one of only two chairs apparently designated for visitors, M'Benga reached up to wipe perspiration from his face. "It takes some getting used to, that's for sure. When I interned here, it took me almost two months before I was fully acclimated, and that was after running five kilometers in the heat of the day, every day during my lunch break."

Such a notion held absolutely no appeal for Pennington. Frowning, he asked, "Don't you medical types have some kind of pill or something?" He rubbed the spot his right arm where, a few hours earlier, M'Benga had injected him with something from his portable medikit. "I mean, you can give me something to help me breathe in this ghastly climate, so you'd think someone would dream up something that'd help you deal with the heat."

"It'll be better after the sun goes down," M'Benga replied.

Upon assuming standard orbit, the *Yukon* had been directed by Vulcan Space Central—the organization tasked with overseeing all spacecraft traffic above and around the planet—to land at the main spaceport on the outskirts of Shi'Kahr's bustling metropolis. With the personnel transport secured at a Starfleet landing bay and its three-person crew having received orders to report to the Starfleet liaison office in the capital city, M'Benga had arranged for himself, Pennington, and T'Prynn to be sent via transporter to a point five kilometers outside the village of Kren'than, the settlement Sobon now called home. Local tenets prohibited most modern technology within the commune's borders, necessitating the use of conventional transportation from the beam-in point.

When they arrived, M'Benga and Pennington discovered a simple rail system in place, with a pair of Vulcans waiting beside a hand-powered rail car large enough to accommodate several passengers, including the still-unconscious and stretcher-bound T'Prynn. Even the use of an antigravity unit to maneuver the stretcher had not been permitted, but the Vulcans had been more than willing to lift T'Prynn into the car. The journey to Kren'than had taken more than two hours, with their Vulcan chauffeurs setting and maintaining a steady pace on the hand-cranked controls that set the car in motion. Despite what had to be enormous effort on their part, the Vulcans uttered not a word, never so much as displaying labored breathing as they worked.

Showoffs, Pennington thought.

In the village itself, he and M'Benga were quickly greeted by a trio of healers, all of whom were working in some capacity with Sobon, who apparently had excused himself to his private chambers for extended meditation in preparation for working with T'Prynn. With M'Benga's approval, the healers had taken T'Prynn into the village's small medical ward, a single-story adobe structure that looked to Pennington to have been created from formed mud or clay, with a wooden roof, as was the case with the majority of the settlement's other presumably permanent structures. Neither M'Benga nor Pennington had seen her since that time, though one of the healers had come to tell them that T'Prynn had been settled in her room and that he and his companions were waiting for Sobon to emerge from meditation. For nearly an hour, the two humans had sat in this room, which as far as Pennington could tell was but one room in the large building that operated as the seat of Kren'than's provincial government.

With the sun continuing its descent behind the western range of the L-langon Mountains, the room was growing darker. As if on cue, a door at the back of the room opened, admitting a young Vulcan male carrying a stout white candle in a flat black holder. Pennington guessed him to be in his late teens or early twenties, knowing that his estimate might be off by decades given protracted Vulcan life spans. As Pennington and M'Benga waited in silence, the young Vulcan used the candle to light a pair of oil lamps mounted on the back wall before proceeding to a smaller lamp on the table at the center of the room. His task completed, he turned his attention to M'Benga.

"Doctor," he said, "I am Sinar, a student of Healer Sobon's. He has assigned me to act as your assistant during your visit with us. I've been instructed to inform you that he is prepared and to ask if there is anything you require at this time." As the young Vulcan spoke, and despite the veneer of self-control that all Vulcans employed at all times, Pennington still noted a slight discomfort, as though Sinar would rather be anywhere else but here.

Well, that makes two of us.

Nodding toward Pennington, M'Benga replied, "Some water would be sufficient for now. I trust sleeping quarters have been readied?"

"As Healer Sobon requested," said Sinar. "I will take you there once your business with him has concluded for the evening."

"Then by all means," Pennington said, "let's get this show on the road." When he caught the irritated glare from M'Benga, he added, "I mean, we're ready when you are."

Sinar nodded. "Very well. Follow me."

As he fell in step next to Pennington and they followed Sinar out of the room and down a long, narrow corridor, M'Benga leaned closer and whispered, "These Vulcans aren't like the ones you're used to dealing with. Jocularity and other informal speech mannerisms won't get you anywhere."

"If that's the case," Pennington replied, "then they're exactly like the Vulcans I'm used to dealing with."

M'Benga suppressed a sigh. "All I'm saying is that these Vulcans don't normally interact with humans—or any outworlders, for that matter. Ordinarily, we'd never have been allowed to set foot in the village at all, much less be welcomed into their homes. The only reason we're not under armed guard is that Sobon put in a good word for us, but that doesn't mean they have to like us. They're not familiar with euphemisms or slang or our plain and simple torturing of what should otherwise be a rather straightforward language. If you talk in anything other than formal Federation Standard, in most instances, they won't have the first damned clue what you're saying."

While his first thought was to respond that such was only fair, in that he rarely, if ever, fully comprehended everything a Vulcan might say during the course of normal conversation, Pennington nodded instead. "Understood, mate. I'll mind my manners."

They continued in silence, following Sinar down the corridor, which was illuminated by oil lamps mounted at regular intervals along the left wall. The slight downward slope of the passageway and numerous intersections they passed led Pennington to realize that they were traversing an underground tunnel, likely in a network of such subterranean passages used to connect the village's aboveground structures.

"Interesting design aesthetic," he remarked.

"Not atypical in remote villages and settlements like this one," M'Benga replied. "Underground chambers are better environments for storage, for one thing. The passages also offer shelter during inclement weather, which is probably something of a regular occurrence up here in these mountains. They also offer protection against local predators."

Pennington frowned. "Predators? You mean beasts of some sort?"

"Of some sort," the doctor repeated. "You'll get this advice soon enough, but don't go anywhere up here alone, particularly after dark."

"Oh, that's grand," Pennington said, shaking his head. *What in the name of hell have I gotten myself into?*

After maneuvering several turns in the corridor, inclining upward at a gradual angle, they came upon a large wooden door secured by a simple metal bolt. Sinar reached out and slid the bolt aside, the sound of it echoing in the narrow passageway. He ushered M'Benga and Pennington through the doorway ahead of him before pulling the door closed behind him and sliding the bolt back into place.

The trio now stood in what Pennington guessed was a sort of den or study. Shelves lined the walls, stuffed with books and scrolls, a dozen crystalline vessels of differing sizes, shapes, and colors, plus various other items he did not recognize. A small wooden desk occupied one corner, and a large, ornately designed area rug dominated the center of the floor. On one end of the desk, an oil lamp provided the room's only illumination.

"These are Sobon's private chambers," Sinar explained. "He has completed his meditation and is now attending your friend."

Pointing to one of the odd crystal objects, each of which caught the lamp's light and reflected it in myriad colors across the shelves' other contents, Pennington asked, "What are those?"

"*Vre-katra.* Closely translated, it means '*katric* ark,' " M'Benga replied. Seeing the quizzical expression on the journalist's face, he held up a hand. "It's a long story."

Gesturing for them to follow, Sinar proceeded across the room to the door on the opposite wall. After passing down another corridor, this one decorated with tapestries and paintings, they crossed a larger sitting room and finally came to another door. Sinar paused before it, knocking on its aged wooden surface.

"Come," a raspy voice called out from the other side. Sinar opened the door and led the way into the room.

Pennington paused as he stepped inside, allowing his eyes to adjust to the dim light offered by the single lamp in the room's far corner. A bed was positioned along the far wall, beneath an open window, and lying on it was T'Prynn. She wore the same Star-fleet-issue patient gown in which she had been dressed by M'Benga before departing the *Yukon*. Her hands were clasped across her chest. The irregular, infrequent rising and falling of her chest were the only indications that she was not dead. Con-spicuously absent was any of the Starfleet medical equipment, all of which had remained on the *Yukon*.

Standing at the foot of the bed, his withered hands held before him and his eyes closed, was the oldest Vulcan Pennington had ever seen. Thin and stoop-shouldered, he had tanned and deeply wrinkled skin, obvious testament to the years he had spent toiling under the harsh Vulcan sun. His hair, stark white, was long and smooth, flowing about his shoulders and descending to the small of his back. His simple black robe reached to the floor, hiding his feet, and was devoid of any decorative pattern.

After nearly a minute of standing in silence and watching the Vulcan say nothing nor move a single muscle, Pennington looked to M'Benga, who shook his head. He was just about to clear his throat or make some other gesture to indicate that they were wait-ing, when the Vulcan's eyes opened, and he turned his head to face them. Despite the man's age, there was no mistaking his in-telligence or focus.

"I am Sobon," he said.

M'Benga replied, "Healer Sobon, I'm Dr. M'Benga, and this is my friend, Timothy Pennington. He also is an associate of T'Prynn's."

"Thank you for helping us," Pennington quickly added, "and for welcoming us into your community." Even as he spoke the words, he realized he likely would be rebuked for undue emo-tionalism or illogic or some other such damned thing.

Instead, Sobon replied, "It has been some time since my last interaction with humans. I had come to realize that I missed the differences between us, which I view as opportunities for exploration, rather than hindrances or inconveniences as so many of my colleagues once believed." Nodding toward T'Prynn, he said, "It is agreeable to see that humans and Vulcans can work together and form friendships, just as I believed when I first traveled to Earth."

For the first time, Pennington actually felt welcome in Kren'than. Reaching up to wipe a line of sweat from the side of his head, he realized he had almost forgotten how bloody hot it still was, even now, after the sun had set. Almost.

"Are you able to help her?" he asked.

Moving from his stance at the food of the bed, Sobon knelt beside T'Prynn. He reached across her body, his curled, wrinkled fingers pressing against three points along the side of her head. "We shall soon see."

Feeling Sten's hands around her throat, T'Prynn howled in unfettered rage, her hands clawing at his face. She felt her nails dig into his skin, and lines of green blood stained her fingers. Sten grunted in pain, though his grip on her throat did not waver. T'Prynn forced her fingers deeper into his flesh, tearing at skin and muscle until he finally relented, staggering backward and reaching for his injured face.

T'Prynn rolled to her side and regained her feet, her strength flagging, her throat aching from Sten's attack as well as implacable thirst. She sucked air greedily, trying to bring her breathing back under control as she fumbled backward, putting space between her and Sten. The wind whipped at her, pelting her exposed skin with blown sand. Looking down at herself, she realized for the first time that her clothing was little more than tatters, held together in some places by individual threads.

Sten bent to the sand and picked up the knife that had fallen there during the struggle. "You grow weak," he taunted, waving the blade toward her. Blood streamed from the ghastly wound she had inflicted on his face, and he stared at her with scorching hatred, his emotions all but consuming him. "Soon you will have no choice but to submit to me. It is inevitable."

"If I'm dead," she countered, "is that truly victory?"

Stepping forward, Sten replied, "If that is all that is attainable, then it will have to suffice."

"No."

Turning to the sound of the new voice, T'Prynn was startled to see an elderly Vulcan male, his long white hair and full-length robe seemingly unaffected by the unceasing sand storm. He stood with hands clasped before him, eyeing them with clinical dispassion. Where had he come from?

"Leave us, old man," Sten said, pointing the knife at him. "This is a private matter and does not concern you."

The aged Vulcan moved until he stood between Sten and T'Prynn. Turning to face Sten, he said, "You do not belong here. For either of you to have peace, you must leave this place."

"Not until I have what is rightfully mine," Sten said, stepping forward.

T'Prynn could not comprehend what happened next. Though the elder Vulcan appeared not to move, Sten's advance halted, and his eyes widened in confusion—perhaps even fear. She watched as he tried to raise the knife, only to see his shock at his seeming inability to move.

Then, simply, he was gone, swallowed by the sand.

Sobon's body jerked, and he wrenched his hand free of T'Prynn's face. His movements cost him his balance, and he would have fallen to the floor if not for Sinar's quick reaction. He caught his mentor, steadying him

"I am well now," he said after a moment, patting the younger Vulcan's hand.

"What happened?" M'Benga asked, his expression a mask of worry.

Pulling himself to his feet, Sobon cleared his throat. When he spoke, his voice was broken and raspy. "Her condition is worse than I first believed. T'Prynn's mind is occupied by two *katras*. Her own, and that of her betrothed, Sten."

"What's a *katra*?" Pennington asked.

Sobon said, "It is the embodiment of a Vulcan's conscious-ness. During mind melds, it is possible to transfer this from one mind to another. Such exchange is supposed to happen on a vol-untary basis, but on rare occasions, it has been done without con-sent from the receiving individual."

"And that's what happened to T'Prynn," Pennington said, re-calling his earlier discussions with M'Benga. "He somehow forced his . . . *katra* . . . into her mind before he died?"

"That is correct," Sobon replied. "She is now what we call *val'reth,* one who hosts another *katra* against his or her own will. Because of the trauma of forcing a meld at the point of death, his *katra* has become entwined with T'Prynn's." He clasped his hands together to emphasize his point. "They are one, though the one still retains the properties of both minds. T'Prynn, naturally, fought this forced union and has continued to do so since the original meld. Since that time, Sten's *katra* has waged war upon T'Prynn's, beat-ing at it and wearing it down. Eventually, his *katra* will triumph, and the result will be a total subsuming of T'Prynn's mind."

"Good Lord." Pennington shook his head. M'Benga had al-ready explained some of this, but the full magnitude of what T'Prynn must have experienced, and had experienced since be-fore he was born, had become clear. Looking to Sobon once more, he asked, "Do you think you can help her?"

"I have created a temporary separation," replied the aged Vul-can, "but it will not last. However, there is a meld ritual that may prove successful. It is called *Dashaya-Ni'Var,* to separate that which has become one. Through this meld, we will be able to remove Sten's *katra* from T'Prynn's mind."

"And do what with it?" Pennington asked, before something clicked in his memory, and he looked to M'Benga. "Those things in Sobon's study. You called them *katric* arks."

Sobon nodded. "A very astute observation, my young friend. A *vre-katra* is capable of preserving a *katra* long after a person's death. The care of such vessels falls to the adepts. Long ago, I, too, looked after many *vre-katra*. If we are successful, Sten's *katra* will be housed in similar fashion."

Frowning, Pennington asked, "And then what do you do with it?"

"That remains to be seen," Sobon replied.

M'Benga asked, "What happens if this . . . separation . . . doesn't work?"

Sobon's eyes narrowed. "Then it is likely that T'Prynn will die."

Despite the lingering heat permeating the room even this long after sunset, the Vulcan's blunt statement sent a shiver down Pennington's spine.

30

"Ambassador, you're tired. You should go home and get some rest."

Looking up from the curved desk at the center of his cramped, dimly lit office, Jetanien saw Akeylah Karumé, one of the diplomatic envoys assigned to his staff, watching him from the doorway. A statuesque human female with brilliant ebony skin and a penchant for dressing in vividly colored attire, she was most attractive by Terran standards. She stood cloaked in shadow, owing to the room's muted illumination as well as the fact that Jetanien had deactivated the display monitors that normally fed him constant updates from a variety of sources. He noted that Karumé was carrying a data slate in one hand, and over her left shoulder hung the black bag she often used to carry whatever personal effects she brought with her to work each day. By all appearances, the envoy was on her way home for the evening.

"It's not that I disagree with your assessment, Ms. Karumé," he said as he reached for the nearly forgotten bowl of Denebian shellfish broth sitting near one corner of his desk. "However, the problems of any given day have a habit of ignoring the civilized strictures of regular business hours." Taking a sip of the broth, Jetanien recoiled at the cold brew, which had congealed into a bitter paste since he had first procured it from his office food slot. How long ago had that been, anyway?

Karumé entered the office and, without invitation, placed her bag on one of the two guest chairs at Jetanien's desk before settling into the other one. "I read the report on your latest meeting with the Tholian ambassador," she said. "Not good."

"To put it mildly, Ms. Karumé," the ambassador replied. He rose from the backless chair designed to accommodate his bulky physique and moved to the food slot for another bowl of broth. "So long as Nezrene enjoys Federation sanctuary, there will be no negotiations."

No matter what concession he had offered, the Tholian ambassador, Sesrene, had been immovable on that one basic point. It was obvious to Jetanien, even from the limited contact afforded the two diplomats via the subspace communications link, that his Tholian counterpart was most upset at the thought of whatever information Nezrene might now be sharing with the Federation. Jetanien had tried to reassure Sesrene that no collusion against Tholian interests was in the offing, but there was no penetrating the thick cloak of xenophobia that seemed to cover most Tholians.

Fairly troubling, he reminded himself, *considering your whole reason for being assigned to this station is to resolve such disputes.* Perhaps in time, if and when Nezrene's efforts began to produce results, there would be new opportunities to reach out once again to the Tholians—assuming that they opted not to do anything rash in response to perceived threats.

Tholians acting rashly? The sour thought echoed in Jetanien's mind as he took his fresh broth from the food slot. *Perish the thought.*

"So," Karumé said, her nose wrinkling in apparent response to the broth's odor, "what do we do now?"

"About the Tholians?" Jetanien asked, retaking his seat. "Nothing—for the moment, anyway." He took a long drink from the bowl and sighed in contentment as the warm broth slid down his throat and its vapors drifted across his nostrils. With his free manus, he indicated the assortment of files and data slates covering his desk. "There are other pressing matters demanding our attention, my dear."

"The Romulans," Karumé said, nodding thoughtfully. "I read that report, too."

Emitting a string of satisfied clicks, Jetanien nodded in

approval. "You are nothing if not efficient and thorough, Ms. Karumé. It's but one of the many reasons I am grateful for your presence on my staff." He paused for another sip of his broth before continuing. "If the Romulans are emerging from their proverbial shells to investigate our interest in the Taurus Reach and they learn even a fraction of what we already know, then you can be sure it will have repercussions throughout the quadrant. The Romulan Empire is unlikely to stand idle and leave to us whatever treasures are to be found here.

"Then there are the simple questions of how long they've been here and how much they know," he added, setting aside his broth. "Not just about the Taurus Reach but also about Starfleet and the Federation in general. It's been more than a century since the war; each side naturally will want to know how far the other has advanced." Shaking his head, Jetanien rested his manus on his desk. "This on top of the noise the Klingons keep making. If the Romulans are preparing some kind of new offensive, we may well be looking at a two-front war."

Karumé leaned back in her chair. "Any word yet on how Starfleet Intelligence is reacting to the *other* news about the Romulans?"

Jetanien released an irritated grunt. "If you mean this idea of Romulans and Vulcans possibly sharing common ancestry, as you might imagine, those in the business of being paranoid are doing exactly that. Even as we speak, comprehensive stratagems for the hunting and exposing of covert Romulan agents are being developed. The Vulcans in particular seem very distraught about this notion, though, of course, there's a segment of their society that has always known about this." Shaking his head, he added, "For a race known for its collective intelligence and enlightenment, Vulcans are almost human-like in their propensity for keeping secrets."

"The societal implications alone could be overwhelming," Karumé said. "It took decades for humans to accept the Vulcans after they came to Earth, and xenophobia escalated for months in the wake of the Xindi attack, even after that threat was neutralized. For something like this, with a brutal enemy being related to one of our most trusted allies?" She shook her head. "Imagine what could happen."

Finished with the broth, Jetanien set the bowl aside. "I'd like to think your people have come a long way in that time, Ms. Karumé, and that such narrow-minded prejudices are a thing of your past."

"You and me both." Leaning forward in her seat, Karumé frowned as she studied the files on his desk. "What is all that? Since when do you keep real paper files?"

"I don't," Jetanien replied, holding up a leather-bound notebook for her to see. "Long ago, these belonged to a dear friend of mine—a human, believe it or not, named Selina Rosen. One of the most dedicated people I've ever known, she loathed computers and instead made copious use of real books and paper. She did all of her writing by hand, and only when something was intended for public dissemination did she give her notes to an assistant for transcription." Indicating the collection with a wave of one manus, he added, "When she died, she left instructions for all of this to be delivered to me. It's provided much inspiration over the years."

"So, you cart all of this around with you from assignment to assignment?" Karumé asked. "Seems more than a bit impractical to me."

Jetanien grunted in understanding. "When I was much younger, I considered it little more than an eccentric affectation, but as I've grown older, I've come to appreciate the almost visceral connection Selina had to her work." Leaning closer to Karumé, he added, "It's something I've tried myself from time to time, and I have often thought of incorporating the practice into my daily routine."

Snorting in mock derision, Karumé replied, "Well, don't look at me. I've seen your handwriting. Besides, I like computers and their accessories just fine, thank you." She rose and went to the food slot on the far wall, where she entered a sequence on the rows of buttons on the control pad beneath the unit. A moment later, the door slid up to reveal what Jetanien recognized as a cup of coffee—brewed with a hint of vanilla, if his nostrils did not deceive him—along with a new bowl of the Denebian shellfish broth. After handing the broth to him, she returned to her seat, nodding toward the collection. "So, why are you poring over all of that, anyway? Feeling nostalgic?"

"Hardly," Jetanien countered, holding the piping-hot bowl of broth between his manus. "At the prime of her own career, Selina was a member of Earth's diplomatic contingent. This was before the Federation was founded, my dear, dating to the Coalition of Planets. She was a member of the team that helped to negotiate the language and parameters of the original treaty between Earth and the Romulans. Her notes on that period are fascinating reading, Ms. Karumé. You'd do well to avail yourself of the wisdom contained here."

Karumé's eyes narrowed as she regarded the ambassador. "Wait a minute, this is starting to make sense now. Are you telling me you've found something that can help us today?"

"Perhaps," Jetanien replied, pleased with himself and with Karumé for her deductive skill. "In one of Selina's journals, there are several entries detailing correspondence she shared with a Romulan named D'tran. A former military officer who left the service to enter politics, he was a junior senator assigned to the Romulan diplomatic team working to ratify the treaty. Contact between him and Selina was, of course, wholly unauthorized, carried out in total secrecy."

Frowning, Karumé shifted in her chair as though seeking a more comfortable position. "To what end?"

Jetanien rolled his shoulders, the closest he could come to a shrug. "Back-channel communication. It seemed that D'tran, like Selina, felt that the original treaty was too limiting and laced with animosity. Rather than laying the foundation for future cooperative spirit between the two powers, the armistice served as little more than a fence erected between two spiteful neighbors, much like the Neutral Zone itself. Even after the treaty went into effect and the Romulans went into seclusion, Selina and D'tran maintained sporadic contact for a time. According to everything I could find in her journals, the communications protocol they used was never discovered."

"But you found it," Karumé said, nodding toward his desk. "Somewhere in all of that, she wrote all about it, didn't she?"

"Indeed, she did," Jetanien replied. The hours he had spent ensconced in his office, rummaging through the long-dormant files and journals, had finally yielded something he thought he could use. From the assortment of papers and files, he retrieved one battered, scuffed leather journal. "It's all in here—the ciphers they used and how they hid their messages among other subspace communications traffic. The methods were so simple as to be laughable, which is probably why they worked so well."

He waited, watching as Karumé's eyes widened in realization. Holding up a hand, she regarded him with equal parts confusion and disbelief.

"You can't seriously be thinking of trying to use that?"

Straightening his posture, Jetanien nodded. "Absolutely. Think of the possibilities, Ms. Karumé. Our two governments have spent the past century staring at each other across the vast gulf of space, each waiting to see what the other will do. Now, the Romulans are here, lurking in the shadows and possibly sizing us up once more for war. If an option exists—any option—that might avoid that, are we not duty-bound to pursue it?"

"You don't even know if there'll be anyone on the other end," Karumé countered. "For all we know, this D'tran is dead, like your friend. Maybe he was discovered and imprisoned or even killed decades ago."

Jetanien nodded. "I have considered those possibilities, of course. The way I see it, either D'tran will answer, or he won't. Perhaps he left information to a trusted protégé, as Selina did, and that person will answer. If their government has discovered the existence of the protocol, the worst that can happen is that they won't answer any message of mine, which is what is currently happening with the official overtures the Federation is sending. That leaves me no worse off than if I were to do nothing."

Karumé finished her coffee and said, "Well, when you put it that way, I say give it a shot, and see what happens."

Jetanien released a satisfied grunt. "I think you would have enjoyed knowing Selina, Ms. Karumé," he said as he laid the treasured journal on his desk and began flipping through its pages, searching for the key entry. "I am quite certain she would have liked knowing you."

Karumé returned the smile. "I'll take that as a compliment, Ambassador."

"As you should, my dear," the Chel responded. Having found the journal entry he sought, he reached for his desktop computer interface. "Now, as you say, let us see what happens."

Even as he began the task of formulating a message that might be appropriate for reestablishing contact with Selina Rosen's Romulan counterpart—or his replacement—after the time that had passed since his friend's death, Jetanien could not help considering the potential held by this simple action. Might it lead to the first true diplomatic relations between the Federation and the Romulans in more than a century? If so, would history one day list him as the arbiter of a new era of trust and cooperation between the two former enemies?

The very idea filled Jetanien with more excitement and hope than he had felt in weeks. There was much work to be done, he decided, as he pushed away thoughts of rest. Sleep could wait.

31

Atish Khatami stepped off the turbolift and onto the *Endeavour*'s hangar deck, beholding the scene of chaos before her.

Perhaps *chaos* was too strong a word, she decided as she began moving among the dozens of people occupying the vast chamber. Cots and containers of supplies that had been stored here were now in use. Moving among the people were the familiar blue tunics of *Endeavour* medical personnel, as well as the red shirts worn by members of the ship's security division. Other members of the crew also had been drafted for working parties, helping to organize the sudden influx of new passengers the *Endeavour* had acquired.

"Captain," a voice called out above the fray, and Khatami looked up to see Commander Stano crossing the deck toward her. The first officer's expression was all business as she sidestepped other crew members.

Nodding as Stano drew closer, Khatami asked, "Is that all of them?"

"Yes," the commander replied. "Transporter control reports the last eleven colonists just completed beam-over. I've got an engineering crew standing by to beam across and see if we might be able to repair the damage and restore environmental control."

Khatami shook her head. "No. We'll take the ship in tow and tractor it to Pacifica. Once we get there, we'll assist in any way we can with repairs, but I don't expect we'll be hanging around that long."

Footsteps echoed along the deck to her right, and she turned to see Dr. Leone walking toward them. Like Stano, the chief medical officer had tabled his usual sardonic manner, now all business as he tended to his latest batch of patients.

"We've finished treating the most serious injuries," he said, reaching up to brush sweat-dampened hair from his forehead. "A lot of radiation burns from the engine overload and some broken bones and assorted lacerations and other bruises, all sustained during the attack. We've stabilized all of the radiation patients, and none of the other injuries is life-threatening, but a few of them will be sore for the next couple of days." His expression changed, and Khatami knew the doctor was readying for the transition back to his normal behavior even before he hooked a thumb over his shoulder. "Sleeping on those cots won't be much help," he said. "If you want, I can set up a torture rack in sickbay. It'd be less painful."

Smiling despite herself, Khatami said, "That won't be necessary, Doctor. My compliments to you and your staff. As for the billeting situation, Commander Stano is taking care of that, but this will have to do for now. Make sure they have access to whatever they want or need from ship's stores."

"All the reconstituted chicken they can eat," Leone replied. "They were better off with radiation poisoning. Anyway, that's my report."

"Thanks, Tony," Khatami said as the doctor turned and made his way back to where his staff had set up a central point for treating the *Roanoke*'s passengers.

"He's always going to be like that, isn't he?" Stano said, eyeing Leone as he went back to work. "I mean, I knew he could be a smart-ass, but all the time?"

Khatami replied, "Yes, and I like him that way, Kathy, so leave him be." She knew from experience that Anthony Leone's attitude was a gauge not just to the state of the crew but of any other situation in which he found himself. So long as the doctor maintained his sense of humor, things were not as bad as they might seem.

"Whatever you say, Captain," Stano replied, obviously unconvinced but apparently unwilling to press the matter further.

Sighing, Khatami reached up to wipe her eyes, which still stung from lack of sleep. She had been awakened by Stano with the report about the distress call from the *Roanoke,* a colony transport ship en route from Alpha Centauri to Pacifica, one of the more popular destinations for settlers in the Taurus Reach. The *Endeavour* had tracked following the coordinates provided by the ship's captain, Zachary Clavell, to find the *Roanoke* adrift in space, its life-support systems damaged and its engines destroyed. The vessel's complement of fourteen crew and ninety-six colonists had been at the end of their rope, the onboard supply of oxygen all but depleted by the time the *Endeavour* arrived. Quick work by the starship's transporter crews had taken care of the immediate danger, beaming over every person from the *Roanoke,* after which security and medical personnel had coordinated the transfer of evacuees from the *Endeavour*'s emergency and cargo transporters to the hangar deck.

According to the *Roanoke*'s captain, the ship had come under fire from a lone Klingon battle cruiser, the assault taking out the life-support systems and disabling the engines. Rather than destroying the transport vessel outright or even boarding her for the purpose of looting her cargo, the Klingon commander seemed satisfied to condemn the injured ship's crew and passengers to a slow, lingering death from freezing or asphyxiation, whichever came first.

Angered by the wanton callousness of the attack, Khatami shook her head. "Where is Captain Clavell?"

Stano pointed and waved. A short, burly man dressed in an orange jumpsuit and black boots returned the gesture and made his way in short order.

"Captain Khatami," the man said, extending his hand. "I'm Zach Clavell, captain of the *Roanoke*. You have no idea how happy we were to see you."

Khatami shook the man's hand, noting how tired he looked. The skin beneath his red-rimmed eyes was dark and puffy, and he had not shaved in several days. His hands and face were dirty, as was his unkempt hair, and there were stains and even a couple of tears in his jumpsuit. Khatami made a point not to wipe her hand on her trousers. "Glad to be of service, Captain. Can you tell me what happened?"

Blowing out a deep breath, Clavell replied, "We'd heard about some of the trouble out here, of course, but the route we were taking to Pacifica had been approved by Starfleet. My understanding is that it's well traveled and frequently patrolled. Space is still pretty big, I guess." He shrugged. "Anyway, we picked up the Klingon ship on our long-range sensors, and it came up on us pretty fast. We received a hail and were ordered to drop out of warp. Since we don't have weapons and there was no way we were going to outrun them, I ordered us to drop to sublight."

As he spoke, his gaze cast downward toward the deck, he put his hands into the hip pockets of his jumpsuit. Khatami recognized the look; it was the posture of a man who believed himself to have failed. In this case, Clavell affected the look of a ship master who had not succeeded in maintaining the safety of his vessel and crew. Never mind that the situation was out of his control and that he had been outmatched against the Klingon ship. It was a sensation nothing could alleviate.

I know how he feels, Khatami thought, recalling once again the day she had been forced by tragic circumstance into the position of commanding the *Endeavour.* Not a single moment had passed since the death of Zhao Sheng that she did not compare herself to her late captain. On many of those occasions, she found herself falling short, but it only motivated her to keep reaching for that standard, impossibly high as it may have been.

"What happened next?" Khatami asked when Clavell paused, obviously uncomfortable with recounting the incident.

"We'd just dropped out of warp when the first attack hit. Our engines were knocked out with their first salvo. From then, we were even more helpless than we'd already been. We watched as the ship circled us, as though its captain was sizing us up before deciding to board us or just finish the job and destroy us." He stopped, swallowing. "I never served in Starfleet, and I've never been shot at before. I don't mind saying I've never been as scared as I was right then."

"It's okay," Stano said, reaching out and placing a hand on the man's shoulder.

After a moment, Clavell nodded. "Then they shot at us again, and I got a report from my chief engineer telling me they'd knocked out life support. Now the clock was ticking. More than a hundred people onboard, sucking oxygen, and the temperature set to start dropping? You know how that goes. Then we get another hail. This time he identifies himself as Captain Kutal, and his ship is called the *Zin'za* or something like that." When Khatami bristled at the name, Clavell took notice. "You know him?"

"More that we know *of* him," Khatami corrected. "He's been making something of a reputation for himself in the Taurus Reach." Kutal and his ship, the *Zin'za,* had been at Jinoteur when the Shedai apparently caused the system to vanish. As a consequence of that, the Klingon Empire knew far more than the Federation would like about the Shedai and the potential harbored by their technology.

Nice understatement there, Khatami mused. *Maybe you're still sleepy.*

"So," Stano said, "they just left you there?"

Clavell nodded. "Kutal said it was an unfortunate misunderstanding, that their sensors mistook us for an enemy ship. He didn't really seem all that choked up about the 'confusion,' of course. Naturally, there were no offers to help, though he said he'd be happy to finish the job if that's what we wanted. Then the communication ended, and they just flew away, leaving us there, adrift and bleeding our atmosphere into space." He paused, covering his mouth as he coughed. "If you hadn't heard our distress call . . ."

"But we did, and everyone's safe now," Khatami said. "We'll get you to Pacifica."

Clavell replied, "That was supposed to be my job."

"And you'll finish that job," Stano said. "You never had a chance against a Klingon cruiser. In fact, you're lucky he didn't just cut you to pieces without saying a word."

"I suppose," Clavell said. He looked up from the deck and gestured over his shoulder. "Captain, I appreciate everything you and your crew have done for us, but if it's all right with you, I'd like to check on my injured."

"Of course," Khatami replied. She waited until the dejected captain was out of earshot before turning to Stano. "The Klingons are getting bolder," she said as she studied the scene before her. Across the hangar deck, the *Roanoke* passengers were settling in. Several dozen had taken advantage of the tables set up to serve as a temporary mess facility, and others had chosen cots in the berthing area and fallen into relieved slumber, their ordeal finally behind them.

"That's one way to put it," replied the first officer. "Tempers are running hot lately, especially after that incident at Starbase 42."

Khatami nodded. The recent attack on the installation orbiting the second planet in the Casmus system was the most egregious assault by Klingon forces on a Starfleet target to date. Klingon invaders, drawn to the system after reports of rich dilithium deposits being found on the third planet, had boarded the station and killed a large number of its crew. They eventually were defeated by a joint mission between the *Starships Enterprise* and *Constellation,* but the cost in lives had been alarming.

"What I don't understand," Stano said, "is why they're targeting civilian ships and then leaving them adrift. What's the point of that?"

Khatami replied, "Maybe because a Starfleet ship responding to a distress call means they're not somewhere else?" It was an alarming thought, especially considering what she knew of recent imperial ship movements. The Klingons were sending more vessels into the Taurus Reach all the time. Even with their resources stretched thin with defending their borders, the ships and personnel they had placed here still outnumbered those supplied by the Federation. "I think we need to alert Admiral Nogura about this. He's going to want more ships."

"I can't say a few more *Constitutions* would go unnoticed,"

Stano said, "or unappreciated. Sooner or later, this kind of constant probing and outright daring is going to blow up into something more serious."

Khatami released a sigh. "I know, but I imagine there's a line even they won't cross, at least not until war's formally declared."

The question needing an answer, she knew, was where that line was drawn.

32

"You know," Reyes said, keeping his voice low as he looked about the courtroom, "I don't think I've ever been in here before."

Sitting to his right, attired, as he was, in dress uniform, Desai leaned close enough to speak almost directly into his ear. "You could've just taken a tour like everyone else. Now, would you please focus?"

Reyes offered a mild grunt, leaning back in his chair. He and Desai were at one of two tables positioned before the raised bench that dominated the front of the courtroom. Just below the bench were a single straight-backed chair and a small shelf with a computer interface, which Reyes knew would be used to record the proceedings and provide as needed a means of retrieving information relevant to the trial from the station's library computer system. The four seats arrayed before him were empty, but in moments, their assigned occupants would enter the chamber and begin the process of deciding how Reyes was to spend the next several years of his life.

Without turning his head, Reyes looked to his right and out of the corner of his eye saw past Desai to the other table before the bench. Seated alone was Captain Sereb, also wearing a dress uniform. The Tellarite appeared to be concentrating on the data slate he had produced from his ever-present briefcase. Sereb had made no further attempts to talk to Desai or to Reyes himself after their aborted meeting in Reyes's quarters three weeks earlier. Since then, according to Desai, at least, the attorney had been content to remain in his office, preparing and refining his prosecution strategy. Desai had carried on in similar fashion, interrupting her own work for meetings with Reyes as she polished the avenues of defense she would pursue.

Here's hoping all that work was worth it.

Behind the tables reserved for counsel were rows of chairs for observers, all of which were unoccupied. Despite the fact that Tim Pennington's explosive story for FNS had laid open several of Operation Vanguard's closely held secrets, there still were many facets of Starbase 47's true mission in the Taurus Reach that remained classified. For that reason, Admiral Moratino had ordered the court-martial to be carried out behind closed doors. Reyes had no problem with that, as he had no desire to be on display before his crew and any gallery of curious onlookers the trial might attract.

"Here we go," Desai said after a moment, returning Reyes's attention to the front of the room as a Starfleet lieutenant—a Vulcan female he did not recognize—entered the courtroom from a door to the left of the bench. Her back was ramrod straight as she marched across the room to the computer terminal and activated it. The rows of multicolored lights on the unit's face began to flash in rhythmic patterns.

"Computer," the Vulcan said, "commence recording."

"Working," an emotionless female voice replied from the terminal. *"Recording activated."*

Turning her attention to the rest of the room, which, of course, consisted only of Reyes, Desai, and Sereb, the lieutenant said nothing for a moment, waiting until Reyes heard the sound of another door opening behind the Vulcan. This one granted access to the bench itself, and Reyes felt a twinge in his gut as Admiral Gillian Moratino and a trio of male officers filed into the room.

"All rise," the Vulcan said, her voice neutral yet firm. Behind her, the officers moved to stand before the bench's four seats. All were human, all ranked commodore or higher. The board's other three members were men, none of whom Reyes recognized. One of the two admirals was an older man, with stark white hair and pale, wrinkled features, while the other was much younger and of

Latino heritage. The panel's lone commodore was a weathered
Asian man, who peered at Reyes over a pair of anachronistic rim-
less eyeglasses.

"All persons having business with this general court-martial,"
the lieutenant continued, "stand forward, and you shall be heard.
The Honorable Gillian Kei Moratino presiding."

Despite the weeks of confinement, along with the long days
and nights spent in conference with Desai, the idea of facing an
actual court-martial had seemed somehow surreal to Reyes. Only
now, as Admiral Moratino reached for the wooden striker resting
on the bench and used it to tap the ancient ship's bell before her,
did it finally hit home that this was really going to happen. He
was about to be tried by a board of his peers and, if found guilty
of the charges against him, likely be sentenced to prison for a
considerable portion of whatever life remained to him.

Too late to cry about it now.

"This court is now in session," Moratino said, directing her gaze
to Desai and Sereb. "Commodore Reyes has provided an official
statement, which has been read to the board members and entered
into the official record. Does counsel wish to raise any objection?"

"No objection, your honor," Sereb replied. Desai shook her
head, repeating the Tellarite's answer.

Moratino next turned to Reyes. "Commodore Reyes, the
board for your trial currently consists of Admiral Franklin Komack, Commodore Jeong Hynu-Su, and Admiral Alejandro
Perez. Do you object to the selection of any of these officers serving in this capacity?"

"No, Admiral," Reyes said, staring straight ahead. Of the four
officers making up his court-martial board, only Admiral Komack possessed any knowledge of Operation Vanguard prior to
his selection for this trial. The admiral was not in the project's
chain of command and was therefore deemed capable of remaining impartial in this matter.

Nodding, Moratino asked, "Do you have any objections to
Captain Sereb serving as prosecuting attorney or to myself as
president of this court?"

"None, Your Honor."

Hell of a time to ask.

"Very well," Moratino said. Looking down to the young Vulcan, she prompted, "Lieutenant T'Nir."

Standing as she had since first taking up her station by the computer interface, her face impassive as she looked toward the rear of the courtroom, T'Nir said, "Charge: willful disobedience of a superior officer. Specification: in that on stardate 1528.4, Commodore Diego Reyes did defy standing orders by revealing classified information to unauthorized personnel. Charge: releasing classified Starfleet intelligence data to unauthorized personnel. Specification: in that Commodore Reyes did allow a member of the press to distribute to the Federation News Service restricted information vital to the interests of Federation security, with that information being published via public news outlets. Charge: conspiracy in the second degree. Specification: in that Commodore Reyes, through purposeful action or lack of action and with knowledge aforethought, did allow unauthorized persons to disseminate classified information."

Reyes stood silent as the charges were entered into the trial's official record, each word cutting into him with the unforgiving torment of a dulled blade. Everything he had once upheld as right and proper, every oath he had ever sworn, seemed to fall to dust in the face of the blunt, cold offenses of which he now was accused.

"Commodore Reyes has entered a plea of guilty to the charge of willful disobedience," Moratino said after the charges were entered, "and not guilty to the remaining charges. Does the commodore wish to change his plea?"

He saw out of the corner of his eye that Desai was looking to him, but Reyes did not turn his attention from the bench. "No, Your Honor."

The admiral nodded. "Very well. The plea of guilty for the charge of willful disobedience is so entered and accepted. You may all be seated." Once everyone had taken a seat, Moratino looked to Sereb. "Captain, is the prosecution prepared to make its opening statement?"

Sereb once again rose to his feet. "I am, Your Honor." The Tellarite moved toward the witness stand, a lone chair on a small dais at the center of the courtroom.

"Members of the court, the facts of this case are straightforward. Commodore Reyes ignored his obligation to superior officers in his chain of command, defying their lawful orders and instead taking matters of Federation security into his own hands." His attention focused on the bench, he began to walk a circuit around the stand, gesturing with his pudgy arms as he talked. "He did so without regard for the larger, sweeping ramifications, not only to the Federation itself but also to our allies and even our enemies. By allowing the disclosure of classified information about ongoing Starfleet operations and interests in the Taurus Reach, Commodore Reyes may well have triggered an upset in the balance of power, the consequences of which likely will be felt for years to come. His actions reflect immense discredit not only upon himself but also upon all of Starfleet and, indeed, the United Federation of Planets."

He had tried to prepare himself for the impact Sereb's opening remarks would have on him, but Reyes still felt his anger rise as he listened to the lawyer's cold, stark assessment about what he had allowed to happen.

I didn't allow *it to happen,* he reminded himself. *I made it happen. I wanted it to happen.* He felt the unbridled need to scream the words. *It was necessary. It was right.*

Perhaps it was, perhaps not. Would any of that matter, or would the truth—not about what he had done but *why* he had done it—be just another obstacle for Captain Sereb as the attorney pushed the court-martial toward a conviction?

Glancing toward Desai, who, like the board members, appeared to be hanging on the Tellarite's every word, Reyes could not help the pang of doubt that began without warning to gnaw at him.

Rana's got her work cut out for her.

33

The ancient computer interface crackled to life, filling the subterranean chamber with the echo of a moderate hum beginning to radiate from somewhere within the millennia-old equipment.

"I'll be damned," said Lieutenant Commander Mahmud al-Khaled as he stood next to Ming Xiong, observing the proceedings. Beneath his feet, the leader of the *U.S.S. Lovell's* Starfleet Corps of Engineers detachment could feel a low vibration coursing through the cavern's stone floor. Somewhere, underneath however many meters of solid rock, something was happening as a result of their efforts in this room. "Any idea what it's doing?"

His head poking out from the neck of his Starfleet-issue field parka, Xiong did not look up as he studied his tricorder. "Whatever it is, it's very localized. I'm only detecting power readings within a sphere of less than one hundred meters."

"That's barely enough to account for this complex," al-Khaled said, watching the steam from his breath as he spoke. "At least the parts we know about, anyway. Still, it's a start." Despite the warmth generated by the portable heaters they had brought from the *Lovell,* the cavern maintained a bone-chilling cold.

Standing at the console, Nezrene appeared to be leaning against it for support, but al-Khaled had quickly realized that the Tholian was, in fact, adopting a posture that allowed her greater access to several contact points embedded within the console's onyx crystal surface. Those points were all but invisible to the naked eye, but Xiong had learned how to identify them with Nezrene's assistance. Beneath the Tholian's appendages, numerous controls and displays—all obviously designed for physiologies quite different from that of humans—now were visible, emanating from within the console itself. Along the wall before Nezrene, other displays were active, also ensconced within another slab of the enigmatic opaque crystal. Unlike the tactile interfaces to which al-Khaled was accustomed and which he, in fact, preferred, nothing like that existed here. Everything was contained inside the dark panels, which, for the most part, resisted scanning attempts and foiled any efforts to create technical schematics of the equipment's interior components.

"Nezrene," Xiong said, stepping closer, "are you feeling anything? Sensing any kind of reaction?"

The Tholian replied, "I am aware of increased power generation. Our access attempts have apparently resulted in the execution of some form of standard activation protocol. I am detecting what I perceive to be limited instructions being conveyed from this interface to other nodes, all of which are engaging in their own initiation procedures."

"Start-up diagnostics?" al-Khaled asked. "That would make sense, especially since most of this equipment hasn't been in operation for thousands of years." He paused, then added, "Well, except for what happened the last time we were here."

"Don't remind me," Xiong said. "It took me days to stop shaking, and it wasn't because of the cold."

Al-Khaled nodded, recalling vividly the events of the *Lovell*'s last visit to Erilon. Working with Xiong, the ship's engineering cadre had spent several days on the surface of this icebound world, the majority of that time within this same set of caverns. When the mysterious Shedai entity had arrived, seemingly from nowhere, and commenced attacking the landing party, only some last-minute, panic-stricken ingenuity on the part of al-Khaled and other *Lovell* engineers had saved the entire Starfleet contingent from being annihilated.

A beep sounded from one of the pockets in his own parka, and al-Khaled removed the glove on his right hand in order to retrieve his communicator. Flipping open the unit's antenna grid, he said, "Al-Khaled here."

"How's the weather down there?" asked the voice of the *Lovell*'s commanding officer, Captain Daniel Okagawa.

"Balmy," al-Khaled replied. "We're thinking of going out for a picnic later this afternoon, once the temperature makes it to within ten points of a positive number."

The sound of Okagawa chuckling was hollow and indistinct when channeled through the communicator's speaker grille. *"Well, according to the readings we're getting up here, you might just be able to do that. There's been some kind of power-generation equipment come online in just the last few minutes, fifty-nine meters below your present location."*

Exchanging surprised expressions with Xiong, al-Khaled said, "Really? What are we talking about?"

"Nothing too crazy," Okagawa replied. *"We've been able to confirm that it's not the same system we detected the last time we were here. Whatever it is, it doesn't appear connected to the global defense system, or whatever it was that almost blew up the planet. So, thanks for not doing that."*

"It's early yet. Give us time."

Al-Khaled paused as Xiong stepped closer and gestured toward the communicator. After holding it up for his friend, the lieutenant asked, "Captain, are you able to determine what the active systems are? We're not getting anything that detailed down here."

"At first blush, it looks as if it might be a computer or communications system. Maybe both. We're picking up what we think are attempts by individual computer nodes to connect to a central hub and to each other, including the equipment at your location."

Now Xiong looked pleased. "If that's true, then it's the biggest breakthrough we've had yet. Learning how to interface with such a system may well be the key to getting control of everything on the planet. After that, we may eventually learn to interface with companion systems on other worlds."

"That is unlikely," Nezrene said, calling out from where she still stood at the Shedai console. "Without the guidance and control from the First World, there are no Conduits, no pathways to link the worlds that once made up the Shedai realm."

"First World?" Okagawa repeated. *"Does she mean Jinoteur IV?"*

Xiong nodded. "That's correct, sir. Jinoteur is the key. Or, rather, was the key. With the system gone, we have no way of knowing whether the network that once connected their planets can be reestablished, or if there might be another planet somewhere in the Taurus Reach capable of providing the same function and control."

"One step at a time," al-Khaled said, holding up his free hand. "Let's not get ahead of ourselves. We can't do anything until we prove we even have real access to anything on this rock. Nezrene, are you able to confirm what the *Lovell* sensors are picking up? What is it you think you're tapping into?"

"I believe your captain is right," the Tholian replied after a moment spent in silent communion with the console. "I am seeing communications pathways, both for connecting to other locations on this planet and for broadcasting into space. Some of it is easy to understand, though there are other aspects of the system that I am unable to transcribe."

"Can you access any of those pathways?" Xiong asked, and when he spoke, al-Khaled heard the excitement in the younger man's voice.

Nezrene nodded, or at least affected the Tholian equivalent. "I believe so." Her left appendage moved to rest on another area of the console, and her movements became still for a moment, during which several displays on the crystal wall before her flared to life. Strings of incomprehensible script scrolled past, almost too fast for al-Khaled's eyes to follow. Then Nezrene said, "I believe I have found one such pathway."

An instant later, Okagawa's voice came over al-Khaled's communicator. *"We're picking up a new signal, Mahmud. From up here, it looks as though the computer node at your location is trying to connect to other nodes in the planetary network. So far, we're not seeing that it's having any success."*

"It could be something as simple as not employing the correct communications protocol," al-Khaled offered. "Nezrene, are you able to see anything? Where are you—in the system, I mean?"

It took an extra moment before the Tholian replied, "I must admit, this is fascinating. If I concentrate and focus my thoughts on the tasks, I can see them being carried out within the network. It is as though I am traveling the pathways myself, moving from one point to another in the system."

"Just as you suspected, Ming," al-Khaled said, smiling. "This could be it; we may have finally found our way in."

Though appearing satisfied at their progress, Xiong still seemed skeptical. "It took us four days to make it this far." He frowned, shaking his head. "We need more time."

"You've got three more days," Okagawa said over the communicator. *"After that, my orders are to pack up this field trip and get you back to Vanguard. We're here on borrowed time as it is."*

Al-Khaled nodded in agreement. That Admiral Nogura had—over the strenuous objections of Ambassador Jetanien—authorized Nezrene to travel with the *Lovell* to Erilon was but one complication to this mission. If the Tholian Assembly learned that its compatriot had fled the station that had provided him sanctuary, it might feel compelled to extradite her, possibly by force. For that reason, Nezrene's presence on the *Lovell* and her departure from Starbase 47 had been kept tightly guarded secrets.

There also was the *Lovell* itself to consider. With the *Endeavour* out on security patrol and the *Sagittarius* too small for Nogura to consider for a mission of this type, it had fallen to the all-but-ancient *Daedalus*-class vessel to transport Xiong, his team, and his equipment to Erilon. Despite the array of improvements and upgrades to which it had been subjected, the *Lovell* was nothing close to a ship of the line. It would stand no realistic chance against enemy attack. Still, in Nogura's mind, the gains for carrying out Xiong's research had outweighed the risks. The admiral had therefore approved a brief expedition back to the frozen planet, which had been chosen for its proximity to the station as well as the fact that Xiong, al-Khaled, and their teams were familiar with the layout of this Shedai structure.

"We'll make the most of the time we have left," Xiong said, "but we're just scratching the surface here. Even if we can gain further access, we still don't know the language of the computer software, assuming that the Shedai developed their technology along the concepts of hardware and software. It could take us months to decipher any meaningful portion of it."

"You can do that back on Vanguard," Okagawa countered. *"Make recordings of everything, and if there's something we can haul back with us, tell Mahmud, and they'll start disassembling the place."*

"Understood, Captain," al-Khaled said, cutting off any further protest from Xiong. "Al-Khaled out." He pocketed the communicator and patted Xiong on the shoulder. "Don't worry about it. We've done some good work here, and we've still got a few days, so let's make them count. After all, we don't know when we might make it back here."

Xiong nodded, and al-Khaled saw the concern in his friend's eyes. "Yeah. That's what worries me. That, and wondering if the Klingons will figure this out before we do."

34

Pennington bounded up the steps to the main floor of Sobon's home, where he found M'Benga sitting on a decorative stone bench before a small garden. Like Pennington, the doctor was dressed in a light brown soft suit like those typically worn by Vulcans who spent great periods of time in the unforgiving desert. The clothing's color was such that M'Benga almost blended in with the garden's serene surroundings.

"You sent for me, mate?" Pennington asked. "Tell me you've found where they hide the swimming pool in this place."

Turning from where he had been examining the garden's array of plants, M'Benga replied, "Afraid not." He rose from the bench, brushing his hands together. "Sinar tells me we have a visitor."

"We?" Pennington asked. "As in you and me? Who would be coming to see us here, of all places?"

"That's the question, isn't it?" M'Benga indicated for Pennington to follow him. "Sinar said she'd be waiting in Sobon's study."

Falling into stride alongside the doctor, Pennington said, "Speaking of Sobon, how's he doing? Rough night last night."

M'Benga nodded. "I'm told he's resting. That last meld took even more out of him than the first one."

"I figured it would be hard," Pennington said as they proceeded down the hallway toward the elder Vulcan's study. "I just didn't think it would be so hard. On him or on her."

He and M'Benga had not been allowed into T'Prynn's room during Sobon's latest attempt to meld with her the previous eve-

ning, but they had not needed to wait long to learn the results of
the Vulcan's efforts. As on the first evening, Sobon had emerged
from the meld visibly shaken and physically weakened, requiring
the assistance of Sinar even to go back to his bedchamber.

"Apparently," M'Benga said, "this Sten has embedded himself so far into T'Prynn's mind that he's become part of her, as
vital to her existence as her own consciousness. If I understood
Sobon correctly, simply going in with the idea of removing him
as a single piece, if you will, won't work. The way he describes it,
he's executing a series of 'probing' melds with T'Prynn, as a
means of helping her to erect mental barriers or finding places to
hide within her mind, away from his attacks. It also somehow
involves diverting Sten's *katra*. To me, it sounds as if he's sending
it away, making it chase shadows, whatever." Shaking his head,
he added, "I don't understand any of it, but in order for her to
achieve peace, Sten will have to be forcibly driven from her.
That's what the *Dashaya-Ni'Var* ritual is supposed to accomplish."

They came to the door leading into Sobon's study, and Pennington slid aside the bolt securing it. He stepped into the room
and stopped as he came face-to-face with T'Prynn.

"What in the name of . . . ?" he began, feeling his jaw slacken
before he caught himself.

"Greetings," offered the Vulcan woman standing before them.
"I am T'Nel."

On closer inspection, Pennington realized that this, of course,
was not T'Prynn, though the resemblance was remarkable. She
was somewhat older, but Pennington noted the similar soft lines
of the woman's jaw. The same dark hair was arranged in a shorter
style, which likely was practical for the Vulcan desert environment. Her eyes were a different color, much darker, though they
peered at him with the same power and focus he recalled from his
encounters with T'Prynn.

Stepping around Pennington, M'Benga said, "Hello. I'm
Dr. Jabilo M'Benga, and this is my friend, Timothy Pennington.
We were told you wanted to see us."

T'Nel nodded. "I am T'Prynn's older sibling. Healer Sobon sent for me upon your arrival, as he believes I may be of some assistance."

"You live here, in the commune?" M'Benga asked, looking around for a place to sit but foiled at every turn by more of Sobon's books, scrolls, and other papers.

"No," T'Nel replied. "I live in the village of Ha'tren, several kilometers from here, though T'Prynn and I did live here for a time."

Gesturing toward the door, M'Benga said, "Would you care to walk outside?" To Pennington, he said, "It's not too hot yet."

"That is acceptable." As the trio moved back into the corridor, T'Nel said, "In our youth, we were quite satisfied living here. I mentored under Healer Sobon, and T'Prynn followed her interests in botanical and agricultural sciences. Indeed, many of the gardens around the commune were first planted by her."

Pennington smiled at the images that suggested. "I never pictured T'Prynn as having a green thumb. Somehow, I like that."

"The pigmentation of T'Prynn's thumb is the same as the rest of her epidermis," T'Nel said, "though I suppose the pigmentation of Vulcan blood might evoke such a description. Still, it is somewhat inaccurate."

They emerged from the main entrance to Sobon's home and into the courtyard that formed the commune's center. Outside, Pennington saw a few villagers tending to gardens or washing clothes by hand in large stone basins. Two younger Vulcan males were working on a roof, replacing what looked like clay shingles. As M'Benga had promised, it was warm, but the heat of the day was still a few hours away.

His eyes tracked along the high stone wall that formed the village's perimeter—installed, Pennington was told, to prevent entry by any of the "predators" M'Benga had mentioned on their first night here—and then he turned to look to the south at the heavy wrought-iron gate that was the commune's main entrance. Beyond the threshold and just visible on the left side of the gateway was the nose of the Starfleet shuttlecraft that had been sitting there since the first morning Pennington and M'Benga had spent here. The Starfleet security personnel who had arrived in the shuttle were polite enough, as Pennington had discovered when he walked to the gate to investigate their arrival. According to the lieutenant who was the team's leader, an attractive blonde with an Australian accent and an apparent invulnerability to every bit of charm Pennington had been able to muster, the detail had been sent to ensure that T'Prynn remained in the village, at least until such time as she was declared medically able to travel. They, of course, were forbidden to enter the village without permission, but that did not stop them from monitoring the comings and go-ings of the residents.

"How delightfully fascist," Pennington had observed during that first morning, earning a disapproving glare from the attractive young lieutenant.

Now, turning his attention back to T'Nel, he asked, "I under-stand that you're a healer?"

"That is correct," she said, clasping her hands behind her back as the trio began to walk a circuit around the courtyard. "Though I am not nearly as accomplished as Healer Sobon. Still, the *Dashaya-Ni'Var* will require two healers working in concert, and he feels my familial connection to T'Prynn may be of some benefit."

"So," M'Benga said, "you're obviously familiar with what happened to her."

"I was there when it happened." T'Nel paused, nodding to one of the workers tending to a garden as they walked past. "T'Prynn and Sten were betrothed as children, as is customary among our people, though she always resisted that tradition. She always was rather conflicted, expending much energy trying to reconcile what she perceived as inconsistencies in our culture. Though Vulcans are taught from a very early age that they possess the right as individuals to make their own life choices, several of our most time-honored traditions seem at odds with this philosophy. Marriage, of course, is one such tradition, and T'Prynn never was able to come to terms with the idea of marrying Sten."

"She resisted him?" Pennington asked, frowning. "Turned him down?"

T'Nel replied, "In a manner of speaking. She lived here for a time, as a youth, learning under Healer Sobon's tutelage and trying to come to terms with those facets of our society with which she had taken such fervent issue. For a while, she was at peace, and when the time came for her and Sten to be united in matrimony, T'Prynn asked Sten to release her from their bond. He had always loved her, had always wanted her, but to T'Prynn, he seemed too controlling, too dominating. It was not what she wanted from a marriage, and after his refusal to release her, she challenged him to ritual combat in order to fight for her release."

"Koon-ut-kal-if-fee," M'Benga said. "Marriage or challenge."

"Yes," T'Nel confirmed. She said nothing for a moment, then turned so that she faced Pennington and M'Benga. "You understand that these are not matters normally discussed with outworlders, but Sobon has spoken for your trustworthiness."

"I'm her doctor," M'Benga said. "I want to help her, any way that I can. To do that, I need to understand things that I admit are beyond my expertise."

Resuming their walk, T'Nel said, "That is logical. During the challenge, when they were in physical contact, T'Prynn was winning the combat. He was near death, at her hand, when Sten initiated the meld. He knew he was about to die, and in his last moments of life, he forced his *katra* into her mind. The meld was interrupted when T'Prynn killed him. Since that day, she has been *val'reth*."

"My God." Pennington shook his head as he tried to imagine what T'Nel was describing.

T'Nel said, "In the years following the meld, T'Prynn was able to erect and maintain mental shields to combat Sten's *katra*, but keeping those in place required much effort. Now it appears that those barriers have failed, and she and Sten are once more locked in mortal combat. Essentially, they are struggling for control of her mind. She attempted to find a cure for her condition, of course, but none was to be found. Finally, she chose to leave Vulcan, for reasons that remain known only to her. I have not seen her since that time."

"Fifty years of fighting off that bastard," Pennington said, feeling overwhelmed by what he had just heard. What must it be like, he wondered, trying to live with the essence of another person living inside one's own mind, dueling with whatever it was that defined one as an individual? The very notion was too much to take in, at least not all at once.

His eyes shifting to the dozen or so *vre-katra* scattered among the books and other items on the shelves of Sobon's study, he asked, "T'Nel, this ritual Sobon is trying, do you think it can work?"

"I admit that I am unfamiliar with the *Dashaya-Ni'Var*," T'Nel replied. "It comes from a time before Surak, and there are no accounts of its practice in modern times. Most adepts will not even acknowledge its existence. I suspect that only a small number of healers and adepts possess the mental skill required to carry out the ritual, and even fewer would be willing to risk such an undertaking. Fortunately, Sobon is one such individual."

"What will happen if Sobon isn't successful?" M'Benga asked.

Once more, T'Nel paused, and Pennington noted the slight shift in her otherwise passive expression. There was something new just beneath the surface of her composed veneer. Resignation, perhaps? Pennington could not be sure.

"T'Prynn has spent many years battling Sten. She has never yielded. She never will yield. If the *Dashaya-Ni'Var* proves unsuccessful, I believe T'Prynn will continue the fight within her mind so long as she is able."

She did not say it, but Pennington knew what came next. T'Prynn would never submit to Sten. She would die for that choice, and she would die fighting, trapped within the inescapable confines of her own mind.

35

"Ensign Ribiero, please describe to the court your primary duties."

From where he sat at the table he shared with Rana Desai, Commodore Reyes watched as Captain Sereb, once again in full theatrical mode, circled the small dais on which sat Ensign Gisela Ribiero, one of Starbase 47's junior communications officers. Though she faced away from him and toward Admiral Moratino and the other board members, Reyes still could see the nervousness and uncertainty wracking the young ensign's body. He doubted that her short career in Starfleet had been sufficient to prepare Ribiero for anything as disconcerting as the court-martial of her commanding officer.

Trial by fire, kid. I'm sorry about that.

"I'm assigned to the station's primary communications control center," she replied, hints of her native Portuguese still evident as she spoke. "We handle the receipt of all incoming communications, both real-time and prerecorded."

Behind her, as he paced a circuit around the dais, Sereb asked, "And as part of your duties, are you not often tasked with the screening of all communications to ensure that they do not violate station security protocols?"

Ribiero nodded. "Yes, sir."

"In particular, are you tasked with ensuring that incoming and outgoing civilian communications traffic complies with these security protocols?"

"That's correct, sir."

Leaning to his right so that he could speak almost directly into

Desai's left ear, Reyes whispered, "He loves the buildup, doesn't he?"

Desai's only response was a muted grunt, her gaze never wavering from the proceedings unfolding before her.

It had gone this way for the past two days, with Sereb calling witnesses and starting out with the mundane, matter-of-fact questions to lay groundwork for the line of questioning he actually wanted to pursue. The senior staff had been called to testify during the first two days of the trial, and all of them had offered little to nothing in the way of damaging testimony. The reasoning for this was simple, in that Reyes had acted to insulate all of them from any fallout from his decisions and actions. Therefore, Commander Cooper and the rest of the command staff had been unable to speak to any direct action Reyes had taken in violation of Starfleet regulations.

However, Sereb still had managed to find some way to make even the most innocuous statements appear damning toward Reyes, establishing a pattern of apparent secretive conduct and furtive conspiring to undermine the lawful operation of the station and its crew. Because none of his people knew anything about what Reyes was doing, he must have been acting with deliberate intent to circumvent regulations and protocols. While Desai had objected several times during different rounds of questioning and Admiral Moratino had sustained some of those objections, Sereb still had done his job, sowing the seeds of doubt in the minds of the court's board members.

He's a crafty bastard, Reyes thought. *I'll give him that.*

"Ensign," Sereb said, now pausing to stand before Ribiero, "you are currently assigned to Gamma Shift, are you not?"

Again, Ribiero nodded. "Yes, sir."

"Gamma Shift is the least busy, in that it is scheduled from twenty-three hundred hours to oh-seven-hundred hours the following morning, correct?"

"Yes, sir."

The burly Tellarite looked up from his questioning, locking eyes with Reyes for a moment, and the commodore was certain that the smug blowhard might have smiled at him if he had not chosen instead to continue his pacing. "As such, is it typical to receive visits to the communications center by members of the station's command staff?"

"Objection," Desai said, rising from her seat. "Calls for speculation."

Moratino nodded. "A bit borderline, Captain, but I'll sustain."

Clearing his throat, Sereb said, "I'll rephrase the question. Ensign Ribiero, for what reasons might a member of the station's command staff visit the communications center?"

"There are occasions when Commodore Reyes or Commander Cooper has been handling some urgent matter and wishes to oversee communications directly. There have also been instances when one of them has to provide an eyes-only decryption key for an encoded message from Starfleet Command. Things like that."

Sereb, pacing again, waved his right arm. "So, suffice it to say that such visits are not the norm."

Oh, for God's sake, just get on with it, already. Despite the exasperation he was beginning to feel at this latest example of Sereb's courtroom drama, Reyes forced himself to remain still, his hands clasped before him on the table while maintaining a stoic expression, just as Desai also was doing.

"Walk us through the events of stardate 1528.4, Ensign," Sereb said. "You were on duty in the communications center. At approximately oh-three-hundred hours, who else was present?"

Knowing where this was going, Ribiero faltered for a moment and even cast a glance over her shoulder toward Reyes, which earned her a stern glare from Sereb before she answered, "I was alone, sir. It was my turn to stand watch while the others were taking their mid-shift meal break. The first one back would relieve me so I could go and eat. It's standard practice, sir."

"So, you were alone at oh-three-hundred hours," Sereb said, continuing to pace. Looking toward Reyes again, he continued, "And did you receive a visit on this evening?"

Ribiero nodded. "Yes, sir. Commodore Reyes entered the center and asked me how things were going."

"And how *were* things going?"

Even from his angle behind and to the left of her, Reyes saw Ribiero's jaw tighten. She did not appreciate this game, either. "They were fine, sir. They're always fine at that time of night."

Sereb grunted. "What happened next?"

"The commodore ordered me to take my meal break, sir."

Pausing before the trial board, Sereb directed an expression of feigned astonishment to the board members before turning toward Reyes and Desai. "He ordered you away from your post?"

"Not exactly, sir," Ribiero replied. "He said that he had a classified message to transmit and that it was urgent and eyes-only and that it would be recorded in the official log as such. It's happened before, sir."

"So, you're saying the commodore makes a habit of circumventing security protocols with regard to classified communications?"

That brought Desai out of her chair again. "Objection, Your Honor. Calls for speculation."

"Sustained," Moratino replied. "Captain Sereb, watch your footing here."

"I apologize, Your Honor," Sereb said before returning his attention to Ribiero. "Ensign, Commodore Reyes ordered you away from the communications center so that he might transmit a classified message. Did he offer any clues to the nature of the message, the receiving party, or whether he might require assistance?"

Ribiero shook her head. "No, sir. The commodore is familiar with our equipment."

"Did you take this opportunity to remind him of station security procedures with respect to communications?"

"Yes, sir, I did, but Commodore Reyes provided an authorized override code that allows him to bypass such restrictions."

Again, Sereb paused, this time holding up one pudgy finger. "Ah, his command override authority. As I understand such protocols, they're normally reserved for emergencies, are they not?"

"That's correct, sir." The ensign now was visibly nervous, doing her best to maintain her bearing. Reyes felt nothing but sympathy for her. It was not her fault that she sat before these officers in this way. She had done her duty in every measurable respect. He wanted to stand and shout that to the board members, wanted to cram the words down Sereb's throat, but even as the thoughts festered in his mind, he felt the gentle touch of Desai's hand on his arm, warning him to stay seated and keep his mouth shut.

"Yes, sir, and the commodore informed me that there was such an emergency."

Sereb glared at her. "And you took him at his word?"

The question seemed to take Ribiero off guard, but for the first time, she seemed willing to push back, if only a little. "Of course I did," she said, a slight edge creeping into her voice. "I had no reason to suspect he'd be lying."

"No, of course not," the Tellarite replied. "You were carrying out your duties, as was expected of you. You had every reason to trust that your commanding officer was doing the same, rather than using his rank and position to carry out illegal acts under cover of official business."

"Objection," Desai snapped, pushing herself to her feet. "Your Honor, is the prosecution asking a question or providing editorial commentary?"

"Sustained," Moratino said, and this time, there was no mistaking the irritation in the admiral's voice. "Captain Sereb, my patience is beginning to wear thin."

The prosecutor nodded. "Understood, Your Honor." To Ribiero, he said, "Ensign, as of this moment, do you know the contents of the message Commodore Reyes sent from the communications center?"

"No, sir," Ribiero replied.

"Isn't there a record of the message in the comm center log?"

The ensign shook her head. "Not of the message itself, sir. Just a record that the message was transmitted, the time and date of the transmission, and the sending and receiving parties."

Sereb asked, "And who were the sending and receiving parties?"

When Ribiero paused this time, Reyes knew she did not want to answer and why. She drew a deep breath before replying, "The sender is listed as Timothy Pennington, and the recipient was the Federation News Service." Even though Reyes knew what the response would be, the words spoken aloud were like kicks to his gut.

Seemingly satisfied with that answer, and perhaps desiring to quit while he was ahead, Sereb turned to the board members. "Your Honor, I have no further questions for this witness."

"Very well." Moratino looked to Desai. "Does defense wish to cross-examine?"

Rising once more from her chair, Desai replied, "No, Your Honor." Reyes thought he sensed a hint of resignation lacing the words.

"You may step down, Ensign," the admiral said. She spent a moment writing something before reaching for the striker. "We'll stand in recess until ten hundred hours tomorrow. Court is adjourned." She rapped the ship's bell, and Lieutenant T'Nir rose from her place just in front of the bench.

"All rise," called the Vulcan as everyone stood and waited for Moratino and the rest of the board to file out of the room. Once they were gone, T'Nir deactivated the computer terminal next to her chair before leaving the room.

Reyes stood silent, staring straight ahead and waiting until Sereb left the courtroom before even turning to Desai. "I really hate this, you know."

"I know," Desai replied, gathering her materials. "But it's necessary if you want your chance on the stand."

"My people don't deserve to be dragged through this," Reyes said. "They don't even know what most of this is about, and I made sure none of them was put in a position to have to do or say anything against regs. Sereb knows that."

Desai sighed. "Of course, he knows that. Remember, the facts aren't in dispute here. All he can do is attempt to demonstrate the scope of what you've done. Since you took steps to protect everyone, all he can do is illustrate that by having all of the witnesses testify that they don't know anything. He's marking time until we switch to the defense phase. That's when he'll cut loose, and you know he's just drooling at the chance to come after you."

"I have that effect on people." Reyes said as the pair of security guards assigned to escort him back to his quarters stepped forward from where they had been standing at the courtroom's rear wall. With them falling into step behind him, Reyes and Desai exited the room, and he paused as he saw Jetanien and Fisher waiting in the corridor.

"Hello, Diego," the ambassador said, bowing in greeting.

"What are you two doing loitering around here?" Reyes asked. He actually was glad to see his two friends.

"We're here to offer moral support," Fisher said. "And if that's not enough, I have a bottle of twelve-year-old scotch I've been saving for a special occasion."

Glancing over his shoulder at his security escorts, Reyes said, "I'm pretty sure I'm not allowed to throw any wild parties while I'm confined to quarters."

"Is there a better time?" Fisher asked. "Don't worry. We've already received approval from Admiral Moratino for a one-hour visit later this evening. Assuming you want the company, that is."

As they began walking up the corridor toward a bank of turbolifts, Reyes asked, "Is this really a good idea? It sounds like the kind of thing they let a condemned man do on his last night."

"Perish your negative thoughts, Diego," Jetanien said, his voice carrying more than a minor rebuke. "Captain Desai has comported herself with distinction to this point, and I have no doubts she will rise to the occasion when the trial turns to the defense."

Looking over her shoulder at the Chel, Desai asked, "How do you know how I'm comporting anything? I haven't seen you in the courtroom."

"My dear, I know everything," Jetanien replied. "Just as I know that there are very few people who possess the unique understanding of the situation here in the Taurus Reach that is required to run this station and oversee its mission. Diego is one such individual." To Reyes, he said, "I firmly believe that you will play a significant role in any success we hope to have out here."

Uncomfortable with dwelling on that line of thought, Reyes sought to change the subject. "I hear you've had your own hands full," he said, eyeing the ambassador. Then, nodding toward his friend's manus, he added, "Or whatever you call those things."

Jetanien uttered a string of clicks that echoed in the passageway. "Indeed, it has not been easy for people in my line of work these past weeks. The Klingons are on the move everywhere, it seems, and the Tholians naturally are proving to be most uncooperative."

Shaking his head, Reyes said, "I don't know how you do it, Jetanien."

"What do you mean?" the ambassador asked.

"I mean juggling so many balls and keeping them all in the air. It's quite a sight to see, you know." He had always been impressed with Jetanien's ability to handle multiple issues, particularly when it came to the nonstop head-to-head game of interplanetary politics, but recent events had tasked even his formidable abilities. Diplomacy was easy when everyone got along, but it was an altogether different animal when things were not quite so picturesque. "You're trying to do the impossible, and it's fun watching you try."

"I'm trying to do the impossible, too, you know," Desai said, punching him playfully in the arm.

Reyes nodded. "It's fun watching you, too."

They came to the row of five turbolifts, and Jetanien and Fisher hung back as Reyes, Desai, and the security detail moved to enter one of the available cars. Pausing at the threshold, Reyes turned to regard his friends. "Listen, I think I'd enjoy that visit." It was the first time since his incarceration had begun that he had requested to see anyone. Even his meetings with Desai during their preparations had been at her bidding. "A change of pace might do me some good."

"Now you're talking," Fisher said, unable to suppress a grin. "And I'll have my scotch in hand."

Jetanien added, "I cannot promise any special vintage spirits, but I do have a vat of—"

Reyes held up a hand. "Don't even say it, whatever it is."

"Well," the ambassador said, "there's simply no accounting for taste."

That elicited a small laugh from Reyes as he boarded the turbolift. "Nineteen hundred hours. You know the address." As the doors slid shut and the lift began to move, he turned to look at Desai.

"You know, for a minute there, I was able to forget about all of this."

Desai smiled. "Good. That's what friends are supposed to help you do."

As the turbolift continued its ascent through the core of the station, Reyes stood in silence, contemplating what Jetanien had said moments earlier. Could he still play a role here, despite all that had happened? Was Starfleet of a mind to forgive his transgressions in the interest of ensuring that the best possible people were employed here, working to unlock the mysteries upon which they had stumbled?

Possible, he decided, *but not damned likely.*

36

"I am Commander Restrene. You are trespassing in a territorial annex of the Tholian Assembly. You must leave this area immediately."

Rising from his seat at the center of the *Lovell*'s bridge, Captain Daniel Okagawa regarded the visage of the Tholian commander now displayed on the main viewer. The Tholian appeared as a bright crimson silhouette standing out against a roiling amber background, the air around it shimmering as a result of the extreme temperature requirements necessary to sustain Tholian physiology.

"Shields activated, weapons armed and ready, Captain," reported Lieutenant Jessica Diamond, the *Lovell*'s weapons officer, from one of the rear bridge stations. "Though I have to tell you, Captain, I think we may be a bit outclassed here."

"Don't remind me," Okagawa said before gesturing toward Folanir Pzial, the Rigelian ensign seated at the communications console. "Open the channel." Once Pzial nodded to indicate that the connection had been established, Okagawa turned his attention back to the viewer. "This is Captain Daniel Okagawa, commanding the Federation *Starship Lovell*. Commander, this planet has been claimed as Federation territory, and we are engaged in a peaceful scientific research mission on the surface."

"Please do not insult our intelligence by maintaining this ridiculous charade, Captain," Restrene replied. *"We both are aware of the Federation's true interest in this planet. Further, we know that you currently are harboring a known fugitive. You will surrender that fugitive and depart this system immediately, or we will be forced to take punitive action."*

He kept his expression neutral, but Okagawa cursed inwardly. How in the name of hell did they know that Nezrene was with them?

"They're always so cheerful and friendly, aren't they?" asked Commander Araev zh'Rhun, Okagawa's first officer, from where she stood on the other side of the command chair, speaking in a voice low enough not to be picked up by the comm system.

Eyeing his Andorian exec, Okagawa replied, "You're one to talk." Turning back to the viewer, he said, "Commander, I will not lie to you. A Tholian citizen is with us, and she is aiding my people in the research we are conducting."

"Then she is committing treason against the Tholian people," Restrene countered. *"Another charge added to her list of crimes. You will transfer her to our custody, Captain."*

Okagawa glanced down at the astrogator before him at the center of the helm and navigation console, noting its depiction of the trio of Tholian ships and their relation to his ship's current position. The ships dropped out of warp almost on top of the *Lovell*, exiting subspace within the orbital track of Erilon's only moon. There barely had been time for sensors to register their approach and opportunity enough only to warn the landing parties down on the planet that trouble was brewing in orbit. Okagawa had ordered an evacuation, but less than half of the personnel on the surface had been transported aboard before the Tholian ships arrived on the scene and assumed an offensive combat formation around the Starfleet vessel.

After drawing a deep breath and knowing how his response likely would be received, Okagawa said, "With all due respect, Commander, I can't do that. Nezrene has been charged to my responsibility." In truth, he had believed it a mistake to bring the Tholian with them to Erilon, but Ming Xiong had insisted, citing her importance to the research he wished to conduct in the bowels of the ancient Shedai ruins. Okagawa had viewed the idea as risky, given the Tholians' general jumpiness about Federation encroachment on planets in the Taurus Reach known to possess Shedai artifacts. The fact that they also were upset at the decision to offer Nezrene sanctuary aboard Vanguard and had made clear their desire to have her extradited, it made sense that they would monitor ship traffic to and from the station in the hopes of recapturing her should she leave her temporary safe haven for any reason. Had they done exactly that, thereby tracking Nezrene to Erilon?

I hate being right all the time.

Restrene's response was to sever the communications link. On the main viewer, his image was replaced with that of the Tholian vessel. An instant later, the foremost point of the smaller vessel's hull glowed red, and a writhing ball of energy spat forth, expanding as it drew closer until it bathed the viewscreen in a harsh crimson shroud an instant before the energy burst struck the *Lovell*'s shields.

Okagawa felt the deck shudder beneath his feet, and he reached back for his chair to steady himself as alarm indicators sounded around the bridge. "Helm, evasive maneuvers! Get me some breathing room. Pzial, notify the landing parties still on the surface that we're breaking orbit."

At the helm console, Lieutenant Sasha Rodriquez said, "Evasive, aye," as she punched in the necessary commands to move the *Lovell* out of orbit. On the viewscreen, the Tholian vessel actually seemed to be breaking off, allowing the Starfleet ship the room to maneuver without harassment.

"Fire a warning shot across their bow," Okagawa ordered. "I don't want them dropping shields and activating transporters."

At the weapons station, Diamond replied, "Aye, sir."

The image on the main viewer depicted the twin streaks of bright blue energy as the *Lovell*'s main phaser banks came to bear, shooting past the forward edge of the Tholian ship.

"That's going to irritate them," zh'Rhun said.

There was no choice, Okagawa knew. Outnumbered three to one and with people vulnerable on the surface, his options were limited. He had to make a stand, a show of strength to demonstrate to the Tholians that he would not simply surrender or even make it easy for them to get what they had come for. Looking down at the astrogator, he saw that the other two vessels were breaking formation, moving closer together at the same time as they closed the distance between them and the *Lovell*.

"I'm picking up power surges in two of the ships," reported Lieutenant Xav, the *Lovell*'s science officer. Standing at his console, the Tellarite was peering into his hooded sensor viewer. "Massive buildup in their secondary power-generation systems."

"Continue evasive," Okagawa ordered. Looking to zh'Rhun, he asked, "Any idea what they're up to?"

The Andorian shook her head. "No, sir."

Beneath his feet, Okagawa felt the deck tremble once again as another disruptor volley slammed into the ship's deflector shields. Zh'Rhun, holding on to the curved railing to maintain her balance, called out, "Transfer power from nonessential systems to the shields."

"Energy buildup is increasing," Xav said. "I've never seen anything like it."

Another strike on the shields sent reverberations through the deck plating, and Okagawa even felt the effects channeled through the arms of his chair. "Diamond, fire at will. Target to disable, if at all possible." Even under the circumstances, he had no desire to take lives if it could be avoided. Damaged vessels were easier than dead people to discuss and perhaps reconcile, assuming the Tholians felt like discussing anything with the Federation ever again.

One problem at a time, Captain.

Overhead, the lighting flickered for the briefest of moments as the phaser systems drew power. Okagawa watched on the viewscreen as the blasts struck the shields of one Tholian vessel, which promptly broke off its own attack, changing course and veering away.

"Captain," Xav called out from the science station, "the two ships actually look to be maneuvering into position to join or link up in some manner."

Confused, Okagawa swiveled his chair toward the science

officer. "Is one of the ships damaged? Are they attempting a rescue of some kind?"

"No damage I can see, sir," the Tellarite replied. Then another alert tone sounded above the rest of the bridge's omnipresent background chatter, and Xav looked up from his station. "Captain, new sensor contacts. Two Klingon ships approaching at high warp."

Scarcely believing what he was hearing, Okagawa turned toward the science officer. "Are you serious?"

Xav nodded. "Yes, sir. They're coming in at full impulse, shields up and weapons armed."

Still gripping the bridge railing, zh'Rhun said, "The day just gets better and better."

"They're targeting the Tholian ships," Xav reported.

"Onscreen," Okagawa ordered.

The image on the viewer shifted once more to depict the now-familiar shapes of two Klingon *D-7* battle cruisers. At the forward edges of the vessels' nacelles, the ships' main disruptor banks glowed with the power of barely harnessed energy.

"Get us the hell out of the way," Okagawa called out, gripping the arms of his chair even as Rodriquez worked her controls. Despite the *Lovell*'s inertial dampening field, his stomach still told him when the ship banked to starboard, answering the skilled touch of Rodriquez's hand and clawing for distance.

At the science station, Xav shouted, "They're opening fire!"

Angry red energy spat forth from the first one, then both of the Klingon cruisers as they homed in on their targets, the oddly conjoined pair of Tholian ships. Multiple plumes of disruptor fire slammed into the smaller vessel's shields before overpowering those defenses. Another salvo, following on the heels of the first, pushed through the floundering deflectors and punched holes in the hull of one Tholian ship. Shuddering beneath multiple devastating hits, the vessel broke away from its companion only moments before its hull came apart. The vacuum of space snuffed out the intense fireball that ripped through the ship, spewing debris in all directions. Seconds later, the other Tholian vessel followed suit, its frame buckling beneath a relentless onslaught of Klingon disruptor fire.

"Captain," said zh'Rhun, her tone one of warning, "if we don't get out of here . . ."

Okagawa nodded. "I know, I know." To Rodriquez, he said, "Helm, plot us an evasive course back to Erilon." He could not leave without the people still on the planet's surface.

"The Klingon ships are separating," Xav said. "One is going after the last Tholian ship, and the other . . ." He turned to look at Okagawa. "Captain, the other is making for orbit. I'm picking up sensors directed at the planet."

After exchanging alarmed glances with zh'Rhun, Okagawa looked first to Xav and then to the main viewer, which now showed an image of the blue-white world that was Erilon, with a Klingon cruiser speeding toward it. Both Klingon ships were ignoring the *Lovell*? Okagawa did not know whether to be relieved or insulted.

"What the hell are they doing?"

Running down the corridor, Mahmud al-Khaled was ripping open the closures on his parka with his free hand, reaching for his phaser even as he held his communicator close to his mouth.

"We're detecting multiple transporter signatures, Mahmud," said the anguished voice of Captain Okagawa. *"Take cover, and do whatever you have to do to defend yourself. We're on our way!"*

"Acknowledged," al-Khaled replied, skidding to a halt in the winding tunnel as he saw the first flashes of transporter beams, immediately noting that they were unlike any Starfleet transporter he had ever used.

"Intruder alert!" he called out, his voice echoing down the winding tunnel as six columns of fiery red transporter energy appeared less than ten meters in front of him, coalescing into humanoid figures far too tall and muscular to be humans. Al-Khaled heard his warning repeated by other members of the landing party as the figures took on substance, and he recognized them as Klingon warriors, each brandishing a disruptor pistol.

Al-Khaled aimed his phaser and waited until the transport cycle completed before he fired.

The single blue beam lanced across the open space, catching the Klingon at the front of the group full in the chest. The warrior staggered beneath the force of the attack, crumpling and falling unconscious to the tunnel's rock floor. Al-Khaled fired again, backpedaling the way he had come as the remaining five Klingons aimed their own weapons at him. His second shot missed, punching into the stone wall behind one of the Klingons, but by now, they had sighted on him and were firing. A hell storm of disruptor energy flooded the tunnel as al-Khaled dashed around a bend, finding temporary cover out of his adversaries' line of sight. Continuing to move and with his communicator still in his other hand, he keyed a control on the device and held it up once more. "Al-Khaled to landing party. Intruder alert. Klingons have entered the complex. Take appropriate defensive measures, and wait for the evacuation signal."

A disruptor bolt tore into the rock behind his head, and al-Khaled ducked, looking over his shoulder to see the first of the Klingon soldiers rounding the bend several meters behind him. Recalling the layout of the underground complex, he knew that he was perhaps fifty meters from the main chamber, where Ming Xiong, the Tholian Nezrene, and other members of the landing party had spent the majority of their time working with centuries-old Shedai equipment. The large number of people working in that area and the activity taking place there would draw no small amount of attention, but al-Khaled saw no reason to lead his pursuers in that direction. He might be able to divert the Klingons, perhaps even buy his companions some extra time to secure the valuable research they were performing and ready their defense until they could be beamed to safety by the *Lovell*.

Another disruptor bolt struck the smooth wall to his left, and al-Khaled dodged to his right. Several meters ahead of him, an opening beckoned. He remembered that it was some kind of anteroom, empty of anything distinguishing as far as Shedai technology was concerned but offering another path toward the chamber in which Xiong and the others should be.

Whatever you're going to do, do it now.

Stopping his headlong flight down the tunnel, al-Khaled turned and fired his phaser back the way he had come. He was not really trying to hit any of the Klingons but instead wanted to make them halt their pursuit and seek cover. He pressed the phaser's firing stud again and again, unleashing a torrent of energy down the tunnel. Shadows flitted against the walls, indicating frantic movement as his pursuers stopped and threw themselves aside to avoid being hit.

You can't win a standoff, his mind chided him. *Do something.*

Without really thinking about it, al-Khaled adjusted his phaser's power setting before aiming the weapon at a spot along the tunnel's roof several meters in front of him. When he fired this time, a thinner, more vibrant beam spat forth, penetrating the ceiling. He moved the continuous beam around in a rough approximation of a circle, and within seconds, the results of his effort became apparent as tons of loosened rock tumbled from the gap he had created. The sound of the avalanche cascaded through the confined space as rubble rained into the tunnel and quickly blocked the passageway.

Satisfied at his makeshift work while at the same time knowing that it would only slow the Klingons for a few moments at best, al-Khaled lunged through the opening in the tunnel wall and into the anteroom. Entrances to three tunnels converged here, and it took him a second to recall which one led to the main chamber. As he made his decision, he heard footsteps echoing in the narrow corridor just as a figure rounded a bend in the tunnel. It was Xiong, still wearing his Starfleet parka and carrying his phaser in his right hand while toting a satchel and his tricorder slung over his left shoulder. Behind him, Nezrene skittered along the tunnel's smooth floor, trying to keep up. Another Starfleet crewman, an ensign named McCown from Xiong's Vanguard-based research team, completed the haphazard group.

"Mahmud!" Xiong called out as he caught sight of al-Khaled. "What's going on?"

Hooking a thumb over his shoulder to indicate the tunnel he had left behind, al-Khaled said, "Klingons. A pair of ships showed up and blasted three Tholian ships that were already giving the *Lovell* trouble." He nodded toward Nezrene. "The Tholians were after their friend there, but I have no idea what the Klingons are after."

"Are we evacuating?" asked McCown, his expression one of unfettered worry, his breath coming in rapid gasps, visible in the tunnel's chilled air.

Al-Khaled said, "Any time now, I'd think. We need to keep moving, though. The *Lovell* will home in on our communicators." Something crashed in the tunnel behind him, and he turned at the sound. "They're breaking through the barricade I made. We need to get out of here—now." Pointing toward the other tunnels leading from the anteroom, he said, "That way." The first heavy footfalls echoed in the passageway, and al-Khaled saw shadows on the walls. "Move!"

Nezrene was the first to enter one of the tunnels, and al-Khaled was right behind her when the first disruptor bolts screamed through the chamber. He heard the energy of the blasts tearing into the smooth walls even before the guttural cries of anger and determination reached his ears. He turned and saw two of the Klingons entering the anteroom, and he fired his phaser, sending them dodging for cover. Out of the corner of his eye, he saw Xiong running down another of the tunnels, with McCown following him. Then vicious crimson energy tore through the air and plowed into the ensign, punching a hole through the man's parka and ripping into his back. McCown howled in agony, stumbling over his own feet and crashing to the ground in a disjointed heap.

"No!"

Al-Khaled's cry drew the Klingons' attention, and they turned toward him, once more raising their weapons. He fired at them again, and one of his shots hit a soldier in his left shoulder and spun him around, carrying him off his feet and sending him to the tunnel floor. His companion ducked, and al-Khaled fired after him, missing but giving himself enough time to scamper down the corridor.

He heard the sounds of the Klingons' remaining companions plunging into the tunnel behind him, but he did not turn to look. Instead, he ran at full speed down the corridor, sprinting in an effort to catch up with Nezrene. A frantic beeping echoed off the narrow walls, and al-Khaled realized that it was his communicator. The next instant, he felt the distinctive tingle of a transporter beam beginning to envelop him.

Al-Khaled materialized in one of the *Lovell*'s transporter rooms, confronted by the anguished face of the crew member on duty, Ensign Brian O'Halloran. Standing just off the transporter pad were other members of the landing party, no doubt retrieved just before his beam-up. To his right on the transporter pad was Nezrene, and lying on the floor to his left was the unmoving form of Ensign McCown.

"Medic!" al-Khaled shouted as he knelt down next to McCown, his fingers reaching for the younger man's throat in search of a pulse while he tried not to think too much about the ghastly wound in his back. Other members of the landing party stepped forward in a bid to help, but he ignored them, just as he only partially heard O'Halloran calling into the intercom and requesting that a medical team be dispatched to the transporter room. Nothing else mattered, not while he madly probed McCown's neck for a pulse.

He found none.

"Bridge to transporter rooms!" the voice of Captain Okagawa shouted through the intercom. *"Do we have everyone or not?"*

Fighting back anger as he continued to stare at the unmoving body of Ensign McCown, al-Khaled called out, "O'Halloran! What's going on?"

"The Klingon ships are breaking orbit," replied the ensign. "They never fired the first shot at us." Reaching across the console, he once more reactivated the intercom system. "Bridge, this is transporter room two. I have eight retrieved here. Six plus the Tholian and one casualty."

Over the speaker, al-Khaled heard another voice respond, *"Transporter room one here. We have nine. Only one sustained injuries, but they're not critical."*

"That's only seventeen," Okagawa's voice snapped. *"Who's missing?"*

Looking around the transporter room, al-Khaled already knew the answer, but still he asked the question. "Where's Xiong? He was near my location when I was beamed up."

A moment later, the voice from transporter room one replied, *"He's not in our group, sir."*

"Son of a bitch!" al-Khaled growled, lunging from the transporter pad and moving around the console, all but elbowing O'Halloran out of the way. Hitting the comm switch, he said, *"Lovell* to Lieutenant Xiong. Come in, Xiong." There was no response, but al-Khaled repeated the call even as he reset the transporter controls and scanned for life signs on or beneath Erilon's surface. None revealed itself. Feeling his temperature rising, he ripped open the parka and shrugged out of it, letting it drop to the floor as he resumed his work at the console. "Bridge, I can't get a lock on Xiong's communicator signal. Are you scanning for him?" It took almost fifteen seconds before science officer Xav replied with the words Mahmud al-Khaled did not want to hear.

"We're not picking up any human life signs anywhere, Commander. He's either dead, or he's not down there."

37

It was too hot to eat, Pennington decided as he stared at his bowl of soup. Except for an hour before sunrise and a few hours after sunset, it seemed it was always too hot to eat. As far as he was concerned, Vulcan was the great weight-loss secret of the Federation.

Sitting at a table on the veranda outside Sobon's home, Pennington gazed across the courtyard, watching members of the village going about their work. As always, they were unaffected by the heat, which was still oppressive even at this elevation. Even M'Benga seemed to have become acclimated to the temperatures in the time they had been here. The only person who still seemed to be suffering was Pennington himself.

I always was slow on the uptake.

"Would you like more water, Mr. Pennington?"

He looked up at the sound of the new voice, finding himself eye-to-eye with a young Vulcan girl standing next to his table and carrying a stone pitcher. Pennington guessed her age to be no more than fifteen years, at least as they would be measured on Earth. She was dressed in a smaller version of the soft suit worn by almost every member of the commune he had encountered. Her long black hair was drawn up into a ponytail and tied with a leather thong, and her face was tanned and free of the age lines that eventually would crease her smooth skin in the years to come.

He held out the oversized mug he had selected for use during his meal. "That'd be lovely, my dear. Thank you." As she began to pour, he said, "I don't think I've seen you around here before. What's your name, if you don't mind my asking?"

"I am T'Lon," the girl replied. "My mother works as one of the keepers of Healer Sobon's house, and I assist her on days when I am not in school."

Once she had filled the mug, Pennington took a long drink, relishing the taste of the cool water. Drawn from a well fed by an intricate aqueduct system running down the mountain from an underground spring, the water possessed a vital, refreshing flavor, which seemed odd when Pennington remembered what he was drinking. He had taken the opportunity during his early-morning walks to investigate the aqueducts, fascinated by the craft embodied in the system's design and admiring that it—like everything else created by the citizens of Kren'than—was accomplished without any form of mechanization.

I could learn to like this place, he thought, not for the first time. Though he was a citizen of a culture where nearly every facet of day-to-day life was inexorably intertwined on some level with modern technology, there was something to be said for the simpler, matter-of-fact existence of this village's residents. There was an appeal, Pennington had decided, to *not* being connected to the entire galaxy or even to the neighboring village without getting up and walking to that destination under your own power.

If it could only be fifty degrees cooler, and if they maybe had a pub or two, it would be almost perfect.

He realized after a moment that the young girl was still standing at the table, looking expectantly at him. "I'm sorry," he said, straightening his posture in his seat. "Is there something else? Have I done something wrong?"

T'Lon shook her head. "No, you have not acted improperly." Gesturing toward the sheaves of parchment lying on his table, she asked, "I was curious about what you might be writing."

"That's a good question," Pennington replied, glancing down at the papers and grimacing at the sight of his handwriting. "Judging by the looks of these, I'd say my pen was having an epileptic fit." He looked up at T'Lon, who stared at him. "I'm sorry," he said, holding up one of the papers. "My writing is a bit out of practice. I've gotten used to dictation or even a keyboard. Anyway, I suppose you could say it's a travelogue, an account of my time here." He had taken up the notion as a means of passing the time, writing something about each day he spent among the people of Kren'than. It was an enjoyable exercise, admittedly made more so because of his having to write everything in longhand. No electronic devices, including the portable data manager that was his life's blood as a reporter, were allowed within the village's confines. The tenet forced him to get back to basics, and he relished the tangible connection to his work as the ink flowed from the pen onto the parchment, guided by his will as he transcribed thoughts and feelings.

No bloody idea what I might do with it, but I'll worry about that when it's finished.

When T'Lon remained in place after another moment without saying anything, he asked, "Do you have another question?"

The young Vulcan nodded. "I wished to ask whether you would be willing to answer a question about T'Prynn."

Surprised by this, Pennington shifted in his seat. "Do you know her?"

"No, though I have mentored under the guidance of her sister, T'Nel. I wished to inquire about her current condition." Lowering her gaze, she added, "We are not given much in the way of information, though many of us are curious."

Pennington smiled at the child's inquisitiveness, able to relate to her youthful, passionate desire to know about everything that might be happening around her. He had been like that at her age, a trait that had often gotten him into trouble with his parents, his teachers, and pretty much anyone irritated by his insatiable curiosity.

"What would you like to know?" he prompted.

After pausing for a moment, T'Lon finally asked, "Has she ever spoken of our village?"

"No, I can't say that she has," Pennington replied. "To be honest, I don't really know her all that well. I know almost nothing about her personal life. For example, I didn't know she had a sister until I came here."

T'Lon did not frown, but her expression shifted just enough that Pennington was able to discern her confusion. "I do not understand," she said. "If you are not T'Prynn's friend, then why did you travel with Dr. M'Benga to bring her here?"

"That's an excellent question, my dear," the journalist replied, sighing as he reached up to wipe perspiration from his forehead. "I guess you could say that our relationship is . . . complicated, but I've recently come to care a great deal for her, for reasons I'm not really able to explain." Shaking his head, he added, "I truly hope she recovers from her illness, so that we can talk about it."

T'Lon asked, "What will you do if T'Prynn does not recover?"

Releasing a small, humorless grunt, Pennington shrugged. "I really don't know." Suddenly feeling uncomfortable, he looked at her and asked, "I understand that T'Prynn once lived here but left when she was very young. Do you know anything about that?" As he spoke, he gestured toward one of the table's other empty chairs and gestured for her to sit.

T'Lon took the seat, setting the water pitcher on the table. "It is tradition that residents not speak openly about those who have chosen to leave the village. I know only that she was dissatisfied with life in Kren'than and left the commune in order to seek answers to questions that could not be found here. She is not the only one to have done this; there have been stories of others following similar paths."

"Have any of them ever returned?" Pennington asked. "You know, perhaps because they did not find the answers they sought, or maybe they did and decided that life here was preferable to whatever it was they found beyond the village?"

"A few have returned," T'Lon replied. "The commune has never turned anyone away, but when someone requests reentry, the village elders proclaim that person *ri-gla-yehat,* what you would call 'the Unseen.' They are admitted back into the commune, but they serve a probationary period where they are never approached or addressed by other members of the village. It is as though they do not exist."

Shocked by what he was hearing, Pennington frowned. "That doesn't seem very compassionate."

"Compassion is an emotional response," T'Lon countered.

"Damned right it is." Catching himself, Pennington cleared his throat and shifted in his seat. "And how long does this probation last?"

T'Lon paused, then replied, "In human terms of time measurement, approximately twelve of your years."

"Twelve *years*?" Pennington repeated, flabbergasted. "That's a bloody long time to walk around with a scarlet V stitched on your clothes." When the young Vulcan's right eyebrow arched in what he recognized as a quizzical expression, he held up a hand. "Bad joke. Tell me where the logic is in treating people that way?"

"It is believed that one who has left the village and then returned must first demonstrate a renewed commitment to our way of life," T'Lon replied. "The probation is a means of cleansing the mind and body of any remnants of the society they chose to embrace at the expense of the commune." After a moment, she said, "I must confess, I do not understand the logic, myself."

Before saying anything else, she looked around, as though verifying that their discussion was not being overheard. "I, too, have grown curious about what lies beyond the village. I wish to visit the cities, perhaps see the science academy, the temples of Gol, Mount Seleya. I may even wish to travel to other worlds. I admit to being intrigued by your planet, Mr. Pennington."

"Nothing says you can't do all of that," the reporter said. "My understanding of Vulcan culture is that it's based on self-determination. It's your choice what you do with your life, right?"

Obviously nervous at the turn the conversation had taken, though doing her level best to maintain her veneer of stoicism, T'Lon replied, "Such questions have troubled me. If the Vulcan way is enlightenment and expansion of the intellect through the pursuit of logic, why must I then be punished for what to me seems nothing more than natural curiosity? I was born in this village, and I have lived my entire life here, and yet if I choose to leave, I will be ostracized and openly shunned if I choose to return."

It was an odd dichotomy, Pennington had to admit, one for which he had no answers or even advice to offer. Even if he did possess such wisdom, would it be appropriate to share it with T'Lon or—for that matter—any other resident of the commune? He was a guest here, after all, and his gut told him that dispensing such guidance, solicited or not, would not be welcomed by the majority of people who chose to call Kren'than home.

Then a disturbing thought struck him.

"T'Lon," he said, growing more troubled as he considered the notion that had so abruptly manifested itself, "do you know what will happen to T'Prynn if she recovers? With respect to her being here, I mean. How will she be treated by the village?"

"Should she choose to remain here, she likely would be proclaimed *ri-gla-yehat* by the elders."

"Even if she doesn't decide to stay here," Pennington said, "and assuming that Starfleet doesn't come swooping in here to drag her away in irons the moment she wakes up, she's probably going to be here for at least a little while. She'll have to recuperate to some degree, right? In that event, how will the villagers treat her?"

T'Lon replied, "She will not be denied any required medical care, but any other interactions will be subject to the elders' proclamation."

"So, for all intents and purposes," Pennington said, "she would be alone."

"Correct." T'Lon looked up as the sound of a bell chiming echoed across the courtyard. "I must go now," she said, rising from her seat. "It is time for afternoon studies. Thank you for your time, Mr. Pennington. It was a most illuminating discussion."

"Indeed, it was, my dear," the journalist replied. "Thank *you*."

As the girl departed, stepping down from the veranda and heading across the courtyard, Pennington leaned back in his chair and reflected on their conversation. It seemed obvious to him that T'Prynn, should she recover from her ordeal, would find herself in a situation not at all unlike the one he recently had faced—rejected, alone, shunned by the very people she once had called family and friends.

No one deserves that, he thought. *Not even the person who made your life hell.*

Finally, it seemed—and assuming that she ever recovered to the point where it became an issue—that Pennington and T'Prynn would have something in common, after all.

Dust clogged her lungs, but she forced herself not to cough lest she give away her location. Feeble light offered by the string of luminescent bulbs hanging along the jagged stone wall made pathetic attempts to cut through the odd, luminescent fog permeating the tunnel. The lights were old, still powered as she remembered by a weak solar battery system somewhere outside the mine, and offered T'Prynn only a few meters' worth of visibility in either direction of the underground passageway. Ahead of her and on the left, she saw a dark opening that she concluded must be another tunnel branching off in a different direction, or perhaps it was a chamber where mining once had been conducted.

Recalling the warnings her parents had given her about the dangers of coming here, T'Prynn thought of the numerous downward-sloped or even vertical shafts descending far below the surface. These were supposed to be covered to avoid accidental falls, but one could never be certain of the safety of the abandoned tunnel network, making it a place to be avoided. This had not prevented curious children from venturing into the mines, of course, after finding a way to circumvent the security barricades erected across each entrance to the deserted facility.

The tunnel or chamber—whichever it was—might make a hiding place, if only for a time. No matter where she hid, Sten would find her, just as he always did. Still, T'Prynn needed only a short respite, a chance to bring her breathing under control and to check the extent of her injuries. She left the main tunnel, and the walls immediately began to veer away from her, disappearing into the ubiquitous fog and telling her that she had entered one of the chambers that had served as one of the mine's primary excavation areas. How far below the surface had she descended? T'Prynn had no idea, just as she did not know how she had come to be here in the first place. The answers to those questions, along with so many others, eluded her.

"T'Prynn!"

The voice came from behind her, and T'Prynn turned in time to hear footsteps approaching from somewhere in the fog. A dark shadow loomed in her vision, and instinct made her duck an instant before the whistling sound of something slicing through the air passed over her head. She recognized the blade of the *lirpa* as it swung past, parting the fog before its wielder. Then Sten lunged forward, the fog moving away from him as though shed like an unwanted cloak. In his hands, he hefted the *lirpa,* the end with the weapon's curved blade aimed toward her. His expression had lost all semblance of self-control; instead, he radiated fury and determination.

"Shall we continue," he asked, his tone mocking, "or are you finally ready to submit?"

Her own *lirpa* lost, perhaps somewhere in the mines, T'Prynn's reply was to reach for the knife at her belt and draw it from its scabbard. The gesture seemed to satisfy Sten, and he even smiled as he waved his own weapon, its blade describing an arc through the lingering mists.

"Excellent," he hissed through gritted teeth an instant before thrusting forward with the *lirpa*.

T'Prynn backed away, avoiding the attack and working to put distance between herself and her attacker. Conscious of her surroundings, she tried to sense when or if she might trip over a shaft's protective cover or, worse yet, the edge of the shaft itself.

"There is nowhere to run," Sten taunted as he pressed forward, swinging his blade before her face. "You cannot escape. Stand and fight, or give me what is mine."

In the corner of her eye, T'Prynn caught sight of something

dark behind and to her left. Risking a glance, she looked over her shoulder and saw the parapet circling a shaft opening. Its safety cover was askew, pushed aside far enough to permit a body to fall through the gap. T'Prynn stepped to her right, trying to give it a wide berth while keeping her attention on Sten.

She sensed his attack before he moved. When he did spring forward, she was ready for him and ducked to her right, his move exposing his left flank. T'Prynn swung at him with her knife, feeling the blade meet resistance. He grunted, and she realized that she had sliced into skin and muscle tissue. Sten fell away from her, growling in rage and pain, and the knife was yanked from her hand. The *lirpa* faltered in his hands, and he jammed the weighted end into the ground to maintain his balance. Still aware of the open shaft, T'Prynn scrambled away just as Sten regained his footing, once more bringing up the *lirpa* and readying for another attack.

"Sten!"

The new voice, raspy and perhaps even weak, called from somewhere to her right, and T'Prynn saw the flickering light of flames cutting toward her through the fog. Carrying the torch was an old, seemingly withered Vulcan, his robes identifying him as a healer. Who was he? T'Prynn had seen him before but could not identify him.

"Leave us, old man," Sten warned, stepping forward and bringing his *lirpa* up. "This does not concern you."

Instead of replying, the elder Vulcan thrust the torch at Sten, his strength and speed belying his age. The flames nearly caught Sten in the face, and he ducked to avoid them, but the healer pressed his attack, forcing his opponent to dodge and weave in order to avoid the fire.

"You're beginning to annoy me," Sten growled, forcing the words between his teeth. The blade of the *lirpa* moved toward the elder's head, trying to keep him at bay. The healer was undeterred, swinging the torch back and forth and moving steadily forward. Sten responded by dodging backward, blocking the elder's advance with his weapon.

And then he disappeared.

T'Prynn watched as the fog swirled where he once had stood, his cries of surprise and terror echoing in the chamber even as they fell away. Sten had fallen into the mine shaft. Standing at the parapet, the aged Vulcan dropped to his knees, drawing deep, ragged breaths as the torch fell from his hands. His entire body seemed on the verge of collapsing in on itself as he looked up at her.

"Run, T'Prynn. He is gone, but he will return."

The fog wrapped around the healer, obscuring him until he vanished before her eyes.

Standing to the side of T'Prynn's bed, M'Benga watched as Sobon released an anguished moan and removed his hands from the *katra* points on his patient's face. Despite his decades of self-discipline and emotional control, the healer's expression was one of pain and fatigue as he slumped forward, reaching out and placing one hand on the bed to steady himself.

"Healer Sobon, are you all right?" M'Benga asked, stepping forward to assist the elder. Well aware of Vulcan customs regarding casual contact, he stopped just short of actually placing his hand on the healer's narrow shoulder. Standing at the foot of the bed, T'Nel watched the proceedings with an impassive expression.

"May I get you some water, Healer?" she asked.

After a moment, Sobon looked to T'Nel and nodded. "That would be appreciated." Turning his attention to M'Benga, he said, "I am well, Doctor. Thank you."

"What happened?" M'Benga asked.

Inhaling deep, regular breaths, the healer replied, "The fight within T'Prynn's mind grows ever stronger. Sten's *katra* is growing more determined, taking advantage of her decreasing ability to erect new defenses against him. Through our meld, I was able to force him into another dark, distant recess of her mind, but as before, it is at best a temporary measure. Sten will emerge from his exile and will attack her yet again." Sobon pushed himself to a sitting position and wiped his forehead. "I believe we are running out of options, and I will have to attempt the *Dashaya-Ni'Var* even though I do not yet feel I am prepared to conduct the procedure properly."

Stepping forward with a glass of water that she offered to Sobon, T'Nel asked, "When do you believe you will be ready, Healer?"

"Soon," Sobon replied, shaking his head. "So far, my meld attempts have kept me in a largely passive role. Because of the intensity of the meld locking T'Prynn's and Sten's *katras,* I am limited in how much influence I exert. For *Dashaya-Ni'Var,* I will have to take a more active role in their meld. In essence, I will need to replace T'Prynn's *katra* with my own, in order to draw Sten from her mind."

Frowning, M'Benga said, "Forgive me, Healer, but that sounds dangerous."

Sobon nodded. "It is, Dr. M'Benga. If I am not successful, I may find my own *katra* trapped within T'Prynn's mind, locked in combat with Sten until death releases us all." He paused, taking a sip of his water. "Though I have translated most of the scrolls' contents, I do not think I possess an adequate comprehension of what is involved. At least, not yet."

M'Benga nodded in understanding. Sobon had spent much of his time ensconced in his study, reading through the centuries-old scrolls that he had said contained all that was known about *Dashaya-Ni'Var.* According to the healer, the ritual was cloaked in secrecy, and even the writings were chronicled in an obscure dialect of the ancient High Vulcan language that had not been used since a time before Surak. Simply translating the scrolls' contents had taken him months and remained an ongoing process.

"How much longer can T'Prynn hold out?" M'Benga asked.

After taking another sip of his water, Sobon cleared his throat. "I do not know. Our best course of action may be to proceed regardless of my confidence in my own abilities."

Any action rather than no action, M'Benga thought. As a

physician who had treated his share of life-threatening injuries under risky conditions without adequate equipment and lacking any true sense of whether the patient would survive, he could sympathize with Sobon's reasoning. Standing by and doing nothing guaranteed T'Prynn's death. Even if the only possible alternative lay within the archaic texts, which no modern physician understood and which carried no assurance of success, then there was no choice. None at all.

38

Nogura paced back and forth across the length of his office, ignoring the looks of Commander Cooper, Ambassador Jetanien, and Dr. Marcus. Though he was not a man given to outward displays of strong emotion, this was one of those occasions when some kind of demonstrative response seemed appropriate.

"Damn it!"

The outburst made Marcus—who already seemed a bit shaken, anyway—jump in her seat, and even Cooper flinched a bit. If it affected Jetanien, the ambassador offered no clue. Nogura had to admit that he surprised himself with his reaction. It had been building, of course, from the moment he received the first reports from Captain Okagawa detailing the incident at Erilon. The audacity exhibited by the Klingons angered him— not so much the actions themselves, as they generally were in keeping with what experience had taught him about Klingons. Instead, it was the idea that the empire felt it could, with impunity, direct its ships against Starfleet vessels and Federation interests. It did not ease his mounting irritation to know that the Federation Council and Starfleet Command seemed willing to allow this behavior to continue unchecked. They stubbornly hung their hopes on the diplomats from either side, who even now remained locked in a room somewhere, participating in what Nogura believed was an increasingly preposterous exercise in futility.

No, it was more than that, Nogura knew. The Klingons were more than happy to allow the charade of diplomacy to continue, all while they refined their strategies, deployed their forces, and even sharpened their blades in anticipation of what they saw as imminent war.

We're not there yet, he reminded himself. *But we're not that far off.*

"I apologize for that," he said. After pausing to draw what he hoped was a calming breath, he turned to Cooper. "Commander, what's the latest from the *Lovell*?"

Shifting in his chair, the executive officer replied, "Captain Okagawa reports that they've conducted four separate searches of the entire underground complex, at least those areas that are accessible. They've found no sign of Lieutenant Xiong, living or otherwise. However, *Lovell*'s sensor logs recorded transporter activity to and from the Klingon ship. According to Okagawa's science officer, Xiong was beamed to that ship, and he was alive when it happened."

"They kidnapped him?" Marcus asked, scowling. "I didn't think Klingons took prisoners."

Jetanien replied, "Generally speaking, Doctor, they do not. There have been exceptions, however."

"Don't believe the propaganda," Nogura added. "If there's something to be gained from taking a prisoner, the Klingons will do it as quickly as anyone else. Of course, they don't usually treat their prisoners very well, so you're normally better off if they just kill you outright." Looking to Cooper, he asked, "I assume the *Lovell* attempted to track the Klingon ship?"

Cooper nodded. "They did, Admiral, but by the time they figured out what had happened, the ship was long gone. They tried to track them based on their last-known course heading, but Captain Okagawa reports that sensors showed that the ship employed an evasive flight path, designed to throw off anyone trying to track it."

"I understand Xiong and his team were making some real progress," Nogura said.

Nodding, Marcus said, "They were, Admiral. They'd succeeded in accessing a few of the Shedai computer systems, though that success was largely limited by other factors out of their control. While they were able to inspect local components of what we believe to be the global computer network, they didn't have any luck connecting with other nodes anywhere else on the planet, nor were they successful in reaching beyond Erilon and perhaps making contact with another planet harboring Shedai technology."

"But they did create some form of broadcast off the planet, did they not?" Jetanien asked. "Is it possible that this was detected by the Tholians, and that's what drew them to Erilon?"

Marcus shrugged. "Maybe. Even with the progress we—that is, Lieutenant Xiong—has made, we still know very little about Shedai technology. Still, he and his team learned to use the Jinoteur carrier wave as a means of searching for other locations where Shedai technology was hidden. The Tholians may possess a similar means of detection. We also don't know what it means when a Shedai consciousness—or a Tholian's, in the case of Nezrene—enters these computer networks, as Xiong seemed to believe. Are they projecting themselves in some fashion? Is that detectable somehow to other Tholians, even if they're not connected to these networks?"

"There's a lot we don't know about the Tholians," Jetanien said, "but I do know that they have been affected by the presence of the Shedai. I've seen their reactions with my own eyes. On some level, they were aware of its consciousness." Even as Nogura moved to stand behind his desk, the Chel ambassador adopted the admiral's pacing. "We know that Tholian crystalline physiology is such that their bodies can themselves be used as a sort of short-range transmitter. It stands to reason that they can receive communications in similar fashion, particularly if the source is something as powerful as we believe the Shedai to be."

"Are you suggesting that those other Tholians somehow detected Nezrene *herself* while she was working within the computer?" Cooper asked, frowning. "With all due respect, Ambassador, that seems a little far-fetched."

Marcus shook her head. "Maybe not, Commander. After all, there's a lot we don't know about the Tholians, either. Perhaps they possess some kind of . . . I don't know . . . if not outright telepathy, then at least an ability to broadcast or project themselves over communications frequencies, much as Ambassador Jetanien hypothesized."

Nogura made a show of clearing his throat to get the attention of his three visitors. "People, as fascinating as this discussion is, none of it's of any use in determining the fate of Lieutenant Xiong. I think we can at least entertain the idea that he was deliberately targeted, likely for his knowledge of the Shedai." Such a possibility did not enthuse Nogura, to say the least. Though he had no doubts that Xiong would do his best to protect the secrets he carried, the admiral had seen firsthand the effects of Klingon "interrogation techniques" and knew that every man, no matter his strength of will, had a breaking point. Sooner or later, the Klingons who had taken Xiong would extract from him what they required.

He looked up when he heard a sniffing sound and saw Marcus reaching up to dab a tear from the corner of her left eye. "Doctor, are you all right?"

Marcus drew a deep breath as she straightened her posture and shook her head. "I don't . . . it's just . . . I keep thinking this is my fault."

"You were driven to find answers, Doctor," Nogura said, "which is exactly why Starfleet sent you out here. I knew the risks in sending a team to Erilon, and you didn't talk me into anything I wasn't already considering. Not that any of that matters, as I'm the one who authorized the mission. If anyone's to be blamed, it'll be me." Sending subordinates into dangerous situations was a reality of command, Nogura knew, and he had carried the scars of that harsh truth for most of his adult life. That experience never made such decisions any easier, and the admiral feared the day would come when he might look upon such responsibility with cold dispassion.

Never.

Shaking off the troubling thought, Nogura turned to Jetanien. "Ambassador, what are the Klingons saying about any of this?"

"They claim that the action at Erilon was carried out without their permission," the Chel replied. "As far as they know, or at least are willing to admit, no Klingon vessel is holding any Starfleet officer hostage."

"What a crock," Cooper said, making no effort to squelch his bitterness.

"As hard as it may be for us to believe," Nogura said, "I suppose it's possible that the Klingons have yet *another* renegade ship commander running around out there. Ambassador, you have at least one or two contacts willing to talk to you off the record, correct? What about pressing them for information?"

Jetanien nodded. "I have already attempted to make contact with those parties, Admiral. I await a response."

"Keep at it," Nogura said, then turned to Cooper. "Get the *Lovell* back here. Some of those artifacts and other materials that Xiong wanted for study might be able to help us. If the Klingons took him because they're trying to understand Shedai technology, then maybe they'll put him to work on some other planet." Next, he looked to Marcus. "That's where you come in, Doctor, you and Nezrene. Re-create what they were doing. Maybe if we can understand what they were figuring out on Erilon, it might give us a clue to where to look for him."

He tapped his right forefinger on the polished surface of his desk, the rhythmic thumping accentuating his words. "People, we don't rest until I find out what happened to my man. Understood?"

There were no objections, and Nogura watched as his visitors—his advisors, really—filed out of his office, heading to carry out their respective tasks. Nogura was left alone as the door slid shut, with nothing to do but ponder the consequences of what had transpired on Erilon, how the Klingons might benefit from it, and what it might all mean for a young, ambitious Starfleet lieutenant named Ming Xiong.

39

"Reyes, Diego Matias. Serial number SC-886-3762-TM. Service rank: Commodore. Position: Starbase command. Current assignment: Starbase 47."

Sitting on the witness stand before his court-martial board, Diego Reyes stared straight ahead, his eyes fixed on a small defect in the paneling just above the computer terminal as the machine relayed his biographical information into the trial's official record. As the computer recited his awards and commendations, he could not help but reflect on the rather large period of time the list covered, and the realization—which, for some reason, he had never before pondered—made him feel old.

Check the dates again, his mind chided him. *They're ancient history and of absolutely no help to you now.*

Finally, this was it. After days upon days of testimony by all manner of witnesses, most from the station's crew but also a "few experts" called by Captain Sereb, it now was his turn to take the stand. Most of the other witnesses had served only to weaken the notion that Reyes had conspired with anyone to disobey orders from higher authority or that anyone but him had any prior knowledge of what he had done with regard to Tim Pennington's story. On the other hand, the testimony also had strengthened Sereb's primary angles of attack: the actual release of what should have remained classified information and his patent disregard of established policies and protocols when taking such action. With the framework for the trial's true purpose firmly established, only one task remained: Reyes himself. To that end, he and Desai had formalized a blunt, concise strategy for the testimony he would give. No theatrics, embellishments, or obfuscation of the relevant points. The questions she would ask would be direct, coinciding with the brutal honesty of the answers he would provide.

Let's get this show on the road.

What did he expect to accomplish here today? Desai had asked him that question on several occasions during the time they spent preparing for trial. Did he actually expect to sway the board? He had come to the conclusion some time ago that such a goal was not realistic. As he knew and as had been rammed home by Commander Spires, Sereb, and even Desai, the charges against him were simple and straightforward. He could not deny them, nor would he avoid responsibility for any consequences arising from them. All that remained was for him to make a case for why he had taken the actions that had brought him to this point, in the hopes that some future good might come forth in terms of the safety of innocent lives.

The computer's readings of his awards were finished, and Reyes straightened his posture ever so slightly as he heard footsteps behind him and Rana Desai walked into his line of sight. "Commodore Reyes," she said, "how long have you been involved with Operation Vanguard?"

His right hand resting on the biometric interface built into the chair's arm, Reyes replied, "I was first briefed on the project just under a year ago. I took command of the station two months later."

Desai asked, "What persuaded you to take this assignment?"

"The orders with my name on them and the date I was to report to the station." The response earned him a small, quickly suppressed chuckle from Admiral Komack, but that was the extent of the board's reaction.

Desai kept her focus on Reyes. "Yes, we know that you accepted the orders as issued to you by Starfleet Command, but what about the assignment attracted your interest?"

"I believed in the project's goals," Reyes said. "I didn't understand the science behind it, and I still don't, to a large extent, but smart people help me with the bigger words. What I did understand was the potential that came with learning as much about the meta-genome as we could. That's how I felt in the beginning." Those feelings still were present, of course, at least as far as the honest, forthright pursuit of knowledge was concerned. Such ambition always was a worthy endeavor. It was only the use to which that knowledge was put that could be defined as either right or wrong. Even with what he now knew about the Taurus Reach, he still held on to that simple axiom.

"And how do you feel now?" Desai asked.

For the first time, Reyes shifted his eyes so that he could stare directly at Admiral Moratino. "Scared."

Desai asked, "Why do you feel scared?"

"Because we've disturbed something out here that we should've left alone, but we didn't. Now it's loose and running around out there, pissed off at us."

Desai nodded. "So, is that why you allowed that story to be published? Because you were scared?"

"No," Reyes replied. "I allowed that story to go out because the public had a right to know about the dangers we'd uncovered out here. Secrecy had already cost too many innocent lives."

"But shouldn't your superiors at Starfleet Command be the ones to make that decision?"

"Yes, they should have been." As he answered the question, his eyes moved across the faces of the trial board members, all unreadable. "They should've made that decision months ago, *before* the incident at Gamma Tauri IV. If they had, we might've been able to avoid what happened there."

"Objection," said Captain Sereb from behind him, speaking for the first time since Reyes took the stand. "The defendant is speculating, Your Honor."

Moratino replied, "Sustained."

Unperturbed, Desai continued. "Commodore, you believe that Starfleet's decision to keep the existence of the Shedai classified is responsible for the destruction of Gamma Tauri IV?"

"No. *I* am responsible for the destruction of Gamma Tauri

IV." The decision to invoke General Order 24 and the resulting tragedy were necessary to contain the threat presented by the Shedai life-form. At least, that was what Reyes had thought at the time. Now, after having learned more about the true extent of power and range of influence the Shedai commanded, even the massive, drastic actions taken at Gamma Tauri IV seemed pitiful by comparison. "Starfleet's decision to keep information about the Shedai classified after our encounters with it on Erilon have put other colonies like that one in the line of fire, to say nothing of Starfleet and civilian vessels traveling through the region."

Desai had begun pacing again, circling the witness stand. "So, your decision to make public the incident at Jinoteur IV was to warn them of the Shedai threat."

"Of course."

"Did you do so because you believed the orders you received from your superiors to be unlawful?"

Reyes shook his head. "I don't know if that's the right word. It's not the word I'd use. Ill-advised, maybe?" He had been reluctant to pursue Desai's original notion of attacking the possible illegality of the directives issued by Starfleet Command. To him, it sounded as though he was trying to deflect culpability away from himself and onto others. While he firmly believed that others were at fault for what was allowed to transpire in the Taurus Reach, he remained adamant that such opinions not be used as a basis for his own defense. "I don't doubt that at least some of the people issuing the orders were doing so with the noblest of intentions, but after the incidents on Erilon, I encountered nothing but reluctance when I brought my concerns to their attention. We should have acted sooner, but we didn't. Invoking General Order 24 at Gamma Tauri IV was the best choice from a list of horrible options, and I didn't want to be in that position again because someone else had failed to act."

"What finally prompted you to release the information?" Desai asked, walking a circuit around his chair.

"Fate gave me Tim Pennington and his eyewitness account of the Shedai on Jinoteur," Reyes replied. "Though he did not—and does not now—know anything about the Shedai or Operation Vanguard beyond what he saw with his own eyes, what he saw was more than enough."

"You discussed this with him prior to the story's release?"

"Of course," Reyes replied. "I knew he'd be writing about his experiences on Jinoteur, and I'd already made up my mind before talking to him. He had written the article and was fully expecting that I would either edit it or refuse to allow its transmission at all. When I saw what he'd written, I knew this was the way to alert the public to what's going on out here."

"He wrote about what he saw on a planet deemed off-limits to civilian space traffic," Desai said, "while engaged in activities as coordinated by a Starfleet officer?"

Reyes kept his eyes on the board members as he replied. "That's right. He and another civilian volunteered to place themselves in harm's way in order to assist a Starfleet vessel in distress and ran into more than they bargained for. Afterward, Pennington chose to write about it, because that's what reporters do."

"So," Desai said, stopping before him once again, "after Pennington wrote his story, you took it from him. He did not coerce you?"

"Of course not," Reyes replied.

"Threaten you?"

"Keep dreaming."

"You took his story, proceeded to the communications center, and transmitted it to the Federation News Service. Is that the correct sequence of events?"

Reyes nodded. "It is."

"Tell me, Commodore," Desai said, "if a similar set of circumstances was to arise again in the future, do you think you'd act as you did on this occasion?"

Hesitating not one fraction of a second, Reyes replied, "If innocent lives were at stake? I would. Absolutely."

Desai asked, "Even if it meant defying Starfleet regulations?"

"I swore an oath to defend Federation citizens," Reyes said, "and that duty comes before any other rule or regulation. If that's changed, for whatever reason, then I'm in the wrong business."

Offering him a small smile, Desai nodded. That was it, he knew. She had laid out all of the cards he had asked her to play. Turning to the bench, she said, "No further questions, Your Honor."

Moratino replied, "Very well," and Reyes watched as Desai moved behind him and back to her table. "Captain Sereb, I assume you wish to cross-examine?"

"Indeed I do, Your Honor," the Tellarite replied, and the swarthy Tellarite rose to his feet and moved to the center of the room. "Commodore Reyes, you said you felt scared now that the truth—or at least some of it—about the Shedai has been revealed. Tell me, are you a coward?"

Thanks to Desai's courtroom experience, she had anticipated several avenues of cross-examination based on the questions she planned to ask Reyes during his testimony. This question from Sereb, or something like it, was one of her accurate guesses. Glancing toward the prosecutor as he strode past, Reyes replied, "I've behaved in a cowardly fashion."

Turning toward him, Sereb leaned closer. "You mean you acted in such fashion by your decision to circumvent your chain of command and release this information to the public."

"Are you asking me a question," Reyes said, keeping his voice even, "or trying to jam words into my mouth?"

Sereb grunted before turning toward Moratino. "Your Honor," he began.

Holding up her hand, Moratino nodded. "Commodore, unless you're invoking the Seventh Guarantee in order to avoid self-incrimination, you're bound to answer all questions put to you." Turning to Sereb, she added, "Captain, you will state your queries as questions, not editorials, opinions, or judgments."

"Understood, Your Honor," the Tellarite replied before turning his attention back to Reyes. "Now, Commodore, do you believe you were acting out of cowardice when you decided to circumvent your chain of command?"

"No," Reyes replied. "I was a coward for not doing it sooner."

For his part, Sereb seemed to have been anticipating a response along those lines. "A very noble sentiment, Commodore, though it raises an interesting question. Why not come forward earlier, before the incident at Gamma Tauri IV? After all, several colonies had already been established on planets known to possess the Taurus Meta-Genome. After the incidents involving the *U.S.S. Endeavour* at Erilon, why did you not launch your crusade for truth and security then? As you said before, you might have saved thousands of lives. Where was your nobility then?"

From behind him, Desai called out, "Objection, Your Honor. Argumentative. Counsel is badgering the witness."

"Sustained," Moratino replied. "Watch yourself, Captain."

"It's all right, Your Honor," Reyes said.

The admiral fixed him with a stern glare. "You don't have to answer that question, Commodore. Counsel will rephrase without the fire and brimstone."

"With all due respect, Your Honor," Reyes countered, "I'd like to answer it as asked."

Moratino nodded. "Very well. You may proceed."

Reyes turned toward Sereb, who had moved to his left. "It's a simple question, with a simple answer. I didn't come forward before because I was weak or blinded by duty and regulations, or both. Whatever. Take your pick. We should've taken what happened at Erilon as an obvious warning and acted accordingly. We should've at least informed colony administrators of the threat potential. Most of all, I was wrong about the true nature of what the Shedai represented. All of us were. We had no idea what we'd stirred up, not really, and the people on Gamma Tauri IV paid for that miscalculation with their lives. So, yes, I took it upon myself to act."

"Your Honor," Desai said, and Reyes heard the pleading in her voice, but he ignored her. He had long since tired of the proceedings, angry that it was taking so long to just get to the heart of the matter.

"Did I disobey orders by revealing that threat?" he asked.

"Yes. Did I conspire with anyone else? No. This is entirely on me, just as the responsibility for all of those people who've died since I took command of this station is mine. If only one good thing comes out of this trial, it should be that no one else should have to die because we didn't do our jobs."

Turning toward the bench, he glared at the board members. "And if the price for protecting the people we're sworn to defend is my head on a platter, then take it. Take it, and jam it down whoever's throat you have to back at Headquarters, and make them listen. If this circus can't even accomplish that, then do me a favor, and either throw me in a hole or out an airlock right now. I don't want any part of any organization that can't understand how badly we've turned everything out here into a pile of shit."

Silence engulfed the courtroom, except for the constant warble of the station's power generators far below their feet. Though he forced himself to stare once more at the base of the bench rather than at any of the board members, Reyes still saw Sereb in his peripheral vision. The Tellarite's expression was not one of triumph or smug satisfaction. Instead, it was unreadable. After a moment, the prosecutor cleared his throat.

"No further questions, Your Honor."

It took Moratino a moment before she said anything. Her own features had hardened into an implacable mask, though Reyes refused to move his eyes to look directly at her. Finally, she said, "Captain Desai, do you wish to redirect?"

Her response so low that Reyes could barely hear it, Desai replied, "No, Your Honor. The defense rests."

40

Standing alone in his private quarters aboard the *Omari-Ekon*, Zett Nilric studied the arrangement of clothing he had removed from his closet—the ensemble he had chosen for the next day's wear—and nodded in satisfaction. Every line in the tailored dark blue suit was perfect, every crease a razor's edge. The black shoes he would wear were polished to a high sheen, his reflection clearly visible in them.

It was part of his self-imposed regime to end each day preparing for the next. No matter how crowded his schedule might be and without regard to the lateness of the hour, Zett never retired before updating himself on the coming day's events, completing his own grueling physical training regimen, and ensuring that his appearance would be in keeping with the high standards he set for himself. Though one might argue that such strict adherence to established routine made one predictable to friends as well as enemies, Zett knew better. His habits were his own, shared with no one. He offered no insights into his private life, not to his employers and certainly not to anyone else on Ganz's staff. It required ceaseless discipline to maintain such a well-ordered life and yet keep every detail of that life to one's self, and discipline was the one trait Zett valued above all others. Those who lacked that control were weak, he knew, easily exploited. Fortunately, he was surrounded by such people, offering him numerous opportunities for advancement and personal gain simply by taking advantage of the chaos with which those people lived their lives.

All of that from pressing a simple suit and shining a pair of shoes? Zett smiled as he regarded his obsidian countenance in the small mirror affixed to one closet door. He examined his rows of gleaming teeth, searching for any hint of discoloration or the slightest particle of food that might have remained after his last meal. He saw only perfection, just as he expected.

Perhaps Ganz is right, and you do take yourself too seriously.

Dismissing the errant thought, Zett turned from the wardrobe, approving his own work as he crossed his quarters to the well-stocked bar in one corner. With his daily schedule completed, he now was free to relax, enjoying the single drink he would prepare from his personal supply of exotic liquors and other spirits before going to bed. As he poured a generous serving of a green-tinged liquid into an octagonal glass, he considered his options for the remainder of the evening. Would he listen to some music with his nightcap? Perhaps watch or read something from his considerable personal library? The music, he decided.

Drink in hand, he moved toward the ornate desk in the opposite corner. Carved from a single piece of dark marble, the desk was, like Zett himself, flawlessly organized. Free of clutter, its top hosted nothing more than the simple black portfolio that Zett carried with him each day and a computer terminal from which he could access his personal files, all of which, of course, were encrypted and protected from unauthorized access. Reaching for the workstation, Zett stopped short when the terminal's monitor flared to life, displaying a simple message.

Secure transmission incoming.

Zett glanced at the wall chronometer above his desk. Who would be contacting him at this hour? Not Ganz, certainly. His employer always reached him via their personal communications devices, rather than the *Omari-Ekon*'s comm system. Looking to the display's lower right corner, Zett noted that the transmission was accompanied by a Klingon encoding schema. *Most interesting.*

Using the terminal's keypad interface, Zett requested information on the communication's encryption and came away only mildly surprised that it was one with which he was unfamiliar.

He would have to accept the transmission in order for any decryption to take place, after which his own library of data-capturing processes could begin the task of examining and finding a way to break the encoding algorithm. For a moment, Zett wondered if this communication was being tracked by eavesdroppers on the Starfleet space station. Surely, they would be curious about the source and reasons behind a Klingon communiqué being directed to a private Orion merchant vessel in this manner. He dismissed that thought, knowing that the *Omari-Ekon* was at this moment traveling beyond the range of Starbase 47's sensor capabilities.

They will learn nothing, Zett decided, *and neither will you unless you accept the transmission.* He keyed the control to complete the connection.

On the screen, the simple text was replaced with the visage of a Klingon. Dressed in the standard black and gold uniform of the Klingon military, he appeared to be *QuchHa',* which was what the Klingons called members of their society descended from those who had suffered an odd genetic mutation that had plagued many Klingons more than a century earlier. Such individuals did not possess the prominent cranial ridges that typified the warrior race. However, while this Klingon at first appeared to be descended from that unfortunate stock, Zett still saw a subtle pattern of ridges on his bald dome. Indeed, the only hair on his head was a dark, thin mustache and an accompanying beard, which only covered his chin. Black, calculating eyes regarded Zett as they peered out from the monitor.

"Greetings, Mr. Nilric," the Klingon said, a small smile playing at the corners of his mouth. When he spoke, his words carried a clipped, precise diction that Zett found unusual for a Klingon soldier. *"My name is Chang. I trust I have not caught you at an inconvenient time?"*

A well-mannered Klingon? Zett supposed there were stranger things in the universe, but he could recall none at the moment. "Not at all, but I think you'll admit this contact is rather unusual."

"Indeed," Chang replied, nodding. *"I'm confident that once you've heard what I have to say, you'll appreciate the need for such unorthodox contact and the discretion employed to bring it about."*

Polite and long-winded. Zett decided that Chang had to be a politician, or at the very least a military officer with political ambitions who was now presented with an opportunity to pursue some unknown agenda. None of that interested Zett—at least, not unless there was something from it for him to gain.

"We have a mutual acquaintance," Chang continued. *"An associate of mine, Qahl, has spoken highly of you, particularly your discretion when it comes to sensitive matters."*

He forced his expression to reveal nothing, but Zett felt his stomach tighten at the mention of the Klingon he had met months earlier, to whom he had delivered that mysterious, damnable stone sarcophagus. Qahl himself had not been memorable, his uninspiring presence aboard Zett's ship, the *Icarion,* all but over-shadowed by the enigmatic object the Nalori had acquired on Traelus II. The remote planet in a relatively unexplored sector of the Taurus Reach was home to a nonspace-faring civilization that nevertheless was aware of other inhabited worlds and intelligent species. As such, over the course of the past several years, they had been making their resource-rich world an ever-increasing destination for interstellar commerce.

More important, the planet reportedly was also home to several other artifacts like the one Zett had obtained, though as far as he had been able to determine, it did not possess any of the ancient ruins the Federation and Klingon Empire had found on other worlds throughout the Taurus Reach. Neither Starfleet nor the Klingons—as far as Zett knew, anyway—were aware of Traelus II's potential value to their seemingly never-ending quest to learn the secrets of the ancient civilization that once had called this region home.

They can have it, Zett had decided after his encounter with the sarcophagus. The intense anxiety and, yes, even fear he had felt while in the object's presence were more than enough to convince the assassin that this long-dead race was to be avoided at all costs. If the Federation or the Klingons wanted to tempt the wrath of whatever had once ruled over the Taurus Reach, that was not his concern.

"Qahl is a competent courier," Zett said, "but I know little of him beyond that." Indeed, he was more than a bit concerned about the Klingon dropping his name in such casual fashion. He made a mental note to track down Qahl in short order and see to that lapse. "Never mind him. What do *you* want with me?"

Chang nodded. *"My superiors wish to make use of your particular talents, Mr. Nilric. You will understand their desire to remain anonymous, at least for the moment. However, I am authorized to negotiate on their behalf, and they are prepared to pay handsomely for your services."*

Zett held up a hand. "Chang, I've met Vulcans who don't take this long to get to the point."

"Very well," Chang replied, his voice losing some of its near-lyrical cadence. *"As you know, the Klingon Empire has placed a price on the head of Commodore Diego Reyes. My employers want you to utilize your considerable skills to resolve this issue."*

Zett all but laughed out loud. "Your employers have a sense of humor I can admire." He leaned closer to the desktop monitor. "Why?"

"The Earther's actions at Gamma Tauri IV are an insult to the Klingon Empire," Chang replied. *"For this, he must pay— with his life."*

Frowning, Zett asked, "Don't Klingons usually like to handle these sorts of things themselves? Honor and all of that?"

Chang sneered in response. *"Sometimes honor and protocol must step aside in the name of swift and meaningful justice."* Now it was his turn to lean closer. *"Not that any Klingon needs to explain himself to anyone."*

Having had his fill of seemingly contradictory and frankly confusing philosophical discussions on this topic with more than one Klingon, Zett said, "I honestly couldn't care less about any of that. Surely, your employers understand that the commodore is under heavy guard at all times and is likely to remain so until his court-martial is completed. That says nothing of the fact that he's also incarcerated aboard one of the most powerful Starfleet space stations in the quadrant."

"A challenge for a person possessing your specific gifts," Chang countered. He reached forward to something Zett could not see, and an instant later, a string of numbers appeared on the lower part of the computer screen. *"I trust the offer I've provided is sufficient for you at least to consider taking this contract?"*

Eyeing the numbers displayed on his monitor, Zett could not help agreeing with the Klingon. It was indeed a nice figure. It would have to be; if he was successful in carrying out this plan hatched by Qahl's superiors, he quickly would become one of the most wanted fugitives in this part of the galaxy.

"Very well," he said after a moment. "I'll think about it."

Chang's face broadened into a smile wide enough that Zett thought the Klingon might well carry Nalori blood in his veins. *"Excellent. I shall await your answer, but I must recommend against delaying your decision, Mr. Nilric, for nothing will come of nothing."*

What is he babbling about?

The communication ended, leaving Zett alone to bask in his room's sudden silence, undisturbed as he pondered the job and the considerable amount of money he had just been offered. Did Diego Reyes pose that much of a threat to the Klingon Empire? From what he knew of current events, Zett could not agree with that, not that he cared. The more likely scenario was that the commodore had essentially stepped on the toes of Klingon honor, whatever that was supposed to be these days, and somebody wanted face-saving vengeance.

Either way, Zett decided, and with everything else hanging over his head, *I wouldn't want to be Reyes just now.*

41

There was just no other way to say it, Xiong decided. Klingons stank.

In the cramped confines of the narrow underground tunnel leading from the surface of whatever planet it was he had been brought to, the stench was all but overpowering. Xiong had to force himself not to gag as he endured the stench emanating from the bodies of the two Klingon soldiers assigned to usher him through the network of tunnels. He was tempted to ask when either of them had last bathed, certain that the answer would be a date several years before his birth. Even their breath was horrid, a consequence of Klingon cuisine coupled with seemingly non-existent dental hygiene.

Who needs disruptors and knives when you wield that?

He reached up in a vain attempt to wipe away the offending odor attacking his nostrils, and Xiong ended up regretting the unplanned movement, as it earned him yet another strike between his shoulder blades.

"Keep your hands away from your body, Earther," warned one of the two Klingon soldiers as Xiong was shoved forward.

The young lieutenant sighed, electing to say nothing. While he was confident that the soldiers would obey their orders not to injure him, he could not help wondering how greatly the definition of "injure" might differ between Klingons and humans.

Trying to put such thoughts out of his mind, Xiong attempted to focus on his surroundings. The tunnel was a crude one, by all appearances cut from the rock with primitive hand tools. The floor was uneven, and he had to watch his footing, lest he stumble and fall. Likewise, the ceiling was low, requiring him to duck on occasion in order to avoid bumping his head. With their larger physiques, his Klingon escorts seemed to find navigating the tunnel an even greater challenge, as evidenced by the frequent grunts of irritation he heard. Mounts, presumably for primitive torches, lined the walls at more or less regular intervals, though none of them was in use. Instead, cabling had been affixed to the rock, from which hung low-level lights.

The trio rounded a bend in the tunnel, and Xiong realized that the light level was increasing beyond that of the lamps on the walls. He also heard the sound of voices and the low hum of what he suspected was a power generator. Another turn revealed the entrance to a larger chamber, and now Xiong saw a handful of other Klingons moving about stacks of crates, supplies, and equipment. Emerging from the tunnel, the lieutenant was surprised to see that a makeshift worksite had been erected within the cavern, with tables supporting tools, computer equipment, and other objects Xiong did not recognize.

His eyes shifted to study the Klingons in the room, counting seven that he could see, including one female. Seated at one of the tables, with a computer terminal in front of her, she looked up at his arrival. Like her male companions, she wore the standard uniform of a Klingon soldier. Her dark, shoulder-length hair was pulled away from her face to reveal dark, angular features. The ridges on her forehead were noticeable though not as pronounced as he had seen on other Klingon women, and in a bizarre way that he did not fully understand, he did not find her unattractive.

You might want to rethink your priorities, Lieutenant.

Turning to look over her shoulder, she called out, "He is here, my captain." Xiong followed her gaze until he saw a large, swarthy Klingon male emerge from between stacks of packing crates. Compared with the female, this specimen was gigantic. The black hair that fell from his shoulders was longer than the female's, flowing behind him like a mane. Xiong's eyes noted the disruptor pistol and the very large knife suspended from a belt at the Klingon's waist.

"I am Komoraq," the Klingon said, studying Xiong with a critical and—Xiong was sure—disapproving eye. "And you are the Earther who has studied these relics?"

The blunt statement sent a wave of unease through Xiong. He had been suspecting something like this. His capture and subsequent treatment had to be related to his knowledge of the Shedai artifacts, such as those he had been studying on Erilon.

They've found something here, wherever here is, but they don't know what to do with it.

Xiong cleared his throat and said, "Yes, I've studied them. We've made some small progress understanding them and the technology." It was not technically a lie, but even he did not feel convinced by his own words.

Neither, apparently, did Komoraq, who offered a dismissive grunt.

"Your modesty aside, the simple fact is that you seem to be the foremost authority on these people and the power they once wielded. We wish to understand that power, and I've brought you here to assist us."

Xiong tried to affect an expression of uncertainty. "We've only just begun to scratch the surface, but based on what we've found and what we've seen, this civilization is orders of magnitude more advanced than yours or mine. You know what happened to the Jinoteur system, right?"

The Klingon nodded. "Indeed, as well as Palgrenax, Gamma Tauri IV, and even the planet from which you were taken. We've made some discoveries of our own, here and on other planets, but I'll admit we lag behind the Federation." His eyes bored into Xiong. "That is why you are here, Earther. We have similar Shedai technology on this rock, though we are unable to do anything with it. Even the artifacts discovered on Palgrenax and Lerais III offered more insight." He gestured toward the Klingon female. "My wife believes that this is because of what happened with the Jinoteur system. Is she correct?" As he asked the question, Komoraq's left hand rested on the handle of the far-too-large knife on his hip.

Feeling his anxiety rising, Xiong replied, "We don't know."

The Klingon wasted no time, waving to one of the guards flanking Xiong. "Kill him."

"Wait!" Xiong blurted, holding up his hands. "I said I didn't know, but it is a possibility we've been exploring." That was somewhat truthful, but he hoped it was enough of a feint to forestall his execution, if only for a few moments. "Since the system's disappearance, all of the alien technology we've encountered has gone dormant. We suspect a connection, but we've had no way to test the theory, since we had only limited success even accessing the equipment in the first place."

"It is because humanoids are not biologically compatible with the technology," the Klingon female said, moving to stand beside her husband. "Correct?"

Xiong shrugged. "Maybe." He kept his expression neutral, careful to reveal no clue to the Klingon woman that she was indeed on the right track. "We've only just begun to test that concept, though." Another small obfuscation.

"Then it's fortunate that I brought you here, rather than killing you outright on Erilon," Komoraq said. He indicated his wife with a nod of his head. "Lorka?"

To Xiong's guards, she said, "Bring him," before turning on her heel and marching off, cutting a path through the stacks of crates and equipment. Xiong felt a massive hand on his shoulder, directing him to follow Lorka, and he and his escorts set off after her. As they made their way around a large container inscribed with long strings of text written in Klingonese, Xiong knew what he would see even before it came into view. Still, he could not help a gasp of surprise as he beheld what the Klingons had found.

It was a series of control consoles, nearly identical to those found on Erilon, Ravanar IV, and other worlds where Starfleet research teams had discovered remnants of Shedai civilization. Like those with which he had been working before his capture on Erilon, these consoles seemed active, receiving power from a portable generator. Xiong could only assume that, also like those on Erilon and—presumably—every other world containing such technology, these systems were all but useless without the guiding force once provided by the now-departed Jinoteur system.

A Tholian stood before them. It was dressed in an environment suit much like the one worn by Nezrene, though this one was a metallic red in color. At his approach, the Tholian turned and appeared to regard him through the narrow slits in the suit's helmet covering. Xiong heard a chorus of lyrical twitters, indecipherable gibberish until the translator incorporated into the Tholian's suit offered up its rendition.

"Why have you brought this outsider here?"

Ignoring the Tholian, Lorka said to Xiong, "This creature has proven to be of limited use to this point. Its physiology has allowed us to gain some access to this equipment, but it lacks any knowledge of its ancestors or their technology. That is why you're here. You will work with it." Turning, she reached for a small equipment box sitting on the rocky floor next to the console. From it she extracted what Xiong recognized as the tricorder confiscated from him at the time of his capture. "Your research and discoveries on Erilon should prove most helpful in that regard, yes?"

So, Xiong decided, this Klingon woman was no fool. Not a simple soldier, he suspected, but likely one of their scientists. As such, she would not be easily duped, and he would have to take great care in what he said or—more important—did not say.

"With time," he said, hoping not to appear too eager to please. "There's still so much we don't know."

"Then I suggest you get started," Lorka said, tossing him the tricorder. "But rest assured, Earther, patience is not one of my husband's numerous virtues. The moment he senses that you are attempting to deceive or misdirect us, or should you try to escape, you will die."

42

Despite the sensation that the collar of his dress uniform was choking the life out of him, Reyes did not reach for it, did not move to run a finger between it and his neck. Instead, he remained fixed at his position of attention, staring straight ahead as the members of the court-martial board resumed their places on the bench. Out of the corner of his right eye, Reyes saw Desai and Sereb, both standing as well. Below the bench, Lieutenant T'Nir stood facing them, her expression implacable as usual.

The happy fun group.

Admiral Moratino and the trial board had spent nearly three days deliberating behind closed doors, and Reyes—with Desai's help—had tried to take some comfort from the protracted waiting. According to her, it was a good sign, indicating that the board did not view the charges against Reyes and the actions he had taken as a simple matter of good or bad, right or wrong. As far as he knew, no Starfleet flag officer had ever stood trial on charges on this magnitude, not with ramifications such as those that might still come about as a result of the events that had occurred and that continued to unfold in the Taurus Reach. In Desai's estimation, the members likely were proceeding with utmost care, perhaps aware of the historic nature of the ruling they would hand down and the precedent such a decision might set for the future.

Or it could mean that they just haven't found the perfect deep, dark hole in which to bury me.

As the board members moved to stand before their seats, Reyes allowed his gaze to flicker to each face, trying to gauge any clue or hint from their expressions. None of the officers showed any outward signs of emotion, their features fixed and neutral as they awaited instructions from Moratino. Without being asked, Lieutenant T'Nir reached for the computer terminal next to her chair and activated the unit, once again recording the court proceedings.

"Commodore Reyes," the admiral said after everyone was in the proper place and she had rung the ship's bell to bring the courtroom to order, "the board has reached its verdict. Are you prepared to hear this decision?"

Here we go.

It had all come to this. The hours spent in earnest preparation, the cold, ruthless prosecution by Sereb and the equally impassioned defense mounted by Rana, the testimony Reyes himself had provided while on the witness stand, and now the trial board's deliberations were past them. All that mattered now was how, or even if, Sereb or Desai had managed to influence the board with their arguments. Though Reyes had always fancied himself a good judge of people and their possible reactions to given situations, he had found himself powerless to produce even the slightest notion of which way the board might be leaning, and that was before they had secluded themselves for their private discussions.

Well, now's your chance to find out, he mused, chastising himself. *Get on with it, already.*

Steeling himself, Reyes nodded. "I am, Your Honor."

Without further delay or preamble, Moratino said, "On the charge of conspiracy, this court finds Commodore Reyes not guilty."

Not really a surprise, Reyes knew. Of the charges against him, everyone had told him this was the one least likely to be upheld. Still, it was a moment's relief actually to hear the decision spoken aloud. His plea of guilty to the charge of willful disobedience had already been entered and accepted. Reyes forced himself to stand rigid and still as he waited for the final charge and findings to be read.

Without even the slightest change in her tone or cadence, Mo-

ratino said, "On the charge and specifications of releasing classified information to unauthorized personnel, this court finds
Commodore Reyes guilty as charged."

There it was, the final, most damning charge against him, the
one even Rana herself had expressed doubts about their ability to
overcome. Despite all of his mental and emotional preparation,
Moratino's every word was like flame scorching his flesh. From
his right, Reyes heard Desai's subtle yet sharp intake of breath.
His heart pounded in his chest, and blood rushed in his ears, and
Reyes felt his knees begin to quiver. He locked them into place,
refusing to present even the slightest sign of weakness or reaction. A glance out of the corner of his eye told him that Desai also
was struggling to maintain her own bearing.

"Does the commodore wish to make any further statement
before the court proceeds to sentencing?" Moratino asked.

What the hell am I supposed to say now? Only sheer force of
will prevented Reyes from asking the question aloud. No, he decided. He had already taken full advantage of the opportunities
afforded to him to speak on his own behalf. There was nothing
more to be said and no need to delay the inevitable any longer.

Reyes shook his head. "I have no further statement, Your
Honor."

Relaxing her posture, Moratino said, "I do have something to
say before sentence is read. Commodore Reyes, I'd like you to
know that the questions presented to this court-martial were not
easy ones to answer. We've dealt with issues typical and yet vital
to the maintaining of proper discipline, order, and leadership that
are hallmarks of Starfleet service. At the same time, we've addressed concerns about the very safety and security of the Federation, whose people and principles we all are sworn to honor
and defend.

"While it would be easy to characterize this trial as a matter
of addressing the simple unlawful actions of a single officer, to do
so overlooks the larger issues that brought about those actions.
Many of those issues are matters of a scope far greater than can
be adequately addressed in this forum.

"However, we are left with certain moral absolutes, which we cannot dismiss and against which we can tolerate no willful disregard, especially when such action results in the alarming or disruption of the very people we are sworn to protect. Starfleet's chain of command is in place for practical, time-tested reasons, as are its regulations and principles. Particularly now, when the Federation faces challenges and obstacles in regard to which its fate has yet to be determined, and with the very likely possibility of war with enemies to our way of life, those principles must be honored. No matter how well intentioned their actions might be, we cannot allow our officers—above all, officers of the rank and experience held by Commodore Reyes—to defy those principles. Likewise, such actions must be appropriately punished, as an example to all who wear our uniform and affirm the oaths we hold so dear.

"Commodore Diego Reyes," Moratino said, her gaze now fixed on him, "it is the ruling of this court that, effective immediately, you are stripped of all rank as well as all allowances and privileges accorded to officers of flag rank. You will be permitted an appropriate time to put your personal affairs in order, after which you will be remanded to the Starfleet detention facility in Auckland, New Zealand, on Earth for a period of no less than ten years, with credit for time already spent in confinement as well as the transfer to Earth."

The words rang in Reyes's ears, pounded his skull, raked across his flesh. No amount of preparation or reflection, none of the nights he had lain awake pondering such possibilities, had been sufficient to offset the plain, blunt force of the judgment Moratino placed upon him. In the eyes of all lawful authority, he was a criminal, branded and stained for all time. Nothing he did from this point forward, no thought, word, or deed, would ever change this simple, harsh truth.

"Upon completion of that sentence," Moratino continued, "you will be dismissed from Starfleet with forfeiture of all allowances or benefits. Transfer to Earth is to commence at the earliest available opportunity, and you will be permitted confinement to your quarters until that time. Mr. Reyes, do you understand the sentence I have just imposed?"

His mouth having suddenly gone dry, it took an extra moment for Reyes to summon the spit necessary to offer even the simplest reply. "Yes, Your Honor."

Perhaps not in approval or satisfaction as much as simple acceptance, Moratino nodded. "Very well. Guards, you will secure the prisoner to his quarters, where he will remain until further notice. This court stands adjourned." She reached forward and took up the wooden striker ringing the bell one final time before laying it to rest.

Reyes stood motionless, waiting as Lieutenant T'Nir deactivated the computer unit and the board members turned and filed out of the room. He turned to see Desai regarding him, tears threatening in the corners of her eyes. Over her shoulder, Captain Sereb made an effort to avoid eye contact as he replaced his belongings in his briefcase. Finished with that, the Tellarite rose to his full height and turned to face Reyes, his deep-set eyes studying him for several moments before the lawyer turned and exited the room without uttering a single word.

A Tellarite who's a good sport? Reyes could not help the wayward thought. *Now I've seen it all.*

"Diego," Desai said, her right hand moving as though to reach for him, but she brought it back to her side as the pair of security officers moved to flank him. "I . . . I don't know what to . . ."

Drawing a deep breath, Reyes made a show of looking about the empty courtroom before his eyes returned to her. Neither he nor Desai spoke.

There was nothing to say.

43

T'Prynn buckled as Sten slammed into her, the weight of his body carrying them both to the sand. She kicked and bucked beneath him, twisting as they tumbled down the slope, sand stinging her eyes and getting into her nose and mouth. Sten's hands reached for her throat, and she struck out, knocking away his arms. Releasing a cry of rage, she punched him in the face. He grunted in pain, and she felt his grip loosen. She kicked at him, her foot catching the inside of his knee. His leg collapsed, and he rolled off her.

T'Prynn came up on one knee, her stance unsteady as she gulped air into her burning lungs. All around her, the wind howled, blowing sand across her body and stinging her exposed skin. Holding up a hand to shield her eyes, she saw him lying on the sand beside her on his stomach, already scrambling to his feet, and with a single awkward movement, she lunged forward with the knife in her right hand, driving the blade into Sten's thigh. He screamed in agony, twisting away from her and allowing himself to tumble down the side of the dune.

The attacks were coming more frequently now, offering her almost no respite. With each successive engagement, she grew weaker, with no means of replenishing her flagging strength. Conversely, Sten appeared for each new clash bearing no injuries or signs of their previous encounters. His strength and determination continued unabated, fueled by the rage of being denied that which he believed was rightfully his.

Looking about, T'Prynn saw nothing but endless rolling sand dunes, offering no paths of retreat or sanctuaries in which to hide.

Her only recourse was to stand and fight, again. Submission was not an option, not so long as breath entered her body. She heard footsteps churning through the sand and turned to see Sten running toward her, once more brandishing a *lirpa,* which had—like Sten himself—seemingly appeared from the very air.

"T'Prynn!" he yelled, his face contorting into a mask of rage.

T'Prynn scrambled to her feet and backpedaled, looking for the weapon she was certain she had dropped during the fight. Nothing but windswept sand surrounded her. Sten was scrambling up the dune now, holding the *lirpa* over his head as he charged. Then he stumbled as a yawning pit seemed to appear in the sand at his feet, spiraling open like a massive iris. T'Prynn watched the sand within the circle fall, disappearing into blackness. Shouting in alarm, Sten tried to lunge to one side, but even his remarkable reflexes were not enough to keep him from dropping into the pit. As he disappeared from sight, T'Prynn still heard him calling her name, the echo of his voice fading into the darkness that had claimed him.

Standing next to M'Benga near the door to the bedchamber, Pennington watched as Sobon's eyes snapped open and he pulled his withered hands from the *katra* points on T'Prynn's face, breaking the meld. His breathing was accelerated, and perspiration had broken out on the Vulcan healer's forehead.

"There is not much time," Sobon said, his voice low and weak. "We must begin the *Dashaya-Ni'Var.*"

From where she stood at the foot of the bed, which had been turned so that its left side no longer rested against the wall but allowed for a person to access that side, T'Nel moved without prompting to the small table in the corner of the room, retrieving what Pennington recognized as a *vre-katra*. Perhaps it was one from Sobon's study, the oversized crystalline vessel appearing to weigh quite heavily in the Vulcan woman's hands. "It is ready, Healer."

Leaning closer to M'Benga, Pennington asked, "They're

doing it? Now?" He regarded Sobon again. "He doesn't look as if he's up to this."

"We're out of time," the doctor replied. "If he thinks they need to go in now, then he's worried that T'Prynn won't last much longer. Besides, T'Nel will be with him."

Pennington nodded, recalling what Sobon had explained to them over dinner one evening more than a week earlier, though he did not pretend to understand any of it. T'Nel would participate in the meld, following Sobon's lead into the depths of T'Prynn's tortured mind. Her task would be to guide T'Prynn—or her *katra,* at least—to a place of relative safety. Meanwhile, Sobon would attempt to engage Sten's essence directly, forcing a joining of their two *katras.* Unlike T'Prynn, whose mental powers had been far outmatched by Sten's during the meld he had initiated in the midst of their ritual combat five decades earlier, Sobon was counting on his own much greater experience to give him the advantage over Sten's unrequited lust and unwavering rage.

The two humans said nothing more as T'Nel positioned the *vre-katra* next to Sobon's left hand, while his right hand remained on the bed, next to T'Prynn's head. Then T'Nel moved to the opposite side of the bed, her movements rapid but not hurried. As expected, neither Vulcan's face revealed any outward sign of emotion.

"Let us begin," Sobon said, his voice barely a whisper as the wrinkled fingers of his right hand reached once more for T'Prynn's face, seeking the contact points. On the opposite side of the bed, T'Nel touched her fingers to her sister's head in similar fashion, and Pennington watched as Sobon and T'Nel closed their eyes at the same moment.

"Terau-kashkau-Veh-shetau," Sobon said, his features tightening as he recited the ancient Vulcan invocation, the basic translation of which Pennington now understood to mean "Our minds are merging, becoming one." The words were offered in a dialect that, according to Sobon, had not even been spoken aloud with any regularity for more than two thousand years. Despite himself, the reporter felt his pulse quickening as he listened to the

Vulcan master continue to recite a litany of incantations in the obscure dialect, now joined by T'Nel, who also was invoking the ritualistic text in synchronicity with Sobon.

Something flickered in the corner of Pennington's left eye, and when he turned his head toward the source, he could not help the gasp of surprise that escaped his lips.

Beneath Sobon's left hand, the *vre-katra* was glowing, emitting an ominous crimson pulse.

"T'Prynn."

She jerked at the sound of the new voice, turning to search for its source until her eyes fell upon Anna Sandesjo, standing less than ten meters from her. She appeared just as she had the last time T'Prynn had seen her, before she boarded the doomed freighter *Malacca*. In her hands, she once more wielded a *bat'leth,* the ceremonial bladed weapon that signified her Klingon heritage.

"Anna?" T'Prynn said, confusion washing over her. How was Anna here now? Despite her uncertainty, T'Prynn could not deny the relief washing over her as she beheld her lover, the strains of prolonged battle seeming already to fade. She no longer heard the wind rushing in her ears, and even the sand seemed to have quelled. "I do not understand." Had Anna come to take her from this place? The idea of leaving behind the war she had waged for far too long was like a siren's call.

"All will be explained in time, T'Prynn," Anna said. Moving her right hand from the pommel of her *bat'leth,* she held it out to her. "Come with me."

T'Prynn extended her own hand, her knees weak as they supported her battered body. Soon, she realized, she would rest, in the comforting embrace of the one person with whom she had been able to find even momentary peace. Her hand slipped into Anna's, and T'Prynn felt the other woman's fingers wrap around her own. Warmth erupted from her very touch, cascading through her being and pushing away the pain that had been her constant companion.

"Come, T'Prynn," Anna said, an instant before her features stretched and contorted into those of Sten, the *bat'leth* in her hand morphing into the familiar shape of a *lirpa*. T'Prynn felt the grip around her hand tighten as Sten's eyes widened in the all-consuming rage that was now the sum total of his existence.

"Submit."

Releasing a howl of rage, T'Prynn lashed out, catching Sten across his temple. How dare he invoke Anna's image, defile it for his own twisted pleasure? Was it not enough that he hounded her mercilessly, stalking and assaulting her without remorse or respite for what seemed like eternity? Now he conjured the image of the one person she had cherished, had *loved,* in his fight against her? The thoughts infuriated T'Prynn even further, and she channeled that wrath into strike after strike, ripping free her hand from Sten's grip and using it to pummel him again and again. The *lirpa* dropped from his other hand and moved to protect his head. T'Prynn ignored the gesture, pounding him until her hands ran slick with her own blood. Sten stumbled backward over a dune and fell to the sand, rolling away from her. She did not follow, standing on the rise, all but consumed by the ferocity of unchecked emotion boiling within. Her pulse rushed in her ears, the sounds of her labored breathing drowning out even the intensifying wind.

Then T'Prynn felt a hand on her shoulder, and a new, softer voice seemed to whisper in her ear, easily heard even over the wind. "Come with me, my sister." Turning toward the voice, she beheld T'Nel, her older sibling. "We must leave this place now."

T'Prynn's first instinct was to jerk away from this new arrival. Another perverted deception invoked by Sten, of this she was certain. Would she be forced to battle her sister as well? Who else might Sten pull from the depths of her mind only to turn against her? "No!" she shouted, screaming to be heard over the wind. "It is a lie!" She turned and scrambled up the side of the dune away from the image of T'Nel, looking for any place to hide. A gaping hole appeared in the sand ahead of her, dark and forbidding but offering perhaps her only chance of escape. T'Prynn lunged for it without hesitation.

"T'Prynn!" shouted T'Nel, still close enough behind her that T'Prynn could hear her breathing, but she ignored the cry. She threw herself forward, reaching for the widening chasm, only to feel arms wrapping around her waist and dragging her to the sand. "No! You can't!" Her fingers clawed at the sand as she tried to pull herself to the void that was her salvation. "You must come with me, T'Prynn. I will take you away from here."

"Lies!" T'Prynn growled, wrenching herself free, but even as she regained her feet, T'Nel was on her again. "Release me!" she cried as she felt T'Nel's hands on her, pulling her farther from the hole. Then she sensed movement in the corner of her eye and looked up to see Sten standing nearby, once more looking clean, refreshed, and free of injury, as he always did whenever he came for her. Once more, he held a *lirpa* in his hands, the weapon's blade carving a path through the air.

"Let me go!" she screamed at T'Nel. Instead, she felt her sister pulling her away from Sten even as he advanced toward them, *lirpa* held high.

"T'Prynn," T'Nel said, her grip unrelenting. "We must go. Now!"

Sten shouted, "Leave her! She is mine!" He swung the *lirpa* as he drew closer, its blade gleamed in the unforgiving desert sun. T'Nel released T'Prynn, and both women ducked to avoid his attack. T'Prynn felt the weapon catch her sleeve, slicing the material as easily as it moved through the air, and she threw herself down the side of the rolling hill, scrambling to retreat.

"Sten!"

All three of them stopped at the sound of the new voice, and T'Prynn turned to see Sobon, the elder Vulcan who had intruded upon her consciousness, helping her with increasing frequency to escape Sten's unceasing campaign. Sobon stood on the wind-swept sand, waiting with hands clasped before him in a meditative stance.

"You," Sten said, pointing his *lirpa* at Sobon. "You stand between me and what is mine. T'Prynn has defied and dishonored me for the last time."

"She is not yours," the healer replied, his voice even. "She rejected you and accepted the ritual challenge. You are the one without honor, for not releasing her from the sacrament. It is time to correct that mistake."

Sten, having long abandoned all semblance of discipline and bearing, actually laughed at that. "If you feel you can rise to the challenge, elder, you are welcome to try." The words were scarcely out of his mouth before he lunged forward, *lirpa* swinging for Sobon. T'Prynn could only watch as the blade cut through the air, aiming for the elder's neck. Sobon stood unmoving, waiting for the attack. When the weapon made contact, the aged Vulcan's body shifted, dissolving and allowing the blade to pass unhindered through him. The momentum of the swing carried Sten off balance, and as he lost his footing, Sobon leaped forward, reaching out to capture Sten's head between his hands.

The instant his fingers touched Sten, both Vulcans' bodies were enveloped in a blinding field of red energy. T'Prynn reached up to shield her eyes from the intensity of the glare as Sten cried out at the contact, jerking in apparent pain. Sobon stepped closer, countering Sten's attempts to break free and moving with the speed and strength of a man half his age as he reinforced his hold on the other Vulcan. His expression remained passive, though T'Prynn could see the strain on his features.

"Dashaya-Ni'Var-kashkau-Veh-shetau-Sten," Sobon said, and Sten shrieked, his eyes screwed shut and his mouth hanging open in new distress. At the same time, T'Prynn felt something tugging on her own consciousness, and a wave of dizziness washed over her. She stumbled, feeling herself beginning to plummet toward the sand, only to have her fall arrested by hands on her shoulders. Looking up, she locked eyes with T'Nel, seeing the concern in her sister's eyes.

She's real.

"Come with me, T'Prynn," T'Nel said.

T'Prynn turned her gaze back to where Sobon and Sten remained locked in their odd embrace. Sten's every attempt to break the elder's grip went unheeded, with Sobon's body shifting in and out of phase and not allowing any of Sten's blows to land. *"Dashaya-Ni'Var-kashkau-Veh-shetau-Sten,"* the healer repeated, his tone carrying more force this time. The crimson energy field that had enveloped them both now seemed to stretch, as though trying to pull away from Sobon's body and taking Sten with it. The younger Vulcan screamed in protest, and now his hands found purchase around Sobon's throat. For a moment, it appeared that Sobon's body would shift again, freeing itself from Sten's grip, but both Vulcans instead remained in place.

"What's happening?" T'Prynn asked, her hands reaching up to press against her temples as she felt something pulling against her own consciousness.

"Sobon is separating Sten's *katra* from yours," T'Nel replied, "but he is growing fatigued. Sten is still very powerful."

T'Prynn watched as Sobon faltered for the first time and dropped to one knee, though his hands remained fixed on Sten's face. Sten stumbled forward, trapped in his opponent's grip even as his own hands seemed to tighten around Sobon's neck. Sobon's only reaction was to keep repeating the strange phrase in that incomprehensible Vulcan dialect. Each time he spoke the words, Sten's body spasmed in obvious pain, but he did not weaken. Likewise, T'Prynn also felt something reaching into her, as though trying to extract something from the depths of her being.

"He needs help," T'Prynn said, shaking T'Nel's hands from her and rising to her feet. Sunlight glinted off metal to her right, and she turned to see Sten's *lirpa* lying in the sand. With no idea what she might do next, she ran to the weapon and hefted it, feeling its comforting weight in her hands.

Ahead of her, Sobon continued to recite the strange incantation, the blazing red energy field stretching and twisting as it moved around him and Sten. Sobon removed his left hand from Sten's face, extending it over his head, and the field followed it. This time, Sten's body also seemed to elongate, as though bonded to the energy field the elder had conjured. Summoning whatever energy drove him, he pulled himself from Sobon until they were connected only by the fingers of the older Vulcan's right hand,

and when he turned, his eyes fell upon T'Prynn. She felt his rage pulsing through her, forcing its way into her, but she ignored it as she stepped closer and with a single thrust drove the *lirpa* blade into Sten's chest.

Sten's body convulsed, his face contorting into an expression of terror and agony. He reached for the *lirpa,* hands wrapping around the staff in a feeble attempt to extract the blade, but his fingers slid uselessly along its length. He went limp, but instead of his body falling to the sand, it was drawn into the crimson energy field Sobon still commanded. The field traveled along Sobon's body and down the length of his left arm, before leaping from the Vulcan's fingertips and disappearing as though it had never existed.

The wind stopped. The sand settled. Even the sun seemed to dim. Of Sten there was no trace. Only Sobon stood before her, his expression one of calm and welcoming, before he, too, vanished before her eyes.

She felt T'Nel's hand on her arm as her sister said, "You're free, T'Prynn."

Pennington watched as Sobon's body jerked, the red hue of the *vre-katra* beneath his left hand pulsing with ever-growing fury. Sobon's breathing had become shallow and erratic, and M'Benga stepped closer to gauge his condition. His fingers twitched on T'Prynn's face, and Pennington was sure he heard the healer mumble something in ancient Vulcan.

Then the *vre-katra* went dormant, the pulse fading to nothingness just as Sobon opened his eyes, drawing a deep breath.

"Healer Sobon," M'Benga said, stepping closer. "Are you all right?" Without waiting to be asked, the doctor reached for a carafe of water and poured some of its contents into a glass, which he handed to the Vulcan.

Stepping around the bed, Pennington watched as T'Nel opened her eyes, pulling her hands from T'Prynn's face. Unlike Sobon, who appeared on the verge of collapse, she looked visibly shaken but otherwise unaffected. "T'Nel?"

She reached up to wipe some of the perspiration from her forehead. "I am uninjured, Mr. Pennington."

"Did it work?" he asked, his eyes moving from her to T'Prynn to Sobon and the *vre-katra* and back again. "What the hell happened?"

"T'Prynn and Sten are no longer linked," Sobon replied, his hand hovering over the *vre-katra,* which appeared now to be nothing more than an inanimate hunk of glass or crystal. "All that he was is now contained within."

Pennington scarcely dared to believe what he was hearing. "That's it? It's over?"

Standing over T'Prynn and doing his best to judge her condition without benefit of his medical equipment, M'Benga said, "She doesn't appear to be in her coma any longer. Her respiration and heart rate are elevated. If I had to guess, I'd say she was in a self-healing trance."

"You are correct, Doctor," T'Nel said. "She'll remain that way while her mind adjusts to Sten's absence. There's no way to know how long this healing might take. She could awaken tomorrow, or days or even weeks from now."

"Will she be okay when she wakes up?" Pennington asked.

Sobon shook his head. "There is no way to know. She may have suffered damage during the *Dashaya-Ni'Var.* We will know when she awakens."

Looking to M'Benga, Pennington could see his friend struggling to remain silent, no doubt frustrated at being unable to utilize any of his modern equipment. It was likely that he could ascertain T'Prynn's condition and likelihood for recovery within seconds.

"What the hell are we supposed to do now?" he asked.

Sobon was, as expected, impassive as he sipped his water. "We wait."

44

Xiong watched the display on his tricorder, his heart racing in time with the increased activity the device was detecting. Finally, after several days of effort, the first sign of progress was manifesting itself.

"I think we've got something," he said, stepping closer to Tasthene, his Tholian companion and fellow captive. The Tholian was standing before one of the ancient Shedai consoles, his crystalline appendages resting on the gleaming onyx surface and making use of the contact points he had found there. The equipment pulsed with life, radiating a power the young lieutenant figured it had not exuded for thousands of years.

At the console, Tasthene said, "I feel odd, as though I am touching an active power conduit."

Xiong nodded. "In essence, that's exactly what you're doing." He had observed a similar scene with the mysterious Shedai being on Erilon months earlier. Since then, he had been working to solidify his theory that the enigmatic species, by virtue of its wondrous crystalline physiology, was capable of channeling electrical impulses both within and beyond their physical bodies. So far, it was only a hypothesis, one he had been unable to investigate given the notable lack of Shedai test subjects. However, the revelation that the Shedai and the Tholians shared an ancestral connection within their DNA offered Xiong new hope for furthering his research. The experiments he and Nezrene had conducted on Erilon had lent credence to his theories.

And now he had Tasthene.

"This is not at all like what I am used to," the Tholian said. As

Xiong had learned during their time together, Tasthene was his people's equivalent to a computer systems engineer. In his role, he had designed and built such mechanisms for a wide variety of uses, including those aboard Tholian military spacecraft. "Even our most advanced prototypes offered nothing like this."

Before them, the console's array of thirteen graphic displays teemed with images. Most were static, but strings of indecipherable alien text and colors scrolled across four of the screens, moving too fast for his human eyes to follow. "Can you make out any of that?"

Tasthene uttered another string of clicks. "Some, but most of it is in a language I do not understand. At least, I do not think I understand. Though I have never before seen this script, at some level, it is recognizable, but I am unable to explain how that is possible." Lifting his left arm from the panel on which it had been resting, the Tholian continued, "These readings are from a subterranean power plant hundreds of kilometers below us, as well as a computer storage and environmental control system. The other systems I do not recognize, and the information regarding them appears to carry a sophisticated encryption scheme." After a moment, he added, "All attempts to move beyond the planetary network are proving ineffective."

Studying the information being relayed to his tricorder, Xiong frowned. It was true that Tasthene's efforts had resulted in far more success than what he had been able to do by himself on Erilon. Still, the vast interstellar network the Shedai once had used to showcase their power and supreme rule over the Taurus Reach, if it had not been destroyed by whatever action had resulted in the disappearance of the Jinoteur system, remained dormant. He had suspected that this might happen, though he had chosen to remain optimistic. Tasthene's report dampened that hope.

"Do I take from your expression, Earther, that you have not yet been successful?"

The voice intruded on his thoughts, and Xiong turned to see Lorka regarding him with an expression of disdain. Her large, muscled arms were folded across her chest. Behind her stood two more Klingons, flanking what appeared to be an oversized packing crate. How long had she been standing there? He chose to assume that Lorka had overheard several minutes of the conversation between him and Tasthene.

"We've made some progress," he said, indicating his Tholian companion and the consoles with a nod of his head, "but we're limited with what we can do here. Accessing the global network to any meaningful degree would take far more power than we could ever generate. Access to the subterranean power source is impossible because of an incredibly complex encryption method, the likes of which I've never seen before."

Seemingly unimpressed, Lorka asked, "What about the planetary defense system?"

It was Tasthene who responded, stepping away from the console and turning to face the Klingon. As he did so, the millennia-old equipment once again went dark, no longer benefiting from the Tholian's contact.

"The defense system is protected in similar fashion," Tasthene said. "Even if we were able to access it, without the proper key or other decryption method at our disposal, there would be no means of utilizing any of it, to say nothing of gaining entry to the larger network used to communicate and send information across the Taurus Reach."

"I'm not interested in that," Lorka countered. "At least, not at the moment. The weapons system is the first priority."

Releasing an exasperated sigh, Xiong pointed to the console. "We don't even know what we're looking at. Tasthene might understand a fraction of the information we're getting to. There's nothing with which to compare it, nothing for a universal translator to grab onto. We need more time."

"Perhaps you recall what I told you the last time you made such a request," Lorka said. "My husband grows more impatient by the day, but he has come into possession of something that may prove helpful to you." She nodded toward Xiong and told her two subordinates, "Bring it in here."

Xiong looked past her, catching the look of uncertainty the two Klingons shared before—in what Xiong took to be a somewhat reluctant fashion—bending and straining to lift the container sitting between them and bring it closer. He felt a sudden, unexplained hint of unease, even paranoia, tingle at the back of his mind. Though he already felt fear, of course, given Lorka's threats to kill him, this was something else.

The guards set down the crate at Xiong's feet, and he noted that even Lorka took a step back before saying, "We believe the contents of this container to be another artifact. If those who possessed it are to be believed, it may well prove useful to our research."

Without asking permission, Xiong ran his hands along the crate's surface. Determining that it was not locked, he raised the lid, beholding what he could only describe as a stone sarcophagus within. "What is it?"

"Unknown," Lorka replied. "No attempt to scan it has been successful." As she spoke, Xiong noted that she appeared to swallow a nervous lump.

What the hell is this thing?

Despite his curiosity, Xiong sensed his own agitation growing as Lorka directed the guards to remove the lid from the sarcophagus. He felt his jaw slacken as he beheld the stone casket's contents.

Lying on a bed of lush, thick fabric that reminded Xiong of an ornate tapestry sat a large crystal. Nearly the size of a human head, it had been cut to resemble a dodecahedron. Its clear, colorless exterior formed a solid shell around a smaller, violet crystal sphere at its center. The smaller crystal was about the size of a large grapefruit.

As he studied it, the inner crystal flared to life, emitting a vibrant aura that radiated through the clear outer shell and bathed the interior of the sarcophagus with a brilliant lavender hue.

"Oh, my God," Xiong said, unable to control his reaction. "I've never seen anything like this." There was no way to determine with certainty that the crystal was a Shedai artifact, but there was no mistaking its apparent lineage. Looking up, he watched as Tasthene stepped away from the crate, his entire body seeming to tremble in panic as he beheld the crystal.

Was it a true missing link, perhaps the very sort of key for which he had been searching since his earliest examinations of Shedai technology? The challenge now facing Xiong was two-fold. He could not waste this opportunity to learn something new, though he also would have to do everything in his power to avoid giving too much to his Klingon captors. Somehow, he would have to find a way to balance those two goals, at least for as long as it might take for Starfleet to find him, if they were searching for him at all.

You have to do all of that and not get yourself killed. Good luck.

45

Draining the contents of his coffee cup, Reyes relished the brew's rich flavor. He reached toward the table before his small sofa to set down the cup but pausing in mid-motion. As he examined the cup, he considered the odd notion that had just come to mind.

"I'll bet the coffee there tastes like crap."

Sitting next to him with her legs curled beneath her, dressed once again in the uniform she had earlier discarded, Desai released a tired sigh followed by a small, humorless laugh as she shook her head. "Your sense of priorities never ceases to amaze me, Diego."

"I've had plenty of time for ponderous reflection," Reyes said, rising to his feet and crossing the room to return the empty cup to the food slot. Deciding against another cup, he turned back to Desai. "Any word on Xiong?"

Desai shook her head. "Nothing. Jetanien's still pursuing a few back-channel options, but the Klingons flatly deny taking any prisoners."

"That's SOP for them," Reyes said. Still, Ming Xiong was Starfleet's foremost expert on all matters related to the Taurus Reach. If the Klingons—or the Tholians, for that matter—wanted insight into the progress the Federation had made in understanding the secrets of the Shedai, Xiong was the prime candidate to provide that knowledge.

"Nogura's not buying it, either, if that makes you feel any better," Desai said after a moment, "but there's not a lot he can do. With tempers running hot at the negotiating table, the Klingons are looking for any excuse to unleash open hostilities. The fact that they're not going to get their chance at you isn't making them want to play any nicer."

Reyes nodded. "I know." The Klingons' calls for his extradition were inconsequential. Every day brought closer the specter of war between the Federation and the Klingon Empire. He had seen his share of combat against Klingons during his career, and it was not something he relished seeing again, but he particularly did not welcome the idea of seeing it from within a prison cell.

Glancing to the chronometer on his desk, he noted the lateness of the hour—or the earliness, depending on one's point of view. It was 0230 hours. They would be coming for him soon, he knew. The prospect of a lengthy passage to Earth was not something he had looked forward to during the best of times; that he now would make that trip as a prisoner made the notion almost unbearable to contemplate. "I don't suppose they could just put me to sleep for the entire trip, could they?"

It had taken only three days for a ship to become available for the journey. In this case, it was to be the *U.S.S. Nowlan,* a Starfleet *Antares*-class transport configured for ferrying passengers rather than cargo. With a maximum speed of warp five, the voyage would take nearly three months, though Reyes knew the ship was equipped with enough amenities to make the trip bearable. He already had been assured that he would be allowed full use of the transport's recreational facilities. After all, he would be the vessel's only passenger, and what else were they going to do with him?

Turning from the food slot, Reyes found Desai standing before him, a sad, resigned expression darkening her delicate features. Her eyes had begun to water as she reached for him and pulled him to her. "It's almost time."

"I know," Reyes replied, stroking her hair with one hand as she buried her head against his chest. He rested his chin on her head, and they stood like that for a moment before he said, "Rana, I don't think I ever thanked you."

Raising her head so that she could see his eyes, Desai regarded him with a small smile that Reyes could tell was forced. "Thank

Admiral Moratino. She's the one who approved the conjugal visit."

Her words had the desired effect, and Reyes laughed despite his heavy heart. "I'll be sure to do that." The admiral had approved his request for a single overnight guest on his last night before boarding the transport to Earth. Indeed, Moratino had been more than generous with regard to his situation while he waited for the ship that would take him to prison. He had wondered about that for a time, but she had not offered any reasons. Rather than spend any more time questioning the leniency she had shown, Reyes chose to focus on sharing this last evening with Rana, the first such opportunity they had enjoyed in months. Though an understandable pall weighed over them, they had managed to keep it at bay for a few hours.

"I guess this means our secret's finally out," Desai said, placing her hand on his chest.

Reyes released another dry chuckle. "I hate to break this to you, sweetheart, but along with the price the Klingons have on my head that cat's been out of the bag for a while. If you don't believe me, ask Tim Pennington whenever he gets back." After a moment, he moved his hand beneath her chin, raising it with his finger. "What I meant was that I never thanked you for standing by me, for going to the mat for me *and* with me. You had the rule book and duty on your side, and still you were there for me."

"I did my duty by defending you," Desai countered. "Right or wrong, I wanted to make sure you had your say." She tapped his chest with one finger. "I suppose it didn't hurt that I'm in love with you, you idiot."

"It's always something," Reyes replied.

Desai's expression fell, and a single tear dropped from her left eye, beginning a slow descent down her cheek. "What am I going to do without you, Diego?"

Reyes wiped away the tear with his thumb and leaned forward to kiss her forehead. "I'm not leaving you, Rana." He drew a deep breath. "And who knows? You might be able to get my sentence reduced on appeal, or I can get an early release for good conduct. Either way, I'm hoping you'll be waiting for me when it's over."

"I'll be here," she said, her voice soft and sounding as though it might break under the strain of fighting to keep her emotions in check. She tightened her arms around him once more, and they remained in that embrace, enjoying the moment and each other. Then the sound of the door chime intruded on the comforting silence.

"Come," Reyes said, loosing his hold on Desai.

The door slid open to reveal one of the security guards stationed outside his quarters. She stepped aside, allowing entry for Dr. Fisher, who strode into the room dressed in his regular-duty uniform despite the hour. In his right hand, he carried what looked like four old-fashioned bound paper books.

"I heard you weren't accepting visitors," Fisher said, "but I figured you'd make one or two exceptions."

Reyes nodded, offering a slight smile. "Jetanien already beat you here, back around dinnertime." He had passed on his request to Admiral Nogura and Commander Cooper declining all visitors. As far as he was concerned, he was now a distraction to the starbase's complement and mission, and the sooner he was away from here, the sooner the men and women he had once commanded could return their full focus to their jobs and the difficult missions Starfleet would continue to give them.

Eyeing Fisher's uniform before glancing to Desai, he said, "I'm starting to feel a little self-conscious." His hands moved to smooth nonexistent wrinkles from the dull gray jumpsuit he had been given to wear—standard attire for a prisoner being transported.

"At least it's not orange," Fisher said. His eyes moved to Desai. "Good evening, Rana." Then he frowned. "Or is it good morning?"

Desai shrugged as she crossed her arms. "Neither, really."

Nodding in understanding, Fisher held up the books and offered them to Reyes. "Some light reading to help pass the time."

His eyes narrowing in mock suspicion, Reyes replied, "Beware doctors bearing gifts." He took the proffered tomes, holding them gently and running his fingers over their smooth leather covers. "They're beautiful, Zeke."

"Not first editions or anything," Fisher said. "I had the quartermaster make them up. I know you prefer real books to data cards, and I didn't know what kind of access to a data terminal you might have, anyway. Besides, these'll look better on your shelf."

Opening the largest of the books, Reyes closed his eyes and took in the musty smell of what should be centuries-old paper but that he knew had only recently been created. How did they do that so convincingly? Closing the volume, he turned it and its companions so that he could read the titles embossed on their spines. *"The Count of Monte Cristo? Rita Hayworth and Shawshank Redemption? Sunrise on Zeta Minor?"* The first he had read as a boy in school long ago, whereas he had never heard of the other two, comparatively shorter works.

"They're about prison breaks," Fisher explained.

Desai added, "Those might prove educational."

Chuckling at the gallows humor, Reyes eyed the fourth book. *"One Day in the Life of Ivan Denisovich?"*

"He spends ten years in prison, too," Fisher replied, "but I figure you'll have it a hell of a lot easier than he did."

"I sure hope so," Reyes said as he crossed the room to where a small black bag sat on his dining table. The bag contained the very few personal effects he would be allowed to carry with him, including—among other things—a collection of photographs and a few books from his own library. The rest of his belongings would be packed and transferred to one of the station's cargo stores until he provided a final destination for them. He had packed no clothing or personal-hygiene items, as all of that would be provided for him aboard ship as well as upon his arrival at the penal settlement. "Your taste in gifts is about as good as my fashion sense." He moved back to where his friends stood and patted Fisher on his arm. "Thanks, Zeke. I mean it."

"I needed something big enough to hide the hacksaw blade," the doctor retorted. Then his expression softened, and he reached out to grip Reyes's shoulder. "Now, listen to me, Diego. I know you did what you thought you had to do, and who knows? Maybe some sense will get knocked into people's heads as a result. Until that happens, you're not alone, do you understand me? You've got friends."

Reyes smiled again. "I know," he said before the door chime sounded again. "Come," he called out.

When the door opened this time, it was to admit Lieutenant Beyer and Ensign Tseng, the pair of security guards posted in the corridor. Beyer regarded Reyes with an apologetic expression clouding her fair features.

"I'm sorry, Comm—I'm sorry, sir," she said. "It's time to go."

Nodding, Reyes replied, "Okay." By mutual agreement, Desai would remain here, rather than accompany him to the hangar bay. He reached for Fisher, drawing his longtime friend into a firm embrace, a gesture shared by brothers and comrades in arms who had lived long enough to see far too much and come through it all because of the uncommon bond linking them.

"Take care of Rana for me, would you?" he asked as they stepped apart.

Fisher's own expression had grown somber. "You got it."

Turning to Desai, Reyes saw the tears that now flowed without restraint, streaming down her face. Without a word, she moved to him, gripping him in her arms and pressing her lips to his. Reyes was terrified to move even the slightest bit, for fear that his own emotions would force themselves to the surface and overwhelm him. They stood like that for several moments, neither willing to move, until Reyes heard a subtle, polite throat-clearing sound from Beyer.

"Sir."

Looking to where the lieutenant stood, her face communicating her fervent desire to be anywhere and doing anything else, Reyes said, "I know." Feeling the lump grow larger in his throat, he crossed the room and took his bag from the dining table. He wiped a tear from his eye before returning to Desai and the others. To Beyer, he said, "All right, Lieutenant. I'm ready."

Beyer offered a formal nod. "As you requested, we've cleared a route to the hangar deck that'll be free of spectators. We'll get you to the *Nowlan* without fuss."

"I appreciate that, Lieutenant." It had been a personal request, one that did not have to be granted, but he had suspected that it would be honored when he learned that Beyer had volunteered to stand the final watch before Reyes's transfer to the transport vessel.

Flanked by the guards, he made his way to the door of his quarters, preparing to exit them for the final time. Then he heard Desai call out from behind him.

"This isn't over, Diego," she said. Turning to face her, Reyes saw the sadness in her eyes, now coupled with new determination. "We've still got the appeals process. I'm already starting on that, and I'll be in touch as soon as I can."

Taking one last look at her, burning her face into his memory, Reyes offered what he hoped was an encouraging smile.

"You'll know where I'll be."

46

For reasons he could not understand, Pennington was nervous.

"What the bloody hell's wrong with me?" he asked as he wiped his sweaty palms on his trousers. "The last time I felt like this, I was picking up my prom date and meeting her father for the first time."

"Did the father like you?" M'Benga asked, standing next to him as the pair waited outside the door to T'Prynn's room.

Pennington shook his head. "Not one damned bit."

"An excellent judge of character, it turns out."

The pair exchanged amused glances, and Pennington tipped a finger to the side of his head in salute.

He and M'Benga had formed a casual friendship during the weeks they had spent here, thanks to both men's easygoing natures. Pennington had learned that the doctor's reserved demeanor housed a sharp wit and an almost encyclopedic knowledge of literature and history, allowing him to pepper his sarcastic remarks with references so arcane as to force the journalist to the nearest computer terminal in order to keep up.

The sound of the door's bolt being slid aside echoed in the hallway, and Pennington and M'Benga composed themselves as it opened to reveal T'Nel.

"T'Prynn is ready to see you now," the Vulcan said, opening the door wider and moving to one side, allowing the men to step into the room before she left, closing the door behind her.

Seated in a straight-backed chair near the window was T'Prynn. She wore a simple sleeping robe, and a thick, ornately decorated blanket had been laid across her lap, covering her from her waist to her feet. Her dark hair had been pulled into a knot at the top of her head, and her hands were clasped in front of her. With a typically Vulcan stoic expression, her alert eyes studied both men from head to toe as they stood before her. Pennington realized for the first time that her cheeks had sunken, if only slightly, evidence of the weight she had lost, even though her metabolism and other body functions had slowed during her coma to the bare minimum necessary to sustain her. She looked exhausted, and Pennington also noted the slight, irregular facial tic in her right cheek, even though she faced them at an angle, her right side somewhat obscured from direct view.

"Good afternoon," he said.

"Mr. Pennington," T'Prynn replied, her voice somewhat raspy. "Dr. M'Benga. It is agreeable to see you both. Doctor, I've been told of the care and treatment you provided me throughout my incapacitation, not only on the station but during the journey from there to Vulcan. You have my sincere thanks."

M'Benga nodded. "I was just doing my job, Commander."

"I'm told, Mr. Pennington, that you also took an interest in my condition. I must admit that I am at a loss to understand this."

"You're welcome," replied the journalist, offering a smile. Then he shrugged. "I don't know how to explain it, except to say that at the time, you looked as if you could use a friend." He felt his stomach lurch as he considered the woman before him, the architect of his professional downfall. As temporary as that expulsion might have been, it had arguably marked the lowest point in his life, surpassing even the ending of his marriage or the loss of his lover, Oriana D'Amato.

Now that she was here, there was much that he wanted to say, but this did not feel like the appropriate time. He thought he might try to visit her later in the day, or perhaps tomorrow, if she felt up to having visitors.

T'Prynn seemed to process that, then nodded as the tic made another appearance. "Very well. You also have my thanks."

"How are you feeling?" M'Benga asked.

"Weak," the Vulcan replied. "Except for a persistent head-ache, I am experiencing no pain. Healer Sobon tells me that there are a number of neurological issues that must be addressed before I can be declared fully recovered." She unclasped her hands, and Pennington noted that her right hand remained limp in her lap as she raised her left hand to gesture toward her legs. "I retain all of my cognitive functions and senses, but I am unable to walk, though I possess all nerve sensation. I am only able to effect lim-ited movement with my right arm, and you have already observed the minor muscle spasms in my face."

M'Benga crossed his arms. "These are residual effects of the coma, I take it?"

Nodding, T'Prynn replied, "Indeed. Healer Sobon has told me that my brain essentially went into a form of hibernation, as a means of protecting higher functions from permanent damage caused by the neurological imbalance triggered by the coma. Once the *Dashaya-Ni'Var* was complete, my brain slowly began to restore that functionality, but its progress is slowed because of the intensity of the meld and the effort required to remove Sten's *katra*. Sobon is confident that I will be fully recovered in a few weeks, perhaps a month."

The first hints of the afternoon heat encroaching on the house's temperate climate were affecting Pennington, in the form of perspiration forming on his forehead. After wiping it away, he regarded his damp hand. "A month, you say? I don't know if I have enough fluids in my body to hold out that long."

"It's likely that Starfleet will insist on your extradition, Com-mander," M'Benga said. "They'll argue that you're well enough to travel to a Starfleet medical facility in order to complete your rehabilitation, during which you'll almost certainly be under ar-rest. I can't imagine a court-martial is far off, either."

The right side of T'Prynn's face twitched again. "Healer Sobon will resist such a request, on the grounds that he'll wish to observe my neurological recovery, which he'll no doubt perform via one or more mind melds."

"I have no reason to argue or disagree with Sobon's diagnosis or treatment suggestions," M'Benga replied.

Pennington could not help smiling at his friend. "Look at you, being a bloody rebel and all."

Raising his right eyebrow in fine Vulcan fashion, the doctor replied, "My concern is for my patient, and that's the way it'll be until she's discharged from my care."

"Your dedication to your duty is commendable, Doctor," T'Prynn said, "but as I will be remaining in Healer Sobon's care for some time, I see no reason for you to stay here. Starfleet surely has better uses for a man of your august talents."

M'Benga nodded, reaching into a pocket and producing a piece of folded parchment. "It appears so," he said, holding it up. "This was delivered to me via messenger from the Starfleet security contingent outside the commune. I'm to report to the Starfleet liaison in Shi'Kahr once I'm finished here. It looks like I'm receiving new orders."

"Back to the station?" Pennington asked.

Shrugging, M'Benga replied. "I don't know, but I guess I'll find out soon enough."

"Healer Sobon has already contacted the Starfleet liaison office in Shi'Kahr," T'Prynn said, "and informed them that you will arrive in due course. They will continue to post security details here until he declares me recovered, at which time I will surrender myself to Starfleet. You are relieved of your responsibility for me, Doctor, without any prejudice. Indeed, Sobon also has communicated a request to Starfleet that you be awarded a commendation for your devotion to duty."

She paused, and though her expression revealed nothing, Pennington noted in T'Prynn's body language that she was coping with something—perhaps a wave of disorientation, fatigue, or even nausea. For a moment, the journalist imagined what the Vulcan must be experiencing, helpless to do anything except react to whatever fits and starts her strained body and mind subjected her to. In a sense, she had been at war for decades, he knew. Was it unrealistic to assume that her recuperation would not take longer than a few days or weeks, as Sobon predicted? What, if any, long-term effects of her protracted torment remained to be discovered? Would T'Prynn ever achieve complete recovery?

"I suppose that's it, then," M'Benga said, nodding in final agreement. "I'll honor your request, T'Prynn. However, I hope you'll contact me and let me know how you're doing."

T'Prynn nodded. "I will do so, Doctor. Thank you."

Much to his own surprise, Pennington found himself saying, "If you'd like the company, I wouldn't mind staying. I need material to finish my book, and it's not as if Starfleet cares if they ever see me again."

"Yes, I've been told about your news features," T'Prynn said. "I imagine they make for most interesting reading." When she said nothing else for a moment, Pennington wondered if the Vulcan also had been told about the court-martial and conviction of Commodore Reyes or even the worsening political climate between the Federation and the Klingons. He decided that for now, unless she broached either subject, it likely was best not to mention them.

T'Prynn, with some difficulty, adjusted her position in her chair, and this time, the lack of mobility in her legs and right arm was apparent. Pennington could not help but feel sympathy for her, though he knew she likely would dismiss his open display of such emotion.

"As I said to Dr. M'Benga," she said, "I appreciate your concern, as well as your offer, but it is not necessary. I will have everything I require here, and Sobon's staff will tend to me during my recovery."

Pennington recalled his conversation with young T'Lon and the hardships endured by those who returned to Kren'than after having chosen to leave the village for whatever reason. "It might not be the easiest path to travel, staying here, what with things being the way they are and whatnot."

Understanding his veiled statement, T'Prynn nodded while casting her gaze down to her folded hands. "Indeed, but it is a burden that I am prepared to carry. I consider it a measure of recompense for the care I have been given." When she looked at him again, Pennington saw something come over the Vulcan, as though she had made a decision. "You and I have had something of an adversarial relationship, Mr. Pennington, and that is my doing. While I would like to think that the actions I took served a greater good, I know now that there may have been other avenues to explore, options that might have spared the injuries done to you. While this may not be sufficient in your view, I hope you will accept my apology."

Seeing her now, weakened and vulnerable, and in the wake of what they had shared, Pennington realized that he could no longer hold on to the anger he had felt toward her. With his reputation restored, was there really anything left for which to hold her accountable? Would doing so accomplish anything?

No. Let it go.

"Thank you, T'Prynn," he said, his voice soft. He glanced at M'Benga, who was nodding in approval.

T'Prynn slumped in her chair, and M'Benga moved forward to help her. She raised her left hand, halting his advance. "I'm fine," she said, "but I am growing fatigued. T'Nel will assist me in returning to bed."

Pennington said, "I think that's our cue, then."

"Yes," M'Benga replied. "Thank you for seeing us, T'Prynn."

"Think nothing of it. I wish you a safe journey back to Starbase 47, gentlemen." Reaching beneath her blanket, she said, "Mr. Pennington, there is something I'd like you to take with you." Her hand emerged and extended toward Pennington. In her palm, the journalist recognized the familiar bronze finish of the mandala.

Frowning in confusion as he took the disc from her, he said, "I don't understand."

"A reminder," T'Prynn replied. Straightening her posture, she regarded them both as she held up her left hand and offered a traditional Vulcan salute. "I wish you both peace and long life."

M'Benga returned the gesture. "Live long and prosper, Commander."

"Goodbye, T'Prynn," Pennington added, swallowing a lump in his throat as his fingers caressed the mandala. Would he see her again? He found it unlikely, given Starfleet's-intentions to- ward her.

Then again, she *was* T'Prynn.

47

Reclining against the chair's padded backrest at a table in a quiet corner of Manón's Cabaret, Nogura sipped his wine and watched the subdued hive of activity taking place around him. Members of the station's complement and civilian personnel occupied most of the other tables, as well as chairs, sofas, and floor cushions arranged about the nightclub's interior. A low buzz generated by numerous conversations hovered in the air, the words themselves just beyond his hearing, and he took note of the few furtive glances cast in his direction from other officers. It was easy to comprehend the subject of at least some of the conversations: him.

Well, he conceded, *perhaps not you specifically.*

Most of the discussions likely revolved around the man he had replaced, along with the events that had transpired to bring about that replacement. It went without saying that Diego Reyes had been respected by his crew, to say nothing of the feelings carried by any close friends among them. Nogura was certain that a sizable percentage of Starbase 47's population supported the former commodore, whether they agreed or disagreed with the decisions he had made and the actions he had taken. Doubtless, some of those people would believe that the sentence imposed on Reyes was too harsh. They had that luxury, of course.

Bringing his glass to his nose, Nogura closed his eyes and savored the wine's supple aroma before taking another sip. He was adjusting to a more comfortable position in his chair, content to wait quietly for his meal, when he heard a familiar voice from behind him.

"Admiral Nogura, I hope I am not disturbing you."

Turning in his seat, Nogura looked up to see Ambassador Jet-anien regarding him. The Rigelian Chel, despite facial features that did not lend themselves to a wide variety of expressions, still managed to appear more than a bit disconcerted.

"Not at all, Ambassador," Nogura replied. "Would you care to join me?" Even as he asked the question, he realized that the chairs already at the table would not accommodate the Chel's unique physiology.

Jetanien, however, having obviously encountered this situa-tion on more than one occasion, was already taking action. A simple wave to one of the cabaret's staff produced two more em-ployees as if from thin air, carrying a backless chair better suited to the ambassador's special seating requirements. Jetanien thanked them and perched on the seat, across from Nogura.

"Excellent service here," the admiral remarked.

"I am something of a regular patron," Jetanien replied. He indicated Nogura's plate and its partially consumed meal. "Eat-ing alone can be unhealthy, you know. Drinking alone also has its share of negative benefits."

Smiling, Nogura held up his wineglass, swirling its contents. "Hazards of rank, I suppose." Long ago, he had adopted the cus-tom of enjoying a quiet drink with his evening meal after a long day's work. It did not matter to him that he usually dined in soli-tude; such was the fate of a flag officer serving without peers at any duty station. "Besides, I can hardly blame the crew for giving me a wide berth. I can't imagine any of them feel particularly comfortable approaching me, even in such a casual atmosphere as this." He waved his free hand to indicate the nightclub's inte-rior.

Jetanien made a sound that sounded like water draining from a sink. "I doubt that any of them harbors any true ill will toward you, Admiral. After all, you played no role in Commodore Reyes's court-martial and subsequent conviction."

"Nevertheless," Nogura countered, "I'm the one Starfleet sent to replace a man they respected." He released a small sigh. "Damn shame, too. What a waste of a good officer."

"One could argue that the commodore's intentions were honorable, Admiral," Jetanien said, resting his oversized hands on the table.

Frowning, Nogura shook his head. "You know what they say about good intentions and the road to hell." He glanced across the table before adding, "Well, maybe you don't."

"I do indeed, sir," the ambassador replied. "Despite his motivation, Commodore Reyes was still in the wrong, legally speaking. Morally speaking, that is a topic all its own. I do not know what I might have done were I in his position, but I'd like to think that he was acting on behalf of a greater good."

It was an interesting viewpoint, one Nogura found hard to fault. Of course, Jetanien and a select few members of the station's senior staff had all been briefed on Starfleet's true mission in the Taurus Reach from the beginning. For Jetanien now to state that he believed Reyes to have been acting toward a higher, more august purpose, would that not also constitute an admission that earlier decisions and actions taken in the name of security—some by the ambassador himself—were less than moral? Were they perhaps illegal?

Let's save that particular can of worms for another day, shall we?

A server approached the table and set down before Jetanien a large bowl of what looked like something that might have been retrieved from one of the station's waste-extraction centers. A faint aroma wafted from the bowl, and Nogura could not help wrinkling his nose in mild protest.

"I apologize if the odor is bothersome," the ambassador said as he brought the bowl to his mouth, "but they make a pickled *keesa* beetle broth here that is unmatched in flavor."

Nogura shrugged. "*Unmatched* is as good a word as any," he said, wiping his nose and draining his wineglass. "Ambassador, can I assume that you didn't visit me this evening to counsel me on my dining habits or to discuss the former Commodore Reyes? Have you heard anything new from the Klingons with respect to Lieutenant Xiong?"

Emitting an irritated snort, Jetanien shook his head. "Lugok maintains that no prisoners were taken from Erilon. Either he's an accomplished liar, which I doubt, or else he's not being kept informed with regard to this situation."

Nogura frowned and leaned forward to glare at the Chel. "So, what are you doing about it?"

A deep, resigned sigh escaped Jetanien's birdlike mouth. "At the moment, nothing. Lugok has gone quiet, apparently on orders from the High Council. All diplomatic relations have been frozen."

"It's not just you and Lugok," Nogura replied, "but you know that. The truth is, no one on either side is talking to anyone about anything, and everyone's getting itchy trigger fingers." After taking a moment to listen to the gentle, almost soothing buzz generated by the conversations of other patrons, Nogura finally leaned back in his seat. A dull ache had begun to manifest itself behind his left eye, an early warning of an impending headache.

The least of my problems, he conceded.

"I appreciate your efforts, Ambassador," he said, "but the unfortunate reality is that as far as the larger picture is concerned, Lieutenant Xiong—regardless of his unique knowledge and capabilities, is a single man." He waved a hand in the air above him, gesturing toward the ceiling. "All of this—our mission, whatever secrets might still be waiting for us to find out there—is liable to become very unimportant in the coming days and weeks, and Xiong's probably nothing more than one of the first casualties in a conflict that will see him joined by countless others."

Jetanien gave an irritated grunt and said, "I find it hard to disagree with you Admiral, given current events, but consider this. What if the Klingons *do* have Xiong and by some miracle and with his assistance—coerced, of course—discover some dreadful weapon that can be turned against the Federation?"

"If that's the case, Ambassador," Nogura replied, "then I imagine the war will go very quickly, and very badly, for us."

48

The spoon, which was more like a small shovel or a gardening tool than an eating utensil, was almost too large for his mouth, though Xiong had learned the trick of balancing the heavy metal bowl in his left hand. This allowed him to concentrate on forcing down whatever it was in the bowl that had the nerve to call itself his evening meal. It was a pallid, cold gruel, as tasteless as it was devoid of color. He had eaten it twice a day every day for however long he had been Komoraq's unwilling guest, trying to imagine that the bland paste was anything else.

As always, the effort failed, and Xiong instead tried to preoccupy himself with studying his surroundings as he brought another spoonful of the vile concoction to his mouth. He sat on a small box, leaning against one stone wall of the chamber that had been his home since arriving on this planet. Across from him was the wall dominated by the Shedai control consoles, dormant except for those few occasions when he and Tasthene, working together, had been able to make some limited progress accessing the ancient apparatus. Tasthene stood before the console, regarding him as he ate.

"You act like one of my children when they dislike the nourishment I would prepare for them," the Tholian said.

Xiong laughed. "You sound like my mother. She would never let me be excused until I'd finished." Holding up the bowl, he added, "Of course, her cooking was better." He shook his head. "I can't imagine what she would have done with fifty-three of us," he said, recalling Tasthene's stories of his large family.

"Offspring can be very taxing," Tasthene said, "but the rewards outweigh the challenges." Listening to the Tholian's words, Xiong knew that the memories of his lifemate and his children were what saved his friend, the strength he needed to get through the situation he now faced. He had a reason to live, motivation to find some way of escaping this ordeal and one day returning home.

And what do you have, besides your ever-unquenchable thirst for knowledge?

Forcing away the taunting question, Xiong dropped his oversized spoon into the bowl, metal clanging against metal and echoing in the chamber. The action did not go unnoticed; within seconds, Xiong heard heavy footsteps coming in his direction. Then a shadow fell across him as a Klingon guard moved into view from around one of the ubiquitous stacks of packing crates.

"You are finished?" the guard asked.

Xiong nodded, holding the bowl out for the Klingon to see. "My compliments to the chef."

The sarcasm naturally was lost on the guard, who offered a disapproving scowl as he examined the bowl and its partially consumed contents. Then he directed a derisive sneer at Xiong. "I see that time has not strengthened your inferior Earther palate." Taking the bowl, he added, "This is a standard prisoner's ration, containing every essential nutrient needed to keep you alive."

Having already had some variant of this conversation more times than he could remember, Xiong countered, "If that's the case, then it's no wonder you don't keep that many prisoners. Most of them probably kill themselves once they find out what's on the menu."

It was as close to friendly banter as he and his guards had managed to force during his stay. The guard released a small, growling laugh before heading back to the small desk from which he and his companion kept watch over the lieutenant and Tasthene.

With nothing else to occupy time until the guards returned to take him to the oversized packing crate that served as a makeshift prison cell and his "bedroom," Xiong picked up his tri-corder. "I think I'll take another look at that artifact," he said as he made his way across the chamber to the enigmatic stone sar-cophagus sitting alone in a corner of the room. Its lid had been removed, allowing Xiong an unobstructed view of the crystal it cradled.

What are you?

It was a question he had asked countless times since first laying eyes on the mysterious object, sitting atop the multihued, elaborately patterned cloth lining the casket's interior. The crystal had resisted all sensor and scanning attempts, with Xiong unable to detect the presence of even the slightest energy signature emanating from the object. As far as his equipment was concerned, the crystal simply did not exist. One of the first things he had done after receiving it from Lorka was to test how it reacted when placed in proximity to the Shedai control equipment, and the results were disappointing. While he had been able to detect minute reactions to the archaic equipment, it had been even less than those received by Tasthene's direct interfacing with the console, defying Xiong's theory of a form of biometric association via the crystalline physiology of both the Shedai and the Tholians.

A momentary shiver down his spine broke Xiong from his reverie. Once again, and as had happened every time he came into proximity of the crystal, he felt an inexplicable, illogical sen-sation of dread wash over him. Rather than outright fear, he thought of it as an impression of foreboding. Whatever this object was, instinct told him that it was wrong.

No, he corrected himself. *Not wrong. Evil.*

He shook his head, disappointed with himself. As a scientist, Xiong knew he should be guided by knowledge and logic rather than emotion, but he could not deny the instinctive desire to flee this place, to get as far away as possible from the crystal and whatever it might represent. He forced the ridiculous notion back to the depths of his mind. It was an object, he reminded himself, nothing more.

Heavy footfalls behind him made him turn away from the sarcophagus, and he felt his body tense in anxiety and anticipation as Lorka entered the chamber, the now-familiar pair of Klingon bodyguards accompanying her. Her expression, as always, was one of determination, though Xiong noted an altogether new quality to the way the female Klingon carried herself. Gone was the obvious disdain with which she normally regarded him and Tasthene. Instead, the lieutenant sensed a sort of subdued excitement, as though she might be concerned with allowing her true feelings to become known, either to him or just to her subordinates.

"You will come with me," she said, pointing at him. "Bring your scanning equipment." With a nod, she indicated Tasthene. "The Tholian as well."

Frowning, Xiong crossed the room to the small worktable he had been given to use, on which sat his tricorder and the Klingon equivalent of a portable computer terminal. "What's going on?" he asked as he slung the tricorder over his left shoulder and allowed it to rest along his right hip.

Lorka ignored him at first, instead barking orders in native Klingonese to her guards, who moved quickly to replace the stone lid on the sarcophagus before lifting the large container between them. "We have discovered a new chamber," she finally said to Xiong. "One that our scanners had not been able to detect. It contains technology similar to this." She indicated the Shedai consoles with a dismissive wave before turning on her heel and marching out of the room. A third guard, the one who had overseen his meal, gestured for Xiong to follow her. Glancing over his shoulder, Xiong saw Tasthene shuffling across the dirt floor, guided at gunpoint by another Klingon sentry.

Even with the illumination provided by the strings of work lights suspended in the corridor, he almost lost sight of Lorka as she made her way around corners and forks in the tunnel. Xiong was unable to keep track of the twists and turns in the narrow subterranean passage as he all but ran to keep up with the Klingon woman, who covered ground in long, rapid strides. He only caught up to her because she stopped before what appeared to be a hole in the tunnel's rock wall. Light from a portable lamp filtered into the passageway from inside whatever room lay beyond the wall, and Xiong stepped closer until he could look through the hole. When he did so, he was unable to suppress an audible gasp.

"What is *this*?"

Lorka stepped through the hole and into the room, and Xiong did not wait for an order or an invitation to join her. Once inside, he was able to get a better view of the new chamber's contents. The room itself was unremarkable, carved, as were all of the others, from the bedrock, the walls too smooth to have been created by normal excavation equipment. Lining the far wall was a single console, similar in most respects to every other specimen of Shedai technology Xiong had encountered. As expected, the console itself was dark and lifeless, its smooth black surface free of blemishes or dust despite having likely been sealed away in this room for uncounted millennia. A wall of flat obsidian stood before him, over the console, also dormant, but none of that surprised Xiong. He had seen it all before.

It was the pedestal that commanded his attention.

"Do you know what that is?" Lorka asked.

Xiong estimated that the column rose about a meter from the chamber's smooth floor. It was octagonal, seemingly carved from a single piece of transparent crystal. At its center was a slim pillar of lavender crystal, which caught the light from the portable lamp. The column flared at its top, expanding into a concave bowl, at the bottom of which Xiong saw a pentagonal base that also was formed from the darker inner crystal.

"Oh, my God," he whispered, realization dawning.

From behind him, Xiong heard Tasthene scurrying across the dirt floor until the Tholian stood beside him. Though his companion's expression would be unreadable with or without the environment suit, Xiong still noted the hesitant manner in which Tasthene approached the pedestal. He seemed almost afraid to get too close.

"Do you know what it is, Tasthene?" he asked. "Is it at all similar to any control mechanism your people might've created?"

Tasthene uttered a string of clicks and chirps that translated as "I have never before seen anything like this. However, it seems familiar to me, somehow, just as I feel I should recognize the other Shedai artifacts we have studied."

"It seems obvious that the item in the box is intended to be used in conjunction with this base," Lorka said, her tone one of contempt.

Xiong nodded. "Of course, it's obvious, but what's *not* obvious is the purpose that this thing serves. For all we know, we're holding the key to some kind of planetary self-destruct system." Memories of what had befallen Palgrenax and had very nearly happened to Erilon were never far from his mind, particularly as he had tried to access and navigate the ancient, unknown control systems, all the while worried that he might invoke whatever final defensive protocol awaited his first careless action.

"Are you afraid to die, Earther?" asked one of the Klingon guards from where they stood near Lorka.

"I'm afraid to die because of simple stupidity," Xiong countered, reaching for his tricorder and activating it. He held it before the pedestal, unsurprised by the unit's readings. "Scans aren't penetrating, but I can at least confirm that it's made from the same crystalline material as that thing in the box."

That seemed more than enough for Lorka. "Excellent." Turning to the guards who had carried the sarcophagus from the other Shedai chamber, she barked another series of commands in her own language. Xiong watched as the Klingons once again exchanged meaningful glances before reaching for the stone container and removing its lid. Taking care not to touch the crystal with any part of their bodies that was not required to lift it, the Klingons raised the oversized object from its resting place and carried it to the column. They paused, looking at each other before casting looks toward Lorka, who snapped another command in Klingonese at them. The guards reacted as though lashed with a whip, moving to the column and setting the crystal sphere into its base.

Xiong heard the distinctive *click* an instant before intense white light erupted from the crystal and the column on which it rested, bathing the entire room in its glow. The effect was followed by the Shedai control console flaring to life, its rows of indicators and graphical displays scrolling in rapid fashion across the opaque crystalline surface. A low, constant hum reverberated about the room, and Xiong was sure he felt a vibration playing across his exposed skin. In his hand, his tricorder began emitting a shrill series of signal tones.

"Whatever it is," he said, "that thing is having one hell of an effect." He nodded toward the crystal sphere and its pedestal, which now resembled an orb sitting on a scepter and waiting for the hand of the god that might now wield it. "Tasthene, can you access that console?"

By way of reply, the Tholian scurried across the floor until he stood before the now quite active console. He paused, as if to familiarize himself with the scrolling streams of data, all rendered in glyphs and text that so far had defied Xiong's attempts at translation. Then Tasthene placed his appendages on the console, his body immediately stiffening in response to the new contact. He said something that at first sounded unintelligible to Xiong's ears, but before he could ask, the Tholian repeated the response.

"I am detecting a host of new pathways into the planetary computer network," he reported, the long fingers on both hands playing across the obsidian panel. "I am not certain, but from what I can discern, we may well be able to access every subsystem from this location."

"How is that possible?" Lorka asked, stepping closer and pushing Xiong out of her way. "How are you able to make such a determination?"

"I do not know," Tasthene responded, and Xiong heard the fear in the Tholian's voice carried through the translation. "I seem to be guided more by . . . instinct . . . than any cognitive function or actual knowledge. I cannot explain it."

"What about data-storage banks?" Xiong asked. "Are you seeing anything like that?"

Tasthene replied, "I believe so. There are what appear to be vast catalogs with indexes to much larger caches of information. It will take some time to decipher, of course, and there may be some form of data encryption that I am not yet detecting."

"Incredible," Xiong said, breathing the word. "Everything we've been searching for might be right here. The technology, the history of the Shedai, the key to the meta-genome—it could all be at our fingertips." Could it really be that simple? After so much prolonged searching, might a single artifact hold the key to everything?

There has to be something more to it.

After a moment, Tasthene's body jerked, and he emitted a series of agitated chirps. "I am also registering a form of communications signal, broadcasting outward from the planet."

The graphics displayed on the massive black panel shifted, warbling and dissolving, only to be replaced by a new image coalescing into focus. It took several seconds for Xiong to recognize the new representation as a star map. Thousands of stars littered the picture, shining in a broad spectrum of colors. More Shedai text crawled across the image, accompanied by indicators pointing to what seemed to be hundreds of the stars being depicted.

"What is this?" Lorka asked.

Tasthene replied, "It appears to be a map of the Taurus Reach. I believe the highlighted stars represent systems that at one time fell under Shedai influence. As far as I am able to determine, the signal currently being broadcast is extending in all directions. It is possible that the intent is to connect to other planets with similar technology."

"The network," Xiong said, whispering the words and looking up to confirm that Lorka had not heard him. If he correctly understood what he was seeing, the map represented locations of every Conduit on any planet in the Taurus Reach. Hundreds, perhaps thousands, of planets appeared to be indicated on the map. By the looks of things, the enigmatic race's influence was indeed as far-reaching as indicated by the Shedai Apostate, as told to Ensign Theriault.

And here we are, he mused, *insects to be crushed under their heel if we keep getting in their way.*

Could the sphere be trying to establish contact with the network of Conduits that had gone dormant in the aftermath of the Jinoteur system's disappearance? He frowned as he turned and once more beheld the crystal, resting on its column and pulsing with light and new life, which he found disconcerting, to say the least. What was the sphere's purpose? It stood to reason that access points such as this must also be present on the other worlds where Shedai artifacts had been found. Were there other similar spheres to accompany them? If so, why? To what end? Given the abilities the Shedai had commanded, for what possible use might this physical manifestation of their power be needed?

Again, Xiong felt that nonsensical, enveloping sensation of trepidation beginning to wash over him. His pulse racing in his ears, he exchanged looks with Lorka. Despite her normal bravado, he was only somewhat surprised to see that her own expression seemed to mirror his own.

"Remove it!" she shouted, waving to the two guards who had been easing away from the pedestal. At her command, they lunged forward, gripping the sphere in their massive hands and yanking it free of the column. The very instant the separation was made, the control console went dark beneath Tasthene's hands, and the room was plunged once again into near silence.

Perhaps angry with herself for her outburst, Lorka now seemed to be having difficulty regaining her composure. Did she also sense that all was not as it appeared to be with regard to the crystal?

"We will proceed," she said after a moment, "but we shall do so without undue haste." As though for Xiong's benefit, she added, "Progress is worthless if all we accomplish is destroying this planet."

Xiong nodded, doing his best to keep his own excitement in check. From the moment Tasthene had reported the signal broadcast, he had begun thinking of its other possible uses.

The trick now, Xiong knew, would be getting an opportunity to test his idea.

49
INTERLUDE

Fools! What have you done?

Despite the vast distance separating her from them, the Shedai Wanderer heard the cries of terror and anguish as an entire civilization died. It came only moments after she detected a sudden, potent surge of power through what remained of the Conduits. It was a familiar sensation, one she had experienced several times, the last while dealing with the *Telinaruul* who had enslaved the primitives on the forest-green world. She had been left with no alternative on that occasion, forced to annihilate the planet lest it and the treasures it held fall into the hands of the interlopers. With a thought, she had reduced it to dust.

Somewhere, far away from the lifeless orb the Wanderer was forced to call home if only for a time, another world had succumbed to a similar fate, but by whose hand?

Extending herself across the Void, she sought any sign of her kind—the Apostate, one of the *Serrataal,* anyone—but found nothing. Had *Telinaruul* overreached, their arrogance finally triumphing their insatiable curiosity? It was a possibility, though one the Wanderer could not confirm without traveling yet again, and her strength was far from ready for such a journey.

There was another prospect, of course, that the native inhabitants of a world controlled uncounted generations ago by the Shedai had stumbled on technology they did not understand and could not control. It had happened on other, isolated occasions, long ago, when Shedai rule was new to this part of the galaxy. Some worlds had resisted or openly rebelled, and in those few instances, those *Telinaruul* also had paid for their insolence, their destruction serving as an example to others who would reject destiny.

How far we have fallen.

The Shedai would return to their former grandeur; of that the Wanderer was certain. What continued to concern her was how far the *Telinaruul* had advanced while she and her people had lolled in slumber. If and when the Enumerated Ones returned, what would they face? A galaxy waiting for guidance and harmony or adversaries who long ago had forgotten what it meant to live under the all-encompassing wisdom of the Shedai?

Another rush of power pushed itself through the compromised Conduits, and the Wanderer felt it touch her consciousness, unsure what she was sensing. It was not nearly as formidable as other Voices she had encountered, but there was an incontestable, unsettling quality to the pulse unlike anything she had ever experienced. Its raw, brutal aura seemed to reach out to seize her consciousness, and in that instant, the Shedai Wanderer was afraid.

What is this? The question drifted into the Void, nearly drowned out in the face of the awesome entity that now commanded her attention. Was this some new enemy? The Wanderer had no answer, though on some level of which she was only fleetingly aware, she perceived other facets of this new presence— something old, something ancient, something angry. Perhaps it was some long-forgotten rival to the Shedai, swept from history by apathy and shortsightedness and now returned to seek some form of retribution.

Despite the discomfort she felt in the face of this mysterious new Voice, the Wanderer still was able to comprehend some aspects of the song it sang. There was a rough, unpracticed rhythm to the pulse she felt, indicating unfamiliarity, even hesitancy. It suggested something the Wanderer had been afraid of since rising from her own long sleep: the *Telinaruul* might have found a way to interact with Shedai technology.

No, she decided. *It cannot be possible.*

Extending herself into the vast gulf of space, the Wanderer searched for the source of the Voice. Even this escalated her sensations of dread and confusion, as though her very actions were being turned back on her. Never before had she faced such primitive, base emotion channeling through the Void. This was different from the obsession demonstrated by the Apostate or even her own drive and determination to see the Enumerated Ones returned. This was altogether different. This new Voice appeared driven by a single, unwavering purpose.

Fear. Absolute, merciless terror.

As abruptly as it had appeared, the Voice was gone. Nevertheless, its residual presence remained, taunting the Wanderer.

This could not go unanswered.

50

For perhaps the thousandth time, Carol Marcus stared at her computer monitor, upon which was displayed a cross-section of the Taurus Meta-Genome. Her eyes traced over every detail, savoring the wealth of information that promised so much and yet seemed determined to defy every effort to understand it. In the three years that had passed since its initial discovery, the meta-genome remained largely an enigma. Its matrix consisted of several million base pairs of biochemical information and featured molecules made of elements unknown to current science.

Starfleet geneticists had taken little time to determine that the genome was of artificial design and that only the smallest portion of it was devoted to the creation of living organisms. What remained unexplained was the purpose of the rest of the complex genetic segments. Though there had been some limited success deciphering fragments of the meta-genome, true understanding remained elusive.

Irritating little bastard, aren't you?

Marcus recalled the excitement she had felt upon first reading the voluminous information pertaining to the genome, collected since Starfleet's first forays into the Taurus Reach. The encounters with the Shedai by the crew of the *Sagittarius* on Jinoteur IV had confirmed the suspicions she harbored from that first day: the mega-genome, if ever it could be translated and understood, was the key to uncounted medical and other scientific advances that until now had largely resided in the worlds of fiction. Reading the report from the captain of the *Sagittarius,* detailing the astounding discoveries made by the vessel's chief medical offi-

cer, Marcus believed that the doctor's findings were but the tip of
the proverbial iceberg. Healing injuries, repairing damaged or
lost organs and limbs, perhaps even replacing them with organic
rather than biomechanical substitutes? Fascinating, to be sure,
but Marcus had been envisioning scenarios on an even grander
scale. The Jinoteur system had been artificially created, as far as
all sensor readings could determine, with the meta-genome as its
catalyst and with every planet and moon and even the star itself
infused with the unique, peculiar energy waveform the Shedai
were able to summon and control. Based on the age of the system,
the Shedai had possessed this power for at least five hundred
thousand years and likely far longer. If the power to create planets
and the stars that sustained them could be understood, harnessed,
and employed with due care, concerns stemming from population overages and resource shortages would become as quaint as
the notion of suffering from simple ailments such as influenza or
cancer.

It's all here, at our fingertips, Marcus mused as she studied
the image. *It wants to tell us everything; we simply don't understand what it's trying to say. Ming, I really wish you were here to
help me with this.*

As quickly as it had blossomed, her excitement at what she
was seeing began to fade. It was difficult to maintain such enthusiasm these days, and Marcus still felt pangs of grief whenever
her thoughts turned to Xiong. His conspicuous absence, both
from the Vault and from anything having to do with the covert
facility's primary mission, continued to be felt by the rest of the
staff. In many ways that Marcus had only just begun to understand, Ming Xiong was the heart of his project. The rest of the
team fed off his passion, his unbridled zest for learning everything the Taurus Reach had to offer. Now that he was gone, a pall
had fallen over the entire effort, which already was showing signs
of distraction and even disenchantment once the true nature of
what they sought had become known.

There was also the guilt, from which Marcus had been unable
to shake or absolve herself. It emanated from the knowledge that

she had lobbied so hard for Xiong to be sent on the mission that had gotten him killed or perhaps captured by the Klingons, which might well be a fate worse than death. Admiral Nogura did not see it that way, but she knew from experience that the station commander was doing what all effective leaders did: accepting the responsibility, for better or worse, arising from decisions made even at the behest of others. While she could admire Nogura's unflagging devotion to duty, she did not think it fair for him to take the blame for acting in good faith based on what should have been sound counsel from a trusted advisor.

You let ambition get in the way of prudence, she chided herself. *Again. What the hell kind of scientist does that?* Glancing at the wall to the left of her desk, she saw the picture mounted there in an antique wooden frame, depicting her and her son, David, smiling for the photographer. *What the hell kind of parent does that?* How, then, in years to come, when he was old enough to ask her about the work she did, would she justify her impulsiveness, well intentioned though it might have been?

She had taken great pains to present to David the virtue of patience and considering all of the angles of a problem and the ramifications of possible solutions before taking any kind of action. The boy's father, while intelligent, could also be stubborn and impulsive, sometimes choosing a less-than-ideal course of action based on incomplete understanding of a situation. While instinct and even luck had sometimes aided him by filling in the gaps resulting from such an approach, Marcus knew that it was not the wisest manner in which to resolve an issue. She feared the day would come when he was wrong. Likewise, she did not want David mimicking that behavior, especially at such an early age. Would he understand and use that knowledge as he grew older to avoid making similar mistakes of his own?

The beeping of her desktop intercom drew her attention, and she reached for the control. "Marcus here."

"Dr. Marcus, this is Dr. Gek," said the voice of Varech jav Gek, a civilian Tellarite scientist assigned to the Vault. *"We've got something out here that I think you're going to want to see."*

"What is it?" she asked, reaching up to rub her eyes, which felt as if they were being polished with sandpaper.

Gek replied, *"It's easier if we just show you, Doctor."*

Marcus sighed in minor annoyance and said, "On my way."

She exited her office and moved toward the Vault's central laboratory workspace. Glancing toward a wall chronometer, she realized that this was the time normally scheduled for the current shift's meal break, so the area was largely deserted. Dr. Gek appeared to have the run of the place, moving between workstations with the speed and agility of someone half his size. The Tellarite was dressed in a dark blue jumpsuit typical of a member of the Vault team, over which he wore a standard-issue white lab coat. Standing to one side of Gek's worktable was Nezrene, working again with the piece of Shedai technology brought back from Erilon. One of the Tholian's appendages rested on the section of polished onyx, which had been configured such that the energy it received and any electronic impulses it generated were recorded by the Vault's self-contained main computer. Marcus saw that the console was active, flashing its streams of indecipherable text and graphics.

Upon seeing her, Gek smiled, his entire face seeming to expand. "Dr. Marcus, I think we've made an interesting discovery." Unlike most Tellarites she had encountered in her travels, Gek was almost insufferably jovial. His knowledge and expertise were almost as formidable as his unrestrained exuberance, which could become annoying at times. She had tried to talk to the doctor about his behavior once or twice but had finally relented upon realizing that Gek's resilient good cheer was a good counterbalance to the rest of the team's notable melancholy.

Reaching the work area, Marcus crossed her arms as she regarded Gek. "Something with the Shedai artifact?"

The Tellarite nodded, his excitement such that Marcus worried that his head might just separate from his neck. "Indeed. We believe this equipment has picked up a signal broadcast from a similar device."

Marcus blinked several times as she processed that statement.

Feeling her pulse quicken, she stepped closer. "Are you serious?"

"Absolutely," he replied, motioning for her to step closer to one of the lab's computer workstations. "It's nothing that was aimed at us. At least, I don't think it was. Rather, it seems to have been an omnidirectional signal, lasting twenty-seven-point-four seconds. The computer's working on plotting its origin point, but according to Nezrene, it's definitely Shedai."

Turning to the Tholian, Marcus asked, "You're sure of this?"

Nezrene emitted a warbled string of animated chitters, after which the translation device in her environment suit said, "Yes, Doctor. This equipment reacted to the signal and attempted to generate what I believe to be a preprogrammed response to receiving contact. Naturally, it was unable to do so, as it is not tied into any sort of communications equipment but only a passive feed from the station's sensor array."

"Do you have any idea what the signal is trying to accomplish?" Marcus asked.

The Tholian replied, "I believe it is a form of hailing message, designed to attract the attention of Conduits on other Shedai worlds. Since the Conduits remain inactive, it is unlikely that the location originating the broadcast will receive a reply."

"What about the individual Shedai that are supposedly out there?" Marcus asked, remembering what she had read from Ensign Theriault's report of the Jinoteur incident. "Isn't it possible that they might pick up on this, too?"

After a moment, Nezrene said, "It is very possible, Doctor, but their ability to respond would depend on whatever resources they have available to them. Without the Conduits, such resources would be extremely limited."

Yeah, but it's not as though the Shedai are weaklings, even without resources, Marcus mused.

Gek's computer terminal beeped, and when the Tellarite turned to inspect it, Marcus saw the look of satisfaction on his face. "The computer's determined the signal's origin point," he said, reaching for the workstation and entering a series of commands. In response to his query, the terminal's monitor shifted to an image of a star map, and Gek pointed to it. "It looks to have originated in the Mirdonyae system. Based on the distance, that signal was first broadcast more than three weeks ago."

"What do we know about that system?" Marcus asked. "Other than that it appears to be yet another world that interested the Shedai for one reason or another?"

Gek shook his head. "Almost nothing. It's in a sector of the Taurus Reach we've not yet explored, but it's close to areas where the Klingons have been traveling."

That would make sense, Marcus decided. The Klingons were conducting their own investigations into the Shedai, but their efforts were motivated by the desire to obtain weapons or some other artifact that might give them a military advantage over their enemies. They had completely bypassed any constructive uses for the ancient Shedai technology, and as far as Starfleet Intelligence was able to determine, the empire knew nothing of the meta-genome or any of the awesome potential it carried.

"What else can you tell me about the signal itself?" Marcus asked. "Any idea what it might be trying to say?"

Nezrene replied, "Based on everything we know or have been able to translate, it appears to be nothing more than a simple hail. However, we have detected another element embedded in the signal, but it seems to have no relation to the signal itself."

Frowning, Marcus reached up to rub her chin. "Another element, like a header or leading sequence or perhaps an encryption key?"

"No," Gek said. "It's wholly separate from the main signal and looks as though it was deliberately implanted in such a manner as to suggest that whoever put it there was trying to hide it. They did a pretty good job of it, too. Only when I compared it to similar transmissions made by our people on Erilon did I pick up the difference." He reached once more for his computer. "I've isolated the signal. Listen."

He touched a control to initiate a playback, and Marcus listened as a long tone was emitted from the terminal's audio ports.

It stopped abruptly, then was followed by a series of similar tones of varying duration. A gap of silence followed this beat, and when a fifth tone was played, Marcus realized that she was hearing the four tones playing in a loop.

"That's the signal for the entire twenty-seven seconds," Gek explained. "The whole thing repeats four times during that loop. I was just about to ask the computer to analyze it."

Marcus nodded. "Do it." She watched as Gek entered the necessary commands, after which only a few seconds passed before the computer beeped.

"That was fast," Gek said, frowning as he leaned closer to the screen. Then his eyes widened in surprise. "Oh, my."

"What is it?"

Clearing his throat, Gek turned to her. "According to the computer, there are several possibilities, but the first one is the most intriguing. It's saying that the tones may be letters from something called Morse code, a primitive signaling scheme developed centuries ago on Earth. The code uses differing sequences of long and short sound bursts to represent letters and numbers, and the computer says that the string we're hearing translates in Morse code to the letters 'M' and 'X.' How does an ancient code from Earth wind up in a . . ." The words faded even as the Tellarites eye's widened, at the same moment as Marcus felt her jaw go slack.

Oh, my God.

"MX," she repeated. "Ming Xiong."

51

"Glad we could be of service, Admiral," said the image of Captain Daniel Okagawa, from where he stood on the bridge of the *U.S.S. Lovell*. *"Give us a call if we can ever be of further assistance."*

Standing with his arms folded before the viewscreen in his office, Nogura offered a cordial nod and smiled. "We appreciate everything you and your crew have done for us, Captain. It's a shame Starfleet's decided they need you elsewhere. I'd rather gotten used to having you around."

It was true that he had been something less than confident upon getting his first look at the dilapidated *Lovell,* which itself had been assigned to Starbase 47 as a temporary replacement for the ill-fated *U.S.S. Bombay*. The ship had already visited the station on an earlier occasion, and circumstances had led to the engineering crew learning some tangential facets of the starbase's top-secret mission. When the situation called for a ship to serve in a stopgap capacity until a formal replacement for the *Bombay* could be dispatched, Commodore Reyes had requested the *Lovell*. He was able to take advantage of its primary mission for the Corps of Engineers as cover for assignments to planets within the Taurus Reach known to harbor Shedai technology and other artifacts. Both the ship and its crew had wasted little time impressing the hell out of him.

On the viewscreen, Okagawa said, *"Well, somewhere someone needs a tunnel bored through a planet, or perhaps their sewage system needs a good dredging. Call us if your toilets get backed up."*

That actually elicited a small chuckle from Nogura, a rare

occurrence. "However it happens, here's hoping our paths cross again. Until then, safe journeys to you and your crew, Captain."

"And best of luck to you, Admiral. Lovell out."

The image on the screen shifted from Okagawa himself to an exterior view of space beyond the station, with the *Lovell* finishing its undocking maneuver and moving away from Vanguard's primary hull. Nogura watched as the ship turned on its axis, dwarfed even by the massive doors to the docking bay it had just vacated, its impulse engines flaring to life as they pushed the vessel away from the station.

From behind him, he heard Commander Cooper tapping on the data slate, which seemed to have become an extension of the executive officer's hand in recent weeks. "I've just received an update on the *Akhiel,* Admiral. She's due to arrive within thirty-eight hours."

Nogura turned from the viewscreen and made his way across the office to his desk. "Excellent. We'll certainly have plenty of work for her captain and crew, won't we?"

"You've got a knack for understatement, sir," Cooper replied, moving to one of the two chairs before Nogura's desk as the admiral gestured for him to take a seat. "Captain Whitsitt likely won't have time even to authorize any shore leave before we turn them around and send them out again."

It was not a notion for which Nogura held any real enthusiasm, but it was a simple reality of their current operational tempo. Because of other commitments and needs throughout the quadrant, Starfleet had been unable to assign a true replacement for the *Bombay* until now. The *Lovell,* despite its effectiveness and that of its crew, simply had not been able to fill all of the requirements for vessels assigned to the station. What was needed was another starship possessing capabilities on par with what the *Bombay* had brought to the table. As no *Miranda*-class ships currently were available, Nogura had decided on a frigate that could handle the cargo transportation requirements for which the *Bombay* had been selected, as well as providing a greater degree of offensive and defensive power. Nogura also had asked that a fourth ship be assigned to the station—preferably a *Constitution*- or *Saladin*-class cruiser—but that request was still being considered by Starfleet Command.

Maybe we should stop making so many neighbors mad at us.

"What's the latest on Cestus III?" he asked, leaning forward and reaching for the nearly forgotten cup of coffee on his desk.

Looking down at the data slate now perched on his lap, Cooper replied, "The outpost was almost completely destroyed. With the exception of a handful of survivors, all Starfleet personnel and civilian colonists were killed—more than five hundred casualties in all. According to the report submitted by the *Enterprise*'s captain, a previously unknown species called the Gorn claimed that the Cestus system lay within their territory and viewed our establishing the outpost as an aggressive action against them." He tapped the data slate's display window with the stylus in his right hand before adding, "Captain Kirk's report on Gorn physiology and technology makes for some very interesting reading."

Kirk again, the admiral thought. The young starship captain had more than his fair share of vocal supporters within the upper echelons at Starfleet Headquarters, and there was little to dispute about the man's abilities and performance to this point. Still, Nogura was not yet convinced that Command had not erred in giving Kirk one of the most advanced vessels in the fleet. He conceded that he might not be giving the captain the benefit of the doubt and was possibly unfairly comparing him with Christopher Pike, the man he had succeeded as captain of the *Enterprise* and an exceptional, consummate officer in his own right. In truth, since taking command of the *Enterprise*, Kirk had already rung up an impressive list of accomplishments.

I'm going to have to keep an eye on that young man.

"So," he said, leaning back in his chair, "now we have the Gorn to worry about, on top of the Klingons and the Tholians and even the Romulans, though they seem to have gone quiet as of late."

Cooper shrugged. "Hard to say with the Gorn, sir. After Kirk's little adventure with the ship that led the attack on Cestus III and that weirdness that came after, an arrangement was made for us to leave the planet to them. In turn, they've agreed to give us a wide berth, and vice versa. That should keep things manageable on *that* front for the time being."

It was probably the best possible outcome from such a tragic series of events, all of which had stemmed from simple lack of communication and trust. While Nogura was relieved that the Federation would not have to deal with yet another enemy during this most difficult of times, the arrangement with regard to Cestus III did have one other facet. "The planet was selected for its proximity to the Klingon border. Without the long-range sensor array we were establishing there, it'll be harder to track Klingon ship movements in that sector." That ability would also have proven quite useful to Starbase 47, as Klingon activity to and from the Taurus Reach also would have been detectable.

His reverie was broken by an alert indicator from his desktop computer terminal. Nogura glanced to the display, and his eyebrows rose in surprise. "Well, what have we here?"

Cooper frowned. "Sir?"

Without responding, Nogura reached for the terminal's compact keypad interface, pressing the control to transfer the information from his desktop unit to the wall viewscreen. "This report just arrived from the *Sagittarius*. They're on fast patrol out to the Aleriq system, and their long-range sensors picked up shock waves similar to those generated by the destruction of Palgrenax. Same energy signature." Walking back to the viewer, he pointed to the computer-generated map of the Taurus Reach. Rendered in a simple two-dimensional vector-line graphic, the region appeared as a triangle, wedged between territories belonging to the Tholian Assembly and the Klingon Empire. "*Sagittarius* couldn't get close enough, so their information is somewhat spotty." He pointed to the area of the map dominated by Tholian space. "It's a good distance inside their territory. We don't even have a name for the affected system. We don't even know which planet we're talking about."

"But the shock wave was the same?" Cooper asked.

Nogura nodded. "It appears so. According to the reports and theories put forth by Lieutenant Xiong, all known Shedai technology should have gone dormant after the Jinoteur system did . . . whatever it was that it did. So, if someone—Tholian, Klingon, us, or a player to be named later—didn't fumble their way into one of those underground complexes and press the wrong button, then are we talking about a Shedai?"

"Remember what Ensign Theriault told us about how they're able to move through that network of Conduits?" Cooper asked. "We don't know how many of them escaped before Jinoteur disappeared. If we're to believe what that . . . Apostate . . . told Theriault, there could be hundreds of them out there, searching for storehouses of Shedai technology. Even if they're limited in what they can do because any control mechanisms that might have resided in the Jinoteur system are now gone, what the hell do beings with that kind of power do once they're off the leash?"

Turning from the viewscreen, Nogura shook his head. "Thank you, Commander, for that image, which is sure to keep me up nights from now on." Of course, he had already lost a lot of sleep thanks to this topic, starting from the first day he had learned that he would be commanding this station. Reports submitted by Commodore Reyes and other members of his senior staff had painted a staggering, frightening picture. The Shedai threat, in whatever form it now took after the astonishing events that had taken place since the beginning of the Federation's investigation into the Taurus Reach, made problems posed by the Klingons, the Romulans, the Gorn, and anyone else who wanted to step up to the plate seem like schoolyard spats by comparison.

What the hell are we going to do?

There was no time to ponder an answer, as his attention was caught by his desktop intercom, followed by the voice of his assistant, Ensign Greenfield. *"Admiral, I have Dr. Marcus on the intercom, requesting to speak with you. She says it's urgent, sir."*

"Put her through, Ensign," Nogura said, returning to the chair behind his desk and pushing the control to activate the intercom. "What can I do for you, Doctor?"

"Admiral," Marcus replied, and Nogura immediately picked up on the excitement in her voice, *"you're not going to believe what we've found."*

52

Reyes had finally gotten to the good part of *Sunrise on Zeta Minor,* with the two fugitives escaped from the underground prison and now on the run from the malfunctioning android prison guard, when his evening of quiet reading went straight to hell.

He lay on the bunk in the single-person quarters that had been his home aboard the *Nowlan* for nearly five weeks, his head propped against two pillows and with the book resting against his bent knees. Reaching to turn the next page, Reyes froze as the silence of his room was shattered by a blaring alarm Klaxon, followed by a male voice booming through the intercom system.

"Red alert. All hands to duty stations. This is not a drill!"

At first, Reyes questioned the term *duty stations* rather than *battle stations,* but just as quickly realized that it was appropriate, given the *Nowlan*'s notable lack of formidable weapons. He recalled what he knew about the *Antares*-class transports, not liking what he remembered. His stomach twitching, Reyes pulled himself to his feet and moved toward the metal desk, which was little more than a shelf affixed to one bulkhead. An intercom keypad was attached to the desktop, and he thumbed the activation control.

"Reyes to bridge. What's going on?"

Instead of a reply from the *Nowlan*'s bridge, he received a response from Lieutenant Ket, the Bolian security guard stationed beyond his door. *"I'm sorry, Mr. Reyes, but your intercom has been programmed to connect only to the comm panel outside your quarters."*

Ignoring that, Reyes, asked, "What the hell's going on?"

"Unknown, sir," Ket replied. *"I know only that Commander Easton has raised the alert level."*

Reyes felt his ire rising but forced it back down. Remembering that he no longer was the commander of any vessel or crew or even an officer deserving the time or respect of a subordinate, he suppressed the urge to respond more harshly to Ket's seemingly dismissive comments. "I understand that, Lieutenant, but maybe you could contact the bridge and get more information? We're out here in the middle of nowhere, after all." It was not a thought that had consumed much of his time since the *Nowlan*'s departure from Starbase 47 for the prolonged journey to Earth, but there were only so many situations that might call for a ship's commander to order his crew to their duty stations. Shipboard emergency was one such possibility, though Reyes's gut told him that it was something else.

The room's overhead lighting flickered at the same time as the drone of the ship's engines changed, deepening as though being requested to generate more power.

That can't be good.

The door to his quarters slid open, revealing the anguished face of Lieutenant Ket staring at him from the corridor.

"Commander Easton reports that they've picked up an unidentified vessel on sensors," the Bolian said, an edge of fear now present in his voice. "It's closing fast, and he's requesting your presence on the bridge."

Unidentified? Reyes wondered if it might be a Klingon ship. He would not put anything past them, not out here, considering the worsening diplomatic situation between the Federation and the Empire, to say nothing of the apparent price placed on his own head.

"Let's get up there, then," Reyes said, jogging to keep up with Ket as the lieutenant ran up the corridor. *Antares*-class transports only possessed three habitable decks to support what he remembered was a twenty-person crew complement, with the bulk of the ship's interior volume dedicated to cargo storage. Rather than turbolifts, the three primary decks were connected by a series of ladders and Jefferies tubes. As they moved up the hallway toward one such access point, Reyes noted other members of the *Nowlan*'s crew moving with speed and purpose, presumably to their assigned station.

Then something slammed into the ship, and the bulkheads and deck plates trembled, groaning in protest. Everything pitched to starboard, and the deck went out from beneath Reyes's feet, defying the vessel's inertial dampening systems and throwing him into the bulkhead to his left. He winced in pain as his shoulder struck the wall, even as he flailed with his other hand to grab something for balance. Ahead of him, Ket fared better, managing to avoid being tossed off his feet and reaching for the entrance to a Jefferies tube to steady himself. All around them, alarm indicators flared harsh crimson, and Reyes heard the pitch of the ship's engines waver yet again.

"Are you all right, sir?" the lieutenant asked as the deck leveled out beneath them.

Reyes nodded, rubbing his sore shoulder. "I'm fine. Let's get up there." If a vessel of any size and armament was indeed attacking them, he did not give the *Nowlan* much chance of surviving long after the initial salvo.

The berthing compartments were on the second deck near the aft section of the ship's primary hull, and the bridge was one deck up and forward. They had only just begun the short ascent to the next deck when the ship shuddered around them yet again. Reyes felt his stomach lurch as the artificial gravity gave way for a moment, and he tightened his grip on the ladder as his feet left the rung on which he was perched. Darkness enveloped the narrow shaft, throwing off his equilibrium, but only for a moment before emergency lighting activated. Now long shadows stretched the length of the passageway, heightening his sense of confinement.

Prison sounds pretty good right about now.

It took only moments for Ket and Reyes to complete the transit to the bridge, climbing the ladder two rungs at a time and emerging at the rear of the *Nowlan*'s command center. Reyes pulled himself through the narrow, circular entry and onto the main deck, after which an ensign assigned to one of the aft stations moved to secure the hatch. At the front of the small, compact room, a large viewscreen dominated the forward bulkhead. The image on the screen was nothing but dense black space highlighted by a handful of distant stars. One of the stars was moving, growing larger by the second as it appeared to be coming closer.

Uh-oh.

Compared with its counterparts on larger Starfleet vessels, the *Nowlan*'s bridge was a sparse, utilitarian affair. Other than the set of consoles at the rear of the room—which seemed configured to handle engineering functions—the only other stations designed for manning by an actual member of the crew were housed in a free-standing console positioned in front of the main viewer and incorporating functionality for helm, navigation, and sensor control. A human female sat at the helm and navigation station, next to a human male manning the sensors. Both wore gold uniforms with lieutenant stripes, and their attention was focused on the status indicators and controls arrayed before them.

Hovering just over their shoulders was a large, muscled man of African descent, the ship's commanding officer, Lieutenant Commander Brandon Easton. A rivulet of sweat ran down the side of his smoothly shaved head, and his own gold uniform tunic stretched across his broad chest and shoulders. The man reached forward and slapped one of the controls on the helm console.

"Engineering, we need more power to the shields, now!" The only immediate response was static coming over the communications channel, to which Easton uttered what Reyes recognized as a particularly vile Andorian oath.

"Report," Reyes commanded, reverting without hesitation to ingrained habits born from years of training and experience.

Easton turned from the consoles, and Reyes saw the look of anxiety on the younger man's face. "We're about to get our asses kicked by whoever that is out there," he said. "It popped up on sensors coming at us like a bat out of hell and didn't let up until it was in weapons range and started shooting at us. All of our attempts to hail it have been ignored. Data banks call it a civilian freighter, but whoever owns it has retrofitted that thing from stem to stern."

Grunting in irritation, Reyes said, "Pirate vessel." Out here, and particularly with larger, more powerful Starfleet vessels occupied with far larger problems, a slow-moving transport was easy pickings. "What's your weapons status?"

"Standard phaser banks fore and aft," the commander replied. "Not that it matters." He waved a hand toward the viewscreen. "We're no match for them. They're armed to the teeth." The man paused, clearing his throat. "This is more than a little out of my league, sir."

Reyes nodded in understanding. The *Nowlan* might be a low-profile transport ship with a crew smaller than the staff Reyes had been assigned while in command of Starbase 47, but Easton was still the one in charge and still the one responsible, no matter what happened. Knowing what it meant for the commander of a ship, *any* ship, to have to ask another officer for assistance or guidance while facing a tough situation, Reyes exchanged a knowing look with the younger officer before hooking a thumb over his shoulder and turning to Ket. "Get on that console, Lieutenant. Open a hailing frequency to that ship."

"Aye, sir," the Bolian replied, snapping into action.

"Commander," the female at the helm console called out, "they're coming around again."

"Continue evasive," Easton ordered before looking to Reyes again. "They can carve this ship up like a holiday roast. The only question is why they haven't done it yet."

Ket reported from the aft bridge station. "Channel open, sir."

Casting aside his current status of prisoner and once more embracing the persona that had defined him for his entire adult life, Reyes cleared his throat. "Unidentified vessel, this is Commodore Diego Reyes, commanding the *U.S.S. Nowlan*." He shrugged, mouthing an apology to Easton before continuing. "We are on a peaceful mission and pose no threat to you. Please state your intentions." He waited with the rest of the bridge crew for a response, wondering just what the hell he might say if and when anyone actually answered him.

The reply to his query came in the form of another salvo rocking the transport. Reyes was thrown to his right and reached for Easton's command chair to keep from falling. Easton grabbed the back of the sensor officer's chair, and everyone held on as lights, monitors, and consoles across the bridge flickered in the face of widespread power disruptions.

"Shields are down," reported the man at the sensor console. "Forward phaser banks are offline."

Another salvo slammed into the ship, this time throwing the helm officer from her chair and slamming her to the deck. The alarm sirens wailed once more, deafening within the compact bridge. Still gripping the center seat, Reyes kept his feet and, without thinking, lunged for the helm, his eyes rapidly taking in the console's various status readings.

"Damage report!" Easton ordered from where he knelt next to his fallen helm officer. Reyes glanced down at her, unsure if she was unconscious or dead. The odor of burnt circuitry assailed his nostrils, and he glanced around the bridge in search of the source. Nothing presented itself, but Reyes was sure that the last attack had overloaded systems across the ship. Without shields, the *Nowlan* might survive one more salvo, but Reyes doubted it.

The rattled lieutenant at the sensor station replied, "Hull breach on Cargo Deck Five, but it's contained. I'm also reading a coolant leak in engineering."

That would explain them not responding, Reyes knew. A coolant leak almost certainly meant an evacuation of that entire area of the ship, at least until the engineering crew could don oxygen masks, if not full environment suits.

A crimson indicator flashed on his console, and he called over his shoulder, "Here they come again." It took another few seconds before the lieutenant manning the sensors looked up from his station and said aloud what Reyes's gut was already telling him.

"All of their weapons are hot."

"No response to our hails!" Ket shouted over the Klaxon from the rear of the bridge. "I've tried sending out a distress call, but they're jamming our signals!"

This is it.

The lone thought echoed in Reyes's mind as he watched the mysterious, unidentified ship growing larger on the main viewer, its blunt bow dominated by a pair of disruptor banks glowing fiery red.

"Here it comes!" Easton shouted. "Brace for impact!"

An instant later, the warship's disruptors flared again, spitting forth hellish new spheres of barely harnessed energy, which filled the screen a heartbeat before the twin blasts struck the *Nowlan*'s unprotected hull.

When the ship trembled this time, Reyes knew it was the beginning of the vessel's death throes and the end of everything else.

53

The words on the data slate taunted her. They danced before Desai's eyes, remaining sharp and distinct as they hovered defiantly before her, refusing to be washed away by her tears.

Transport Nowlan *destroyed. Suspect attack by pirate vessel. No survivors.*

It was a preliminary report, received from the Federation News Service, courtesy of the station's main computer, and offering no details about the identity or allegiance of the attacking vessel. Admiral Nogura had arrived at her door before she read the article, to inform her personally about what had happened. Unfortunately, he had possessed only slightly more in the way of helpful information. The *Nowlan*'s disaster recorder buoy had been detected by the *U.S.S. Gloucester,* a Starfleet ship on long-range patrol in the Taurus Reach, its contents transferred to the vessel and then transmitted to the nearest Federation starbase—Vanguard. As for the recorder, the last log entry captured by the recorder before its launch from the ill-fated transport had been entered by the ship's commanding officer. It contained no clues to the reasons for the attack.

Nogura departed at her request to be left alone. Desai lost count of the number of times she had read the FNS article. Her entire world shrank to nothing more than the compact screen before her, time ceasing to have any meaning as she commanded the device to provide new information. Instead, the data slate tortured her with the same soulless words and callous turns of phrase.

No survivors.

Tears streaming down her face, Desai threw the data slate

across the room, and its molded polymer housing splintered as it slammed into the far wall before dropping to the carpeted floor of her quarters. She brought her knees to her chest and rolled to one side on her sofa, curling into a protective fetal ball.

Diego.

It was ludicrous, but she was certain she still smelled him, on her clothes, in her hair, on her skin still damp with sweat in the wake of their final night of passion. Raising her head, she looked to the end table next to the sofa and saw the framed photograph she had taken of him months earlier. She had caught him in a rare quiet moment, sitting on the grass somewhere in Fontana Meadow—part of the station's terrestrial enclosure—looking down at something that had caught his attention. The corners of his mouth were turned upward in a wistful smile, as though he was enjoying a private joke. It was one of the few occasions when he had not appeared consumed by the burden of command, awash amid the dozens of decisions that had seemed to dominate his every waking minute. Desai never had asked him what he had been thinking just then, electing instead to allow him that fleeting moment of peaceful inner reflection.

And now, of course, she never would know.

Desai buried her head in the sofa cushion, unrelenting emptiness reaching out to grip her. It crushed her heart, driving her into a vast pit of darkness. She was alone here, plummeting ever deeper and making no effort to arrest her fall. What was the point? There was no one to save her and no one waiting for her upon her salvation. So be it.

The door chime sounded, intruding on her grief.

"Go away."

A second chime echoed, wailing for attention. She repeated her call to be left alone, but the door only offered a third signal. Then the door opened, and Desai snapped to a sitting position, her anguish replaced—for the moment, at least—with anger.

"What the hell do you want?"

It was not until she hurled the question across the room that she realized who stood in her doorway. Ezekiel Fisher regarded her from the threshold, his dark eyes narrowed in concern, his mouth pressed shut in an expression of resolve.

"Rana," he said, stepping into the room.

"How did you get in here?" Desai asked, reaching up to wipe her eyes.

Fisher cocked his head toward the door. "Emergency medical override. One of the benefits of being the head doctor around here."

Not in the mood for Fisher's laidback banter, Desai pulled herself from the sofa. "I want to be left alone, Fish."

"I can understand that," the doctor replied, standing just far enough inside the room so that the door slid closed behind him. "I just wanted to see how you were holding up."

"Holding up?" Desai nearly spat the words. Then, realizing that her friend meant well, she reined in her follow-up response and paused, drawing a heavy breath and slowly releasing it, working to bring herself under some semblance of control. "I honestly don't know." Shaking her head, she moved toward the small kitchenette in one corner.

Fisher shrugged, stepping toward her. "That's normal."

Sighing, Desai turned to look at him, for the first time noting the dark circles under his eyes and the unmistakable look of sadness clouding his features.

He knew Diego longer than you did, after all.

A sudden wave of guilt washed over her. Ashamed at her selfishness, Desai felt new tears welling up in her eyes. "Oh, God, Fish, I'm so sorry." She reached out for him, pulling him to her and burying her head in his shoulder. She felt the older man's arms wrap around her, one hand resting gently at the back of her head. Fisher said nothing, standing in silence as she began to cry all over again.

Pulling away from him, she wiped tears from her eyes. "Have you heard anything new?"

Fisher frowned, shaking his head. "No. They've sent the *Endeavour* to investigate, but it'll be a while before they know anything." He paused before adding, "If ever."

"But they're certain it was pirates?" she asked, stepping away from him and reaching for the glass of water she had left on the kitchenette counter. "Not the Klingons or even the Tholians?" Admiral Nogura had already told her as much, but without anything in the way of hard evidence, she was unwilling to rule out any possibility.

"Nogura told me the same thing he told you," the doctor replied. "The ship that discovered the wreckage found no indications of Tholian or Klingon weaponry. The Tholians have denied any involvement, and you know that if the Klingons had anything to do with it, there's no way they're staying quiet."

Taking a sip of water, Desai was forced to agree with Fisher's reasoning. The Klingons had put a price on Reyes's head, but that was for a live capture in order for him to be judged by what passed for their court system. From what little information she had been able to find about the empire's judicial practices—drawn from the logs of a Starfleet captain who had faced trial, conviction, and sentencing at the hands of a Klingon court more than a century earlier—Reyes might well have been spared a worse fate.

Small favors and all that.

Fisher moved toward the counter and the carafe of water. He reached for another glass and paused as his eyes fell across another data slate she had left sitting near one corner. The contents on its screen were legible even from where she stood, so she knew the doctor also could read them. He looked up at her, frowning.

"You're resigning?"

Shrugging, Desai replied, "I was considering it." She took another sip of water. "It was an option for being able to continue acting as Diego's lawyer while he served his sentence and we pursued the appeals process. I'd already placed a request to Starfleet Command for a change of duty to one of the JAG offices on Earth or at least somewhere in the Sol sector." She had wanted an assignment that would put her near him, for professional as well as obvious personal reasons. "From what I've heard, such assignments are hard to come by, so I started researching civilian law firms." She had found one candidate in particular that held an appeal, a small, one-man operation based in Los Angeles on Earth. The lawyer apparently specialized in Starfleet as well as civilian law, having successfully represented the captain of the *U.S.S. Enterprise* during his recent court-martial. Though the lawyer appeared unwilling to take on a partner, Desai had figured there was nothing to be lost by sending a query and gauging his interest.

Fisher released a small chuckle. "You? Come on, Rana. We both know you've got Starfleet in your blood. You might be a lawyer, but you're just as much an explorer as any ship jockey flying off to unknown worlds. Didn't you say you wanted to make good law rather than just serve it? You can't do that from an office on Earth."

"It wasn't about any of that," Desai snapped, regretting the force of her words as soon as she spoke them. Offering an expression that she hoped would communicate her apology to her friend, she said, "I just wanted to help Diego, any way that I could. If that meant resigning from Starfleet, then to hell with it. I . . ." She stopped, blowing out a resigned, tired breath. "I just wanted to be with him, Fish. If he was going to have to go through that, I wanted to be there with him." Casting a dismissive wave toward the all-but-forgotten data slate, she shook her head. "Not that it matters anymore."

Leaning against the counter, Fisher regarded her with that familiar paternal glint in his eyes. "So, what are you thinking of doing now?"

Desai groaned in exasperation. This was not a conversation she wanted to be having at this moment. "God, Fish, I really don't know." She waved a hand in the air to indicate her surroundings. "Are we just supposed to go on with our lives out here like nothing happened? Continue keeping the secrets and the lies that brought us here in the first place?" How many lives had been lost? The crew of the *Bombay*. Those who had died on Erilon and Jinoteur IV, to say nothing of Gamma Tauri IV. Uncounted Klingons and Tholians, as well as innocents on other planets throughout the region. Ming Xiong. Diego Reyes. The list was far too long already and would likely only grow in the coming days, weeks, and months. No matter how well intentioned the cause had been, many, if not most, perhaps even all, of those who had perished had done so in service to a lie. Perhaps Diego's court-martial had served to make more people aware of the tremendous cost that had been exacted out here, and maybe things could change for the better. It was even possible that Desai herself might find some way to continue contributing to the ongoing effort.

"Rana," Fisher said after a moment, "if anything good is coming from all of this, it has to be that Diego opened a lot of people's eyes about what's going on out here. He may have broken Starfleet regulations, but you and I both know that what he did *needed* to be done. If what he did gets us to step back and reexamine those lofty ideals we're supposed to hold in such high esteem—gets us to take a long, hard look at ourselves and just what the hell we're doing—then it won't be a wasted effort."

He placed his hand on her arm. "But for that to happen all the way out here, out of sight and potentially out of mind, it's going to take good people who know the truth to stick with it. Why do you think he let you in on the big secret in the first place? He wanted people he could trust to do the right thing watching his back."

Though Desai had not agreed with everything Reyes told her when he revealed to her the secret mission to which he and Starbase 47 had been assigned, she knew that he had confided in her so that she might ride herd on his conscience. She had done her best to do just that, despite knowing that there were some secrets he would not share with her. Those came later, of course, after he had taken the actions that had led to his removal from service and . . .

Enough.

"I don't know, Fish," she said, feeling the pit of emptiness once again within her.

She felt Fisher's hand on her arm, his grip firm and comforting. "Besides, regardless of what happens with the Shedai, or even the Klingons and the Tholians, the fact is that the Federation is pushing out this way. More colonies, more trade routes, a larger Starfleet presence. They're going to need some good law and good lawyers to help make it." He smiled again. "Diego would want you doing what you love, you know."

"Maybe," Desai said, offering a noncommittal shrug. None that resonated within her as it once had, the way it once had called to her. At the moment, none of that seemed important.

Though her career had always been the driving force in her life, Desi now found herself longing for the man she loved, along with a life that might have been.

What the hell do I do now?

54

Ganz stood naked at the foot of the oversized round bed in his opulent private suite aboard the *Omari-Ekon,* gripping the Andorian by his throat. He held the would-be assassin nearly a meter off the deck, the fingers of his massive right hand closing around the Andorian's windpipe. It required every iota of his formidable willpower to keep his temper in check as he watched the life drain from his assailant's face. The Andorian was doing an admirable job of fighting for his life, striking out at Ganz's muscled arm with ever-waning strength. He reached for the hand at his throat, fingers clawing in a futile attempt to loosen Ganz's grip. His boots kicked out at the Orion's body, but Ganz ignored the weak, frantic blows. Finally, the Andorian's arms fell to his sides, and his body went limp. Satisfied that his attacker was dead, Ganz let the body fall to the floor of his bedroom.

On the other side of the room, Neera was examining the area behind a large, ornate Orion tapestry, from which the Andorian had emerged from hiding in his ill-fated attempt to kill Ganz. She also was nude, having been forced from bed along with Ganz by the sudden appearance of the assassin from behind the tapestry. Moving aside the wall hanging, Neera grunted something inaudible, though Ganz still could make out her irritation.

"You won't find anything," Ganz said, feeling his own anger beginning to mount. He crossed the room to a waist-high polished black bureau and reached for the communications panel set into its surface. He pressed one of its two buttons, the one linked to a similar panel mounted outside the door to his quarters. "Get in here. Now," he growled into the unit.

He had only just retrieved a silken blue robe from where he had cast it across the end of the bed and begun wrapping it around himself when the door to his private chambers slid aside, and the bodyguard stationed outside his quarters came rushing in. He was a muscled Orion male, dressed in leather pants and boots and wearing a disruptor pistol in a holster on his hip. Rather than a shirt, he favored a pair of bandoliers strung in crisscross fashion across his chest.

Upon entering the room and seeing the Andorian's body, the guard recoiled in surprise, brandishing his weapon and leveling it at Ganz. The merchant prince found himself staring down the disruptor's gaping maw, not scared so much as he was angry with himself for not seeing this coming,

"Jahno," he said, looking past the weapon to the face of the guard wielding it. He indicated the dead Andorian with a dismissive wave. "You betrayed me for this piece of filth?" There had to be more to it, Ganz knew. Someone else had dispatched the assassin—likely one of his many rivals—and the Andorian had co-opted Jahno to help him get through Ganz's security. For a moment, Ganz wondered how many other people currently in his employ might be working for one of his competitors.

Before Jahno could answer, something whipped past Ganz's left ear, and he saw a thin silver blade embed itself in the guard's right shoulder. Jahno shrieked in pain, his eyes wide with terror as his free hand reached for the knife. Blood streamed from the wound, running down his bare chest and right arm. Then Neera was lunging across the room, her lithe nude body slamming into Jahno and driving the guard to the floor. She reached for her knife, ripping it from his arm, intensifying the flow of blood.

"You traitorous pig," she spat, glowering down at him as she sat astride him, the edge of the blade tracing a line across his throat. "I'll gut you like the worthless animal you are." Reaching for the disruptor Jahno had dropped, she placed the muzzle of the weapon in Jahno's right ear.

"Who are you working for?" Ganz asked, stepping closer. He nodded toward the dead Andorian. "Who sent him to kill me?"

Jahno was trying yet failing to stem the flow of blood from his shoulder. His expression was a mask of anguish and fear as his gaze shifted between his employer and the person who held his very life in her hands. "I don't know who hired him," he hissed between gritted teeth. "He was the only one who paid me. I never talked to anyone else."

"You're lying!" Neera said, emitting a feral growl as she poked the point of her knife into the wound. Jahno's body jerked, and he cried out in pain.

Leaning closer, Ganz said, "So, you're saying this one person gave you enough money to turn you against me?" Perhaps Jahno really did not know who was behind the assassination attempt. In truth, Ganz did not care. What unnerved him was the apparent ease with which one of his people had been turned. The Andorian, whoever he had been, was nothing more than a tool employed by one of the numerous enemies Ganz had made over the years. Torturing Jahno, himself nothing more than a pawn no matter who paid him, would be a waste of time.

"Finish it," he said, glancing to Neera. He stood in silence as his lover drew the edge of her blade across Jahno's throat. The Orion responded with a gurgling sound as blood flooded his esophagus and he inhaled it into his lungs. His body convulsed in a series of violent spasms, and his eyes bugged out of his head.

Rising to her feet, Neera stood over him, watching him suffer for several seconds. Then, without looking to Ganz or even speaking a single word, she aimed the disruptor at the guard, thumbing the weapon's power level before pressing the firing stud. A harsh, brilliant orange burst erupted from the disruptor's muzzle, enveloping Jahno. The hellish energy tore apart his body at the molecular level, erasing it from existence in the space of a few heartbeats, his cries of agony echoing about the bedroom as his body disintegrated.

"That's the third time in less than a month," Ganz said, grunting in mounting irritation as he moved back to the bureau and poured himself a glass of Altair water from a crystal carafe. Compared with the Andorian, the two previous attempts had been amateurish, with both prospective assassins detected in the midst of conducting their initial reconnaissance while posing as patrons on the *Omari-Ekon*'s gaming deck. Zett Nilric and his subordinates had taken care of them without attracting attention from any of the other customers, though neither had provided the names of their employers before dying. Ganz had no way of knowing if he was being targeted by one rival or several.

"It's not as though you've never had people after you before," Neera said as she crossed to the bathroom for a washcloth to wipe the blood from her knife. Satisfied that the blade was clean, she returned it to the scabbard stitched inside the robe she had been wearing before retiring. Rather than donning the robe itself, Neera chose to recline naked across the bed. "You had to expect that some of your enemies would step up their attempts once we left the station."

Ganz nodded from where he stood next to his bureau, having dispatched a message to Zett Nilric to send two new guards to be stationed outside his quarters. He was forced to agree with his lover's assessment. From the moment the *Omari-Ekon* was forced to surrender the relative safety that came with being docked at Starbase 47, his rivals would have been planning ways to eliminate him. Destroying the ship itself seemed like the easiest way to accomplish that goal, but Ganz knew that to most of his competitors, the trading vessel was worth more if captured intact.

"They'll only get bolder," he said, watching the low lights play over Neera's glistening jade skin as she rolled onto her stomach.

"Even with Starfleet stepping up their patrols?" she asked. Propping her chin on her folded arms, she looked up at him.

Ganz nodded. "Absolutely. I'd do the same thing." In the wake of the destruction of the transport vessel bearing Commodore Reyes to Earth, Starfleet had stepped up its boarding and inspection of merchant vessels operating in Federation space. More than a few "independent contractors" had found their ships impounded and themselves arrested after being caught ferrying contraband. "I know how to beat Starfleet at its own game."

"You're not the only one," Neera replied, her tone one of caution. "You're not even the best there is." Then she offered a leering smile. "Though I'll admit you do possess formidable skills, in a *number* of areas."

Smiling at the overt innuendo, Ganz nevertheless remained restless. "It's not just my competitors, of course. You see how easily Jahno was turned. How many others might be in line behind him?"

Neera shrugged. "What about Zett? If anyone stands to gain from your untimely demise, it's him. I've told you before that I don't like him."

"And I've told you that I don't like him, either," Ganz countered, taking a seat next to her on the edge of the bed. "But he's loyal." Reaching out to stroke her hair, he added, "Besides, I think he's scared of you."

"If he's not," Neera said, rolling onto her side to face him, "then he should be." She laughed at her own joke. Ganz always liked the sound of her laugh.

After a moment, he said, "I think we need to rethink Nogura's offer."

Neera frowned. "You're assuming he's willing to let you return to the station at all. Simply agreeing to his offer now won't be enough, not after the way you turned him down the first time." Her arm moved until it rested on Ganz's thigh. "You need to present him with something he does not have, cannot get through other means, and cannot refuse."

Now it was Ganz's turn to smile. "Always the shrewd one, but there's something else to consider. We have to be careful how we approach this. If anyone finds out, they'll think we're selling out to Starfleet." Such a perception, unfounded or not, would be a death knell for his various lines of business.

"Then we'll just have to make sure that doesn't happen," Neera replied, running her hand across his leg. "So, what do you intend to offer Nogura?"

"There's really only one thing he'll view as having any worth," Ganz said, "and we both know what it is." Something that—if the information given to him at the time he took possession of the item was correct—would prove invaluable to continuing Starfleet interests in this region of space.

Releasing a tired sigh, he said, "Contact Tujeta Larn on Arcturus. Tell him to pull it from whatever hole he's buried it and get it here as soon as possible."

"Very well," Neera replied, nodding in approval, "but it can wait a while, can it not?" Her fingers delved beneath the folds of his robe.

Ganz smiled as he lay back on the bed and allowed Neera's hand to continue its unfettered wandering, overcome as always by the raw magnetism she exuded with every fiber of her being. "I suppose it can."

55

Eyeing the selection of fruits and nuts arrayed on the plate, T'Nel nodded in approval. They would satisfy nutritional requirements for the morning meal, she decided.

She placed the plate on a serving tray, which contained eating utensils, a woven cloth that would serve as a napkin, and a tall glass of spring water, and carried it out of the kitchen. As she did while performing this task each morning, she offered greetings to members of Sobon's staff she passed while making her way to T'Prynn's room. One or two were cleaning, and another tended to the large garden at the center of the house's main floor. It was a routine that rarely varied, which was good. T'Prynn's recovery would benefit from such structure, particularly when T'Nel returned to her own village and the patients and other work she had left behind in order to care for her sister.

For a moment, T'Nel considered the possibility that T'Prynn might choose to return to Ha'tren with her, at least for a time, but she just as quickly dismissed that possibility. If she was well enough to travel, one of the Starfleet security contingents that had remained on watch outside the village walls likely would take her into custody. While Vulcan had not disallowed her extradition from the planet, the government had elected not to interfere with the Kren'than community tenets regarding sanctuary and who was allowed to enter the commune. Instead, they had decreed that T'Prynn could be extradited upon Sobon's agreement that her recovery was complete or if he revoked her status as living in asylum in the village. Since that time, the security details had been steadfast in their diligence, with teams arriving and departing via shuttlecraft at six-hour intervals throughout the period T'Prynn had spent under Sobon's care. T'Nel knew of the charges Starfleet had leveled against her sister, just as she knew they had successfully convicted her former commanding officer of similar crimes. None of that was important to T'Nel; what mattered now was T'Prynn's continued recuperation.

As she navigated the narrow corridor leading to the house's bedchambers, T'Nel's eye caught the open doors leading to rooms formerly occupied by the outworlders, Pennington and M'Benga. They were gone now, of course, having returned to Shi'kahr and secured transportation for the long voyage back to their space station. She missed her conversations with the Earth men. M'Benga, in particular, was a fascinating individual, a human who had dedicated a significant portion of his life to learning how to care for Vulcan patients. The doctor obviously had benefited from his time among Vulcans, and she had noted how he had easily adapted to life here in Kren'than. Though outworlders had never been allowed to reside permanently in communes such as this, T'Nel wondered if Sobon might not have made an exception for M'Benga, had the physician thought to ask. She thought not, recalling the other aspirations of which he had spoken during some of their talks. Still, T'Nel decided, it might have proven beneficial to have the doctor present as T'Prynn's recovery continued.

She knocked at the door to T'Prynn's room. When no response came, T'Nel listened for movement through the door and heard none. She knocked again, louder this time, and again there was no answer.

"T'Prynn," she called out, loudly enough to be heard through the door. "It is I, T'Nel." When there was no response this time, T'Nel opened the door.

T'Prynn was not in the room. Instead, Sobon lay on the bed, dressed in a simple white sleeping robe, his hands clasped across his chest.

"Good morning, my child," said the elder Vulcan. "May I presume that the meal is for me?"

Curious about this odd development, T'Nel entered the room. "Forgive me, Healer Sobon, but I do not understand. Why did you not answer when I knocked on the door?"

"You asked for T'Prynn," Sobon replied. "I am not T'Prynn."

Setting the tray on the edge of the bed near Sobon's feet, T'Nel examined the room. T'Prynn's bed clothing had been folded and placed on the nightstand next to the bed, and an inspection of the wardrobe revealed that one of the soft suits T'Nel had brought for her was missing.

"Where is T'Prynn?" she asked.

Sobon rose to a sitting position, swung his feet over the tray, and lowered them to the floor, a maneuver of surprising agility for a Vulcan of his advanced years. "I do not know," he said as he inspected the breakfast tray and decided on one of the fruit slices. Taking a bite, he nodded in approval. "The *liral*'s flavor is most robust this morning."

"Healer Sobon," T'Nel said, sensing the first hints of concern. "Is T'Prynn still in the village?"

"Again, I do not know, my child," Sobon said, taking another bite of the *liral* slice. "Though, were I to engage in speculation, I would say that she has left."

T'Nel looked through the window toward the village's front gate and saw a Starfleet shuttlecraft, fifty meters beyond the perimeter wall and sitting on a patch of flat ground. Outside the shuttle, three humans in Starfleet uniforms milled about. "Are the Starfleet officers aware of this?"

"I suspect not," Sobon said, reaching for another piece of fruit. "While their sensor equipment can monitor biological readings and determine the current location of each of the village's residents, they are not so sensitive as to be able to distinguish between individuals. I imagine T'Prynn was aware of this when she asked me to stay in her room last night as she prepared to depart and to remain here until you arrived this morning."

For the first time, T'Nel felt genuine emotion stirring within her. Training suppressed it, of course, but it was there. "Healer

Sobon, do you mean to say that you assisted T'Prynn in a bid for her to escape the village?" How was such a feat even possible, given her sister's compromised condition? Had she progressed more rapidly than she had allowed others to believe?

Was it her imagination, or did she see the ghost of a smile on Sobon's face? "T'Prynn did not discuss her evening's agenda. She asked only that I remain here." After a moment, he added, "However, upon returning to my study, I expect to find several items missing, such as a small rucksack, a vessel for carrying water, a portable hand lamp, and perhaps one or two maps. An inspection of the kitchen may reveal that several days' worth of dried fruits and vegetables is gone as well."

Her eyes narrowing as she comprehended the true scope of Sobon's words, T'Nel said, "I do not believe Starfleet will view that as plausible deniability, Healer."

"That is Starfleet's concern," Sobon countered, "not mine."

"How would she even be able to leave the village undetected?" T'Nel asked, confused. "Surely, she could not get past the Starfleet security team."

He rose from the bed, and his withered hands smoothed wrinkles from his robe. "You seem to forget, my child, that T'Prynn is a formidable Starfleet officer in her own right, as well as an intelligence officer. It seems logical to conclude that she possesses the knowledge and skills to deal with such obstacles. Now, if you will excuse me, I must proceed with my own schedule for the day."

With a final glance out the window, T'Nel turned back to the elder Vulcan. "I do not understand. Where would she go?"

Almost to the door, Sobon stopped and turned back to face her. "T'Prynn seeks answers to many questions. Perhaps she decided that now was a good time to search for those answers."

"Once Starfleet discovers she's missing," T'Nel replied, "she will be considered a fugitive. Any opportunity for leniency in the face of the charges against her will be lost."

"I have no reason to believe that T'Prynn is unaware of that, T'Nel," Sobon said, "but you know as well as I that she would never allow that to impede her, and you also know that whatever it is she has decided to do, she will only be satisfied by doing it on her own. That has always been her way."

Indeed, T'Nel mused. T'Prynn never had allowed anything to interfere with her pursuit of whatever goal she had set. Now that she had emerged from the ordeal that had consumed her for so many years, it was logical that T'Prynn would set new goals, which remained known only to her.

Sobon exited the room, leaving T'Nel alone. She stared out the window beyond Kren'than's confines, her gaze taking in the panoramic view that was offered by the surrounding L-langon Mountains. Somewhere out there, she knew, was her sister, pursuing a new journey she believed she could undertake only on her own. Would she return? T'Nel could not be certain, of course, but she considered it unlikely. That, she knew, also was T'Prynn's way.

Peace, my sister, for you have earned it, T'Nel thought. *Peace and long life.*

56

Komoraq cursed the droning dirge of the alarm Klaxon as it echoed through the narrow corridor leading to the *M'ahtagh*'s bridge. His heavy boots clanging against the metal deck grating, he bared his teeth and growled at those few subordinates standing between him and the hatch leading to the ship's command center. Not wanting to risk incurring their captain's wrath, they pushed themselves against angled bulkheads or plunged into open service crawlways to clear a path for him. The pressure hatch's massive doors parted at his approach.

"Silence that insufferable baby wailing," Komoraq snarled as he stepped onto the bridge, on his way to the captain's chair at the center of the room. "Report!"

Standing at the console positioned along the left bulkhead, Lieutenant Kalorg, one of the *M'ahtagh*'s weapons officers, replied, "Federation starship has just entered sensor range, Captain. It's on an intercept course, traveling at high warp. Sensors indicate that it is a *Constitution*-class battle cruiser. At its present rate of speed, it will be in our weapons range in less than two *kuvits*."

"Raise shields," the captain ordered, "Place weapons on ready status."

Had Starfleet somehow determined the location of the Earther his wife held beneath the planet's surface? Pondering his options as he stroked his beard, Komoraq's first instinct was to engage the Federation ship in battle. There would be some controversy, of course, raised mostly by clueless, whiny bureaucrats back on the homeworld. It would pass, particularly when it came to light that the Federation vessel had intruded in space claimed by the empire. The Earther government, with no stomach for confrontation, would happily accept that explanation, content to dishonor those who might die in battle for the sake of protecting their own worthless hides.

"You say the ship is on an intercept course?" he asked.

Nodding, Kalorg said, "Yes, Captain, though their weapons do not appear to be activated."

Perhaps this Earther captain has courage his leaders lack, Komoraq mused. Intrigued by this notion, he turned to his communications officer. "Open a channel, and hail them."

At the communications station, Lieutenant Mondol replied, "Yes, Captain."

"Vessel closing to weapons range," Kalorg reported.

When Mondol turned back to face Komoraq, his expression was a mask of uncertainty. "I have received a response, sir."

Komoraq scowled. "What is it?"

"The vessel's captain has suggested that you engage in disrespectful acts with your mother, sir."

It took an additional moment for the response to register, after which Komoraq ground his teeth together, uttering a low, ominous growl. "Target that vessel, and prepare to open fire."

"They are activating their energy weapons!" Kalorg called out. "They're firing!"

An instant later, Komoraq felt the deck tremble beneath his feet and listened to the protests of the angled support struts along the bridge's perimeter. Most of the energy from the attack had been absorbed by the *M'ahtagh*'s shields, but that did not discount the possibility of damage. "Report," he ordered.

"Minor power loss in the starboard deflectors," replied Kalorg. "The enemy vessel is coming about, altering its course."

"Onscreen!"

Komoraq watched as an image of the small, streamlined vessel sailed past on the viewscreen, the imaging software rendering the Starfleet ship's gleaming hull in sharp relief against the utter darkness of space behind it. At this distance, he was able to discern the vessel's hull markings. Whoever commanded the ship did indeed possess great courage. That, or he was simply insane.

"Fire!" Komoraq shouted. "Aim to disable only!"

To his left, Kalorg said, "They are accelerating to warp speed, Captain."

"Helm, lay in a pursuit course," Komoraq barked. Whereas his initial thought had been to carve the Federation ship into slivers of smoldering metal, all he wanted now was to stare the vessel's master in the eyes. "Have security ready a boarding party. I want to hold that captain's beating heart in my hand." He felt the vibrations in the deck plating as the *M'ahtagh*'s warp engines engaged and the stars on the main screen stretched into multi-hued streaks. "Match its course and speed."

Komoraq watched as the ship on the screen grew larger with every passing moment. The Earther captain now seemed content to run like a whipped *targ*. What was to be gained from such a strategy?

The warbling alert tone from Kalorg's station gave him his answer, as the Starfleet ship seemed to vanish from the viewscreen.

"What?" Komoraq said, straightening in his chair.

"Captain," the weapons officer shouted, his tone one of surprise. "They dropped out of warp, changed course, and are now heading for the planet!"

All around her, Atish Khatami heard the *Endeavour* groan in protest as the starship dropped out of subspace. In front of her, Neelakanta's fingers danced across his helm console. Without any further instructions from Khatami, the ship lunged once again to warp speed, making the shift so quickly that the captain felt herself pushed into the back of her chair as the inertial dampening systems struggled to compensate for the rapid changes.

Mog's going to kill me if I wreck his pretty ship.

"Time!" Khatami called out.

"About fifteen seconds," replied Klisiewicz from the science station. "The Klingon ship is changing course to intercept and accelerating. All weapons are armed."

It was going to be close, Khatami knew. Very close. She was not a fan of reckless tactics like the one she and her crew were attempting. *Constitution*-class starships were not constructed for such maneuvers, even though Mog had assured her that the *Endeavour* was more than capable of meeting the challenge. Despite her chief engineer's confidence, Khatami still harbored visions of the ship shearing apart around her.

Of course, taunting a Klingon ship commander would not normally be considered a prudent course of action, either, but doing so had worked to perfection, drawing the enemy vessel away from its position and allowing the *Endeavour* to approach the planet.

"Closing to transporter range," Neelakanta reported from the helm. On the main viewer, the blue and brown sphere that was Mirdonyae V grew larger with every passing second. Somewhere down there, if Carol Marcus and the Tholian Nezrene were correct, Lieutenant Ming Xiong awaited rescue.

"Coordinates verified?"

Klisiewicz replied, "Verified, Captain. The best we can do is put them down near the entrance to the artifact site."

Damn it.

"Dropping to impulse," Neelakanta reported. "Now."

Once more, the *Endeavour* trembled around her as the ship fell out of warp space, the image of Mirdonyae V filling the viewscreen.

"Lower shields," Khatami ordered. "Transporter room, energize!" Even as she spoke the words, she began mentally ticking off the precious seconds required to complete the process of sending her people down to the surface.

"Captain!" Klisiewicz shouted. "They're here!"

Over the intercom, Khatami heard the voice of the chief on duty in the transporter room as he reported, *"Transport complete, Captain!"*

"Shields!" she ordered. "Helm, bring us about!" They had

delivered their package. Now, they needed to stall for time, and the only way to do that was to smack the Klingon commander once more across the face.

Come and get me.

Feeling the grip of the transporter beam release her, Lieutenant Jeanne La Sala took stock of her surroundings, her phaser rifle aimed ahead of her as she searched for threats. For a brief moment she thought she sensed a hint of dizziness, but she dismissed it as being her imagination, the odd sensation conjured by the decidedly unorthodox method employed to transport her and her five-person team down from the *Endeavour.*

Not my first choice, that's for sure.

With sensors unable to penetrate the Shedai construct from orbit, it fell to a landing party with boots on the ground to search for the missing Lieutenant Xiong, who, according to Dr. Carol Marcus, had been brought to this planet following his capture on Erilon. La Sala was fuzzy on the details, but as she understood it, the industrious young lieutenant had found some covert means of signaling for help, even going so far as to use the Klingons and the Shedai equipment to assist him in the effort.

Finding the planet on which Xiong was being held had been the easy part. Actually finding and rescuing him was another matter altogether. First, there was the Klingon battle cruiser in orbit above Mirdonyae V, the captain of which likely would have something to say about the *Endeavour* swooping in and taking the captive. Captain Khatami was currently addressing that issue, leaving La Sala and her security team to search for Xiong and deal with any Klingons who might be down here with him and who, La Sala suspected, would be equally resistant to the idea of a rescue operation.

That's why we brought presents, she thought, hefting the stock of the phaser rifle to her right shoulder. Studying the area, she noted that the terrain looked almost exactly as described by the transporter chief just before the landing party beamed down. Rolling hills covered with all manner of trees and other vegetation presented a deceptively tranquil setting, but La Sala knew that danger lurked nearby, perhaps beneath her feet, perhaps even ready to appear from the very air.

Focus, Lieutenant.

Looking to one of her team members, Ensign Paul Simpson, she indicated the tricorder in the man's left hand. "Anything?"

"I'm picking up power readings," Simpson said as he studied his readings. "Three hundred meters ahead." He pointed toward the black onyx façade set into the side of a nearby hillside. "In there."

"Once more into the breach, as they say," La Sala replied. It was not hard to remember her previous encounters with the She-dai or their technology, months earlier on Erilon. The first of those missions had ended with the tragic death of her former captain, Zhao Sheng, as well as several other very good people, some of whom she had called friends. The *Endeavour*'s second visit had nearly resulted in utter catastrophe, with their mysterious Shedai adversary almost succeeding in destroying the entire planet. Though Captain Khatami had assured the crew that the Shedai were not a threat on this occasion, that did not stop La Sala from constantly scanning the surrounding terrain, searching for any sign of the crystalline monstrosities she and her people had fought on Erilon.

"I'm looking for them, too," said Ensign Hammond, another survivor of those battles. After a moment, the younger man forced a smile. "I suppose we should be happy that we're just dealing with Klingons this time."

"Yeah," La Sala replied, frowning at the poor attempt at humor. "Okay, let's get on with this." With the barrel of her phaser rifle leading the way, La Sala took point and started toward the entrance to the centuries-old Shedai artifact. "Follow me."

The muzzle of the disruptor loomed in Xiong's vision, looking like a massive, toothless maw as its owner jammed it in his face.

"Move!" shouted the Klingon guard, using the weapon to in-

dicate where Xiong should go. Raising his hands, the lieutenant
followed the guard's instructions and moved toward a far corner
of the chamber, stepping away from the polished black computer
console and around the crystalline pedestal, which at the moment
was not cradling the strange Shedai artifact. Another guard, this
one only slightly smaller than his hulking companion, aimed his
own disruptor at Tasthene, ordering the Tholian to join Xiong.

"What is happening?" Tasthene asked.

Xiong shook his head. "I don't know." One moment, he and
his Tholian companion had been working, just as they had done
for however many days or weeks the pair had been prisoners of
the Klingons. The next, one of their guards, the larger one, had
received some kind of alarmed message via his communicator.
Whatever the Klingon was told, it had set him on edge, and the
next moments were spent with Xiong wondering when and if the
excited guard would shoot him in the head.

"Quiet!" the guard snarled, baring his teeth at Xiong.

From somewhere beyond the chamber, he heard the muted
reports not of a Klingon's disruptor weapon but of what he was
certain was a Starfleet phaser, its deep warbling echoing in the
crystalline corridors. It was accompanied by another and yet another, then answered by a chorus of disruptor fire.

They're here!

Feeling his pulse quickening in hope and anticipation, Xiong
could not help smiling as he realized the true nature of the ca-
cophony unfolding outside the chamber. Somehow, someone had
received the message he had embedded in the test carrier signals
generated by the mysterious Shedai artifact and its unprecedented
access to the primeval technology. Given the limited time he had
been allowed to work with the strange crystal, he was certain his
plan was a long shot, as likely to be discovered by Lorka or Captain Komoraq as by anyone who might be in a position to attempt
a rescue operation.

The other guard moved toward the chamber's entrance,
searching for the source of the commotion. His companion, with
his weapon still trained on Xiong and Tasthene, nevertheless di-

rected his attention toward the doorway. Xiong considered making a move for the weapon, but there was no way he could physically overpower a Klingon soldier.

Tasthene had other ideas.

Emitting a disturbing string of high-pitched shrieks that succeeded in startling the guard, the Tholian abruptly surged forward, raising his upper appendages. Before the Klingon could react, Tasthene closed the distance and promptly drove his right spearlike arm into the guard's chest. The Klingon howled in terror and pain as the arm pushed through his back, spraying pinkish-red blood across the ground and the wall behind him. Using his left arm, Tasthene jammed it upward until the point penetrated the Klingon's head just beneath his jaw, and the Tholian pressed forward, driving the pointed end through the top of the guard's skull. The Klingon went limp, still impaled on Tasthene's crystalline arms as his disruptor fell from his hand.

Startled and even horrified at the scene, Xiong still was able to pull himself together long enough to scoop up the weapon, the disruptor feeling large and ungainly in his hand. He heard heavy footfalls running toward him and looked up to see the other guard an instant before a burst of energy sailed past his head, chewing into the stone wall behind him. He flinched at the attack, ducking to his left even as he held his captured disruptor in both hands and fired. The single burst caught the Klingon in his chest, pushing him back and off his feet. He struck the edge of the computer console before falling lifeless to the ground, a massive smoking hole in his torso.

"Someone's found us," Xiong said, shaking off Tasthene's horrific execution of the guard as he ran across the chamber to retrieve his tricorder. "We need to get out of here." At the set of crates he had fashioned into a work area, Xiong moved aside one of the smaller containers and grabbed the set of tricorder data discs he had secreted there. The discs contained everything he had been able to record about his work here, including the progress he and Tasthene had made while working with the mysterious object from the sarcophagus. The information he had gathered would prove invaluable to Starfleet's ongoing research of the Shedai.

Assuming that we can get it out of here without getting killed.

"Come on," he said as he slung his tricorder over his shoulder. He turned to look for Tasthene, and his eyes widened. He was sure he felt his heart skip a beat as he beheld Lorka standing at the entrance to the chamber. She held a disruptor in her right hand, her arm extended to aim the weapon at Tasthene, who was back-pedaling away from the Klingon woman. Still holding the disruptor he had taken from the dead Klingon guard, Xiong tried to bring it to bear, but he was far too slow.

Without saying a word, Lorka fired.

"No!" Xiong yelled, but it was too late. The single disruptor bolt struck Tasthene in his torso, and the Tholian's spindly, crystalline body trembled as the energy blast enveloped him. His agonized wail echoed off the chamber's smooth obsidian walls, only to be drowned out by the horrific sound of his entire body shattering. Xiong ducked behind one of the packing crates, throwing up his arms to protect his head as most of Tasthene's environment suit disintegrated in an expanding mushroom of crystal fragments blown backward toward the room's far wall.

His hands shaking at the image of Tasthene's ghastly murder, Xiong peered around one side of the crate and saw Lorka stepping into the room, her disruptor moving in a lateral line across her body as she searched for him. She smiled in wolfish satisfaction as her eyes fell on him, and she aimed her weapon.

"Your usefulness is at an end, Earther."

Lunging to his left, Xiong stood and brought up his own disruptor, turning it on Lorka. His shot was badly aimed, passing over her right shoulder. The Klingon did not flinch in the face of the attack, instead adjusting her aim. Xiong ducked, trying to avoid her shot, but then his ears rang with the high-pitched whine of a Starfleet phaser, and Lorka's body was consumed for the briefest of moments by a cobalt-blue sphere of energy. She grunted in surprise before dropping limp to the floor, leaving Xiong to stare wide-eyed at his fallen adversary. Looking across the room, he felt a rush of relief as his eyes beheld Lieutenant Jeanne La Sala entering the chamber, her phaser rifle up and ready for another target. When she caught sight of Xiong, she smiled.

"You the one calling for a ride?"

For the first time in weeks, Xiong felt like laughing, though such thoughts faded as his eyes fell on the countless shards of crystal littering the floor, all that remained of his friend Tasthene.

"That's me," he said, his voice soft as he took in the sight of La Sala. Behind her, members of her security detachment entered the room, a couple of them taking up positions near the entrance to guard against unwelcome visitors. How long had it been since he had last seen her? The mission to Jinoteur, he now remembered. Her short black hair was matted to her head with perspiration, but that did not prevent the security officer from looking as radiant to Xiong as he recalled from their previous meetings. Gesturing toward Lorka, he asked, "She's not dead, is she?" Even as he asked the question, he was disturbed by how much he wanted La Sala to tell him that the Klingon was indeed deceased.

La Sala shook her head. "Heavy stun. No killing unless it's absolutely necessary."

Drawing a deep breath, Xiong ground his teeth. "If only the Klingons felt that way."

"We're not the Klingons," La Sala said.

For all the good that does us.

He waved toward her phaser rifle. "What is it with you and that thing, anyway? Isn't a Type-two enough?"

La Sala shrugged. "Unlike some people, I think size *does* matter." She grinned, bobbing her eyebrows in suggestive fashion before nodding toward the corridor outside the room. "Clock's ticking, Xiong. We need to get gone."

"Okay," he replied, turning to the exit. Then he stopped, seeing the packing crate and the now-sealed sarcophagus it contained. "Wait," he said, pointing to the crate. "We can't leave this."

"No time for that, Ming," La Sala said, worry in her voice.

Turning to look at her, Xiong said, "We can't leave it. It's *important,* Jeanne."

Reluctantly, the security officer nodded. "Okay."

"Incoming!"

In defiance of his weapons officer's warning, Komoraq stood before his captain's chair on the *M'ahtagh*'s bridge, holding on to nothing for support as the photon torpedo made impact against the cruiser's shields. Consoles and display monitors across the bridge flickered as power momentarily dipped, and Komoraq felt his stomach lurch as the ship's artificial gravity and inertial dampening systems wavered for the slightest instant.

"Return fire!" he ordered, punctuating the command by pumping his gloved fist in the air before him. On the forward screen, the image of the Starfleet ship danced in and out of view, as though taunting him.

I will mount their captain's head on my trophy wall, he vowed, relishing the image of how he would exact vengeance for what had transpired here. The Starfleet captain, a treacherous *petaQ* in the finest Earther tradition, had employed misdirection and subterfuge rather than facing him directly, capitalizing on such trickery in order to close to transporter range of the planet. Sensors had detected the transporter signatures, and Komoraq had even ordered his communications officer to warn his wife and the rest of the landing party on the surface, but the response from Lorka had told him he was too late. The Earthers had infiltrated the ancient ruins, no doubt seeking to reclaim their lost compatriot. Meanwhile, the Starfleet ship had turned back toward the *M'ahtagh*, engaging in strafing runs and other craven maneuvers with the obvious goal of keeping his ship from getting close enough to the planet to send down reinforcements. No matter how long he lived or however many times he might engage Earth-ers in battle, he never would understand their predilection for wasting so much effort on the salvation of a single life.

Such weakness ultimately will be their undoing.

"Captain," Lieutenant Kalorg called from the weapons station, "the enemy vessel is altering course again!"

Stepping forward so that he stood alongside the helm console, Komoraq shouted, "Fire at will!"

On the viewscreen, successive bursts of fiery red energy lanced across the void separating the two ships, and Komoraq watched the multiple flares as the disruptor blasts slammed into the Starfleet vessel's deflector shields. For an instant, the field around the enemy ship glimmered, and he was sure he saw one of the bolts pass through the protective barrier to strike the ship it-self.

"Direct hit on their secondary hull," Kalorg reported. "No breach."

The other ship returned fire, brilliant beams of blue energy cut across the void, interspersed with the hot white, elongated orbs of a photon-torpedo barrage. Once more, Komoraq felt the *M'ahtagh*'s shields absorb the hits, though this time, he heard the troubled warbling of the main engines as they, too, suffered the effects of the assault. On the bridge, the most immediate effect of the strike was the loss of the main viewer, the image depicted on it dissolving into a storm of hissing static.

"Shield generators are down to twenty-six percent," Kalorg called out above the din of alarms and the status reports offered by other members of the bridge crew. "Warp drive is offline. Main sensor array is inoperative!"

"Get me a tactical plot," Komoraq ordered. Reaching past his helm officer, he stabbed the controls on the console to execute the command, but the viewscreen remained nonfunctional. To his credit, the young lieutenant manning the helm did not appear af-fected by the chaotic situation, his attention focused on his station as he continued to pilot the vessel. "Where are they?"

"They've broken off their attack," Kalorg replied. Turning

from his station, he added, "Captain, they maneuvered into orbit around the planet and activated transporters again."

Had the Earthers found their precious companion? Komoraq did not care about that any longer. Lorka had found the human to possess value to her research, but he was happy to be rid of the miserable cretin. He could only hope that the Earthers had taken the equally worthless Tholian with them, though he would not have minded killing the irksome rodent himself.

"Bring us about," he ordered, standing behind his helm officer and observing the console's array of tactical displays, which indicated the *M'ahtagh*'s position in relation to the planet and the Starfleet ship. "Stand by all weapons. All available power to the forward shields." Even with his own vessel wounded, he had no intention of breaking off the fight.

"Captain!" Kalorg said. "The enemy vessel is veering away from us." A moment later, he added, "They have accelerated to warp speed."

No!

Komoraq's furious growl echoed around the cramped bridge as he pounded the back of the helm officer's chair with his fist. The Earther captain had apparently accomplished his mission and now was running like a terrified child, rather than remaining here and finishing the fight he had started. *Coward!*

"What is the status of warp drive?" he asked, rage all but smothering every syllable.

Shaking his head, Kalorg replied, "The engineer reports that it will take at least thirty *kuvits* to bring control systems back online."

Too long, Komoraq knew. Turning to Kalorg, he said, "Kill the engineer."

"Yes, Captain," Kalorg replied, saluting as he acknowledged the order.

From the communications station, Lieutenant Mondol said, "Captain, we are receiving a signal from the surface from Commander Lorka."

"Open a channel," Komoraq ordered, his heart racing at the

mere mention of his wife's name. Whatever had transpired on the planet below, his mate had survived.

"M'ahtagh, *this is Science Officer Lorka. Something is happening down here.*"

Frowning, Komoraq replied, "What do you mean?"

"Massive power generation throughout the complex," Lorka replied. *"We are detecting energy readings across the continent."*

Komoraq looked to Kalorg. "What's she talking about?"

At the weapons station, the lieutenant was scrambling to find answers. "I've rerouted navigational and weapons-tracking scanners to substitute for the main array," he said. Then he nodded. "She's right. There's an enormous power buildup across the planet. It is the alien systems, Captain."

"How in the name of *Fek'lhr* can that be?" Komoraq asked.

Then, in one sickening instant, realization dawned.

"Alert the transporter room!" he shouted, pointing to Kalorg. "Get them out of there!"

Scorn. Chaos. Fear. Doom.

The thoughts echoed in the Shedai Wanderer's consciousness as she emerged from the void and fell to the lush, thriving world. Weakened from her journey, she nevertheless was able to sense the presence of *Telinaruul* on the world the Shedai once had ruled. Reaching out with tendrils of her consciousness, she was able to detect the hints of primitive life, created by the Makers long ago and placed here to develop at its own rate. The primeval children were aeons from evolving into anything that might be of any use to the Shedai, but their very existence had been tainted by the arrogant meddling of the unworthy ones who seemed capable of nothing but stumbling from planet to planet and contaminating everything with which they came into contact.

There were only a few of the vermin infesting the planet, the Wanderer knew, along with many more in proximity to the planet, contained within the pathetic vessel in which they traveled among the stars. Still, she sensed the effects of their presence, as she had on the worlds throughout the realm where she had encountered their kind. Once again, they had overstepped their bounds, taking it upon themselves to insert themselves where they did not and would not ever belong. Even in her weakened state, exterminating them would require almost no effort. The *Telinaruul* were not what had compelled her

Drawn here by the fearsome, unexplained Voice that had resonated through what remained of the Conduits, the Wanderer had expected to find the *Telinaruul* having somehow discovered a means of using Shedai power for their own ends. Whatever had reached out to her across the vast gulfs separating stars was here no longer. Probing the dormant mechanisms left behind by the Shedai ages ago, she sensed only the residue of the Voice's passing. If it had originated here, how had it been able to leave? As far as the Wanderer knew, only she possessed the ability to travel among the stars without benefit of the Conduits. Was this some secret harbored by the Makers? If so, for what purpose had they confined this knowledge only to themselves?

Even the vestiges of the unidentified presence carried with them a foreboding that shook every fiber of the Wanderer's being. There could be no mistaking its malevolence, which even after its passing remained entwined with everything it had touched. The dread it seemed driven to summon was palpable, reaching out from the depths of darkness as it searched for . . . *something.*

Feeling the energy of the planet responding to her commands, the Wanderer now knew what she must do. The Voice, whatever it might represent, was an evil without equal, surpassing even that of the Apostate. It, and anything it touched, must be eradicated at all costs.

That purging would begin here.

58

"The three of us are going to have to stop meeting like this," Nogura said as he entered his office to find Ambassador Jetanien and Commander Cooper waiting for him. "People are going to start talking."

The ambassador, dressed as always in the robes of his office, replied, "Thank you for meeting with me so late in the evening, Admiral."

Walking around his visitors on his way to the food slot on the back wall, Nogura shrugged. "I'd only been asleep for two or three hours, anyway. If we're going to keep doing this, we should at least play poker or something." He reached for one of the data cards on the small shelf next to the food slot, selected one, and inserted it into the unit's reader before keying a command sequence. A moment later, the food slot's door slid up, revealing a cup of steaming coffee on a saucer. Glancing over his shoulder at Cooper, he waved the executive officer to one of the chairs in front of his desk. "Commander, I take it you're an insomniac in training as well?"

"It sort of comes with the job, Admiral," Cooper replied, his smile belying the fatigue Nogura saw in the man's eyes. The commander was right, of course; one did not assume the mantle of command if he looked forward to catching a lot of beauty sleep.

"What can I do for you, Ambassador?" Nogura asked as he took his coffee and made his way to his desk.

His manus clicking as though he might be anxious, Jetanien said, "The Klingons are very angry, Admiral."

Nogura paused in the act of bringing the cup of coffee to his lips. "That's why you got me out of bed? Because the Klingons are angry?" He looked to Cooper. "Make a note of that, Commander. The Klingons are angry. While you're at it, I'd like an update on the status of the station's water supply. Is it still wet?"

"This is anything but a joking matter, Admiral," Jetanien said, punctuating his rebuttal with a series of irritated clicks and grunts.

Waiting until he had savored the first sip of coffee—and making a mental note to commend the station's chief engineer, Lieutenant Farber, for seeing to it that the food slot was able to prepare his favorite blend properly—Nogura returned the cup to its saucer and leaned back in his chair to regard Jetanien. "Perhaps you could be a bit more specific, Ambassador?"

Jetanien stepped closer, until he stood behind the other chair in front of Nogura's desk. "Specifically, the Klingons are unhappy about what happened at Mirdonyae V."

"Ah," Nogura replied, nodding. "Well, they should probably take that up with the Shedai. They're the ones who left a global self-destruct system lying around without an owner's manual." He had read the report from Captain Khatami the previous evening, which detailed the *Endeavour* doubling back to the planet after departing in the wake of the successful rescue of Lieutenant Xiong. The starship's sensors had detected the shock wave emanating from the Mirdonyae system, and Khatami and her crew had seen with their own eyes the vast, expanding field of debris that was all that remained of the fifth planet. By all accounts, the Klingon contingent on Mirdonyae V had fallen victim to its own arrogance and carelessness.

"What I don't understand," Nogura said, "is how the Klingons were able to achieve that level of access to the weapons systems, or anything else, for that matter. According to Xiong, they'd only managed moderate success before kidnapping him."

"They must have been paying attention as Xiong worked," Jetanien replied. "Not that it matters, as they're claiming we triggered the self-destruct, that our people used it as a last-ditch act of desperation when it became evident that they could not defeat the Klingon vessel on their own." He punctuated the comment with what sounded like a belch. "In doing so, they slaughtered a number of Klingons who were not party to the combat, to say nothing of destroying an entire world that the Klingons had claimed in the name of the empire."

"And somehow managed to avoid getting destroyed or at least severely damaged along with the Klingon ship still in orbit when the planet blew?" Nogura asked, rolling his eyes. "That's some trick." Turning to Cooper, he asked, "Commander, I assume the *Endeavour*'s sensor logs corroborate Captain Khatami's accounting of the events?"

Cooper nodded. "Absolutely, sir. The *Endeavour* was well under way when the incident occurred and only knew what happened because sensors picked up the gravimetric disturbance while they were tracking for signs of Klingon pursuit."

That was consistent with Khatami's report, Nogura knew. Her theory was that the Klingon contingent on the planet somehow had accessed the Shedai planetary defense system they believed to be hidden far beneath the surface, perhaps in a bid to bring those weapons to bear against the *Endeavour*. Their unfamiliarity with the technology had almost certainly been their undoing.

"There is the matter of a Starfleet ship attacking a Klingon target," Jetanien said. "Naturally, comparisons are already being drawn to what happened on Gamma Tauri IV."

"Outrageous comparisons, to be sure," Nogura countered. Starfleet's public-relations machine had never fully recovered from the black eye inflicted by the tragic, if necessary, actions taken by Commodore Reyes on that occasion. They, along with the merciless dissection of Starfleet's military policies and rampant debate regarding the appropriateness of such power and authority given to Starfleet officers, had raged through media outlets for weeks after the incident.

"But ones to which the Federation Council and Starfleet Command remain sensitive," Jetanien said, his tone one of caution. "Even if such comparisons are without merit, viewing the incident on Mirdonyae as isolated is enough to make the Klingon High Council most displeased."

"The Klingon High Council can get stuffed, for all I care," Nogura replied. "I'm still not convinced that Klingons weren't behind what happened to Reyes's transport." The notion that pirates had attacked and destroyed the *U.S.S. Nowlan* was not out of the question, but raids against Starfleet vessels by such groups, Orion or otherwise, were exceedingly rare. He could not even recall such an incident within the last twenty years.

"According to them," he continued, "they had no knowledge of those Klingons attacking our people on Erilon, to say nothing of kidnapping Xiong. We're supposed to believe that mob of alleged rabble rousers was acting without any authority from higher command? In that case, we did them a favor by dealing with them ourselves. Formal thanks aren't necessary, but they should feel free to send flowers or perhaps a nice selection of cordials."

Jetanien snorted. "I find that highly unlikely, Admiral. Needless to say, this latest incident will almost certainly incite reprisals."

"That's one way to put it," Cooper said.

"One of the nicer ways, actually," Nogura added, "but I suspect we'll have plenty of time to worry about the Klingons." Rather than allow his concerns over the ever-worsening political situation to consume him just now, he chose to dwell on the relief he felt over the rescue of Ming Xiong, who had survived in fine form the ordeal to which he had been subjected. "What do we know about this new Shedai artifact the Klingons provided Xiong?" While some might view the actions he took while in captivity as collaborating with an enemy, Nogura did not see it that way. He had read Khatami's report following her debriefing of the lieutenant and believed, as she did, that any cooperation Xiong had offered was in the guise of learning what he could about their knowledge of Shedai technology, all while using his expertise either to formulate an escape plan or—as had happened—to broadcast a plea for help.

"According to Xiong," Cooper said, "it's some kind of key or cipher. The access it allowed him into the Shedai computer system on Mirdonyae V is unprecedented, far beyond anything we've obtained on any of our expeditions to other planets with such technology." He shrugged, frowning. "The problem is that we're just looking at more stuff that we really don't understand."

Nogura nodded. "What about the other people Dr. Marcus has engaged to help decipher the Shedai computer systems?"

"A work in progress, Admiral," Cooper replied. "As you know, Starfleet Command's only recently approved your requests to have the specialists she's asked for to be briefed on the project. Now that they'll have full access, things should start moving at a faster pace."

Finishing his coffee, Nogura said, "Let's hope we'll find some way of holding off the war long enough to give them the time they need to finish the job." He knew that the Klingons would simply add the incident at Mirdonyae to the grievances that were rapidly piling up on the negotiating table currently separating the Federation and the Klingon Empire. Would this latest straw break the camel's already straining back and along with it any chance of success for the ongoing diplomatic talks? Experience and cynicism told Nogura that the prolonged cold war between the two interstellar powers was heating up, and the boiling point was fast approaching.

It's a matter of when, not if.

"It's good to see you, Lieutenant," said Carol Marcus, taking in the image of Ming Xiong on the computer terminal in her quarters. Though he looked more than a little gaunt, and there was a noticeable bruising on his face, she was thankful that he appeared not to look too much the worse for wear. "You look pretty good, all things considered."

On the screen, Xiong nodded. *"If it matters I probably feel better than I look. Nothing a few nights' sleep in a decent bed won't cure. That and any meal that's not from a Klingon menu."* A wistful expression played across his features. *"You know, when I joined Starfleet, this wasn't exactly the kind of career I had in mind."*

Marcus could not help laughing. "What, you're admitting that you were dazzled by all that talk of exploring strange new worlds, or whatever it is that's engraved on all the walls at Starfleet Academy?"

"Guilty," Xiong replied, matching her smile. He held up his right hand in a gesture of mock surrender. *"You'll have to forgive me. I was a hopeless idealist back then."*

"And now?"

Xiong paused before answering, and when he did, his expression faded. *"I don't know."* Looking around the small room that Marcus presumed was the quarters to which he had been assigned on the *Endeavour,* he said, *"So much has happened since we began all of this. Even when I received my assignment to Vanguard, I never thought it would evolve into what it has. I was driven by the potential for discovery, what that might mean not just for us but for everyone."* He shook his head. *"But now look where we are. Everything's been warped and perverted. No one cares about the scientific benefits of what we've found. It's all about power and who can get what first."* Looking directly at her, he added, *"What's worse is that I'm now a willing participant. I know that no matter what I believe or want to happen, for now, everything we're doing is simply about doing it before the Klingons can do it."*

"Don't lose sight of what you believe in, Ming," Marcus said, sympathetic to what the man was feeling. "As much as I prefer the pursuit of science for noble goals, Starfleet isn't the bad guy here. Besides, we both knew coming in that figuring out the Shedai and the meta-genome and everything else was as much about not letting anything like a weapon fall into enemy hands as it was about increasing our knowledge. Until everyone in the galaxy can learn to live with everyone else, it's always going to be like that."

Xiong sighed. *"I know, but it doesn't mean I have to like it, just as I don't have to like what all of this has turned me into."*

"You should be proud of yourself, Ming," Marcus said. "Admiral Nogura couldn't speak highly enough about you once he read the reports that Captain Khatami and I submitted. What you were able to accomplish while you were a prisoner is astounding." When she contemplated everything the man had endured during the past months, she could not help but shake her head in wonder. It was a testament to the man's character that he had persevered under such conditions, not merely to survive but also to continue carrying out his mission to the best of his ability, all while preventing enemies from getting their hands on the invaluable discoveries he had made while being held in captivity.

Xiong said, *"I had help, of course. I couldn't have done any of it without Tasthene."* He paused, casting a glance downward. *"I wish I could have helped him."*

"I'm sure you did everything you could," Marcus replied, hoping the words did not sound as hollow to Xiong as they did to her own ears. "And as long as I have my say, everything he did to help you won't be in vain." She watched as Xiong reached up to rub his eyes and stifle a yawn. "Ming, why don't you get some sleep? We'll have plenty of time to talk once you get back to the station. Besides, you're going to need that rest. Thanks to you and Tasthene, we've got a lot of work ahead of us and all sorts of new avenues to explore."

"Point taken, Doctor," the lieutenant said, seemingly relieved. *"Thanks. I'll talk to you soon. Xiong out."*

The screen faded, leaving Marcus alone with her stacks of reports and files, several of which had been created just since her initial conversations with Xiong in the days after his rescue from Mirdonyae V. Based on the reports submitted by the archaeology and anthropology officer as part of his debriefing aboard the *Endeavour* while the starship was en route back to Vanguard, she could not wait to get her first look at this mysterious crystal the lieutenant had brought with him. Why had the Shedai created it? What was its purpose? What abilities did it possess that provided its seeming ability to interface and take control of Shedai computer systems? Of course, the progress Xiong and Tasthene had made while prisoners of the Klingons had raised new questions regarding the advanced nature of Shedai technical advancement. Of greater, arguably tremendous importance was the notion that such achievement appeared linked to the ancient race's apparent mastery of genetic manipulation, as well as their demonstrated ability to affect at will the delicate balance between matter and energy. These were the puzzles that would occupy Marcus, Xiong, and the entire Vault research team in the weeks and months ahead.

59

Jetanien looked up to see Akeylah Karumé standing in his doorway. Rather than one of her usual ensembles, his aide was dressed in what the ambassador recognized as athletic attire. She wore no cosmetics, and her hair had been pulled into a ponytail. The expression on her face was one of undisguised irritation.

"Do you have any idea what time it is?" she asked.

"Even without the chronometer positioned so conveniently on my desk," Jetanien replied, "I am well aware of the time." It was, it seemed, his night for rousing people out of sleep for what he believed to be pressing matters. Diplomacy, he long ago had learned, did not keep regular schedules. "I apologize for calling you at this late hour, but this could not wait. I think, however, that you'll find it worth the inconvenience."

Karumé appeared unconvinced. "Does it involve you dying of some incurable, debilitating disease from which you will suffer great pain before your ultimate, undignified demise while lying in an expanding pool of your own body waste?"

"Another time, perhaps," Jetanien countered, adjusting his posture while sitting on his chair. He pointed to his computer terminal. "I received a rather interesting communiqué this evening." He let the sentence hang in the air for a moment, until Karumé's eyes widened in comprehension.

"The Romulan?"

Jetanien nodded. "Senator D'tran himself, if he's to be believed. Apparently, death has not yet caught up to him." Without any real information to consult, Jetanien could only guess that the senator had to be approaching the upper limits of advanced age even for Romulans, and even that was assuming that their physiology remained similar to their distant genetic relatives, the Vulcans.

Moving into the office, Karumé made her way around Jetanien's desk in order to see the terminal. "Assuming that it's not some kind of ruse, this is incredible, Ambassador."

"Indeed," Jetanien replied. "The message arrived in an encrypted form, and I spent several hours combing through Selina's notes to find the cipher." He had finally found the decryption key buried in the pages in one of his mentor's numerous handwritten journals. The entry was innocuous, deliberately designed not to stand out from the rest of the book's contents. Jetanien had nearly passed it while leafing through the pages. "There are no photographs or other visual references to D'tran in any of Selina's files, so for now, I have no means of authenticating his identity." It made sense, of course, as Rosen and her fellow diplomats had carried out their negotiations with their Romulan counterparts over subspace radio. Peace between the two powers had begun the same way the war preceding it had ended, with no human or ally ever seeing a Romulan in the flesh. D'tran and Rosen would continue their covert communications for years afterward in similar fashion, never meeting in person.

Leaning closer, Karumé nodded to the terminal. "Well? Let's see it."

Unable to resist the temptation, Jetanien emitted a small laugh. "It would seem that you're awake now." On the computer terminal's interface, he tapped a command to replay the message he already had viewed three times. The display shifted from a graphic of the UFP seal to the image of an aged Romulan. Thick gray hair framed a gaunt, angular face, the most distinctive features of which were the stark, penetrating blue eyes peering out from beneath a pronounced brow. Though time may have ravaged the body, all indications were that the mind within remained vibrant.

"Greetings, Ambassador Jetanien," began the recorded message. *"I am D'tran. It seems you have benefited from the rather voluminous record-keeping habits of our mutual friend. I must*

*admit to being more than a bit surprised to receive your com-
munication, given the length of time since my last correspondence with Selina. However, I hope you will accept my sympathies
for her passing. It is one of my life's regrets that I never was able
to meet her in person.*

*"As you know, Selina and I were in agreement that while the
peace accord negotiated between our two peoples was necessary, its terms were lacking with respect to long-term consequences as far as our mutual future was concerned. Despite the
propaganda fed to our citizens, there are many within the Romulan Empire, including more than a few within our government,
who believe that a lasting peace with the Federation is possible,
even desirable. We also accept that many within the Federation
must feel the same way."*

"Well," Karumé said as D'tran paused, "he certainly *talks*
like a politician."

Leaning forward, the elderly senator continued, *"Of course,
there are those among our people who would welcome another
war, perhaps as a misguided opportunity to atone for what they
believe were unreasonable concessions forced upon us when the
peace treaty was enacted. However, I am not alone in the Senate
when I say that this is not a path we wish to follow. A few of my
more ambitious colleagues even harbor fanciful notions of negotiating some form of accord with the Klingons."* A small smile
graced his weathered features. *"The wide-eyed optimism of
youth never ceases to amuse me."*

Jetanien chuckled at that. "I may learn to like this Romulan."

*"Since the recent contact between one of our vessels and a
Federation starship, I have had discussions with trusted colleagues about how best to open new diplomatic channels between our governments. We did not agree with the mission given
to that vessel or to the ship sent to the area of space you call the
Taurus Reach, believing those actions to be unnecessarily aggressive for no purpose other than provocation. For there to be a
lasting peace, we must stop searching for battles that do not need
to be fought in the first place."*

It was what the Romulan said next that caught Jetanien off guard. *"I recall Selina mentioning you on occasion. She referred to you as a gifted prodigy with much potential. Based on what she told me about you, you very well might be someone who can persuade your Federation to engage us the way we wish to approach you—in peace. To that end, I make a proposition: full-faith negotiations, face-to-face, at a neutral site of your choosing."*

He shrugged. *"If you have contemporaries within the Klingon Empire who you feel are up to this challenge, then we are willing to meet with them as well. As Selina might once have said, I leave the ball in your court and await your reply with great anticipation. Until then, my new friend, I wish you well."*

D'tran's image faded on the computer display, and Jetanien looked up at Karumé. "Well, what do you think of that?"

Karumé shook her head, her expression skeptical. "It's either the mother of all cons, or else this D'tran just dropped a career-defining opportunity right into your lap. The question now is, what do you intend to do about it?"

It was a question Jetanien had been mulling for some time before Karumé's arrival. The idea of brokering any kind of extended diplomatic discourse with the Romulans and the Klingons, particularly now, with relations between the Federation and the Klingon Empire teetering on the edge of the proverbial abyss, excited him. As D'tran had said, he might be the one to foster such a cooperation. After his failed attempt to bring together the Federation, the Klingons, and the Tholians with respect to the ongoing concerns in the Taurus Reach, this was just the challenge he needed now.

"Is there another choice?" he said after a moment. "We at least have to explore the possibilities and see where they might take us." Assuming a more comfortable position on his chair, he reached once more to the computer and pressed the control to activate its voice interface. "Computer, provide a list of Class-M planets occupying positions equidistant to Federation, Klingon, and Romulan territory. Include spatial coordinates for all selections."

Jetanien and Karumé waited in silence while the computer processed the request, which took longer than the ambassador anticipated. After nearly a minute, a list of planets appeared on the screen. It was a short list.

"I don't recognize any of these," Karumé said.

"Wait," Jetanien said, pointing to one name. "This one might work. It has no strategic value for any party and possesses no natural resources worth exploiting. It's an inhospitable hunk of rock, with no distractions to fuel unsavory agendas." He released a satisfied grunt. Of those listed, one planet seemed perfect for his needs.

Nimbus III.

60

INTERLUDE

The Shedai Wanderer had found a new home.

Still reeling from the exertion it had cost her to traverse the Void, she took a moment to gather what little strength she was able to preserve. She was weaker now than she had ever been since the collapsing of the Conduits and the departure of the First World. How much longer could she continue like this, without the guidance and support of the First Conduit? Had the Enumerated Ones not heard her cries for help or those of others like her who she knew were scattered among the stars?

As always, her pleas went unanswered.

Surveying her surroundings, the Wanderer could not help but feel satisfaction at what she beheld. Unlike the world she had been forced to sterilize after its infestation at the hands of *Telinaruul,* this planet held much promise. Its lush, fertile environs offering ideal breeding grounds for the nascent life-forms it harbored. Searching her memory, the Wanderer recalled this world as being among those selected for prolonged experimentation and observation, with the ultimate goal of bringing about the next stage in the evolution of the Shedai.

So far, the planet had been spared contamination by *Telinaruul.* Observing the primordial beings that dwelled among its vast undersea mountains and crevasses, the Wanderer sensed that they carried within them the seeds of life given to them uncounted generations ago by the Enumerated Ones. Their potential was palpable, yet at their present rate of advancement, she knew it would be aeons before they rose to a level that might indicate whether those who planted them here were successful. Such progression might be accelerated, of course, should the Enumerated Ones desire it, but without them, this world and the life on it would evolve at its predetermined pace. As such, it offered no immediate assistance to the Wanderer in her ongoing battle.

That is correct, child. There are no others to take pity on you.

Her consciousness convulsed in response to the words of the Apostate, taunting her once more from somewhere in the Void. Summoning precious bits of her flagging strength, she probed outward, searching for some hint to his location. It was a futile attempt. At the same time, the Wanderer drew in upon herself, hoping to escape the Apostate's scrutiny, not just for her sake but also for the burgeoning life this world cradled. If her enemy found it, she knew that he would obliterate it from existence without a second thought.

Worry not, little one. I will find you and the feeble hatchlings you seek to protect.

For a moment, the Wanderer was certain she sensed irritation in the Apostate's words, along with . . . fatigue? Was it possible that her adversary also was weakened, perhaps by attempts at transit without benefit of the Conduits?

I need no such aid. I am all.

Strong words, but they were tainted by something else, something new, an odd quality the Wanderer had never before felt him exhibit. Then she understood.

The Apostate was afraid, but of what?

I fear nothing.

A lie, the Wanderer decided, but what could have this effect on one so powerful? Might it be the furtive, unknown Voice that had penetrated the Void, perhaps even at the bidding of *Telinaruul?* Straining to listen, she detected no overt sign of that presence, either, but the sensation of terror that had gripped her upon first hearing it was still fresh in her memories.

Of course it is. Monsters always frighten children.

The Apostate's goading tone belied his own anxiety, of this

the Wanderer now was certain, just as she was convinced that her enemy harbored his own apprehension about whatever it was that awaited them in the Void. Did that make this mysterious entity her ally? Of that the Wanderer was unsure. All she knew was that she still felt the dread that had enveloped her on the diseased world she had so recently cleansed. Did the *Telinaruul* understand this unknown consciousness? Was it possible that they were able to harness its power to any degree?

She all but shuddered at that thought.

Your weakness will be your undoing, young one.

The Wanderer ignored her enemy and his words, dismissing them as empty, distant, and weak. There were larger concerns, she knew. Somewhere in the Void, something powerful was growing, lying ominously in wait. Would any threat it posed be enough to incite the return of the Enumerated Ones? If that happened, was whatever might oppose them great enough to usurp their will?

Once more, the Shedai Wanderer was gripped by fear.

The Taurus Reach
2267

EPILOGUE

Harsh crimson illumination bathed the bridge of the *I.K.S. Zin'za*, casting most of the room in near-darkness and forcing the animated computer displays that littered the bulkheads to stand out in stark contrast. In the dim lighting, the shadows grew longer, making the walls of the already cramped space seem as though they might be pushing inward and attempting to crush the comparatively fragile beings who dwelled within them. The sensation acted as stimulation to a true warrior's spirit. Anticipation was heightened, hearts beat stronger, and blood raced ever faster through veins as every fiber of one's being prepared for battle.

Captain Kutal would have it no other way.

"Range?" he barked, feeling the rush of expectation as the time for battle approached. Leaning forward in his chair, he studied the immense Federation space station now depicted on the bridge's central viewing screen.

"Twelve thousand *qell'qams* and closing, Captain," replied his tactical officer, Lieutenant Tonar. "Sensors show that the station's deflector-shield generators and weapons systems are online."

On the viewer, the image of the station was overlaid with a series of bright red indicators and other telemetry that offered tactical information about the station as relayed from the *Zin'za*'s sensors. The outpost, one of the Federation Starfleet's newest and most advanced models, was by all accounts more than capable of defending itself against an enemy attack such as the one it currently faced. Of course, the station had not yet endured the ferocity of a Klingon battle squadron, an oversight Kutal intended to correct in the coming moments.

As for the quartet of vessels maneuvering into a defensive formation between the station and Kutal's squadron, tactical scans showed that only one of the ships, the Earthers' closest equivalent to a battle cruiser, appeared to pose any significant threat. Of course, as an experienced veteran of space combat, Kutal knew that a ship's fighting prowess was predicated as much—if not more—on the ability of its crew and the ingenuity of its commander as on its simple technical capabilities. Further, he had seen more than one Earther ship and its master emerge from battle with victories that should have been beyond their reach. That included the battle cruiser that he and his strike force now faced. Kutal vowed that there would be no underestimating his enemy on this day.

"Captain," called out Lieutenant Kreq, the *Zin'za*'s communications officer, from his station along the bridge's left bulkhead, "the space station is attempting to hail us."

Kutal released a low grunt. "Of course they are. Earthers love to talk," he said, sneering as he cast a look over his shoulder to the back of the bridge and the lone figure standing alone there and observing the proceedings. "It seems to be an embedded genetic disposition of their species."

The time for talk had passed. As far as Kutal was concerned, diplomats had already spent far too long delaying what should have been allowed to happen in the first place. Even after it had become clear that the Earthers would present an obstacle to Klingon expansion, the High Council had continued to squander repeated opportunities to vanquish the Federation Starfleet. Studying early battles such as those fought at Donatu V, Axanar, and Kolm-an, to name but a few, and even more recent encounters had shown Kutal where the mistakes had been committed. Even the more recent encounters—including ones in which he had participated—revealed a criminal misjudgment of the Earthers' tenacity and resolve. One day, the Council would have to realize that the only way to deal with the humans was to unleash the full might of the empire in a merciless, unrelenting campaign that could only end with the Earthers and their allies crushed for all time.

Perhaps, after months of repeated delays and other stalling tactics, today was that day.

"Execute envelopment formation *to'qiL maH*!" Kutal barked, emphasizing the command by punching the air with his fist. "Activate the tactical display!"

The image on the main viewer shifted as Tonar complied with the order, now offering a computer-generated schematic that depicted the space station and its quartet of defense ships as well as the *Zin'za* and the five other battle cruisers of Kutal's strike force.

"Target their lead ship with all weapons," he called out. Overcoming the other vessels would be far easier if the most powerful of the Starfleet ships could be disabled or destroyed at the outset. Once that was accomplished, firepower could then be concentrated on the station itself. Whatever armaments it might have, it was still an immobile target, ultimately vulnerable to the sweeping attacks that would be inflicted by his strike force. Kutal smiled. Patience and persistence would rule the day.

He was so caught up in the activities unfolding around him as his ship prepared for battle that it took an additional moment for the captain to realize that his seat was growing warmer. The heat penetrated the thick material of his uniform, gaining intensity with each passing heartbeat. He rose from his chair, growling in confusion and annoyance. "What is this?"

The reply to his question came in the form of everyone on the bridge jerking back from the stations, a few of them cursing or barking as they held their hands up and away from their bodies. Kutal now could see waves of heat radiating from nearly every surface across the bridge, the heat continuing to grow more oppressive in the confined space.

Much to his own disgust, Kutal flinched at the sound of a soft, whining hum that began to permeate the bridge. His eyes narrowing in suspicion, the captain searched for the source of the noise but saw nothing out of the ordinary. The volume of the droning increased to the point where it became uncomfortable, as though a sonic weapon were being aimed at his head.

"Are we under attack?" he asked, shouting to be heard.

Tonar shook his head. "We must be, but I do not know how, Captain. Our weapons and shields have deactivated, as if by themselves!" He pointed to his tactical console. "The Earther vessels have also been disabled. I cannot explain it!"

Finally, the sound began to fade, only to be replaced with a sphere of light that simply appeared before the forward viewing screen and began to grow and stretch into a humanoid shape. To their credit, several of Kutal's warriors drew their weapons, but he commanded them to hold their fire—for the moment, at least.

"What is this trickery?" Tonar asked, his disruptor in his hand and aimed at the mysterious intruder.

When the glow faded, revealing what appeared to be a bearded human dressed in drab clothing, it was obvious to the captain that a real being did not stand before him. Instead, it appeared more as a vision, a ghostlike projection, but what was its source?

It was the ghost who answered.

"My name is Ayelborne, of the planet Organia," the figure said, clasping his hands before him. *"At this moment, the military forces of your empire and the Federation have converged in orbit above my planet, as well as elsewhere in space, ready, if not eager, to wage war. Were you to confine your hostilities to yourselves, we would be content to allow you to destroy each other. However, your conflict threatens millions of innocent lives, and that is something we cannot allow. All of your instruments of violence now radiate a temperature of three hundred fifty degrees. They are inoperative. These same conditions exist within both of your fleets. There will be no battle."*

Of all the impudence! Kutal felt his jaw tighten as he listened to the arrogance spewing from the mouth of this . . . whatever this was. An Earther? Kutal doubted it. As pompous as the Federation often projected itself to be, it did not possess the technology simply to disable an entire strike force as if by magic. Even if such power was in their grasp, why would they inflict it on their own vessels, rather than crippling just those of their enemy?

"What is this transmission's origin?" Kutal barked.

Tonar shook his head. "I am unable to determine its source, sir. It is definitely not coming from the space station or any of the Federation ships."

"As I stand before you now," the interloper continued, *"I also stand upon the home planet of your empire and the home planet of the Federation. Unless both sides agree to an immediate cessation of hostilities, all of your armed forces, wherever they may be, will be immediately immobilized."*

"Who is this mongrel?" Tonar shouted, pointing at the alien with his disruptor pistol. "You dare to challenge the empire?"

The query, repeated in various forms by other warriors on the bridge, was ignored by the projection. Instead, this alien from a planet Kutal did not recognize or recall from star charts or intelligence briefings continued his incessant babbling, offering a litany of spineless whining about how he and his ilk would rather refrain from interfering in the affairs of others but now felt they had no choice but to foist their will upon the empire and the Earthers. He also offered assurances that there would be further contact, during which these Organians would clarify their position and the ultimatum they had levied.

"You will be offered paths to assist you in finding peace with each other," the alien said, seemingly turning to level a withering gaze at Kutal himself. *"The choice of which path to follow is entirely yours to make, and the consequences for your decision will rest solely with you."*

As the final words left his mouth, the projection began to shimmer and contract, with the near-blinding light now returning to envelop him and accompanied once more by the irritating whine that assaulted Kutal's ears. The captain squinted to ward off the worst of the glare, but it faded more quickly this time, and within moments, all evidence that the alien—real or projected—had ever been on the bridge was gone. Only the bridge crew was left, exchanging looks of bewilderment and mounting anger at what they had just witnessed.

"Captain," Kreq said, his youthful eyes wide with puzzlement, "is it possible? An enemy that can defeat the empire with such ease?"

Moving to his chair and realizing at the last instant that it still radiated far too much heat for him to sit in it, Kutal did not reply to the question. What could he say? He had no answers. Who were these Organians? Were they bluffing, or did they truly wield the power they seemed to have demonstrated? Kutal did not discount the possibility of such a people's existence. His tours of duty in the Gonmog Sector alone had provided ample proof.

"Turning to face the rear of the bridge, Kutal directed his attention to the lone human standing there. The man had remained silent throughout the events of the past several months. "What do *you* think, Earther?"

Dressed in dark clothes that almost allowed him to blend in with the shadows, the man stood with his arms folded across his chest. The deep lines on his face appeared even more pronounced under the bridge's severe lighting as he regarded Kutal with an expression that the Klingon recognized on humans as one of uncertainty.

"Well," said Diego Reyes, former and now-disgraced Starfleet officer. He nodded toward the viewscreen and the image of Starbase 47 displayed on it. "Things have certainly gotten a bit more interesting."

The saga of
STAR TREK: VANGUARD
will continue
in
PRECIPICE

ACKNOWLEDGMENTS

First, thanks to editor Marco Palmieri and fellow writer David Mack, for conspiring to create the *Star Trek: Vanguard* series and for having me back for a second helping. Additional thanks to David for leaving so much to work with after the series' third book, *Reap the Whirlwind*. Here's hoping I returned the favor.

Thanks also to Kevin Dilmore, my dear friend and frequent writing partner. Life dealt us a few curveballs this time around, requiring Kevin to recuse himself from participating in the writing of this novel in order to see to more important concerns. Rest assured that the book you're reading follows very closely to the outline we developed together, and his influence is present all throughout these pages. I hope I didn't screw it up too bad, dude.

I once again offer my sincere appreciation to Alex Rosenzweig, fan extraordinaire, who contributed much in the way of assistance with respect to the *Star Trek* timeline. Given the period of time over which the events of this novel unfold, along with the fact that they take place in concert with a host of other happenings during this period in *Star Trek*'s "future history," it's always nice to get the insight of someone who really knows this stuff. Any flubs, goofs, or other missteps in this area are the author's, despite everything Alex did to keep that from happening.

Much appreciation is extended to the fine folks responsible for maintaining the Memory Alpha (http://www.memory-alpha.org) and Memory Beta (http://startrek.wikia.com) Web sites, which offered more than a few helpful nuggets of knowledge on a variety of topics researched during the writing of this book. Keep up the awesome work!

Salutes are offered to Jeanne M. Dillard, Josepha Sherman, and Susan Shwartz, authors of various *Star Trek* novels over the years, several of which provided a few choice tidbits of Vulcan and other lore that ended up sprinkled throughout *Open Secrets*.

A glass of Saurian brandy is raised to Dorothy Jones Heydt, an old-school fan who created a comprehensive Vulcan language in the 1960s and coined the term *Ni'Var* in a *Star Trek* story she wrote for the fanzine *T-Negative*. Also included in this toast is Claire Gabriel, one of the contributors to Bantam Books' *Star Trek: The New Voyages* in 1976. Claire arguably "popularized" the term *"Ni'Var"* in her story of the same name, which appeared in that book.

Also appreciated is the work of Kenneth A. Hite, Ross A. Isaacs, Evan Jamieson, Steve Long, Christian Moore, Ree Soesbee, Gareth Michael Sharka, John Snead, and John Vick, all authors and contributors to the sourcebook *The Way of Kolinahr: The Vulcans,* for Last Unicorn Games' now-defunct *Star Trek: The Next Generation Role-Playing Game.* The book provided much inspiration during the plotting of T'Prynn's arc.

And finally, many thanks to the loyal readers and fans who make this job so rewarding. A writer's work is often carried out in solitude, and while we certainly write for our own satisfaction or because it's something we simply have to do (like, you know, breathing), it's still nice to see our efforts read and enjoyed by so many people.

Until next time!

ABOUT THE AUTHOR

Dayton Ward. Author. Trekkie. Writing his goofy little science-fiction stories and searching for a way to tap into the hidden nerdity that all humans have. Then an accidental overdose of Mountain Dew altered his body chemistry. Now, when Dayton Ward grows excited or just downright geeky, a startling meta-morphosis occurs. Driven by outlandish ideas and a pronounced lack of sleep, he is pursued by fans and editors, as well as funny men in bright uniforms wielding tasers, straitjackets, and medi-cation. In addition to the numerous credits he shares with friend and cowriter Kevin Dilmore, Dayton is the author of the *Star Trek* novel *In the Name of Honor* and the science-fiction novels *The Last World War* and *The Genesis Protocol*, as well as short stories that have appeared in the first three *Star Trek: Strange New Worlds* anthologies, the Yard Dog Press anthology *Houston, We've Got Bubbas, Kansas City Voices* magazine, and the *Star Trek: New Frontier* anthology *No Limits*. Dayton is believed to be working on his next novel, and he must let the world think that he is working on it, until he can find a way to earn back the advance check he blew on strippers and booze. Though he currently lives in Kansas City with his wife and two daughters, Dayton is a Florida native and still maintains a torrid long-distance romance with his beloved Tampa Bay Buccaneers. Visit him on the web at http://www.daytonward.com.

ANALOG
SCIENCE FICTION AND FACT

A full year of engaging reading delivered right to your door!

Discover the unbeatable combination of stimulating fiction, provocative editorials, and fascinating science articles in every issue of **Analog Science Fiction and Fact**.

Subscribe today and enjoy a full year of reading delivered right to your home for less than the cost of a single novel. You save 72% off the regular price!

1 year (12 issues), only $12*

To subscribe, fill out the order form below or call
TOLL-FREE, 1-800-220-7443 (M-F 8am–7pm, EST)
to charge your order. (We accept MC, VISA, AmEx, Discover.)

Mail to: Analog • 6 Prowitt St. • Norwalk, CT 06855-1220

YES! Start my subscription to Analog (AFF) right

away. My payment of $12.00 (U.S. funds) is enclosed.

Name _____
(Please print)

Address _____

City _____ State _____ Zip _____

* We publish 2 double issues, in Jan/Feb and Jul/Aug, which count as four issues towards your subscription. Allow 8 weeks for delivery of first issue. WA Residents: Add applicable state and local taxes to your total order. For delivery outside U.S.A., pay $22.00 (U.S. funds). Includes GST.

XFAF67

STAR TREK® LIVES!

Visit the many worlds of
Star Trek books online at

www.simonsays.com/st

- Discuss the fiction
- Find out about upcoming books
- Chat with the authors and editors
- View the updated *Star Trek* backlist
- Read excerpts
- View exclusive content

It's a big universe.
Explore it.

SS/ST

Asimov's
SCIENCE FICTION

Enjoy a full year of award-winning science fiction!

Asimov's Science Fiction magazine delivers novellas and short stories from the leading science fiction and fantasy writers, plus candid, no-holds-barred book reviews and guest editorials. Subscribe now and enjoy a full year of captivating science fiction reading for just $1.00 per month. You save 72% off the regular price!

1 year (12 issues), only $12*

To subscribe, fill out the order form below or call TOLL-FREE, **1-800-220-7443** (M-F 8am–7pm, EST) to charge your order. (We accept MC, VISA, AmEx, Discover.)

Mail to: Asimov's • 6 Prowitt St. • Norwalk, CT 06855-1220

YES! Start my subscription to Asimov's (ASF) right away. My payment of $12.00 (U.S. funds) is enclosed.

Name _____
(Please print)

Address _____

City _____ State _____ Zip _____

* We publish 2 double issues, in Apr/May and Oct/Nov, which count as four issues towards your subscription. Allow 8 weeks for delivery of first issue. WA Residents: Add applicable state and local taxes to your total order. For delivery outside U.S.A., pay $22.00 (U.S. funds). Includes GST. **XFAS67**